Douglas Ash

THE DEVIL IN VELVET

Books By John Dickson Carr

THE
DEVIL IN VELVET

by

John Dickson Carr

HARPER & BROTHERS
Publishers · New York

For

Lillian de la Torre

CONTENTS

THE DEVIL IN VELVET

CHAPTER I

THE MIST DOOR OPENS

SOMETHING woke him in the middle of the night. Perhaps it was the heavy, stifling air of closed bed curtains.

In his half-doze he could not remember drawing the curtains of the bed, which was three hundred years old. And it floated through his mind that he had swallowed rather a large dose of chloral hydrate, as a sleeping draught. Hence he might not have remembered.

Yet the drug still seemed to hold him. Memory, which he tried to summon up in the dark, gave back only images behind thick shifting gauze. When he essayed to remember words, they were as silent as puffs of smoke from cracks in a wasteground.

A drift of smoke showed him his own speech now.

"My name is Nicholas Fenton," he said to himself, to restore clarity out of chloral. "I am a professor of history at Paracelsus College, Cambridge. In this modern year, which the calendar gives as 1925, I am fifty-eight years old."

Now he realized that he had whispered the words faintly. Memory, briefly, awarded him a gauzy vision of last night. Yes, last night.

He had been sitting downstairs in the drawing room, and in the house which he had rented for the summer because "nobody" would be in London then. Across from him, on an oak settee with brocaded cushions, had sat Mary. Mary wore a cloche hat, to indicate a brief visit, and had a glass of whisky and soda in her hand. Mary was very much younger than himself, of course, and almost beautiful.

"Mary," he had said, "I've sold my soul to the devil."

Nicholas Fenton knew that she would not laugh, or even smile. She merely nodded gravely.

1

"Have you?" she asked. "And what did the devil look like, Professor Fenton?"

"Do you know," he answered, "for the life of me I can't remember? He seemed to change into all shapes. The light was dim; he was sitting in the chair over there; and my infernal eyesight ... "

Mary leaned forward. Mary's eyes possessed a quality which in his earlier days he would have called smoky: their colour a grey deepening almost to black, then again to a darker smoky-grey elusiveness as though they were shadowed in her young face.

"Did you really sell your soul, Professor Fenton?"

"Actually, no." His dry chuckle was barely audible. "In the first place, I cannot quite credit the reality of the devil. He might have been only a hoaxing friend, with a talent for stage effect. I should not put it past Parkinson of Caius, for instance. In the second place ... "

"In the second place?" prompted Mary.

"Except perhaps in the case of Dr. Faustus," mused Fenton, "the devil's bargains have always been too easy for him."

"How so?"

"Contrary to popular saying, he is not a gentleman. His victims are always simpletons against whom he plays with cogged dice. He has never yet encountered a man of wit. If I *have* made a bargain with him, then the devil has fallen into a trap and I have beaten him hands down."

He had intended to smile at her, indicating that she must not take him too seriously. Whereupon—or so it seemed to the half-drugged man now lying upstairs amid drawn bed curtains—whereupon that scene in the drawing room became even more dreamlike.

What Mary held in her hand was not an ordinary drinking glass. It appeared to be a silver goblet, highly polished. As she tilted the goblet to her lips, the light flashed and dazzled on its surface, sending the reflection straight into Fenton's eyes. Light, they say, is cold. Yet this reflection shot across with a palpable heat, as of wrath.

And was there a short, sharp movement, as of a visitor, in one corner of the room?

No; it could only have been illusion. Mary held an ordinary drinking glass.

"What gift did you ask of the devil?" she inquired. "That you might be young again, like Faust?"

"No. That does not interest me." This was only, say, one-fourth

2

untrue, since Fenton had always firmly told himself he was as young as ever.

"Then was it . . . what stupid people have called your obsession?"

"In a sense, yes. I asked to be carried back through time to a specific date in the third quarter of the seventeenth century."

"Oh, you can do it," Mary whispered.

Often he wished that she would not sit there and look at him with such grave, attentive eyes. Often he could not understand what she found interesting in the conversation of an elderly stick like himself.

"You are the only historian," said Mary, "with sufficient knowledge of minutiae to do it. Carry yourself cleverly, especially as regards phraseology, and none will suspect you."

Now where on earth, he wondered, had she picked up that term "carry yourself cleverly"? It was common usage in the seventeenth century.

"And yet," continued Mary suddenly, "I don't understand this."

"I don't understand myself. But, if the devil keeps his bargain . . . "

"You mistake my meaning. In this way: you must many times have wished, before this, to be carried back into the past?"

"Oh, yes. 'Wished' is a mild word. God!" unexpectedly whispered Fenton, and felt a cold tremble. "How I longed for it! How I writhed on a bed of nettles, as men scarify themselves for money or women for social position! But it was only academic curiosity, I thought."

"Then why do you wish for it now?"

"First, curiosity has reached a point past endurance. Second, I have a mission. Third, I never knew it was so easy to whistle up the devil."

The expressionless Mary seemed interested in only one part of this.

"Mission, Professor Fenton? What mission?"

Fenton hesitated. He touched the pince-nez on the nose of his mild, donnish face. Automatically he ran a hand over his high, arched skull, where some strands of dark-red hair were still brushed back. In person he was a little over middle height, stoop-shouldered from bookishness, and very lean.

If he stopped to think about it, Fenton knew, he was a frail man to throw himself like a swimmer into the dark waters of the past, full of cries and sounds unknown, a-rush with currents that might break his bones among rocks. But he resolved not to think about it.

"In this house," he said, "on June 10th of the year 1675, a certain person at last died of poison. It was a slow, brutal murder."

3

"Oh," said Mary, putting down her glass on a side table. "Please forgive me, but have you authenticated evidence for all this?"

"Yes. I even have a folio-size portrait engraving of each person in the household. I could recognize any one of them who came into this room now."

"Murder." She repeated the word slowly. "And who were these people?"

"Three were women, all of them beautiful. Not," Fenton added hastily, "that this has influenced my decision in any way." Quite suddenly he sat up straight. "Did you hear an odd kind of laugh, then, very low-pitched, from the direction of those bookcases?"

"No."

Under the sides of Mary's cloche hat two edges of her black bobbed hair showed glossy wings against the milky-white complexion of her face. It seemed to Fenton that her eyes had hardened.

"Then, for another example," he said quickly, "there was the owner of the house. Er—curiously enough, he bore the same name as my own. Nicholas Fenton."

"Some ancestor of yours?"

"No. He was no relation whatever; I've traced it carefully. Sir Nicholas Fenton was a baronet. His line died out in the latter part of the next century. Mary, who committed that murder?"

"You mean you don't know?" Mary asked incredulously.

"No! No! No!"

"Please, Professor Fenton! You mustn't get excited. Your voice . . ."

"I beg your pardon." Fenton controlled himself, though his insides were again cold and trembling. "The reason I don't know," he went on in his usual mild tone, "is that three sheets are missing from Giles Collins's manuscript account. Someone was arrested, tried, and executed after a confession voluntarily given. But the pages containing this account have been lost or stolen. We can be certain only of two persons who were not guilty."

"Oh?" said Mary. "Who were they?"

Her companion grimaced.

"One of them was Sir Nicholas himself. The other was a woman; her name not given, but from the details it is easy to guess her identity. I know it because there are notes at the end. We must accept this; otherwise we have no eyes to see through."

4

"But surely," Mary protested, "there must be some published account of this murder case besides that of Giles Collins?"

"So I had supposed. But it's not in Howell's *State Trials*, of course. It's not in the first volume of the *Complete Newgate Calendar*, because Captain Johnson merely chose his cases and did not list them. For nine years—yes, nine years!—I have searched libraries and advertised to obtain some book, some pamphlet, even the broadsheet which was usually published at the time of a hanging. There is none."

"Nine years," whispered Mary. "You never told me." In some fashion her face seemed to grow shadowy and smoky, like her hair and eyes. "There are three women in this, you said. I daresay your 'Sir Nicholas' was hard in love with one of them?"

"Well . . . yes."

Now how had the child guessed that? For Mary, at twenty-five, he regarded merely as a child because she was the daughter of his old friend Dr. Grenville, of Paracelsus.

"You still don't understand," he insisted. "G—the devil help me, I have done everything! I have even taken up a headachy course of reading at criminology and medical jurisprudence, because this was an affair of poison. I think I can deduce the name of the murderer." His voice rose. "But I don't *know*."

"And so," Mary's shapely shoulders moved, "you are now so desperate that you must go back into the past and find the truth?"

"I have a mission, remember. I may be able to prevent the murder."

No clock ticked in the muffled silence.

"Prevent the murder?" Mary repeated.

"Yes."

"But that's impossible! This is a small thing, if you like, against the march of all the ages. But it's already happened. It's a part of the stream of history. You can't change. . . ."

"So I was reminded," he told her dryly. "Nevertheless, I wonder!"

"Did your satanic friend tell you this? What did he say to you?"

How difficult, how extraordinarily difficult, it had been to describe to Mary an interview which had seemed as normal and even casual as that of two men talking in the smoking room of a club! For the devil had paid him a quiet visit that night, not an hour before Mary arrived. His visitor, unattended by any of the lurid ceremonies usually described, had sat in a tapestry chair far across the drawing room.

5

What Fenton had told Mary was quite true. The light being dim—it was a small bulb in a table lamp darkened by several thicknesses of imperial-purple silk—Fenton saw only that unstable ever-varying outline, and heard soundless words.

"Yes, Professor Fenton," his visitor had said amiably, in English of a faintly archaic flavour, like the gentleman he was not, "I think I can arrange this matter to your satisfaction. Others have requested it before you. The date you mentioned, I believe, was . . . ?"

"It was May 10th, in the year 1675. Just a month before the murder."

"Ah, yes. I will make a note of it." The visitor mused. "Those were rough and bloody days, if memory serves me. But the ladies!" Here he revolted Fenton by smacking his lips audibly. "Dear sir, the ladies!"

Fenton did not reply.

"It is unfortunate," continued the visitor, in a distressed voice, "that two gentlemen must discuss matters of business. But you know my conditions and my—er—price. Come! Can we not strike a bargain now?"

Fenton smiled. He had no very high opinion of his visitor's intelligence. Of his power, yes. But not his intelligence.

"You go too fast, sir," Fenton objected mildly, and ran his hand over the very thin hair on top of his head. "Before we strike any kind of bargain, I should prefer you to hear my conditions."

"Your conditions?"

Towards Fenton, out of the dark tapestry chair, there seemed to flow a wave of such huge arrogance that it threatened the room and even the house. Fenton, who hitherto had felt no fear or even awe, was momentarily frightened. But the wave of feeling dwindled into a kind of bored politeness.

"Let us hear your conditions," yawned the visitor.

"First, I wish to go back to the past in the character of Sir Nicholas Fenton."

"Of course you do." The visitor seemed surprised. "However! Granted."

"Next, since I cannot discover a great deal about Sir Nicholas, there are further conditions. He was a baronet, yes. But baronetcies in those days, as you are aware, were sometimes worn by the oddest of bedlamites."

"True, true! But. . . ."

"I must be a man of wealth and noble blood," Fenton continued.

6

"I must be young, I must at no time suffer any illness, bodily or mental affliction, or deformity of any kind whatever. Nor must you create any accident, or other circumstance, to deprive me of anything I have mentioned."

For a second Fenton thought he had gone too far.

Out of the dark chair flowed a wave of pure childish annoyance, as though a small boy had stamped his feet on the floor.

"I ref—" There was a sulky pause. "Very well. Granted."

"Thank you. Now I hear, sir, that one of your favourite jokes is to tamper with dates and clocks like an old-fashioned detective story. When I give you the date of May 10th, 1675, it is the time I mean. Nor shall there be any jugglery of fact. For example, you will not have me imprisoned and hanged for this murder. I shall live out my life, exactly as Sir Nicholas did. Granted?"

Though the childish heel-drumming had gone, anger remained.

"Granted, Professor Fenton. Surely there is nothing else?"

"Only one thing more," said Fenton, who was sweating. "Though I shall be in the body of this Sir Nicholas, I must retain my own mind, my own knowledge, memory, and experience, just as they are in this year 1925."

"One moment, if you please," his visitor interrupted in a rich, soothing voice. "Now there, I am afraid, I cannot accommodate you completely. You observe that I deal plainly with you."

"Be good enough to explain."

"Essentially," purred the visitor, "you are a kindly and good man. That is why I want your sou—your company. Now Sir Nicholas, I confess, was at heart much like you. He was good-natured, generous, and easily touched to sympathy. But, being of his age, he was cruder, of different temperament, and given to fits of violent rage."

"I still fail to understand."

"Anger," the visitor explained, "is the strongest of all emotions. Now if you yourself—Professor Fenton, in the body of Sir Nicholas—were to lose your own temper violently, then Sir Nicholas would take over your mind as long as the anger fit lasted. You would become Sir Nicholas for that time. Yet, as part of the bargain, I solemnly tell you that his wrath fits never lasted for more than ten minutes. If you accept this, I grant your condition. What do you say?"

Again conscious of the sweat on his forehead, Fenton considered this to find a catch in it.

7

But there was none. In late middle age Fenton was a trifle inclined towards fussiness, and he fussed and fussed with the rack of pipes beside him. A man in a rage, admittedly, might do much damage in ten minutes. But Fenton's other conditions, already granted, protected him from harm of any kind. They were like heavy nails, driven in after long thought, to seal up the door against the devil.

Besides, he become violently angry? He, Nicholas Fenton? Damn the visitor's impudence! He never became angry. It was monstrous!

"Yes?" insinuated the visitor. "Agreed?"

"Agreed!" snapped Fenton.

"Admirable, my dear sir! Then we have only to seal the bargain."

"Er—I was wondering," Fenton began, but added hastily: "No, no! Not another condition! I merely wished to ask a question."

"My dear friend!" cooed the visitor. "Ask, by all means."

"I daresay it would violate the rules, and be outside even your power to grant, if I were to change history?"

The wave of feeling which flowed towards him was one of childish amusement.

"You could not change history," the visitor said simply.

"Do you seriously mean," insisted Fenton, "that with all the resources of the twentieth century, with infinitely detailed knowledge of what is going to happen, I could not alter even political events with a crash?"

"Oh, you might alter a small and trifling detail here and there," said the other. "Especially in domestic matters. But, whatever you did, the ultimate result would be just the same. You are at perfect liberty," he added politely, "to try it."

"Thank you. I promise I shall try it!"

And then presently the devil had departed, with little less ceremony than he had come. Nicholas Fenton had a good space of time to sit down again, and calm his nerves with a soothing pipe of John Cotton, before Mary's visit.

When he had finished telling Mary every detail of that conversation, she did not speak for some time.

"Then you did sell your soul," she said at length. It was a statement rather than a question.

"My dear Mary, I hope not."

"But you did!"

8

Here Fenton felt rather ashamed of himself. He felt that his tactics had been a little unsporting, even against the Father of Evil.

"The fact is," he said hesitantly, "I had up my sleeve, so to speak ... er ... an ace of trumps which will ultimately defeat him. No, don't ask what it is. Perhaps I have talked great nonsense already."

Abruptly Mary rose to her feet.

"I must be going," she said. "It's getting late, Professor Fenton."

Fenton was conscience-stricken. He must not keep the child up after ten o'clock, or her parents would worry. Nevertheless, even as he escorted her to the front door, he felt piqued that she made no comment.

"What did you think of it?" he asked. "A while ago, you seemed to approve."

"I did," whispered Mary. "I do!"

"Well, then?"

"You see the devil," she said, "as your mind tells you to see him. All your interests are concentrated like a burning glass on history and literature alone. You see him as a combination of the clever, worldly man and the cruel, naïve small boy: I mean, just like a person of the later seventeenth century."

Then she ran down the few short steps to the southern side of Pall Mall. Fenton was left holding the door open to a damp if not rainy night. A twinge of his old rheumatism stirred with pain. Closing and locking the door, he returned to the dim drawing room.

There was not a soul in the house, not even a dog to keep him company. A certain elderly and energetic woman, Mrs. Wishwell, had promised to come in each morning to get his breakfast and tidy up. Each week she and her daughter would give the house what she had enthusiastically called "a real good clean."

Go to bed now? Fenton knew he could not sleep. But he had anticipated that beforehand. His doctor had given him a medium-sized bottle of chloral hydrate, which he had hidden—rather furtively—in the carved-oak sideboard of the drawing room.

Professor Fenton was an abstemious man. Carefully he poured out, as a nightcap, the one whisky and soda he allowed himself a day. Going over to the sideboard, he found the bottle of colourless liquid and added an overly generous dose to the whisky. Afterwards he sat down, leaned back in a comfortable chair, and sipped the mixture.

9

Its effects, he reflected after about ten minutes, must be coming on too quickly. Outlines began to blur. He could scarcely . . .

And that was all he could recall, until something waked him in the middle of the night, or it might have been early in the morning, with the bed curtains drawn and half stifling him. His heart was beating thickly, and he remembered a warning from his doctor. To drive what he supposed to be the chloral from his brain, he forced himself to lie back and reconstruct the events of last night.

"Extraordinary!" he muttered, speaking aloud after the fashion of lonely men. "What a curious dream! No; perhaps not curious. But I must have drunk that infernal stuff much earlier in the evening than I can remember now."

Automatically he ran his hand up over his head. His hand reached the back of the neck, stopped suddenly, groped again, and then stopped altogether.

Even the remaining strands of hair brushed across his skull were now gone. His head was shaved like that of an old-fashioned convict.

Not quite closely shaved, however. There was a faint bristly stubble, which felt as though there might have been hair all over the head.

Sitting up straight in bed, Fenton noticed that for the first time in very many years he had not put on his pyjamas, and that he wore nothing at all.

"Look here, now!" he said to himself, but not aloud. Rolling to his left—the bed sheets seemed oddly coarse and raw—he touched the bed curtains. Despite pitch-darkness, he guessed this to be the bed and the room in which he had chosen to sleep. The bed curtains were thicknesses of unbleached linen, which would have on their outer sides a design woven in heavy red thread. He had seen the bed some days earlier, when he had rented the house, and had sat on the edge of that bed with his feet firmly planted on the ground.

Though still muddle-witted, he nodded gravely. He threw aside the bedclothes, flung back the curtains with a wooden rattle of rings, and swung himself round to sit on the edge of the bed. He must find his pince-nez on the bedside table; afterwards he must grope past the edge of the table and reach the electric switch beside the door.

But Fenton's next gesture would have been really strange—if he had noticed it at the time.

Mechanically he reached along the side of the bed, and found what the undersurface of his brain knew would be there: a loose ankle-length

10

garment of padded silk, with a small trim of fur round the collar and sleeves.

The bedgown, yes. Mechanically he put it round him, pushing his arms into the sleeves, and made a discovery which did rouse him. His whole figure, long and lank and lean, had now altered. He was thick of chest, with a flat stomach and heavily muscled arms. But, when he swung his feet over the side of the bed, his legs did not seem long enough to reach the floor.

From the throat of Nicholas Fenton, professor of history at the University of Cambridge, rose a purely animal snarl which seemed of heavier pitch than his usual light-baritone voice. He did not even know whether he had spoken, or another.

Sheer panic caught him. He was afraid of the darkness, afraid of himself, afraid of primeval forces unknown; and he sat there in a sweat of hot and cold, with his legs grotesquely dangling as though over a gulf.

"Jump!" a great voice seemed to be crying. "Wencher, rakehelly, gamester, jump!"

Fenton jumped, jolting his heels because it was not a long distance to the floor.

"Where am I?" he shouted back. And then: "Who am I?"

Nobody answered him.

Every curtain must have been sealed against the windows, so dense was the dark. Fenton staggered a little. His bare right foot touched what felt like an old slipper of very hard leather; a pair of slippers, he discovered by exploration, and he put them on.

The whole room was pervaded by a faintly unpleasant smell, intensified by stuffiness. What was it he had wanted? Ah, yes. His pince-nez and the light switch. But suppose . . .

Clutching hard to the bed curtain as a guide, he edged his way towards the head. Yes, there was a table of some sort against the wall at the head of the bed. He stretched out his hand, and touched human hair.

This time he felt no impulse to cry out, no flinch to a crawling skin. He knew what he had touched, of course. It was the great peruke, or periwig, whose heavy curls fell down over the shoulders; it stood on its high wig block, ready for the morning.

Fenton nodded. If that were so, there must be something else. His fingers slid towards the right, encountering a large kerchief of silk folded several times. It was probably of bright vivid colours, like his bed gown.

11

On impulse he whipped it up, shook it out, and (with surprising dexterity, for such shaky hands) bound it round his head like a flattened turban. Even his reading, his intense study of small detail, told him that every man of quality concealed his shaven head in this fashion when he lounged at home en déshabille.

Though the breath whistled through his lungs—strong lungs, those of a young man, unbrushed by even the faintest whiff of poison gas from the second battle of Ypres—he imagined himself to be quite calm. Yet he made another test.

Though he groped carefully over the table, he could not find his pince-nez. Edging his way round the table, he attained the rather ill-fitting door. There was no light switch beside it. On the door he encountered not even a porcelain knob; only a wooden latch whose inner side curved outwards and downwards like a claw.

"Quite!" he said aloud. The utter banality of the word made him want to laugh.

On the table there had been a candle in its holder. But there was no match . . . that is to say, no tinderbox. He could not, literally and physically could not, remain here in darkness until morning. Nevertheless, if there had happened what he suspected yet still doubted, there must be someone else in the house.

Someone else. The imagined faces which swam before him . . .

Professor Fenton lifted the latch and threw open the door.

Again darkness. But he had chosen the large bedroom at the back of the house. He must be facing straight down the upstairs passage with the unexpectedly small bedrooms on either side. Some distance away, on the left, a thin line of yellow light shone under the sill of a door.

Fenton walked straight ahead, albeit on shaky legs. The same faintly unpleasant smell pervaded this passage as well as his room. Gaining the door of the room with the light, he did not trouble to knock. He lifted the latch and opened the door halfway.

It was as though veils were dropping away from his now-sharp eyesight, as though he had stumbled through a long tunnel in space to find this door.

Against the wall opposite the door stood some kind of table or perhaps dressing table. A single candle, in a painted china holder, cast (to him) only a dull little glimmer with blurred edges. It brushed the gold-leaf frame of an oblong mirror, propped against the wall with its narrow side on the dressing table. •

Someone sat in an oak chair before the mirror, back towards him. But

12

he could make out little, since the narrow back of the chair—of some yellow woven material pierced by lines of tiny round holes—cut off his view even from the mirror.

He knew only that it was a woman, since her long black hair was let down far over her shoulders, and pressed against the back of the chair. Stop! It was as though she had been expecting him. She did not start or even move at the wooden clunk of the latch, or the creak of the opening door.

For an instant, a finger-snap's time, he dreaded to see her face. If he saw her face, he felt, it would close irrevocably the last barrier between his own life and a century two hundred and fifty years gone by.

But the woman gave him no time, even if he had wished it. She rose to her feet. Pushing the chair back and well to one side, she turned round fully to face him. And for seconds he could only look at her in stupefaction.

"Mary!" he said.

CHAPTER II

SCANDALOUS BEHAVIOUR

OF TWO LADIES

"NICK," the woman answered, with a strange intonation on that one word.

The sound of his own voice unnerved him. He could only stare. Mary Grenville had never in her life called him Nick. And yet, despite that inflection, it was her voice. Furthermore, despite differences from the subtle to the . . . well, to the shocking, he felt rather than knew it was Mary.

Since he had always towered over her, it was more than disturbing to find her only half a head shorter than himself. No, stop! His own height must now be about five feet six inches. And she was not a child. No, not in any sense! It startled Professor Fenton that he should ever notice the obvious reasons why she was not a child.

She stood there in an elaborate bedgown of yellow silk, somewhat soiled, but trimmed with white fur round the very loose sleeves and round a collar whose folds met about halfway to her waist. She had drawn it about her carelessly but tightly. By that dim candlelight her very white skin seemed to have that smoky, shadowy quality he had first remarked last night.

Mary held her head a little back and up. What unsettled him was her smile, especially when it broadened; that, and the expression in her grey eyes.

Then he thought he understood everything.

"Mary!" he said, with ordinary modern pronunciation. "You've

14

been carried back too! I didn't dream that conversation last night; you were not being polite when you sympathized! You've been carried back too!"

But it was the wrong approach.

All the woman's coquetry and insinuation fell away. She shrank back from him, with fear in her eyes.

"Nick!" she cried out, as though begging him not to joke. "What black-more's tongue d'ye speak? Pay your service to another, if you be struck stark mad!"

The last sentence sounded exactly like, "Pye your sarvis to anather, if ye be strook't staark maad!" And suddenly Fenton remembered certain gramophone records he had made himself. With so many stage plays and letters of the age written or dictated phonetically, it was possible to reconstruct their speech as well as any man could. Often he had imitated it for the amusement of the high table at Paracelsus.

Drawing himself up, he made her a deeper and more courteous bow than Sir Nicholas Fenton would have made.

"If it be not too troublesome to you," he intoned in her own speech, but gently, "may I beg to explain myself, madam?"

She understood well enough. But still it was the wrong approach. Breathing in hard gasps, the woman almost spat at him.

"Mad!" she said. "This frenzy for wine and the doxies has spilled the wits out of your head, as it hath done for my Lord Rochester!"

"I must be a devil of a fellow," thought Professor Fenton, much disquieted. But he guessed the proper tactics at last.

"Hold your clack!" he suddenly roared at her. "God's body! Must you skreek out like a carted dell if a man but use you with court civility?"

The woman's right hand, raised as though to shield herself, dropped to her side. The tiny candle flame wavered, amid drifts and weights of shadow. The woman shook back her long hair, fleecy and yet cloudy black. She straightened up. Her whole expression became languishing, pleading, humble; and ever-ready tears started to her eyes.

"Nay, now, forgive me," she pleaded in a soft voice, though he knew her white flesh held a tiger cat. "I was so distracted, that you did put me to lie in a chamber opposite your wife's . . . sweetest, I scarce remember what I said!"

"D'ye heed me?" shouted Fenton, still acting his part and feeling

15

rather pleased with himself. "Am I drunk? Durst you say I am? Or mad?"

"Sweetest, dearest; I owned I was wrong!"

"And I own, for my part, I have led no very admirable life. Well! We can mend that. But let's pretend, for the comedy's sake," and he laughed loudly, "that we begin all anew. That we have never met, and do not know each other. —Who are you?"

Her long eyelashes lifted in brief wonder; then they drooped. Her expression became sweet and sly-lipped.

"If you don't know me, sir," she answered—with a slight emphasis on both you and know, while she smiled—"then in all faith no man on earth knows me!"

"A plague on't, now! *What is your name?*"

"I am Magdalen York, whom it is your pleasure to call Meg. And who is 'Mary'?"

Magdalen York.

In Giles Collins's manuscript there had been considerable mention of "Madam Magdalen York." The "Madam" did not necessarily mean she was married, but only a lady of quality; as the polite "Mrs." of the playhouse dubbed the actress respectable. But this woman only slightly resembled the contemporary likeness of her, probably the fault of the engraver. She was . . .

"Sir Nick," softly wheedled the woman called Meg. She hovered near him, clearly wondering whether to insinuate her arms round his neck or stand clear. Then, as she glided away from the dressing table, for the first time he saw his own face in the mirror.

Striding forward, he picked up the painted china candleholder and held the light close.

"God's body!" he swore.

This time the engraver had done well. Out of the darkling glass, under a close-wound headdress of dull brown silk streaked with white, peered a swarthy but not unhandsome face, with a long nose and a very thin black line of moustache over a good-humoured mouth.

"*Sir Nick. Fenton, born 25th Dec'r, 1649; dy'd*—" Why, he could not be more than twenty-six years old! Only a year older than Mar . . . than this woman Meg. New, startling thoughts crept into the mind of Professor Fenton in the shape of Sir Nick. Under his bedgown, which was brown in colour and sewn with scarlet poppies outlined by silver thread, he flexed his arm muscles and sensed his flat belly.

16

"Come, now," coaxed Meg from behind his shoulder. "You'd not feign madness again?"

"Why, no. I but wondered," and he passed a hand over his jaw, "if I were badly shaved."

"As though that mattered a Birmingham groat to me!" Her tone changed. "Sweetest. You'd not truly . . . mend your way of life?"

"Did you not wish it so?"

He turned round, setting down the candle on the table, so that he faced her and the dim light fell fully on Meg York.

"As touches other women, surely!" She was serious now; her face a little flushed, but her voice soft. "I have loved you—oh, most monstrously!—these two years past. You'd not leave me?"

"Could I leave you?"

"We-ell! For discourse' sake . . ." murmured Meg.

Detached, as though considering the floor without curiosity, she carelessly allowed the front of her yellow bedgown to fall open. Under it she wore not even the seventeenth-century ladies' nightgown or the short smock they sometimes preferred.

It is regrettable to state that desire gripped Fenton like a strangler. The intense sense of her physical nearness made his head swim. "This will never do," thought the Cambridge don. The high-backed chair was near him. With as much dignity as he could, which was not great, he backed towards it and sat down. He had not allowed for his shorter stature, and the seat of the chair bumped him unexpectedly.

All this time Meg watched him furtively, through half-closed eyes, and uttered the ghost of a laugh which might have been a giggle if it had passed her closed lips.

"You a reformed rake?" she murmured. "Oh, fie!"

Women have a peculiar sense of humour.

Then her laugh vanished, through the flush remained on her face.

"I told you before," she said. "I was so extravagant vexed at you, for putting me to lie in a chamber opposite your wife, and thereby causing a great noise of scandal should we be discovered, that I swear I could have killed you! But I have forgot that. I have forgot all. Why should we care what she thinks?"

"Why indeed?" he asked in a hoarse voice.

Fenton's nerves were jumping like a hooked fish, his arms a-tremble. He got to his feet, and Meg stretched out her arms. But he never touched her . . . that is, at this time. Meg, her eyes seeming half-glazed, nevertheless flung a quick look over her shoulder.

17

"The door," she whispered. "Oh, fool, you have forgot to shut the door! —Hark! Did you lend ear to *that?*"

"Some noise! . . . What matter? . . . I . . . "

"You've never heard the scratch of a tinderbox, then?" she inquired. Her tone was whispered fury, and she stamped her foot on the floor. "My sweetest cousin, your lady wife, will be across the passage before you may count ten on your fingers. Pray sit down; do!"

Afterwards Professor Fenton had a confused notion that he had uttered words, some late Restoration oaths he was not even aware he knew. For a moment he had imagined Sir Nick took possession of him, because his memory blurred.

But he sat down, and Sir Nick vanished.

He tried to concentrate on purely academic matters. When Meg drew her lips back, her teeth were even and as white as a hound's, although only the most fastidious ever troubled with the teeth save for an occasional scrub with a soapy twig. Doubtless it was the harsh, gnawed food. All the same, Meg's body was white and clean in an age when . . . stop! This only led his thoughts round in the old circle.

Snap went a door latch across the passage, and another. There was the moving gleam of a candle, and a rustle of taffeta, as someone else entered the room.

"Sweetest Lydia!" crooned Meg, with eyes of childlike innocence, and her bed gown wound round her.

"Then this will be the woman," reflected Fenton, not daring to look over his shoulder, "whom I have—er—idealistically cherished for nine years."

Bracing himself, he did look round.

Lydia, Lady Fenton, was fully dressed as though for a court ball. Her "sky-and-pink" taffeta gown was sleeveless, the low-corsage pushed outwards in heart shape and edged with Venice-point lace, the waist slender, and ankle-length skirt only a little flared. Lydia's soft, light-brown hair was arranged round her head in a sort of very thick cap, down over the ears as well and wide at the sides with a few trailing curls: a fashion set by Louise de Kéroualle.

Her figure was comely, too. She was not as tall as Meg; even so, Fenton knew there would be high heels concealed by the blue-and-pink gown. Lydia Fenton would have been extraordinarily pretty if it had not been for one thing.

18

Her arms, shoulders, and breast were smeared with coarse white powder. Rough-and-ready cosmetics turned her face into a white-and-red mask, as though enamelled. Against a corpse-white face, the smears of red stood out against her cheekbones, and the mouth was heavy scarlet. She wore two "patches," microscopic bits of black paper cut into the shape of hearts or diamonds or Cupids, one pasted beside the left eyelid and one at the corner of the mouth.

The effect was almost horrible. Enamel for a worn-out old woman of seventy had been raddled on the face of a twenty-one-year-old girl. It was as though an old waxwork had stepped down from its stand.

"Sweetest cousin!" intoned Meg, pronouncing the word cozen.

With a somewhat unsteady gait, Lydia moved towards the mantel-piece on her left. There, first tilting the candle, she set it upright on the mantelshelf. It must be remembered that Fenton could still not see her face well. But she had fine blue eyes, strained with tears, inside the mask.

Then Fenton did a strange thing. With one hand he picked up the high, heavy back of the chair, and brought its legs down on the floor with a crash.

"Our Gracious Liege, Charles the Second," he intoned as though in a trance. "By the Grace of God King of England, Scotland, and Ireland, Defender of the Faith. And, "—the trance lifted—"he sleeps now at Whitehall Palace."

"Or elsewhere," tittered Meg, lifting one shoulder in astonishment. "What matter?"

Lydia ignored Meg altogether.

"Sir," she addressed Fenton in a low, sweet voice, "you will confess I have endured much. But that you and this creature, within three yards of my door . . . "

Meg had backed against the dressing table. Her mouth was a pink O of shocked innocence and surprise.

"Oh, filthy! Hideous!" Meg shivered. "Fair cousin! Sure you would not think that Nick and I—"

Still Lydia did not look at her. Perhaps this was what made Meg pause in mid-flight, or perhaps it was the behaviour of Professor Fenton. Bowing low to Lydia, he lifted her hand and kissed it.

"My lady," he said very gently, "I am not unaware of my weakness or cruelty towards you. May I ask your pardon on my knee, thus?"

19

Then he rose up again. "I am not the boorish oaf, with indifferent learning and no wit, you must suppose me. May I have leave to alter my conduct?"

In Lydia's blue eyes there was an expression which, for a moment, stabbed his heart with pity like a physical pain.

"You beg my pardon?" she whispered. "I beg yours, with all my heart."

Then a touch of horror went past her eyes.

"You swear all this?" she begged. "You'd not put a trick upon me?"

"I swear it by what knightly honour is left to me."

"Then rid yourself of her," said Lydia, clasping his hand in both of hers. "Do not suffer her to stay here: not a night, not an hour! Sweet heart, I beseech you! She will destroy you; I know it! She will . . ."

Without hesitation Meg snatched up a hand mirror from the table and flung it at Lydia. The glass, missing both Lydia and Fenton, sailed across the room through the open door and crashed in the passage outside.

"Really," thought Professor Fenton of Cambridge, "these people seem to have no inhibitions whatever." Yet, despite himself, he found his own neck veins swelling with the blood of wrath.

"Bitch!" screamed Meg.

"Punk!" retorted Lydia, meaning harlot.

"Whey-face!"

"Fireship!"

"Fireship, eh?" repeated Meg, in a cool fury of perspiration at this deadliest insult of all. Whirling round, paying no attention to the set of her bedgown, she indicated on the dressing table the litter of used handkerchiefs, jars, and unguent bottles with whose aid she had removed her cosmetics.

"And is it I who have the French sickness, then," she inquired, whirling round again, "that I dare not show my face save under thick enamel? Foh! Or is it the seeming innocent, the virtuous wife—daughter of a mad Independent, granddaughter of a hanged and damned regicide—who is truly a danger to men because she hath . . ."

Once more Meg paused.

Fenton could feel the furious congestion of his face, the blindness that was blackening his eyesight as well as his mind or soul. With both hands he whirled the heavy chair overhead as though it were made of plywood, to smash it down on Meg York's head.

Meg, for the first time really terrified, screamed and backed away and fell on her hands and knees, with her long hair sweeping forwards to hide her face. Her clawed fingers sent up puffs of dust from the bright carpet.

What saved her life was partly that Sir Nick lusted for her too much, and hesitated to kill; and partly that Professor Fenton, as though fighting to shut down a coffin lid with some rolling horror inside, felt the struggle cease and the lid click shut.

Fenton's arms and legs were shaking as he lowered the chair to the floor. Nausea crept up inside him. Catching sight of his own white face in the glass, with the curved black eyebrows and narrow line of moustache, he did not recognize himself and looked round wildly for someone else. Then he grew steadier.

"I hope I did not frighten you, madam?" he said hoarsely—to Lydia, not Meg.

"A little," answered Lydia. "But not as much as you do think." She lifted her eyes. "You will turn her away?"

From behind Fenton there was a faint, mocking titter.

Meg, still on all fours between the edge of the table and the edge of the bed, looked at him past the line of her long black hair. Her eyes were narrow and she laughed with her lips closed. He knew that, except for one black moment, this queenly slut had been enjoying it all.

Fenton strode towards the door. He felt, with justice, that he had experienced quite enough for one night.

"It shall be as you desire," he said to Lydia, and pressed his hand on one bare shoulder. "But . . . not tonight. This night, dear wife, I lie alone. I must think how things are like to go. And above all," he snapped, as he turned round in the doorway, "a sweet good night to both of you!"

Though he slammed the door behind him, he forgot that a wooden latch was unlikely to hold. The door banged, and then stood an inch open; pale vertical light slanted out into the dark passage. Fenton, shuffling a little way towards his own bedroom, resting his head against the wall panel and tried for a time to think.

Had any man, he wondered, ever faced so formidable a problem?

Twice that night Sir Nick had almost—almost, if not quite—gained control. And not alone by anger. Silkily, casually, the devil had mentioned anger. Now the devil (who must in the future not be underestimated) had not mentioned physical desire, which somehow

21

seemed vaguely connected with anger and could be just as powerful. But physical desire was granted by implication, it became automatic, if you stipulated strong health and the age of twenty-six.

He was begining to understand a little of Sir Nick's character. Sir Nick lusted for Meg York, and would never turn her out or suffer her harm. But Sir Nick also loved his wife, and would never turn her out or suffer her harm either. Could a man at the mental age of fifty-eight control this? But fifty-eight was not really old; did he want to control it? Dimly Fenton realized (with horror) that in his heart he shared Sir Nick's feelings too.

And he had promised to get rid of Meg next day.

But this was not his real problem. No, not by a jugful! His real problem, set down in the neat script of Giles Collins's manuscript, was this:

Unless he could prevent it, Lydia would die of poison in exactly one month. She was the victim. And the person he had long suspected of being the murderess, from certain details in the manuscript, was Meg York.

Fenton, in creaky leather slippers, stumbled towards his bedroom door.

CHAPTER III

LYDIA IN BROWN;

AND POISON

WHEN he awoke next morning, he had this time no feeling that he had been dreaming. He knew very well where he was.

A dull light of morning shone behind the bleached-linen bed curtains, which were again closely drawn and heightened the faintly unpleasant smell in the room. But seldom had Fenton felt so happy or elated or refreshed. Tightening his muscles under the snarled-up bedgown, he drew the air deeply into his lungs.

Why, it was amazing that a man should feel so refreshed at fi ... no, twenty-six. Better still! His troubles of last night seemed no heavier than the feather you scarcely feel. Kick Meg out of the house, and save Lydia's life! It was as simple as that.

Even if Meg were not guilty, it would be good riddance.

"The world, the flesh, and the devil," he mused aloud; "I have challenged all three." Professor Fenton smiled. "But I also have, 'Si la jeunesse savait, si la vieillesse pouvait,' which is a good combination to defeat them."

Instantly, as though at a signal, the curtains towards the left were both thrown wide open.

In the aperture stood a lean, smallish man dressed in sober dark clothes, but of fine quality and with silk stockings to his breeches, as befitted his position. The man stood with head bent a little forwards, hands clasped together in front of him. It needed only a flash of the engraver to tell his identity.

He was Giles Collins, Sir Nick's servant-cum-clerk. His fiery red hair stuck up straight over a long lean face like a Puritan's, but he

23

had a bawdy-looking eye and mouth. His native impudence led him to talk back to his master as far as he dared. But, as Fenton knew from sources other than Giles's own writing, he was the most faithful servant alive.

"A good morning to you, sir and master," he said obsequiously.

Rolling over on his side, Fenton braced himself for the phrase and accent he must use.

"Halloa, ye cursed rogue," he growled out in what he correctly imagined to be the morning voice of Sir Nick. "Are you about your business so soon?"

"Ay; that I am. And yours too. And you, I observe," said Giles, "were again boozy last night. Come! Will you not don a proper night habit, even when I set it out for you?"

"'Tis a cursed nuisance."

"True, in some ways true!" agreed Giles wisely, but with a low-minded smile twisting round his mouth. "Ah, these ladies! When Madam York does this,"—his description was more full and pungent than need be recorded—" or when Madam York does that . . ."

"*Hold your tongue, damn you!*"

Redheaded Giles shrank together like a deflated bladder-on-a-stick, and looked hurt.

"Nay, now," growled Fenton, "I meant no harm."

"And I mean but to serve you well, sir!" Giles said obsequiously.

"As for the slut called Magdalen York, she'll leave this house as soon as we can fetch a glass coach. Where she goes is her own pleasure. I've done with her; d'ye hear me?"

Fenton stopped there because Giles, with his long Puritan face on one side, was regarding him with a look neither of obsequiousness nor of agreement nor of impudence.

"And now what ails you, Giles?"

"Mistrust me not," said Giles. "It is only that I have heard you use those same words so often ere this."

Fenton sat up straight in bed. Softly Giles moved to the table at the head of the bed, where the black peruke—freshly combed and curled to glossiness—still stood on its wig block. Beside it now was a heavy silver tray, with almost as heavy a silver cup containing steaming hot chocolate.

Deftly Giles lifted the silver tray and slid it across Fenton's lap. Just as deftly and quickly he opened all the bed curtains, looping each

24

back on its post near the foot of the bed. Fenton, sipping the chocolate, glanced unobtrusively round the room.

A grey, overcast sky, with a rattle of wind, showed beyond the two windows at the rear. From where he sat he could see only the tops of tossing trees. The window hangings, of heavy dull-white brocade picked out in dull red, were all looped back. On the floor was a carpet of such brilliant and entwined Oriental colours that Fenton shut his eyes. The furniture loomed in hard, uncompromising oak, bringing lack of joy to the anatomy. The low ceiling and the brown-panelled walls seemed to shut him in and press him down.

He grimaced over his chocolate. It was harsh, gritty, and much too sweet; but a young palate can gulp down anything. Giles watched him closely.

"Sir, you must make haste!" the servant-clerk moaned, and wrung his hands. "The hour is late already—"

"How late?"

"Past eight of the clock. And Lord George will be here soon."

"D'ye call that late?" asked Fenton, simulating a yawn and a half-boozy eye. "Be quick, carrot-pate: What's the day and the month? If it comes to that, ecod, what's the year?"

Giles gave him a look. But Giles, with restrained impudence, informed him that it was Tuesday, the tenth of May, in the year of Our Lord one thousand six hundred and seventy-five.

"Then last night," reflected Fenton, "was a part of this morning. Past midnight, of course!" The devil always kept his bargains to the letter, if not to the spirit. And Lord George, naturally, must be George Harwell, second son of the Earl of Bristol; he was Sir Nick's closest friend and boon companion.

"Your clothes, good sir!" said Giles, who was flying from one chair to another on which various vestments were set out. "Sober, yet with just a touch of colour to show your gentility? Black-velvet coat and breeches, black stockings, and your Clemens Hornn sword?"

Moodily Giles paused beside a tall chair over which hung a narrow leather sword belt with a silver buckle.

"There is like to be bloody work this day," he added. "I think you venture too far."

" 'Bloody work?' " exclaimed Fenton. " 'Venture too far?' "

There had been nothing about this in the manuscript; perhaps it had never happened, or had been suppressed for delicacy's sake.

25

"Will you approve the clothes, master?"

Fenton surveyed them. From many pictures he knew exactly how they looked when they were worn. But he had not the slightest idea how to put them on. He gave the only possible command, which was also the proper command for his day.

"Dress me!" he said; and felt like a fool.

Giles led him to a table, rather like Meg's dressing table but in the angle of the left-hand window and the wall. On it Giles had placed a huge silver basin, a monstrous ewer of hot water, a very large straight-bladed razor on its oiled whetstone block (Fenton shied a little), several highly scented soaps in bowls, together with heated cloths and towels.

For once there was a round-shaped chair, with a deep cushion. At Giles's broad and curvetting gesture, he sat down facing the mirror. Neatly Giles unwound Fenton's head covering, with all Giles's airs becoming Frenchified. Very solemnly, without splashing a drop of water, he washed Fenton's hands—each to a point about two inches above the wrist—and dried them with great care.

If Giles had not triumphantly added, "Voilà!" it might not have stirred Fenton's donnish sense of humour.

"Now that is well done!" he said, lifting his right hand from the sleeve and inspecting it. "Indeed it is admirably done, as far as it goes. But doth it go, do you think, quite far enough? What if I had a mind to order a bath?"

Giles's red eyebrows shot up in two half-circles. "Good master?" he said.

"I have it by report," mused Fenton, "that Queen Catherine of Braganza, when she married our king well over a decade ago, had a large bath set into one of her apartments at Whitehall Palace, with a pump to bring up the water."

"Ay; true. But who bathes in Thames water," Giles sneered, "would bathe also in Fleet Ditch." He turned round and spat on the carpet. "A filthy lot, these foreigners!"

"Then don't try to be French, good carrot-pate. You are too much English."

Giles, in a huff, disdained this remark.

"We have a bath," he pointed out. "And a full half-dozen times a year, for aught I can tell, Big Tom must fetch it up from the cellar

26

because my Lady Fenton or Madam York make such a great noise about the matter."

"Whereas you would be more moderate?"

"I say nothing," declared Giles.

All this time the fingers of his right hand had been working in a soap bowl, almost magically foaming up a scented shaving lather. Then the speechless one continued.

"But the ladies of our house," he said, "can manage—ay, and do manage—to wash themselves without a monstrous great tub and buckets of sweet water from the pump. 'Tis but natural they should desire to wash neck and arms and shoulders, these being exposed in some public place such as ballroom or gaming house or the like. Yet on occasion (I apprehend) they even wash themselves all over."

Here Giles shut one eye in a wink so lecherous, yet so unaffectedly gleeful, that even his leer was not at all unpleasant.

"Giles," said his master, "you are a whoreson old man."

"Old or young, pray who is not?" retorted Giles. "To pretend otherwise were hypocrisy, which we find many times condemned in Holy Writ."

At this point, by some prestidigitation of Giles's left hand, a warm cloth slid smoothly round Fenton's neck. His head was pushed very far back, so that his neck rested with steady cramping pain against the rounded top of the chair back. In this position, where he could see only two joinings of the wall panels and a part of a grimy white plaster ceiling, he felt Giles dexterously applying lather.

"Now to continue my thesis—" observed Giles.

"God's body, will you never have done?"

"Sir Nick, you swear too much. The head back, if it please you." His head was pushed once more, his neck agonized. "Now woman in general, from the high degree of Madam Carwell (which French fireship somehow ensnares His Majesty) to the low degree of Mistress Kitty, our cook, on whom your own lewd eye hath so often been cast . . ."

"Wha'?"

"The mouth closed, good sir, or it will receive lather: thus. Woman, I say, must by nature and art be sweeter of flesh than ourselves, poor devils, whom they cozen and wheedle and tease, so that accordingly, by their behaviour, they are the more often undressed."

27

The lather felt cool and smooth, though its heavy perfume revolted Fenton. He opened one eye.

"Have a care with that razor, Impudence! I had as lief be shaved with a two-handed broadsword!"

"Mistrust me not," murmured Giles. "'Twill be as light as a feather touch."

And in fact it was, Fenton being scarcely conscious of it even on the neck or at the angle of the jaw.

"As regards men," said Giles, "it is but fitting, especially as touches quality, that they should on occasion fully wash themselves. Also, that the windows of a house should often be set open, to take away the scent of the watches of the night."

"Well, then, damme," exclaimed Fenton, sitting up so abruptly that only Giles's deftness prevented a throat-cutting, "why is there such an offensive bad odour in *this* house?"

Giles, wiping off lather on the neckcloth, gave a Frenchified shrug.

"Why, sir, if that matter were my poor fault and not your own . . ."

"Mine? How?"

This time Giles's shrug carried his shoulders almost up to his ears.

"Here's our cellar half full of sewage from the house, and what to do with it?" Giles looked sad. "Here are you, a Member of Parliament, a King's man and the hottest of the Court party. Half a hundred times you have swore, and struck the table when you swore, you would employ your mouth and make interest with Sir John Gilead to have a pipe run not three dozen yards to a main sewer. But always you have forgot."

"Not this time, I'll warrant you," said Fenton, dropping his neck back to agony and a last touch of the razor.

"'Tis true," murmured Giles, "we have a third course open to us."

"Oh?"

"Certes we could have it all pumped out into the street, as Sir Francis North did. But I fear this would sorely vex the neighbours."

Now Giles's remark was not funny. "It's a wonder," thought Fenton, "that more of them didn't die of typhoid, let alone the great or bubonic plague." Nevertheless he roared with laughter.

"Ay," he mused, "Roger North tells the anecdote in his biography of—that is," he corrected himself swiftly, "Mr. North tells it any night you please, when he has taken a pint or two at the Devil, within Temple Bar."

The razor stopped. Fenton sensed that all Giles's sauciness and sermon talk had fallen away, and that the old man felt a shiver of fear.

28

"Now of a surety," Giles said quickly, "you would not take a cup of wine at the Devil tavern? So hard by the King's Head, at the turning of Chancery Lane?"

"And why not?"

Here Fenton made his first large slip, though he did not know it and even Giles did not recognize it for what it was. Fenton's mind, so alert not to betray itself over small points, had let a large one go past unnoticed. He had known of old that Sir Nick was a Member of Parliament and of the Court party; it overjoyed him, since these were his own politics of the era.

But he did not, at the moment, connect these facts with the King's Head tavern. The chilly grey sky seemed to press down on a chilly, ill-odoured room.

"Now bend your head forward over the basin," said Giles, "that I may wash your face."

Twenty minutes later, when he stood fully dressed before a full-length mirror, he looked at the reflection with incredulity. The glossy black peruke, with its curls falling down over the shoulder, would have seemed rather foolish on the head of Professor Fenton in his pince-nez. But, when it framed the broad swarthy face of Sir Nick, with moody grey eyes and narrow line of moustache, the countenance leaped out strong and even formidable.

The black-velvet coat was rather long—halfway to the knee—but comfortable. Though it was loose and never meant to close or be buttoned, it had a short line of silver buttons down the right side. He was given no jewellery, for which he was thankful. His neckband carried only a short fall of lace, down over a long black-satin waistcoat slashed with red. The black-velvet breeches, the black hose: at only one point had there been violent argument.

"Now hark'ee, coxcomb," said Fenton. He gave Giles what he intended to be only a very light push in the chest, to keep the man from fussing round him. But he forgot the power of his arm, and sent Giles flying and sprawling against the base of the opposite wall.

There Giles sat us loftily, folded his arms, and proceeded to murmur a stream of vituperation.

"I will wear all else," pleaded Fenton, "but I will not wear these accursed high-heeled shoes with the bowknots on them."

Giles murmured something indistinguishable, flicking his fingers after it.

"In four-inches heels," said Fenton, "I could not take half a dozen

29

steps without falling flat. As for your coloured ribbands at the knee garter and bowknots on the shoes, I well know these are worn by good brisk lusty men as well as fops and beaux. Yet my love for them is not yet developed."

Giles was understood to murmur something about small popinjays.

"Yet I am a good middle height for our time," Fenton told him stoutly. "Giles, Giles! Have I no honest leathern shoes with flat heels?"

Giles uttered a silent sarcastic laugh.

"Questionless," he said, "you have the old shoes you sometimes wear about the house."

"Good! Go and fetch them!"

There was a long pause, while Giles's red hair stood up like a goblin's.

"Sir Nick would dare the devil and the altar," he said softly. "Sir Nick would fling wine into the face of my Lord Shaftesbury himself. But Sir Nick, the man à la mode, durst not venture into the street in those shoes."

"Go and fetch them!"

Giles rose up, all meekness. He gave Fenton a quick glance in which wonder was somewhat blended with a subtle quality not quite to be identified.

"I fly, sir," he answered, and feathered out of the room with scarce a whisper from the closing door.

Fenton turned round again to the full-length mirror. Automatically his hand fell on the sword hilt, which projected well out from under the coat at his left hip.

Also automatically, his hands slipped under the rather long waist and shifted the belt a shading to the right. From that belt, at the left hip and behind it, two very thin lengths of chain supported and sloped the scabbard. And, since the scabbard was made only of the thinnest wood strips, glued together and covered with shagreen, it was so light that the duellist never even noticed it.

"Clemens Hornn," he said, unconscious that he had spoken aloud. "In past day the greatest swordmaker in England."

His right hand closed round the tight wire-woven grip. He backed away from the mirror. Then he whipped out the rapier.

A low light glittered along the blade. It was not one of your fine old-style Cavalier rapiers, with cup hilt and long quillons but a blade too cumbersomely long. Nowadays men had discovered that an old-fashioned overarm cut was helpless against the lightning thrust of the point.

30

Fenton's sword was still a rapier, though in transition period to the smallsword. Its shallow guard gleamed like a closing flower carved in steel. Its short curving quillons were merely ornamental. It was shorter than the old blades—its edges blunt, half an inch wide down to the tapering, murderous point—but lighter and far more deadly. Thus the fine old blade now suited its day.

Ever since touching the steel, he had been startled to find the sense of pride and pleasure which swept through him: the deep breath, the sense of steadiness and power. For certainly he was no swordsman.

True, from youth to middle age he had been a very competent performer with the fencing foil in a gymnasium. But he could laugh at that now. The foil was a toy; it was too light, with all its complexities and too-easy parries. Such a performer could not stand for twenty seconds against a fighting sword in a crafty hand. At the same time . . .

"In my little chat with the devil," he thought to himself, "there was no mention of duelling. I cannot die before my time; true. I cannot be overtaken by physical illness; true. But a vicious sword-thrust?"

"Your shoes, good sir," interrupted the voice of Giles Collins, striking so like a rapier into Fenton's thoughts that the latter all but dropped the sword in his hand.

You could never tell in what mood you would find Giles. At the moment he was merely obedient. And merry.

"If you will have the goodness to be seated," he said, holding up the shoes like a pair of rare jewels, "I shall put them on. Heyday! I see you practice your secret *botte*."

Fenton's eyes opened at his own image in the glass. His upper lip was lifted, exposing the white teeth in a snarl. The curls of his peruke had slipped a little forward. He stood sideways to the mirror, right foot straight forward with knee bent, left foot sideways and a little behind him, creeping to the right leg. The rapier, so balanced to his hand that it seemed to carry its own weight, gleamed at an unorthodox guard.

Then Fenton woke up, and laughed rather too loudly.

"'Tis no 'secret' *botte*," Giles informed him dryly, "though all the rufflers think it so. Observe how your left foot crept towards your right. Your guard, deliberately, too close to your body. Heyday! *I* know it."

"Oh, I am no swordsman," Fenton said carelessly, slipping the blade back into the scabbard and sitting down so that scabbard and coat could be accommodated.

Again Giles gave him that curious, subtle glance. Giles was about to speak when Fenton withered him.

"I have much of moment to do," he said. The strong, harsh tone struck the servant like a handblow. "Is Lord George Harwell yet come?"

"Nay, sir, I believe not." Giles fitted on the old, disreputable, comfortable shoes.

"Ay; well; should he come, he must wait. I have an errand for you. Render my service to my lady wife—"

Giles's dark eyes bulged under the red eyebrows. "Your wife?"

"Have you ears?" demanded Fenton.

"Assuredly. I but thought . . ."

"Ask of her," Fenton continued, remembering the rules of civility for a mere wife, "if it be not too troublesome, whether she will wait upon me here as soon as convenient?"

The husband must summon the wife; never go to her in public.

"Again I fly," murmured Giles, trying to subdue a leer. As he turned round, Fenton longed to deliver a mighty kick in the seat of his breeches; but Fenton had learned that Giles, though his age might be anything from fifty to seventy, was too agile to be caught.

"Ah," murmured this doubtful jewel of a manservant, "if I may make bold . . . ?"

"Well?"

"Should I by mischance encounter Madam York—"

"Bid her go to the devil!"

The door closed.

Fenton paced the floor. By summoning Lydia, he knew, he was turning loose emotional currents which last night had nearly swamped him. But every moment of this morning had made him bolder, because of his new age and his outward transformation. If for nine dim years he had cherished idealistically a bad engraving, wondering and picturing what the original must have been, he could not but feel a kindness towards her when both were young.

But this (or so he told himself) was of no matter. Pressing his hands to his head, and being surprised to find the hair of the peruke he had forgotten, he brought back that old grind at medical jurisprudence. If last night he had not been so overwrought, he would have seen why Lydia wore so much paint and moved at an unsteady gait.

Sir Nick would be prowling soon. Sir Nick either disliked Lydia or grudgingly tolerated her. Then, at all costs, Lydia and Meg must not be permitted to meet. They acted on each other like fire and loose gunpowder, a hissing flare at which you only scorched your hands, and looked to any powder kegs about you.

32

Quick, rapping footsteps on small heels ran down the bare boards of the passage outside. About two yards from the door the footsteps stopped, as though their owner would draw herself up with dignity. There was a light knock on the door.

"Enter!" said Fenton.

It was Giles who opened the door, though so many emotional currents swirled into the room that Fenton did not even notice him. Lydia stepped hesitantly across the threshold.

"Gad!" Fenton said involuntarily, and frankly stared at her for such a time that she grew discomforted and colour came into her face.

Lydia wore today a gown for the house, of some light-brown material drawn in at the waist, with very tiny ruffles at the sleeves and at the fairly high neck. It had a white bodice, broad and triangular, so that its crisscross of points and laces began in a bow at the neck and ran down to her waist.

But, above all, Lydia seemed to wear no cosmetics that disfigured her countenance. Her fresh-complexioned face, framed in the thick cap of light-brown hair which surrounded her head like a curve, ceased to seem ill or drawn because of the colour in it. Lydia's blue eyes were set wide apart. Her nose was short, her mouth broad and full-lipped, her chin rounded. It was not a type of beauty, as Giles would say, à la mode; it would be considered to lack boldness, or a quality of stariness. But Fenton's heart sailed like a paper dart out of a window. Since Lydia wore low heels, she appeared even smaller.

"Do you," she murmured, and lowered her eyes and seemed to search hard for some petty word, "do you find me pleasing?"

"Pleasing?" repeated Fenton.

He strode close to her, lifted her hand, kissed it, and pressed it against his cheek.

"Last night," faltererd Lydia, "you did that. You have not done it since . . . " She paused.

Now, when very close to her, he could see the faint powder she had applied. It was applied up high on the forehead, near the hairline, and at one side of her cheek. Probably it extended to the arms and shoulders. Even in this bad light, if he could persuade her to lie down, he could decide the matter.

"My lady," he said gently, "will you have the kindness to lie down on the bed?"

At the very same moment, in a snap of sixth sense, he became conscious of Giles Collins.

33

Now Giles would not stoop to clear away chocolate service or shaving service; such menial work must be done by a chambermaid. But Giles stood near the dressing table. His red eyebrows travelled up almost to the hairline, while his mouth sketched a delighted whistle.

"Jackanapes and louse!" roared Fenton, looking about for something to throw. "I'll have thee in the pillory for this! Begone, louse! Begone!"

This time, since Giles had to fly past the bed, Fenton had another chance at a mighty kick. Again Giles dodged. And once more Fenton told himself to remember that these people—shrewd though they might be—were in many respects like children or adolescents.

"Giles," he growled, half in apology, to the wicked grin twisted outside the door.

"Good master?"

"Look to it that none disturbs us."

"Myself shall set watch, Sir Nick."

And Giles latched the door, which had no lock or bolt.

Fenton turned back to the bed. Obediently Lydia had lain down beside the discarded silver chocolate service, though she trembled slightly. Fenton sat down beside her.

"My lady . . ." he began gently.

"Have you no tenderness at all?" she whispered, without opening her eyes. "Call me Lydia! Or," she hesitated, hardly bold enough for a suggestion, "or even . . . dear heart?"

Fenton felt a pang, not for her naïveté but for her intense devotion to the man she thought he was.

"Dear heart," he said, taking her hand and unobtrusively finding her pulse, "do you recall old days? When I took my degree, *magister artium*, at Paracelsus when I was seventeen? And desired to study physick, but that my father thought it beneath me?"

She nodded at this information from Giles's manuscript. Though Fenton had no watch, he needed none to find that her pulse beat was small, frequent, irregular. Gently touching her cheek, he found it cold and faintly clammy.

"Well!" he said. "I would have you know that I did study thus in the way of secrecy. I can cure you. Am I one you intrust?"

The blue eyes opened wide.

"But what else?" she asked. "Are you not my husband? And do I not . . . have a fondness for you?"

34

She spoke with such wonder that Fenton gritted his teeth.

"Why, then," he smiled, "but a few moments more!"

He rose to his feet, the sword scabbard banging the side of the bed before his shoes struck the floor. Hurrying over to the dressing table, he found a clean towel and dipped one end of it into the now tepid water of the ewer. He returned with it, the towel bunched in his hand.

"And now, Lydia," he continued, gently passing the dampened cloth over her forehead where she had put the face powder, "we have only to . . ."

"No! I won't! Not ever!"

The moment that cloth touched her forehead, Lydia shook her head violently and turned her head away. But Fenton saw just what he expected to see: the skin rash along the forehead, rather like eczema, but fainter. It was also under the powder patch on the cheek.

At the same time, he gently touched the calf of her left leg; then the right. Both were a trifle swollen, and must have been painful. Only the stamina of this small twenty-one-year-old girl, her passionate longing for he knew not what, kept her even near to her belief that she was well.

"Lydia!" he said sharply.

She whirled round to face him, partly propped up by the pillow and the wall behind the bed. With swift fingers she flew at the bowknot of her bodice, so that in some fashion the whole gown seemed to fall apart at the top. Lithely she writhed her arms and shoulders out of it. Since a high silk smock impeded her, she ripped it down. Gown and slip lay about her, leaving her uncovered to the waist. Snatching the towel from Fenton, she began to daub at powder on her left shoulder, down the arm, and across the side.

"Now see all my disgrace!" said Lydia. It was only the small eczema-like rash, but tears came into her eyes. "Can I go into a public place without being sensible I am jeered? Are you not disgusted?"

"Not the least in the world," he smiled, and held her glance by compulsion. "Lydia, what do you think is the matter with you?"

But again she turned her face away and sobbed.

"Last night," she muttered, "when that creature—oh, horrid!—as much as said I had the French sickness, I could have died with shame. Oh, she has said it ere that! How could I have got it? God He knoweth, I have never . . . But fear will not go away."

"Lydia!" he said sharply. He put his hands on her bare shoulders, and pulled her up almost to a seated position. "You said you did intrust me. Now look at me."

Then, though he dropped his hands, she did not fall back. But her face was still turned away.

"You have no illness of the kind you think. Nor, in fact, any illness at all that is a part of nature. I can cure you in a day or less." Fenton laughed, but not too loudly to frighten her the more. "Now let me give proof I know. Do you not sometimes have a great thirst?"

"I—I have drunk so much barley water I am like to burst. But how could you know?"

"You often suffer," he said, touching the calves of her legs, "from pain here?"

Lydia looked at him. The blurred blue eyes, the short nose with nostrils now wide, the broad trembling lips, wore an expression almost of awe.

"After you have partaken of food or drink, say a quarter of an hour, do you—not always, but on occasion—fell fierce pains of the stomach, and are violently sick?"

"Oh, horridly! And, oh, in truth I think you know all man may know! But what . . . ?"

He dreaded to give her the reply, but he had no other choice.

"Lydia, someone has been trying, very slowly, to poison you with arsenic."

CHAPTER IV

MEG IN SCARLET;

AND A DAGGER

HE WAS right in dreading to tell her. Even the word "poison," to Lydia as to nearly all other persons, was wrapped in dread and mystery; it struck out of nowhere, and could not be fended off. It was born of sorcery and witchcraft, howling like a wind in the chimney.

Fenton needed a long time to soothe and reassure her.

"Then I . . . shall not die?"

"No! Do you feel like a dying woman?"

"Truly, I don't." She mused on this. "Only a *little* indisposed; no more."

"That is because the poisoner gave you too few doses, and at too long intervals. If you but take the draughts I shall order, there is nothing to fear."

Lydia's hand flew to her forehead. "These—these spots . . . ?"

"They will vanish altogether. They are only symptoms of poisoning by arsenic."

"But who would desire to . . . ?" Lydia began on a shuddering breath. Fenton stopped her.

"We will speak of that anon," he said. "First we must cure you."

Lydia, so overjoyed and delighted and relieved that she could not trouble her head about a mere murderer, simply looked at him and continued to look. Her manner grew quieter. Fenton tried to explain, in the simplest possible words, the nature of a poison and how it worked. But he knew she would not understand; the Royal Society itself would not understand. Last night he had observed that Lydia had a very comely figure. In the present state of her attire, this fact was much noticeable.

"These legends," he was saying, "of bat's blood and toad's entrails and other substances, nauseous yet quite without harm, become laughable in the light of . . . in the light of . . ." He paused. "I beg your pardon. What was I saying?"

"Dearest heart," Lydia assured him tenderly, though somewhat crimson of face, "you were but looking at . . ."

"Ay; true! True, true, true! I had forgot."

Fenton slipped off the edge of the bed and stood on his feet.

"It doth not displease me," said Lydia.

Fenton made one final effort to be paternal. Walking towards the head of the bed, he bent down and very lightly kissed her lips. Then the weights in the scalepans flew wide. Lydia's arms went fiercely round him; or, rather, round that confounded periwig. He bent her head back and kissed her with what might be called some degree of intimacy.

"Nick," she presently muttered, close by the side of his mouth.

"Y-yes?"

"When you first bade me lie down, I thought what Giles thought. Then I bethought myself, 'Here? . . . so publicly? . . . with so many people like to be about? . . .' "

"I know."

"Shall our true rendezvous be for tonight?"

This was folly. It was utter folly for a girl not yet free from poison, albeit a mild attack. But Fenton was rapidly losing his wits.

"Tonight, Lydia, you may feel in no mood for such—"

"I could love you," she murmured fiercely, "if I were dying. Am I dying?"

"No! A fiend's name, no!"

"Then I shall have your company this night?"

"Yes!"

His arms went fully round her. And (such is nature's way) Lydia's skin seemed no longer in the least cold or clammy. The kiss had reached such an intimacy that both were considering it foolish and unnecessary to postpone the rendezvous, when . . .

Giles, in the passage outside, put up a fine long defence. But this

38

was the moment at which the door swept open, and in walked Meg.

And, in that instant restirring of emotional currents, Sir Nick prowled after her like a black dog's soul. Fenton, though shaken and startled, knew another emotion. It was the wrath which could slowly darken his eyesight.

Meg, after one brief glance round the looped-back bed curtains, turned her head away. She walked slowly across the room towards the windows, giving herself time to think how she must meet this situation. Meg's arms trembled a little. Lydia herself was not in the least embarrassed. Even before Meg's glance, Lydia had contrived to writhe herself into the bedcovers so that she appeared to be wearing even less than was actually the case.

"Then you honour us, madam?" Fenton asked, with a heavy snarl.

"In faith I honour you," Meg said coolly.

At the windows, magnificently drawn up, she turned to face them.

Meg's black straw hat had a very wide brim, which forced her to hold her head up, but was a little curved up at the back. Flat along the curve of the hatbrim lay a single golden-coloured plume. Against her black glossy hair, done up in much the same style as Lydia's, her white smoky complexion had never stood out more vividly.

Round her neck, despite the warm weather, she wore a short pelisse of black fur reaching only to her elbows. It was unfastened, to show the top of a gown in vertical stripes of black and scarlet, with a very low bodice edged in small black ruffles. Her small purse, swung at her right hip, was gold-dusted and set with a circle of rubies. Both hands were thrust into a black fur muff, as the fashion was. Her skirt flared in vivid scarlet. Under it she wore so many satin petticoats that, when she moved, she sounded like a wandering rain shower.

"Nick my dear," Meg said airily, "I have ordered your coach for this morning. You'll not deny me, I know."

"Indeed, madam?"

Meg had decided, evidently, to ignore the whole matter and pretend Lydia was not there. Lydia, as though also uninterested, looked at nothingness with dreamy eyes and the suggestion of a smile. It was not in human nature for Meg to refrain from an eye-flick at her; and Meg gave only one gasp of fury.

"I have a mind," she continued carelessly, "to go to the New Exchange. I shall take a turn in the galleries, and perhaps buy a trifle or

39

two. Sweetest, I am so wasteful. Yet twenty guineas, I think, will suffice for today."

"You are sure, madam?"

Meg gave him a quick look of appraisal. He was approaching at a soft, murderous step. With an effort at carelessness, Meg moved out from the windows past the dressing table, and backed towards the left-hand wall. Slowly he wheeled round to face her, his forehead blackening with rage and his lips drawn back from his teeth.

Helplessly Fenton felt the constriction tighten round his chest; he could hardly breathe. Something black, like a hangman's hood, seemed to be settling over his head and addling his brain. He fought against it, but . . .

"Oh, fie!" cried Meg, with a little shivering laugh. "Sure you would not be jealous of the foplings in the New Exchange, all flaxen periwigs and killing ogles, when they follow me. To one (thus) I give my manteau to hold; to another (thus) my muff; to still a third—"

Meg broke off. She had not time to scream or even move.

There was a soft hiss as the rapier whipped out of its sheath, and seemed to make a blur in dim grey light. Its point rested against Meg's body exactly above the middle of her bodice. A hairline less, and it would not have touched her; a hairline more, and it would have drawn blood.

"Before we speak of aught else," a hoarse voice was saying, "you will let fall the dagger in your muff."

"Dagger?" whispered Meg, lifting long black eyelashes.

"The haft projecting beyond your hand, your thumb on the blade: 'tis too plain to be missed."

"Oh, hideous! To think—"

"You will let fall the dagger, or you will have this through your guts. Be easy, madam. The choice is your own."

Sir Nick would do it, and Meg must have seen so. Meg's grey eyes slid round. Sir Nick's thumb and forefinger tightened on the sword grip, to drive it through her body, while Fenton struggled and fought to hold back the arm.

Meg drew her right hand out of her muff. Her expression was cool and rather contemptuous. A small Venetian dagger, dull and unpolished, clattered on the floor boards beyond the carpet.

"I am mightily obliged to you," he said.

The man in the periwig, whose every moment was as swift and light-

40

footed as a cat's, lowered the sword point. He bent down, picked up the dagger, and sent it skimming across the room. Then, straightening up, he let the rapier slip back into its sheath.

"And now," he said, nodding towards Lydia in the bed, "which of us had you a mind to stab?"

Meg's astonishment was unfeigned.

"Why, who but the Roundhead's daughter?" she asked, gesturing towards the bed. "Did I not see her a-running in here? Could I not fancy what was a-doing? Some matters I account no crime."

"God's body, you have the right of it there." Then the voice grew soft. "But don't try it against my wife, Meg, and don't try it against me; or direly you will regret it. Last night, against my wife, you said a foul and untrue thing . . ."

Meg lifted her shoulders and looked perplexed.

"If it served my turn, wherefore not?" she asked. "I do as I please."

"Do you so? —Giles!"

Giles, with a wizened face of terror which held no mischief, slipped into the room.

"Ay, good sir?"

"Let Madam York have the money she desires; look to it." He swung back to Meg. "You may take the coach, but return it. —Stay but a moment, good slut; there is one matter more." His fingers crept again to the sword grip. "George Harwell and I go into the Strand; rather, to Dead Man's Lane; a coach would make snail's walk. If I find you here when I return, if you are not gone forever with all you possess, I will not open my neck to the hangman by using this." He shook the scabbard. "I will summon a magistrate, and have you committed to gaol."

Meg's floppy hat went up and back. "And pray on what charge?"

"That you will discover. But 'tis a hanging matter, you may depend on it. Now go."

"Go for all time? You don't mean it!"

The sword started halfway out. The face before her was swollen and dark. Meg fell back against the wall, sending her hat askew. At the same time, she gave him a glance from under lowered lids.

"I give you one minute," he said, "to be gone."

As though too warm, Meg slipped the black-fur pelisse from her shoulders and draped it across the muff. Her gleaming white shoulders rose up from the black ruffles, above vertical scarlet-and-black, and vivid scarlet. As she adjusted her hat, her eyes grew narrow and again she

41

smiled without opening her lips. The perfume she wore, to men as heady as strong waters, rose up round her. A slight movement could suggest, could remind . . .

"Are you sensible," Meg asked, "that Captain Duroc, of the French King's personal attendance, hath already taken lodgings for me in Chancery Lane? The finest lodgings in London? And hath begged me, on his knees as a man of quality should, that I be kept by him?"

"I wish Captain Duroc all joy of you."

"Nick!" she screamed, half-realizing he meant what he said.

"Half a minute!"

"If you would turn me away," Meg said coldly, "I am not the woman to make protest. But—this very day!" Her voice softened. "Why, 'twould take me that time to gather up my poor stuffs and trifles. Sir, will you not suffer me to remain one night more?"

"I . . . I . . . well! One night more, I dare swear, could do no harm."

(This was the point at which Lydia, now wrapped in his bedgown, sat up straight with a new look on her face.)

"And this I tell you," Meg added. Tears were running down her cheeks; you might even have thought them sincere. "Even though you turn me away, to Captain Duroc or another, we shall come together again. I am much perplexed; I see not why. I have apprehended this only since last night. Yet in some fashion we are bound together, you and I, to live or to die."

There was a silence, while a wind shook the windowpanes and whipped the trees outside in a dead world, yet a very living world. Unexpectedly Sir Nick's voice altered.

"Mary!" it said. "Can it be that—"

Thus Fenton, again fighting down a coffin lid with some horror inside, gained the mastery and held it. He saw through his own eyes, and with his own brain. Yet for the moment he must not loosen one muscle. The woman Meg (even if she were Mary, which he thought doubtful) must leave this house tomorrow, or her influence would smash all.

"Your time is done," he snapped. "Now go!" The scabbard rattled slightly.

Meg, evidently deciding it was too dangerous for more words, rushed past him. Beyond the middle of the room she paused, swung the fur piece round her neck, again adjusted her hat with the golden-coloured plume, and drew herself up.

Though about to speak, she thought better of it. With some dignity she swept out of the room, in a mighty rustling of petticoats. Only someone in the dim passage would have seen her face alter, or seen her secret smile.

Fenton, swaying a little, kept himself steady on his feet.

Twice he had defeated Sir Nick; but what if the other soul grew more powerful? Mechanically Fenton let the sword slide back into the scabbard. All over him he felt the sweat and exhaustion of the contest. Added to it was the strain of playing his part: the words came smoothly enough, from such long reading, but the affected accent drained him more.

Putting a hand to his collar, he discovered only a neckband and a fall of lace. His fine black-velvet coat and breeches seemed heavy yet limp.

"What," he thought, "if we are all ghosts?"

But the chair he touched was solid oak. The hearty prettiness of Lydia, wrapped in his bedgown and now kneeling on the bed facing him, was as real as her physical touch. He walked towards her as steadily as he could.

"Lydia," he said humbly, and put his hands on her cheeks, "you must pardon me for forgetting you while I dealt with . . . your cousin."

Lydia regarded him with eyes of worship, which was embarrassing.

"Forget me?" she repeated. "Dear heart, that was when you remembered me!" Her broad moist lips trembled. "Will she go this time, that creature? Really and truly you are determined?"

"She will go," Fenton answered, with quiet conviction.

Even Giles, who had lost his terror but remained sober and silent, seemed to feel that conviction in a man whose moods were beyond him.

"Now we must study your illness . . . "

"Now what a pother," cried Lydia, "over so small a matter!"

Well, but it was not a small matter. Unless he could change it, and shift the course of history, this girl would die of a heavy dosage of arsenic in the time of one month now less a day. His own wife—or was she his wife? Yes, of course she was! Else the whole tragicomedy had no sense or meaning. His fierce protectiveness went over her like a buckler.

"Now bethink you, Lydia. When did these strong pains of the stomach, and the vomiting, begin to trouble you? Shall I say, at hazard, some three weeks ago?"

Lydia counted back on her fingers, slowly.

43

"True! But for one day, true!"

"What are you accustomed to partake of, in the way of food or drink?"

"When the first pain did come, after dinner, I made haste to my chamber and bolted the door. Afterwards I would not suffer even my chambermaid to be there when I was sick. No one must know," whispered Lydia, trying (with those eyes) to look crafty. "I kept all things dark."

"But, after the first pains . . . ?"

"I did not go down to table. I could partake only of a bowl of sack posset, which the chambermaid carried up to me each day at noon precisely. Yet even the sack posset—not each day, but on occasion—did near to double me up: oh, most horrid!"

For the first time Lydia grimaced with pain and loneliness.

"Lydia, what did you think ailed you?"

The girl looked vague.

"Oh . . . I thought 'twas my death. People are always a-dying; and who can tell the reason?" Lydia hesitated, with an inner struggle. "Nay, the Lord forgive me, I'll not deny it! I'll tell all. Once or twice, 'tis true, I did think of poison. But I thought it must be you, dear heart; and thus, my husband, I could not speak."

Fenton turned away, clenching his fists.

Lydia mistook his mood, which was only fondness for her and shame for the Sir Nick she had married. Nevertheless Lydia cried out.

"Now the Lord forgive me!" and in her speech was a faint inherited twang of the Roundhead "Laard." "The Lord forgive me, but what have I done? Nick, Nick!" She hammered her delicate hands on the bedclothes. "I swear I did but suspect it once or twice, when I had the vapours and was foolish. Now a thousand times I know! Oh, I have done you so much harm already!"

He turned back to her, and smiled and reassured her.

"You have done me harm?" he asked, again putting his hands on her cheeks and lightly kissing her lips. "You will do me harm only if you turn from my questions. Did you, in your illness, eat or drink anything save this sack posset you had each day? *Anything* else?"

Lydia pondered.

"No. Save for the barley water; but that is in a large glass bottle from which all drink."

"This sack posset: how is it prepared?"

"A common sort. Four eggs, well whipped and beaten in a bowl.

44

These poured into another bowl, of half a pint of milk and four pieces of sugar loaf. Then half a bottle of sack. No more."

Moodily Fenton bent down and picked up Meg's dagger from the floor. For a time he weighed the dagger in his hand.

"Giles!"

"Ay, good sir?"

"I believe you are acquainted with our 'secret'?"

"You were pleased to acquaint me, sir, when yesterday you made discovery that . . . "

"Good!" said Fenton. "You will now gather together the kitchen staff, any who might have prepared this sack posset, together with any who might have touched it by means of its being carried upstairs. Gather them together in—in my study."

Giles bowed, still sober and with no trace of impudence.

"You will tell them," continued Fenton, "that my lady hath been poisoned by arsenic; and that I will seek them presently. No doubt, Giles, there will be a great howling and skreeking . . ."

"Howling and skreeking?" echoed Giles. "Ecod, sir! 'Twill be a worse din than at the playhouse, when they flourish for an entrance of witches. These cattle," said the upper servant, "are in want of a roping, a good cat-of-nine-tails. But I'll deal with them, sir; do you judge!"

And he was gone, the door closed, before Fenton could protest.

Lydia, who clearly distrusted Giles, still knelt facing Fenton on the side of the bed; but her blue eyes now laughed and her manner was gleeful.

"I knew it!" she said. "Oh, I was assured of it! When we were married just," she cast up her eyes, "three years, one month, and four days ago."

"Assured of what, my dear?"

"Come here, and I'll whisper a secret in your ear. Nay, closer! Come closer!"

Obediently Fenton lifted the hair of the periwig and did as he was requested. Lydia immediately did such things to his ear as made him jump, albeit the attack was not too displeasing.

"A whoreson trick!" he said, though he could not help grinning. Still weighing the dagger in his right hand, he mock-threatened her. "And where did you learn that?"

"But you taught me," replied Lydia, raising her eyebrows. "I know a hundred such; but now, please, I am in deep earnest." She was; her

45

eyes grew intent and her voice serious. "Nick, I tell you today because you are now different. Nick, I—I spoke of you to my father before we married. He hated you; I own it. Do you know what I said of you?"

"No, Lydia! I had rather you . . ."

Yet Lydia spoke out proudly, unconscious of how grotesque her words must sound.

" 'As gentle as a minister of God,' said I, 'yet bold as an Ironside soldier.' "

There was a pause.

And once more the black soul struck hard at the coffin lid.

There could have been no worse ill luck for these ill-starred lovers. For, in that civil war of Cavalier against Roundhead, now more than thirty years gone by, there had been no more fierce-fighting Royalist than the grandsire of Sir Nick, or his father too.

And—in that purely academic way which can grow more bitter than any current politics—Professor Fenton was as fire-eating a Cavalier as his old namesakes. When he argued against the Roundhead views held by Parkinson of Caius, he really hated Parkinson.

"I am deserving of no such compliments," a too-polite voice observed to Lydia. "Still! Had you said, 'as bold as a Cavalier . . .' "

A sudden frightened look crept into Lydia's eyes.

"No, now, stay!" she begged, putting her hands over her face. "Oh, Lord forgive me! One more word, and again we shall ruin all!"

"As—how, my lady?"

Wearily Lydia let herself fall back on the pillows, her right arm extended and her head resting on it. It was as though she had half-died.

"Nick," the muffled voice spoke drearily, "why did you desire to marry me?"

"Because I loved you."

"So I had thought and hoped. And yet, in this sick house, there can be only brief mention of someone I was brought up to love and honour and admire; and on the instant you fall a-ranting with jeers. Even great Oliver . . . "

" 'Great Oliver,' " he whispered. His left hand tightened on the lower bedpost; his right hand gripped the haft of the dagger. "Do you refer to—Cromwell?"

Even the pronunciation, *Crummle*, spat it out with such a crunch of viciousness that all hatred might have packed into one word. And, in fact, so it was.

"I was born," said Sir Nick, "in the year your holy Roundheads cut off the head of King Charles the First. It was a day in January, I have heard. There was a little snow in the air, but they had cleared the scaffold outside the Banqueting House window. He walked from St. James's Palace, across the Park, up through the passage inside the Holbein Gate, and so turned down the long rooms of Whitehall Palace to the window of the scaffold. There they cut off his head."

Sir Nick, or it may have been Fenton himself, drew a deep breath.

"Never a man died so bravely. Never a man walked so like a king. Never a king so proved that man himself might be noble, though they spat at him and blew tobacco smoke in his face as he passed." Sir Nick, wheeling round, drove the dagger to its hilt through the bedpost, with such an eye that not a wood-chip cracked or shivered. "May God's curse rest on them and all their race!"

Lydia surged up, the bedgown falling back. In her heart she was not first of all interested in this.

"Did you marry me," she asked, "because you boasted, at the Grey-hound tavern, that you would 'tame the Roundhead maid'?"

"No."

"I have heard as much, Nick."

"Then, God's body, believe what you like!"

"Well, you did not tame her," Lydia said unsteadily. "My grand-father was a regicide, as your doxy Meg repeated last night. I was a young maid at the time of the Restoration; they did not take me to see him hanged and drawn and quartered, and his entrails thrown into the fire; but I have heard *he* died bravely too."

"Lydia, Lydia, do you know how few of the regicides were in truth executed?"

"Pah! Do you?"

"Across the council table King Charles the Second pushed a note to my Lord Clarendon. 'I am weary of hanging; let it sleep.'"

"And the Meg creature," said Lydia, ignoring this, "told a foul lie when she said my father was a mad Independent. He was no Inde-pendent, but a Presbyterian moderate; and all such were horrified at killing the King, and did so vote as you may see in the record."

Again she pressed her hands over her eyes.

"Nor was he mad, Nick. All knew it. He was gentle, but great and unafraid. They but shut him up because he would preach the gospel of the Lord as it came to him. From all this, Nick, I cut myself off for you. Oh, that is of small import! But why should *I* live, to what purpose, if your mind and heart are gone?"

"This must stop," Fenton thought desperately. "It must stop!"

He had slid down on his knees beside the bed, hands grasping the sides of it. He knew that he could defeat Sir Nick, because he was still keyed up for the fight and because of his fondness for Lydia. It was the shortest contest, but the hardest. Once, it seemed, a fleshless arm writhed out of the coffin and laid hold in his very vitals.

"Help me, Lydia," he said, stretching out his hands, "help me!"

Though she did not understand, she pressed his hands to her breast, and rejoiced to see the light come back into his eyes.

"Lydia," said the voice of Fenton, breathing hard, "there are things I cannot explain. If you were to imagine . . . nay; don't imagine. But sometimes I am not myself, even when I have had no taste of wine or strong waters. Stay by me—"

"Do I ask aught else?"

"—and cry, 'Go back; go back!' if this senseless anger should move again. It will not, I swear, if you are there. And attend on this, dearest heart," he added gently. "What have you and I to do with these old quarrels of our grandsires? They are blown away. Even their swords and pistols have changed. A Roundhead hath as much respect as he of our Church of England. And so I say, even of Oliver: may his staunch old soul rest in peace."

"Then—God for King Charles!" Lydia breathed passionately, and threw her arms round his neck and sobbed.

And thereafter, if not understanding, there was peace.

"If I might put a question," said Lydia. "Nay; 'tis none to anger you. Why do you embroil yourself today in this 'body politic' or 'matter politic' or whatever it is about men voting and shouting, which I do not understand?"

Fenton stroked her soft, light-brown hair.

"Do I so? I had forgot," he said absently, and felt Lydia start. "Well, then!" he added, "if I do, it is because the same old tragedy is being enacted again."

"How?"

"As thus. King Charles the First died. Cromwell, good Cromwell, rode high in the saddle for near a decade, boasting a strength he did not have. Then he died, as we do, leaving a near-empty Treasury. The brief rickety governments tumbled down after him, leaving a completely empty Treasury. And, in the blessed (or cursed) year of 1660, the old monarch's son—King Charles the Second—returned from exile to rule over us."

"I remember the very night."

"For a time, dear heart, all went well. 'Twas as cheerful as an innkeeper's crying, 'Sit you merry, gentlemen!' In a decade there were some snarls, though all patched up. By and by your Parliament did begin to shew its claws. 'Twas a matter of money and religion, just as under Charles the First. Their great cry was, 'No Popery! No Popery!'"

"Hush!" whispered Lydia, and cast a frightened look round her. "Who can tell what Papist might be listening? Hush!"

Lydia was more terrified than she had been at any time before. She did not see Fenton smile above her head.

"Then I will discourse softly; but speak my mind. Shall I mistrust these men—I had rather you called them Catholics—who poured out gold and life's blood in defence of the King's father? Who would cheerfully see their houses burn, if they could smite back once at a Roundhead helmet? Can I think they mean harm to the old King's son? If I were not of our Established Church, I might myself be a Catholic."

"Now, Lord, you are o'ertaken again!" gabbled Lydia, and held him close. "Go back!" she cried, "Go back!"

"Look into my eyes, sweet girl, and see whether or not I am myself."

"Truly, you—you do seem yourself. But may I speak?"

"With all my heart!"

"The King, poor fellow," said Lydia, "is a weak man . . . "

Again, over her head, she did not see Fenton's broader smile.

"And easily," insisted Lydia, "to be led by lewd women. The Queen is a Papist. She who most ruleth the King, call her Louise de Kéroualle or Madam Carwell or Duchess of Portsmouth, is a French Papist and spy. The King's brother, 'tis open rumour, is become a Papist. Is there no wicked design in this?"

Fenton tilted up her chin.

"Since you apprehend so much, do you know what the King's supposed friends—the council at his own table—have done now?"

"Nick, I have so poor a head for matters politic! 'Tis only you and I . . . "

"They have ratted from him, Lydia, or are about to do so. My

49

Lord Shaftesbury, the little man with the abscess in his side, deserted two years ago, though he still sits at the council board because he thinks himself too powerful to be dismissed. His Grace of Buckingham, a man of parts despite fat folly, deserted too. There are other peers of the realm, skreeking out 'No Popery,' but these are pygmies. Shaftesbury and Bucks have founded what they call the Green Ribbon Club, with its rosette a green ribbon, at the King's Head tavern. Their party you are free to call the Opposition party or the Country party or the Treason party.

"But they do not come at you fairly, as the old Roundheads did. No; not for a moment! Theirs is the method of tongues set a-whispering, to flood London with rumour in twenty-four hours. Theirs is the way of the pamphleteer, the elbow jogger, the little knife if you dissent: all an honest man would call small and vile.

"One thing more I tell you, and have done. We are in a lull before the greatest politic battle of all. Three years more (mark it well!), and . . ."

There was a soft rapping at the door, and Giles appeared.

"The cattle are penned, sir," Giles reported, with a wicked little twist of the mouth which showed he had tasted power and enjoyed it. "They await you in your study."

"Quiet, Giles?"

"Most quiet now, sir."

Lydia had moved to the head of the bed. There, screened from the side by the looped-back bed curtain, she was drawing up the sleeves of her gown and adjusting the bodice. Meanwhile she made faces at him to show she loved him. And, since he had been speaking of the Green Ribbon Club's little knives, a remark of Lydia's still returned and twisted like a little knife in his heart.

"'As gentle as a minister of God, yet as bold as a Roundhead soldier!'"

"O Thou," he prayed to himself, "if only a dry old stick in a boy's carcase could somehow be worthy of that, or live up to it!" But he knew it was hopeless.

"When you have completed your dressing," he said to Lydia, "I direct thus: return to your chamber. There is a bolt inside the door, you said?"

"Yes; a stout wooden bolt. But . . ."

"Lock your door, and open it to no one save you hear my voice.

50

You are to have no food today; only such draughts as I shall order."

A little twitch of fear travelled round Giles's face.

"Nay, sir!" he scoffed, not convincingly. "You don't think . . . "

"But I do think, malapert. 'Tis my only virtue. There is a horror in this house," said Fenton, "more nauseous or deadly than a cellar of sewage. I go to seek it out—now."

CHAPTER V

KITTY IN GREY; AND

A CAT-OF-NINE-TAILS

THE passage outside had only two windows: one at the far end and one a little down on the right, over the staircase landing. As Giles bowed him out, Fenton remembered a new cause for trouble.

"Er—Giles!"

"At your command, master?" answered Giles, sticking round a wrinkled and more malapert face.

"In that manusc . . . that is to say, I call to mind this morning," Fenton corrected himself, "you made mention of a certain Mistress Kitty . . . ?"

"Kitty Softcover, the cook?"

"Tush, that's it! The very name!"

"And upon whom, I also said," added the remorseless Giles, "your own lewd eye hath so often been cast?"

"My meaning, as touches Kitty, runs thus. Are we . . . have we . . . ?"

"Nay, now how should I know?" demanded Giles, pursing out his lips with a look of holiness. "If you are not yourself aware, then only God He knoweth. Yet it seems to me, master, you have acquired a singular delicacy of speech. I but said," the wicked smile came round again, "you often cast your lecherous eye upon her: which fact, under favour, was as plain as a book with large print. Still, I will present them all to you in the study."

It did not strike Giles in the least odd that he should introduce the master of the house to his own servants. But that, as Fenton reflected, was only natural. A man of quality would not condescend to learn

52

the names or faces of lower servants, unless he had special reason to do so.

At the turn of the staircase they descended to the lower hall, and turned round so as to face the front door. And how that lower hall had changed, since he spoke to Mary Grenville in the front room on the left! It was now all black oak panelling and silver sconces, with one carved chest.

And the big front door stood wide open.

Though he had been prepared for it, yet Fenton was startled to find Pall Mall a little sylvan lane. There was a border of lime trees before his own front door. Sweet air stole into the hall. Fenton recalled that one of his neighbours was Madam Eleanor Gwynn, but he could not remember whether she had yet moved from the north side to the south side.

"If you will be pleased, sir . . . " murmured Giles.

"Stay a moment! Is Lord George yet come?"

"Over an hour gone by, sir."

"Did he quiz you; did he make merry?"

"Nay, sir. He is in the stable, and happy. He but said . . . if your hearing be not still too delicate?"

"Now a pox on your sauciness!" roared Fenton, with so vivid an imitation of Sir Nick that Giles darted back as though from a blow. "What did he say? Speak plain!"

"Well! 'If Nick be having only one of them, instead of two,' quoth His Lordship, 'then why is he taking so plaguey long about the business?' "

"But this morning—"

"I replied," softly said Giles, "that you, being a good trencherman, liked oft to partake several times of the same plate. 'Ay,' quoth he, 'there's reason in that. Don't trouble him.' "

Again Fenton glanced ahead. He could see, motionless to the right outside the front door, the porter on guard. He was lofty of manner and carried a tipstaff. He admitted desirable people and turned away undesirables: all without constantly opening and shutting the door, or fussing the occupants inside.

Fenton had always considered this an excellent old custom, which should have been kept up.

"Sir, sir!" implored Giles, beginning to open a door at the back of the hall. "If you will but deign to enter?"

Fenton entered.

53

The study, though small, was well stocked with calf-bound books from folio to octavo. Against one window facing the door a flat desk-table in heavy, polished, dark wood stood sideways to the window. But the East India Company had again done its best in the carpet, and the rest of the furniture was oak.

Even as he went in, Fenton sensed the atmosphere of tears and screams and huffings which must have beaten against these little walls. He thought of Lydia; his nature became harder, more ruthless than Sir Nick's, because it was not wild or whirling; and Sir Nick's anger lasted ten minutes at most.

Four persons were drawn up in a kind of semicircle, each a little way apart, to face him. On a carved cabinet standing against the right-hand wall, the cabinet being about as high as a man, a silver candelabrum held three branches of wax lights.

From a hook beside the door, Giles coolly took down a middle-sized whip with nine leather thongs, each tipped with steel. This was the law, though the cat might be used only on suspicion of serious offence.

"I will point them out to you, sir," said Giles, indicating the semicircle of one man and three women. Letting the thongs of the whip fall, he pointed with the handle towards the man on the extreme left.

"That is Big Tom, the sculleryman," he said.

Big Tom, who lived up to his name both in breadth as well as height, shifted from one foot to the other as though in this way he might get less dirt on the carpet. His face was begrimed out of a mop of hair, as were his flannel shirt, his buff-leather doublet, and his leather apron: he was evidently an odd-jobs man. Though contemptuous of Giles, he eyed Fenton in a worship of awe. He ducked his head, touched his forelock, and only made a gurgle in his throat.

The whip moved to the right, towards the next person.

"Nan Curtis, the kitchenmaid," said Giles.

Nan Curtis, overstout though less than thirty, had a round rosy face now drained of colour by fear, and a down-pulled lip like a baby. She wore a cap, and was tolerably clean save for a few oven stains. She sobbed audibly, and then was silent.

Yet, each time that whip moved, a thicker spasm of repressed fear or anger seemed to beat against these topheavy walls of books, or send a quiver amid three candle flames shining down on silver and polished wood.

54

"Next on the right," said Giles, "we have Judith Pamphlin. Our lady's chambermaid."

Fenton studied this chambermaid, remembering Lydia.

Judith Pamphlin was a thin, tall, harsh-featured virgin in her late forties. Her sparse hair was done into tight curls close to her head. Hands folded, she stood bolt upright in a tight-laced frock of grey wool.

No, Lydia would not like her. And yet . . .

"Finally," said Giles, moving the whip, "this is Kitty Softcover, the cook."

Fenton looked at her coldly and steadily, with hard appraisal.

Kitty seemed the meekest of them all. She was small, plump, and about nineteen years old. Though her loose blouse of coarse linen and her drab wool skirt had suffered from working over fire and turnspit, she had only a faint smut on the side of her nose. What Fenton first noticed was her hair.

It was thick and heavy, of that very dark red colour which seems to ripple with lighter gleams. The candle flames set it a-glow. She raised her head and gave Fenton a brief glance out of eyes so dark blue that they seemed almost black. They were large eyes, too large eyes for the small bold face and overbold nose.

Yet her glance was that of a woman who has been intimate with him: secret, knowledgeable, faintly defiant. Kitty was the only one who spoke.

"Sir, sir, you'd not harm me?" she asked humbly, in a light voice but with so thick an accent that Fenton hardly understood her.

"You all know," he ignored her and turned to the rest, "that your lady mistress is being poisoned with slow poison named arsenic. She partook of it, we think, in a bowl of sack posset prepared in the kitchen and carried up each day. Slow poison does not occur by accident. Who prepared this sack posset?"

"Sir, 'twas me," replied Kitty. Again she gave him that intimate, close-knit glance. "What I know!" it seemed to say.

"You prepared it always?"

"Always," nodded Kitty. Slowly she turned her chin sideways. "But there's many, passing in and out the kitchen, can swear I had no hand in it."

"Who carried the sack posset to my wife?"

He looked at the rigid, harsh-featured Judith Pamphlin, who had now folded her arms tightly across her flat breast. Her lips had become

55

a white, locked line. She seemed debating whether or not to trouble with answering him. When she spoke, her lip opened downwards.

"I did carry it."

"Judith Pamphlin," said Fenton, "how long have you been chamber-maid to my wife?"

"I was her servant long before she had the ill fortune to marry you," replied Judith, with a through-the-nose twang but looking steadily into his eyes. "When you have taken a large cup overnight, and were out of your wits, I have heard you call her Roundhead bitch, scum of the Conventicle, spawn of a regicide."

Fenton looked at her.

"Giles, give me the whip," he said quietly.

Giles handed it over.

Fenton looked back at her with a gaze colder, steadier than Judith's own. These were not Sir Nick's tactics, all bull's roar and have-at-you, which a strong-minded woman could have met. Fenton was beating down her mind and will, slowly, because his mind and will were superior to her own.

Seconds appeared to stretch into minutes, while that cold look went on. Then he saw Judith Pamphlin's eyelids begin to turn and lower. Not far to his right Fenton had noticed a high, heavy chair. As soon as he saw her eyelids flicker, he raised the cat-of-nine-tails high and brought it down with all the power of his arm at the meeting of the chair back with one chair arm. The thongs hissed and thudded, but with no more terrifying effect than the *rattle-clack* of steel tips.

They bit; they gouged raw and ugly wounds into wood, as into flesh; and the heavy chair jumped and cracked.

"Woman," said Fenton, "you will never speak so to me again."

There was a pause. Giles Collins was as white as a ghost.

"Nay," muttered Judith, "I . . . I think I shall not."

"What do you call me?"

"Master."

A shudder went round the group, except for stolid Big Tom.

"Good," said Fenton in the same expressionless voice, and handed back the whip to Giles. "When the sack posset was prepared in the kitchen, were ever you here to see it done?"

"I never once failed to see it prepared," returned Judith Pamphlin, bolt upright but conquered. Her harsh voice sounded shaken.

"How? Did you suspect poison?"

"Nay, not poison. But this slattern," Judith shot out a long thin arm towards Kitty, "hath been lewd and thievish since her breasts grew: she casting eyes on all 'prentices or suchlike, and wheedling them to steal for her." Judith's voice rose. "The Laard's justice condemneth her already to the lake of burning pitch, and the fire that . . ."

"Forebear this Puritan cant. I will hear none of it."

Judith Pamphlin folded her arms tightly, and was again silent.

But Kitty, he noticed out of the corner of his eye, no longer pretended meekness. Her small plump shoulders were crouched, and she turned too-large eyes of hatred on Judith. The small thick upper lip had risen, showing bad teeth.

"This arsenic," Fenton continued, "is a white powder, or," he remembered what it was more likely to be in this age, "it may have been a small white bit from a larger cake. Judith, could the cook have put this into the sack posset without your notice?"

Judith, hating Kitty, but in iron fairness, opened and shut her lips on one word.

"No," she said.

"You are sure?"

"'Twould not have escaped me."

"When you passed abovestairs, carrying the bowl to my wife's room, did any person bid you pause, or try to trap your attention otherwise, so that poison might have been put there?"

"There was none. Not ever."

"So!" said Fenton, after a pause. "You had best hear, then, that I intrust you and I think you faithful. A word aside with you."

Fenton backed towards the door of the study, setting the door half-way open. Judith Pamphlin, who had been standing with her back to the desk at the window—how much that same desk figured in Giles Collins's account!—Judith darted a look of suspicion at him. But, when she marched across the room towards the door, she seemed a little less rigid.

"Precede me," Fenton said curtly, as she stopped at the door.

The woman hesitated long, then ducked her head in obedience and marched out. Fenton, following her out into the dim hall, all but closed the door and set only his fingers inside it.

"Go quickly to the kitchen," he said in a low voice, "and prepare this. One large spoonful, of the sort I have seen in a museu—of the sort to

57

eat soup at table, of powdered mustard. You have powdered mustard?"

Judith did not reply; she merely nodded.

"This in a glass or cup of warm water. To follow it if necessary, salt water or greasy water. Have you," here his immense memory for minutiae faltered, "have you oil of olives?"

Judith nodded.

"This in equal parts with the juice of China oranges," he pronounced it chaney, "and give it often. Barley water in plenty. Hot stones or bricks at the feet. All this should serve. Should my lady wife afterwards be weak, hot cloths to the abdomen and . . ." (No, of course there would be no morphine!) "Stop: have you laudanum?"

Another nod.

"A strong dose of laudanum, powdered and in water, to keep her drowsy for a few hours. By late afternoon, we shall see a different person. Quickly, now! Put on a salver such things as you immediately need; then return here, and tap at the door."

Judith nodded, and turned away.

"Stay now! One moment more!" Fenton added.

"At your command, master."

"I think you faithful. No guilty woman would dare speak as you did. Then why, tell me, does my wife mislike you, and run away, and bolt the door against you when she is ill?"

Unexpectedly, an odd kind of emotion half-stirred behind that emotionless face. Judith Pamphlin touched her cheek.

"Because I am hard-favoured, which is but the Laard's will. Because I would help her, and well she knows I hate you. Because, as in childhood, I would teach her what is the will of the Laard . . ."

"Again, woman: forbear your Puritan cant!"

"I know the will of the Laard!"

"What humility! How wiser than the wisest of men!"

"Nay," said Judith, all but shrinking up, "I am humble, the humblest of creatures . . ."

"Yet you know His will. Attend to me: say but one word of your gibberish to my wife, and I will not have you flogged. You don't fear a flogging." (He knew her, and she sensed that; her eyes moved sideways.) "But I will have you turned into the street, and she will die."

"In some ways," said Judith Pamphlin, again defeated, "you do well." In a queer croak of something like respect she added: "Master."

Then, bolt upright, she marched towards a very small stairway leading down under the main stairs.

For a long time Fenton stood motionless, his fingers inside the door, looking towards the front door and the border of lime trees.

Towards anything that endangered Lydia, he was not angry: he was only merciless. Though he fought against history and the devil together, he swore she should not die. Then who was the author of the mischief?

Plainest of all was Kitty Softcover, despite Judith's statement. There could be no doubt that Kitty was Sir Nick's latest conquest. Fenton did not like her in the least. For all her bodily charm, for all her insinuating large eyes and her magnificent red hair, he sensed that Kitty was as cold as a fish and had the instincts of a magpie. What a fool Sir Nick was!

Compare Kitty, for instance, with Meg York. Compare the redhead dullard against Meg's wit and Meg's physical presence! (Now why was he making such comparisons?)

True, he himself had been the first to suspect Meg. But that estimate had come entirely from reading Giles Collins's narrative. Now that he had seen most of these persons, and weighed them up in judgment, his conclusions about Meg were different.

Meg, of course, might easily commit murder. He had almost seen her do it. But Meg would kill only in one sudden flare of violence, with dagger or pistol; swiftly, before the fit died. Slow, laborious poisoning would not be quick enough for her. She would administer enough arsenic to kill ten persons, or none at all. And in this she was exactly like Sir Nick.

Yet someone . . .

Fenton hesitated. There was another possibility, beside the plain course in Giles's account. He could apply a certain test. Settling his periwig, still butting against history and the devil, Fenton went into the study and closed the door behind him.

Each person stood in the same place. Only the wax lights leaped at the draught of the closing door.

"It would seem," said Fenton, "that Mistress Pamphlin is now cleared. There remain but three of you."

Nan Curtis, the young but too-stout kitchenmaid in the cloth cap, could no longer be repressed. She put her hands to the sides of the cap, as though stricken with toothache, and tears trickled down her cheeks.

"Oh, we are poor wretches in poor plight!" she cried out, so that Fenton could not help feeling sympathy for her. "We are undone, Tom! Tom, we are undone!"

"Nay!" growled Big Tom in heavy bass, and boomed away in so thick an accent that Fenton called Giles to translate.

"Why, sir," smiled Giles, rattling the whip, "his talk runs thus, since he much admires you. 'Harm him or his own? Him, the best swordsman in all England?' "

Fenton was taken aback. "It is increasingly clear," he thought, "that I am notorious for my rapier play. If only they knew the feeble truth!"

"I thank you, Tom," he said with courtesy. "I would wish it so, if I could."

During this time Kitty Softcover watched him openly, and disturbingly as though she saw a different man there. Her eyes were as quick and alert as those of a magpie with a bright new thimble clutched in its beak. She sidled up to Fenton.

"Pray, sir," she begged, with a wheedling look and half-smile, "you say Mistress Pamphlin is cleared. Well! Am I not cleared too? Didst not hear (eh) the bracket-face say *I* put in no poison?" Her voice dropped to an intimate whisper. "Tip us truth, dear Rome-Culle." Up went her voice. "Am *I* not cleared too?"

Fenton looked her up and down, without favour.

"That, good wench, depends upon her eyesight and your own daring. Still! Let us suppose, for discourse' sake, that you are all innocent. Now stand aside."

Kitty showed her teeth. Fenton, ignoring her, went to the desk of polished dark wood set endways to the window. He moved round to the desk chair. For so many years he had conned Giles's script that he had fully memorized it. His mind's eye saw the curling characters of the script flow across in front of him.

"... mid-afternoon of Monday, 9th May [it ran; the 9th May was yesterday], *as I Remember, that Sir Nicholas discouered, in the desk in his Study, a paper packet. On it was writ, in clarkly Hand, the words, 'Arsenick, Deadly Poyson.' Under this was a Mark or Desy'n in blue Ink. Being much surpryz'd, Sir Nicholas did summon me to ask, How came it there? I reply'd, That I knew not. But what make you, saith He, of this Mark here? Why, sir, I make no doubt 'tis the street-desy'n that hangs above the Door of some Apothecary...."*

Fenton cleared the memory of the manuscript from his mind and looked down at the desk. Except in imagination, he had never seen it. It had only one drawer, underneath the flat top. Someone, who for once was not Sir Nick, had put there a "paper packet." He pulled open the squeaky drawer.

Well, it was still there. A little rumpled, but fresh. Heavy whitish paper, about three inches wide, folded lengthwise and tucked over at each end. Rather thick, too. He touched it, and found the contents in powdered form after all. White arsenic, old when Greece was young. And enough of it to satisfy old Locusta herself.

He turned round from the desk, opening out the packet gingerly.

"Here's arsenic," he said. "The poison itself. Which of you finds it familiar?"

Big Tom growled and shook his head. Nan Curtis, after one quick glance of insatiable curiosity, fell to sobbing again. Kitty, who had retreated into the shadow of the high cabinet, muttered words so low-voiced that Fenton nearly missed them.

"Stow your whids, Rome-Culle!" she breathed. "The' talkst overmuch!"

"Now tell me," Fenton addressed Nan Curtis gently, to prevent screams. "These materials for my lady's sack posset: are they drawn from common stock in the house, or are they kept apart in particular for the posset?"

"Nay, sir," sobbed Nan, after pausing to consider what he meant. "They are all kept apart, each in particular. Even the milk is fresh-fetched from the dairy."

"Now here's an admirable thing!" declared Fenton. "Here's a way to explain much! What's the answer, Giles? Do you apprehend it, Giles?"

He said this out of pure devilment. At that moment Giles was leaning round the side of the high cabinet and looking at Kitty, who did not see him. Giles's upstanding light-red hair and Kitty's dark-red gleaming hair stood out against dark wood carved in satyrs' heads. Giles's expression, as his eyes devoured Kitty, was more goatish than the carved heads.

But you could not catch him off balance. He was himself almost instantly.

"Why, sir," he replied, "I call it simple."

"How?"

"Sir, we learn that no poison was dropped into the bowl by . . . by

61

this poor wench. We learn that none touched the bowl as it was carried up. Then, mayhap, the poison was in one of the ingredients before the posset was made."

"Good, fair Giles!" Fenton faced the other three. "Now if this be so, we have a plain way to try it. We descend to the kitchen. We prepare a sack posset prescisely as 'tis done for my lady. And all of you shall drink of it."

Except for a high wind prowling at the window, the study was so deathly quiet that there was not even the scrape of a foot. Slowly, as his meaning penetrated, the lines in their faces altered.

"Ay; good!" Big Tom roared suddenly, and rumbled out some words which were evidently meant for approval.

Nan Curtis, even her cap now tear-drenched, fell on her knees.

"Nay, master, would you kill us all that are but your poor servants?"

"Kill you?" inquired Fenton. "Is my wife dead?"

Holding the paper packet of arsenic in front of them, he slowly refolded it, tucked over the ends, and put it into the deep right-hand pocket of his coat.

"You will suffer," he said, "but a day of cramp; perhaps, if the dose should be strong, a sense that a fire is lit in your belly, and will not be put out. There is one part of the test. Should any draw back, or refuse to drink . . ."

He paused, and then went on. "Nay, I have not done. It may be there is no poison in the bowl. But that I, detecting one reluctant to drink," he touched his pocket, "may conjure into the bowl enough of arsenic to ensure death. So that only the guilty shall suffer, and the innocent take no harm. In either case, one who should refuse to drink . . ."

"I refuse," said Kitty.

Again Fenton looked her up and down, without favour.

"Do you so? Then we must try the other way."

Kitty opened her mouth, showing the bad teeth, but shut it again. She stood with her back to the cabinet, arms outspread on either side, each hand grasping a satyr's head.

"If t' mean tha' cat—"

"Not at all. We must fetch you up before each magistrate, until we find the one who knows. Now I'll lay a gold angel to a lead shilling, by way of wager, that you've already been charged with theft or other offence that's a matter for hanging. You're a handsome mort, overaged

62

at nineteen. Why do you huddle here, over a hot fire in a vile hole, except for safety's sake?"

Kitty's eyes grew narrow and ugly.

"Plant your whids, cokir!" she sneered. "Me a thief? Th' couldst na know!"

"I could not know? Come! You discovered it a pleasure, I suppose, to prattle sweet nonsense into the ear of thick-witted Sir Nick Fenton? Myself, yes! All so artless, that you could laugh inside you and he was befooled?"

Then Fenton's voice lashed out at her like the whip.

"But I am not your 'rich coxcomb,' " he said, "as twice you dubbed me with 'Rome-Culle.' I need not be wary, as you bade me with, 'Stow your whids!' Now you have shouted, 'Have a care what you say, liar,' I know your place in life. —You forget I speak thieves' cant too."

With an effort Kitty threw off both dialect and thick speech.

"What I can speak of you. . . !"

"Then speak it. But first choose. Shall it be the sack posset—or the magistrate?"

There was a sharp rapping on the door of the study, which was instantly thrown open.

"Now, scratch me," proclaimed a genial, hearty, what-does-it-matter voice, "but I've sought you in every nook and cranny of this house except a room with books in it. I take it as a favour, Nick, scratch me if I don't, that at last you ceased pleasuring your wife and clapped on your clothes to meet me. 'Twas to be eight-thirty prompt, d'ye recall? I near died in the waking up. And now . . ."

Here the voice stopped short.

Into the room blew a large breath of the stable and of heavy white wine, but overcoming more offensive air from below. Fenton turned round, and immediately grinned. The engraver made it easiest of all to recognize Lord George Harwell.

George's broad-brimmed beaver-skin hat, which had a low crown with a gold band, was stuck rakishly on his long flaxen periwig. Out of this frame twinkled brown bold eyes, together with a good-sized nose, a narrow line of (blond) moustache, a broad grin, and the suggestion of a second chin.

Though George was two inches taller than Fenton, he had grown a little stout; it impeded, or so Giles wrote, his fine swordplay. Wearing purple velvet, his fingers afire with jewelled rings, with ruffles at his

63

wrist and a fine fall of lace at his throat, the newcomer made the gaudy display he intended.

George sensed there was something wrong here; he frowned; yet he could not quite seem to find it. He and Fenton went through the formula of friendship.

"George!" said the latter affectionately. "May your soul rot as deep among cinders as Oliver's!"

"Nick!" said George, with sincere affection. "May you have the pox worse than Charles Sedley, and every doctor in the world struck dead!"

During these amenities, George had been industriously clearing his shoes of stable mire against the lower edge of the door.

"Nay, pay no heed to my manners," he advised everybody in general, trying to look tragic. "I've been a ruined man since my christening; stay; no jest; dead earnest! I've told people a thousand times—" He paused, and his eyes rested on Giles. "Come! Did I ever tell you?"

"No, my lord," lied Giles, with a deep bow.

"Didn't I? Scratch me!" said Lord George Harwell, with honest brown eyes bulging out. "Well, 'tis no secret. We're good old stock in general. But my cursed granddam was a cursed Germanic frog; my cur— blessed parents wanted her money; they christened me George. (My name is George)." None could now doubt his sincerity. "Foggy Germanic name like everlasting rheumatics. May God send there be never another German George in this land."

"Amen to that," Fenton said grimly. "But I much fear you won't have your wish."

"And how not? If—"

For the first time George really looked at Giles Collins, and saw the steel-tipped thongs of the whip. He placed the elusive sense of wrongness.

"*That's* it!" he muttered. George snapped his fingers, and shifting colours of diamond and ruby and emerald burned against the silver setting of his rings. Kitty, who had again become a truly beautiful woman, could not take her eyes from them.

"Here's a court; here's judge and jury; here's a trial," George said hastily. His sword, with a pierced-silver guard and even a smooth silver grip, blundered and clattered against the door as he turned round. "Nay, Nick, I'll leave you. These things must be done; but I don't like 'em. The stable, now . . ."

From the corner of his eye Fenton saw Judith Pamphlin marching upstairs with a large laden tray.

64

"Don't go, George. My business here is ended, for the moment. —Giles!"

"Sir?"

"Keep them in this room," Fenton nodded at the group, "until I return. Let them be easy; give them chairs; but none is to stir below-stairs, lest matters be tampered with. Lord George and I have business of moment; but we shall be short."

Now that he saw removed (for a time, at least) the prospect of a flogging which could half-kill a woman in twenty lashes, George's rosy face broadened and beamed.

"Scratch me, but there's a fine wench!" he exclaimed, nodding broad-brimmed hat and flaxen peruke towards Kitty. "How d'ye go, m'girl?"

"The better for your lordship's notice, my lord," sweetly answered Kitty, with a low curtsy.

"Hah!" said George, delighted. "Nick, she has wit too! Eh?"

"It is remotely possible."

"But look you, Nick! This 'business of moment.' In your letter you were so cursed _mystérieux_ (as the French say, curse 'em) that I understood no word of it."

Fenton took from his pocket the wrapped-up poison and handed it to him.

"I found it yesterday, hidden unbeknownst to me. Read the inscription."

"Poison!" said George, shrinking back and holding the packet as though it might burn him. "Here, be quick; have it back!"

Fenton took it. Though George always plunged headlong into a fight, saying with tears that he was a man of peace, the presence of arsenic scared the colour from his face.

"D'ye think, now," he said, "that already it might have infected my hand? Causing it to swell up and turn black? Nay; dead earnest! Do ye?"

"Come, man, there's no harm here! Observe how I touch it. Now, then: did you note the mark or design drawn in blue ink under the writing?"

"I . . . to speak truth . . ."

"Well! I made nothing of it, until Giles Collins aided me. 'Twas the street sign above the door of an apothecary, he said."

"Eh? How?"

"The design is like to a mortar, with a pestle above it. Some sign, it might be, as the Blue Mortar." (Here Giles smirked complacently,

65

and contemplated a corner of the ceiling.) "If we fetched in a street porter, he might well know the place itself."

"And did the porter know?"

"At once," said Fenton, quoting the manuscript. "At the sign of the Blue Mortar, in Dead Man's Lane, off the Strand by the Savage's Head. We go there to discover who bought the arsenic of the apothecary."

"Ah, crafty!" nodded George, who was never conspicuous for his shining intellect. "Crafty as a daggle-gown at Westminster Hall! Are we ready now?"

"Yes. I have but to go upstairs, presenting my person to my wife . . ."

George's eyes bulged out. "Ecod, Nick! Not *again?*"

"Your mind, good fellow, is more nauseous than Snow Hill in August. Lydia must hear my voice, and know it for mine. Then . . ."

Fenton paused. Though he could not have said why, a premonition of dread shot through him.

"To the Blue Mortar," he said, "in Dead Man's Lane!"

CHAPTER VI

OF CONFIDENCES AT

THE "BLUE MORTAR"

CRUNN-BANG! went the squeal and clatter of two heavy street signs, as they whacked together overhead in the Strand. *Crack!* went another, like a pistol shot. The crashes and bangs were mingled with a heavy crunch as some sign turned over without hitting anything, or the high-pitched *cree-ak* of another which merely swung.

Thus a high wind whooped down the Strand from Charing Cross. It drove before it the sooty drizzle from chimney pots; it endangered hats and flapped the curls of periwigs; it set the street signs a-dance. They might be old or dirty, these signs, but their avenue brightened as the sun crept out, with crude imagery and blazing colour.

Here a red mouth gaped wide in a face the hue of a new chimney pot. There a green mermaid cavorted above the door of a cookshop. Eyes, dog's heads, three drunken fishes at once, bobbed up and down in flashes of crimson and purple and gold, while wind and soot fought each other and then whirled together.

But the din of the signs was hardly greater than the din made by those who walked or rode. The Strand, once a stately thoroughfare of noblemen's town houses with their backs to the smoky-sparkling Thames, had been invaded by commerce even before the Great Fire nine years ago had gutted the farthest Cheapside and Eastcheap.

Here, where the kennel or sewage ditch sent up heavy vapours from the middle of the street, iron-rimmed wheels crashed on cobbles amid the oaths of drivers. Street hawkers screamed their wares. A tinker beat

67

his call on a brass kettle. They were outdone by the shouts of apprentices, who leaned out over half-doors or walked up and down outside the shops.

"Cloth, sir! Like velvet; pray touch it; yet but one-fourth the price!"

"Lily-white vinegar! Lily-white vinegar!"

"Have you a brass pot, iron pot, skillet, kettle, or frying pan to mend?"

"And a finer bawdyhouse," proclaimed Lord George Harwell, yelling into his companion's ear, "I never saw in my whole life! None such as Mother Creswell's; faugh!"

"Er—better?"

"A true Temple of Venus, scratch me! I'll tell you. . . . Curse it, Nick, take care where you walk! You'll be under those wheels or down in the kennel! Hah! Back again!"

This sort of thing had been happening for a long time, ever since he and Fenton walked east along Pall Mall. They had passed the long wall of very high, thick hedge which bounded Spring Gardens on this side, turning a little southwards, and emerged into a huge open space whose dry earth was scored by the boot marks of soldiery.

"Now look you, Nick!" George began his first protest.

His companion's eyes were glazed and half-closed. As they moved across the open space, he began slowly to turn round and round as he walked. When his eyes encountered anything which seemed vaguely familiar, he would silently open and close his mouth as though confirming its name.

George had begun to grow nervous. He laid a hand on his companion's arm as they neared the equestrian statue of Charles the First across the open space.

"Damme," said George after deep pondering, "but you can't have pot-walloped so much claret before you went from home. I saw you."

Fenton, motioning this aside with a fierce gesture, pointed his finger.

"To the north," he said. "Those are the Royal Mews, where the soldiers are quartered?"

"Ay. As though you'd never heard the tattoo beat from there!"

"To the northeast: the Church of St. Martin's-in-the-field?"

"What else? But . . ."

"And southwards," said Fenton, turning completely round to face a street there, "is King Street. On the left—"

68

He swept his hand towards an old, dingy straggle of red-brick buildings, half-obscured by blowing smoke and grey sky and stretching half a mile between King Street and the riverside.

"Whitehall Palace," said Fenton. He moved his hand to the other side. "On the right, those iron railings and the hedges hide the King's private garden, with all St. James's Park beyond it."

"Nick, Nick, the back of your own house looks on the Park! 'Tis the Park. Where else is one?"

Fenton was still staring straight down King Street, at a square tower of red and blue and yellow bricks, with a weathercock spinning at each corner. Though it stood exactly in the middle of the street, it had a large arch for a way-through to Westminster.

"That is the Holbein Gate," said Fenton, slowly turning. "And to the southwest: that must be a way into Spring Gardens."

Most of George's worry lifted, and he began to chuckle. If Nick professed not to be acquainted with Spring Gardens, the scene of Mr. Wycherley's *Love in a Wood* (and a brisk fellow always got love there, scratch him!), then Nick was not in any fit of moody-madness. Nick was but excellent well drunk. George's chuckle deepened to a roar.

Whereupon, unexpectedly . . .

"Don't mock at me, I beg," said Fenton with a face so pale that George stopped short, mouth open. Fenton moistened his lips. Glancing eastwards towards Northumberland House, the New Exchange, and the mouth of the Strand, he turned back again. He stooped down beside the statue, and picked up a handful of dust and earth. He let it sift away through his fingers.

"I am here," Fenton said.

But George had forgotten all this, as they struggled through the throng on the north side of the Strand. Happily he was about to describe his dream of all bawdyhouses when Fenton, still staring round, nearly slipped under the wheels of a funeral cart with mourners, and had to be hauled back.

"Now hark'ee, Nick," advised George, who was not angry but perturbed, "I care not a groat what any man may do in his cups. That's but in the way of pleasantness. *But* . . ."

"I ask your pardon," said Fenton, trying to get the soot out of his eyes. "My head is cleared of fumes now."

"Good! Then ye'll know better than to gape and gawk and stare, else—"

"I tumble into the kennel?"

"Not so much that. But here's a rough crew, no less: these tatter-demalions, Abram-coves, street rogues, even the porters. They'll . . ."

Across George's voice, drowning it, hooted the noise of a pig-killer's horn. One of the many youthful shoeblacks, lurking in alleys with their mixture of soot and rancid oil, saw the state of George's shoes and darted out at him. The heel of George's hand sent him flying.

"They'll take ye for a country bumpkin newcome to town. Or for a mounseer (which is what they call a Frenchman); and that's worse. They'll put a trick on ye; they'll pelt ye with ram's horns or kennel stuff; they'll come at ye like hornets. Then your face turns black; you lug out your sword; and the devil's to pay."

"I shall take care, George."

"Admittedly," Fenton was thinking, "these great goblin street signs were a matter of simple necessity. Since so many persons can't read, especially the porters, names or numbers would be no good. But what an artistic pride the owners must take in them! The tavern with its red lattice, the coffeehouse with its lantern hanging outside . . ."

Whap went a sword scabbard against the back of his knee. Half the throng seemed to be wearing swords; as they hurried, they kept on tangling or stinging you unless you carried yourself with care.

Fenton, still trying to keep the soot from his eyes and the kennel reek from his nostrils, woke up and really looked. He clutched at his hat, but it was safe. Both his hat and George's were skewered to their periwigs with long golden pins, or they would have flown away long ago.

Another gleam of sunshine pierced down through the haze. Fenton saw a fop being carried in a sedan chair, amid sneers of the tatterde-malions. He saw sober citizens in camlet cloaks, worsted stockings, and buckled shoes.

There would be, he knew, no rich merchants with their gold chains and grave fur gowns. These belonged in the farthest City, where brick houses had been built after the Fire to replace the old wooden ones. Involuntarily he looked upwards, then across the street at the old houses with their gables of black timbers and once-white plaster, far overhanging the path underneath.

A window lattice was pushed open there, then the other side of the lattice. A somewhat comely slattern of sixteen, yawning and with hair dishevelled because she was newly risen, had not troubled to don much attire. She surveyed the street without interest, scratching herself with one hand while she held a tankard of small beer in the other.

"That's it!" burst out George, who had been pondering deeply and now followed the direction of Fenton's glance. "Now I call it to mind!"

"What do you call to mind?"

"Why, man, the Temple of Venus! I desired to tell you . . ."

"Speaking of Venus, George," interposed Fenton, with all his perplexities on him, "what if I told you I have decided to have done with all women save Lydia?"

"Hey?"

"What if I told you that? What would you say?"

George's brown eyes rolled sideways. He gave a huff of his stoutening chest. When he lifted a hand to his neckband, the glitter of his rings was reflected in the eyes of street rogues against the wall.

"Why, then," said George, "I should inquire politely after the health of Meg York."

"True; Meg. She will leave my house tomorrow."

There was a strange expression on George's face.

"Meg—will go? Whence?"

"I cannot say. Oh! Except that she is to be kept by one Captain Duroc, of whom I know nothing."

"Is she so?" muttered George, and his left hand dropped to his sword hilt.

"The question I . . . Hold! We are near to our destination."

Fenton stopped dead in the throng, and nearly had his head knocked off by a barrel of lard on the shoulder of a hurrying porter. The noise was still so great that he was compelled to shout, as he and George had been shouting at all times.

"We must be near, else we have already passed it. Ahead there," and Fenton pointed to a long line of grey gloomy pillars along the south, "is old Somerset House, with St. Clement's facing us beyond."

"*Old* Somerset House?" retorted George, giving him once more a perplexed look. "D'ye know of a New Somerset House?"

"Not yet. That's to say," Fenton deftly corrected himself in his yell, "the place *is* old and dank, you'll confess. Now do you study the left-hand side of the road, and I'll study the right. Dead Man's Lane is beside the Savage's Head, which I take to be a tavern."

71

"Tavern!" said George, and spat scornfully. "The place is a shop; they vend tobacco and make snuff. I have led you to it. Look up at the sign ahead."

The sign, not fifteen feet in front of them, swung and creaked and obediently whirled over to face them. On it was depicted a long, brown, horrible face, presumably the artist's notion of a red Indian, showing two sets of ferocious-looking teeth with a long clay pipe gripped between them.

Dead Man's Lane, like so many lanes and courts and alleys winding back from the Strand, had for its entrance an arch about ten feet high and eight or nine feet across. Its tunnel was of smooth stone, stretching back some twenty feet to support the small house above.

Towards the end, where the tunnel widened into a broader lane, there stood against the wall twelve red-leather fire buckets, in two lines of six each pressed together; grimed, weather-stained, and full of foul water.

Both Fenton and George stumbled inside the tunnel, coughing to get the grit out of their lungs and brushing smuts from their waistcoats. The wind stood still; there was not a breath of it. Well inside this tunnel, the howl and babel sank to a low growl. You could speak in an ordinary tone. By mutual consent the two friends stopped for a breather.

Again George seemed to be pondering.

"Hey, those fire buckets!" he said carelessly, but with a crafty glance at his companion. "Now how did they come there, d'ye think?"

"Come, George! Your wits are surely fuddled."

"My wits, ecod!"

"Why," Fenton told him in a casual way, "since the Fire there have been I-don't-know-how-many royal edicts that each merchant, however small of business, must keep a fire bucket on the premises. Don't you remember, George?"

"I . . . I . . ."

"But truly, good fellow, these fire buckets are a devil in narrow huddlings. They will drench the goods; often, to his great wrath, they will drench the buyer too. Set them quietly away! What constable or even magistrate will trouble his head about them, save at a playhouse?"

"Ecod, you are Nick Fenton!"

The other pretended amazement. "And did you doubt that?"

"Nay, not doubt; but . . ."

72

George's voice trailed. He waved his hands, ruffles flying. When he did not understand a thing, it seemed monstrous and un-English; he turned swiftly from it.

"Now, Nick. As touches the matter of Meg York—"

"I can tell you only she goes tomorrow. And, which I forgot a moment ago, she says this Captain Duroc hath lodgings for her in Chancery Lane. If you desire to keep her . . ."

"Keep her?" roared George, with a huff of anger and deep injury. "Curse you, Nick, I desire to wed her!"

"Wed—Meg?"

"And wherefore not?" Again George puffed out his chest, in the purple coat and white-satin waistcoat with gold buttons. "Meg is a lady of quality, kin to your own wife. She needs no dowry; I have the rhino in plenty." Here George grew embarrassed. "Certes, I know of her relations with you . . ."

"Luckily or unluckily," thought Fenton, "I don't know."

"But give me the name of one high-born lady," challenged George, "saving only Queen Catherine or Lady Temple or—or certes Lydia, who hath not been put on her back a dozen times by some brisk fellow! 'Tis but female frailty, betrayed to unlawful embraces. 'Tis the custom. And I am a man of my time."

Here George shifted his feet uneasily, looking at the dirt floor of the tunnel.

"Nick," he blurted out, "d'ye think she'll have me?"

"Oh, I make little doubt of it. If I hesitate, it is because I wonder whether you are well advised in this." Fenton could not be sure of his own feelings. "God's body!" he said. "Twice in the past twenty-four hours I have been at point of killing the damned woman: once with a chair, once with a sword."

George was vastly amused.

"Bear up, good friend!" he chuckled. "'Tis but the sweet heart's diverting humour."

"No doubt. Yet you may find it less diverting, George, should she drive a dagger through your ribs or . . . or prepare you hot mulled wine with arsenic."

Now remembrance lit up George's bulging eyes.

"Arsenic!" he said. His mind seemed to shy back. "Ecod, that's why we're here! I had forgot." George cast a quick look at his right hand to see whether it had swelled up and turned black, which it had not.

73

Whereupon he turned and strode forwards into Dead Man's Lane.

The lane itself was no more than twelve feet wide, having on its right a high dead wall of darkened bricks which at some places bulged with long cracks. It ended, thirty feet away, in a half-turn to another lane barred by a locked gate, iron-railed and -spiked, which made it all but a dead wall.

On the left ran the long open front of a hay-and-grain dealer's. Though the whole lane had a pleasant stable-like atmosphere, nobody showed face at the hay dealer's. They saw only an empty cart and a long stone watering trough. There were a number of shops in the row, but the newcomers saw only one: a blue door, with a sign of the Blue Mortar.

George swung round.

"Where in all this is the reason?" he asked, a reddish bar of anger across his forehead under the flaxen peruke. "There's none poisoned at your house, Nick, else he would have been took up by a magistrate! You durst not say (I'll defy you!) that Meg—"

His companion's grave countenance stopped him.

"I cannot tell," Fenton said wretchedly. "For a long time I had thought so: I speak plain. Yet today I strongly doubted, and doubted again. Who am I, or any man, to say, 'Such a person would do this,' or 'Such a person would do that'? George, I don't know."

"I'll discover—"

"No! Leave all speech to me."

Fenton pushed open the blue door, into small and dingy premises which had nevertheless a rather large window of wavy glass set in round leaden circles. The wavy glass sent a faint greenish light on the little space before a dark-stained oak counter, with its dingy brass scales. The apothecary himself, a little wizened man who wore his own iron-grey hair under a black skullcap, was behind the counter poring over an open ledger. He looked up through oblong steel-rimmed spectacles as his visitors entered.

"A good day to you, gentlemen," he said, in a voice that creaked like a street sign. He bowed, but with no cringing. "And how may I serve you?"

The apothecary, Master William Wynnel, was at heart a merry, bouncing, excitable little man, who decades ago might have done well as ropedancer or tumbler at Bart's Fair. But long years had set a mask

74

on him. He regarded them with lips pursed out and a look of sad severity, as though his learning were too much for him.

"Master Apothecary, my name is Fenton."

"Have I the honour," said the other, again bowing without obsequiousness, "of addressing Sir Nicholas Fenton?"

"If you are pleased to call it honour, I am Nicholas Fenton."

It did in truth please the old apothecary, who found himself treated as he felt he ought to be treated.

"You are too good, Sir Nicholas! And you are come here . . . ?" The inquiry lifted.

Fenton reached into his big right-hand pocket. Over the packet of arsenic was now the small but heavy purse, with a drawstring, he had taken from Giles before he left home.

"I would buy knowledge," he said.

Opening the bag, he flung out part of its contents. Gold guineas, gold angels each worth ten shillings, broadpieces, silver rolled and rattled on the counter.

Little William Wynnel drew himself up.

"Sir," he replied, "I am apothecary and chymist, this being (I must inform you) a skilled mystery, below only that of the chiurgien or the doctor of physick. Put by your money, I beg, until we discover whether I possess . . . the sort of knowledge you wish."

There was a silence. George, opening his mouth to roar, was stopped by a below-the-counter sign from Fenton. Fenton acted from a precise purpose.

"Your words are just," he said, sweeping the coins back into the bag, "and I am rightly rebuked. Master Apothecary, I ask your pardon."

Both George and the apothecary stared at him. A handsome apology, from a nobleman whose line went back beyond the third Edward, seemed such condescension that it won over the apothecary and all his confidence. He would have told any secret.

"First," continued Fenton, replacing the bag in his pocket and carelessly drawing out the packet of arsenic, "I believe you sold this?"

Master Wynnel took the packet and studied it.

"Indeed I did," he answered promptly. "Had I wished to hide the fact, Sir Nicholas, I would not have marked my shop design so plain. For (I must inform you) it is no offence against the law to sell arsenic. Near all our houses are infected with vermin, viz.: rats, mice, large and small insects or the like, which must be got rid of. 'Tis left to the apothecary, his judgment and cunning questions, to determine the buyer's honesty."

This was true. Nevertheless the old man's eyes shifted and struggled with dread.

"Yet I hope," he said, "there hath been no . . . ill fortune? No . . . no . . . ?"

"None at all," Fenton reassured him, with a smile. "Observe how much arsenic remains! I explore the matter only to teach my household good rules of thrift."

He could just barely hear a stifled gasp of relief. All the apothecary's portentous airs and pursed lips had gone. He was an eager, bouncing little man, eyes glittering behind the spectacles, anxious to help.

"Can you call to mind," suggested Fenton, "the date when this purchase was made?"

"Call to mind? Nay, sir, I can tell you (as we say) *instanter!*"

He flew at the open ledger in front of him, whipped over two pages, and set his finger on an entry.

"The date," said Master Wynnel, "was April 16th. A trifle more than three weeks gone."

"Yet could you know . . . though 'twould be a wondrous thing . . . how much arsenic is gone from the packet now?"

"Wondrous? Nay, Sir Nicholas! Here!"

The apothecary flew at the old brass pair of scales. Putting the packet into one scalepan, he placed a very light pebble on the other.

"Here are ill-balanced scales," he fussed. "I am too poor a man for . . . Still! Let us make it a matter of (say) three or four grains that are gone."

"And the original amount you dispensed?"

"'Tis in my book. One hundred and thirty grains."

Evidently they doled out poison with a ladle. But this would just cover the three-weeks' time, the amount administered, to account for Lydia's symptoms.

"Now the devil fly away with all this!" blurted out George. "What we desire to know—"

"Softly!" said Fenton, with a warning look. "Gently, or you spoil all." He turned back carelessly to the apothecary. "The name of the buyer, now . . ."

"Nay, sir, she would give no name."

The shop, though grimed and dingy, was pleasantly flavoured with

76

the scent of some drug Fenton could not identify. At the ominous word *she*, it was as though a noose had fallen round Lord George's neck.

"Yet she is of your household," the apothecary said to Fenton. "Or so I think."

"True. Describe her."

"The girl, for I dare not call her wench, was of good, meek, modest deportment. Her age may have been eighteen or nineteen. She had a shawl round her shoulders, and clogs on her feet. Ay; and she had most remarkable dark-red hair, which did flame in the sun. I could tell her for honest and virtuous as soon as I clapped eyes on her."

"Kitty," whispered George, and struck his finger tips softly on the counter. "D'ye hear, Nick? Your cook-maid. Kitty."

Fenton's expression did not change.

"Yet surely, Master Apothecary," he said, "you must have pressed her with questions: as, how she came there, who sent her, and so on?"

"That I did, Sir Nicholas!" affirmed the other, leaning over the counter and giving a crafty leer. "As you shall hear! She said to me she wished to buy arsenic, 'as much as should go into the largest pocket.' "

Then the apothecary excitedly acted it out.

" 'Come, my dear,' says I, all a-wheedle, 'now why do you desire that?' She said 'twas for the rats, very large rats. They were a-swarm in the kitchen of the house, she being a poor servant; they ate food, and chewed away wooden stuff as well, and put her in great fear."

"Pray continue."

" 'Then tell me, my dear,' says I, like a father (thus), 'who are your master and mistress?' She replied that they were Sir Nicholas and Lady Fenton. Certes, Sir Nicholas, I had heard much of you because of your swor ... your high repute i' the House of Commons. 'Who bade you go and seek poison?' says I. 'Why,' says she, 'my lady mistress.' "

"Lydia?" muttered George in amazement, and stared at his companion. Fenton remained impassive.

" 'Now then, my dear,' says I, 'a last question.' And I regarded her with cunning wisdom, thus. 'Do you describe for me,' says I, 'your mistress.' "

"Master Apothecary, are you acquainted with my Lady Fenton?"

The little man spread out his hands.

"Sir, sir, have I that honour? No; the trap of it lay thus: not in what she might say, but how she did say it. Would she stammer and hesitate,

77

or speak sweetly plain? Would her eyes shift, or meet mine in candour? Ah, it sufficed even for my cunning!"

"And how did she describe my Lady Fenton?"

"Why, sir, as I should have expected. As being something tall, with lustrous black hair in abundance, with grey eyes oft changing colour, and a skin milk-white."

Now the silence stretched out unendurably.

"That's not Lydia!" said George, in a low, half-strangled voice. "That's . . . that's . . ."

"Softly, George! —Master Apothecary, did the girl chance to mention the Christian name of this lady?"

"Nay, sir, she . . . Stop!" muttered the apothecary, and clucked his tongue. "Lord, I had forgot! 'If you doubt me,' says she, raising a ripe upper lip to smile, and plucking at the buttons of my coat in modest friendship, whilst I—Hem! 'If you doubt me,' says she, 'the first name of my master's true mistress, for the moment, is Magdalen or Meg.'"

Fenton lowered his head.

On the counter, unnoticed till then at his left, lay the apothecary's thick walking-stick of twined carved oak. Absently he picked it up and weighed it in his hand.

Well, he had expected most of this. It was in Giles's record. But he had been compelled to test it, since Meg's name was not mentioned there. It was only hinted at, so very intricately and so like a puzzle that long, close study could alone bring out the hidden meaning.

But then, as Fenton was discovering, so many, many vital things were not in the manuscript! He had to grope in blindness. In fact, the record was all but useless except when . . .

Then, so to speak, the shop exploded.

"Liar!" George suddenly shouted. "Liar! Knave! Jack-fool!"

With a big hand George lunged across the counter for the apothecary's throat. The scales toppled, and went over on the floor with a crash. The apothecary, trying to keep some loincloth of dignity, scuttled along behind the counter in the other direction. He rounded the edge of the counter, and stood behind Fenton.

"George! Softly! Be quiet!"

But George, frenzied and attempting to scare the apothecary still more, did the usual thing and tried to scare him with a lie.

"There's been murder done," he cried, "and you'll be took up, too!

I'll see you at Newgate! I'll see you at Tyburn Tree! I'll see the cart drawn from under you ..."

Then the words ripped out.

"Damn ye, George! Be silent!"

Lord George Harwell stopped dead, left hand in the air and right hand crossed on his sword grip. It was the first familiar tone, or speech, or bearing, or what you like, which he had observed in Nick all that day.

The crooked veins in his temples stood out like blue cords. His face had grown more swarthy, and he was beginning to smile. Sir Nick's hands, set some way apart on a heavy oak cane, gripped it tightly and more tightly, as he held it horizontally against his waist.

Yet to George, more superstitious or perhaps more sensitive than he looked, it seemed that some invisible thing bestrode Nick's shoulders; or was inside him or round him. It was as though this fought to make him drop the cane, yet he would not yield.

"Take care, Nick!" cried George. "When you fall in this mood ..."

Meanwhile the little apothecary, scuttling towards the door to get them away in some fashion, glanced to the left out of the large window. This window, because of wavy glass, was all but opaque to the others. But Master Wynnel, who felt himself under Sir Nick's protection, moved close to it, looking first left and then right.

And he shivered worse than he had shivered before.

"Sir Nicholas—" he began. He turned round, and shied back at the sight of the face that met him.

"Nay, man!" said Sir Nick, in a low soft growl which he strove hard to make kindly. One trembling hand dropped from the cane, and fumbled at his pocket. "Here are a couple of guineas for you; take them!"

It was far more than the apothecary could dream of earning in a month.

"Since I know they tell lies against you," said Master Wynnel, "I'll take them and not deny I need them. But, sir: you must not go from this house as yet. Let me make you comfortable in my poor back parlour."

"Not go from the house? How not?"

"Court gentlemen may not know that off Fleet Street, hard by the Temple, there is a foul district called Alsatia."

"Is it so?" murmured Sir Nick, showing his teeth.

79

"This Alsatia is a legal refuge, a sanctuary, even for those guilty of the foulest crime. The worst is called bully, or bullyrock, since . . . "

George dived at the window, putting one eye to it. Almost immediately he found a space of clear glass.

"The rogue on the left," gabbled the apothecary, "hath drawn back against the shops near the end of the lane. I can't see him now. But the other man, on the right by the arch that leads to the Strand . . . "

"I see him," said George.

The man lounged against the old dark-brick wall, just inside the arch and at right angles to it. He lounged negligently, his right shoulder against the wall; arms folded; legs crossed in such fashion that the tip of one ruined shoe rested on the ground. There was a long broomstraw stuck in his mouth; and, as he chewed it, his lip rolled in a perpetual sneer.

Of body he was very tall and lean. His tattered coat was fastened tightly to his body with pewter buttons to the neck. His rusty greenish breeches were laced to rusty greenish stockings, so that all, including the coat, seemed one tight-fitting garment. In an old scabbard he wore a new sword (its steel-lace guard a-glitter in a shaft of sun) which someone had bought for him. His wide low-crowned hat had a broken brim, but fastened to the side of the crown was a rosette of green ribbon. Under it the broomstraw still rolled with that perpetual sneer.

He was loud-mouthed, without pity or bowels, the dread of all sober men—Bully of Alsatia himself.

CHAPTER VII

OF SWORDPLAY IN

DEADMAN'S LANE

"DO NOT take it amiss!" the apothecary was still begging. "These bullyrocks go from sanctuary only to kill for pay. 'Tis but natural they should be more skilled with the sword than those gently bred . . ."

"Fixed to his hat," said George, "is a green ribbon."

With a heavy arm Sir Nick gently pushed the apothecary aside, took two strides to the window, and looked—where George pointed— across the lane and some way up to the right. He did not look long before he straightened up.

"The Green Ribbon Club," he said. "My Lord Shaftesbury. His Grace of Bucks . . . "

And he broke the cane in his hands with a splintering crack as though a roof beam had gone.

On Sir Nick's swollen face was a look of almost religious ecstasy. Had any invisible presence been trying to hold him back, it was flung out, stamped upon, flown to the wind. But his bearing was quiet and brisk.

"George," he said, "do you remain here and rest quiet. I'll engage Long-legs up by the arch; I'll draw him down, draw him down (eh, George?) until I can engage them both together. Was there ever such an opportunity?"

But this was too much for George, who yelled back at him.

" 'Remain here.' 'Rest quiet.' —'Fore God, Nick Fenton, what d'ye make of me? D'ye forget the time, scarce eight months ago, when we stood back to back in . . . "

"I—I—"

"Heyday! Ye think me grown too fat and slow, eh?"

"Nay, I—I would not insult you so." Suddenly Sir Nick's lips drew back in what he evidently thought was a pleasant grin. "Then you'd stand to't, old friend? Good! Let be! But tuck up your wrist-ruffles, man! Up under your sleeve; that's it! Else they intangle in the guard and you're undone. And never, never wear a sword with a smooth-surfaced grip! Take heed, now, that silver grip don't slip or turn in your hand! Are ye prepared?"

"Yes."

Sir Nick's right hand moved the rapier a few inches from its scabbard, shook it to make sure it was loose, and let it slip back. He shifted his sword belt a trifle.

"I still desire Long-legs with the green ribbon," he snapped. "Do you engage the other one. Now!"

Sir Nick opened the door quietly and went out at his slow, soft tread. George followed him, turning to the left past the round-paned window.

"Oh, Lord!" moaned the apothecary. "Lord, Lord, Lord!"

And grotesquely, in his black skullcap and long black gown, he beat his hands together and danced round the tiny shop in agony.

But an onlooker might not have seen the true reason for his behaviour.

Master Wynnel was the gravest, soberest citizen in this lane or in any lane or alley of the district. He moved at stately pace. His solemn nod was a condescension. Durst he, in skullcap and gown, go a-flying out to watch a common brawl?

And yet, though he had heard much of Sir Nicholas Fenton, he had never seen Sir Nick in a sword fight. Almost he would have given his life to see it.

Human nature won, of course.

"Lord!" bleated the apothecary and dashed out of the shop, running low. He thought, like ostriches and men in his humour, he knew where he could lurk without being seen. Some way up, in front of Marty the hay dealer's ran a long stone watering trough for horses. If he crouched behind it, he could see across to the place where Sir Nick and Long-legs must meet.

Sir Nick, having turned sideways to face the arch, was slowly approaching. Long-legs, still leaning negligently against the arch and chewing the broomstraw, made a sudden move.

82

The man was as quick as a panther, or an acrobat at a fair. A great sideways bound, knees crooked up and feet in the air, carried him exactly before the middle of the arch, barring it. A puff of brown dust went up round his legs.

Sir Nick stopped six feet in front of him. If Sir Nick had glanced towards his right, he would have seen the staring spectacles and black skullcap of the apothecary, hidden beyond the far rim of the watering-trough. From the other end of the lane, near the spiked gate, began a quick rattle of blades; a pause; than a rattle again.

But nobody looked, and nobody turned.

"Now a fool," thought the shivering apothecary, "a fool, seeing Bully's great reach and length of leg in skin-tight rags, would wager a broadpiece to a penny against Sir Nick. Yet . . . "

Seen at close range, Long-legs showed a long mottled face patched with black beard stubble, and an even wider sneer. His eyes were rheumy but sharp under the broken hat. His voice was harsh and loud, but it now put on a mincing accent.

"Would you pass here, little court gentleman?"

"The only pass I make," said Sir Nick, "will be through your rotted guts.—*Who are ye, scum?*"

Long-legs spat out the broomstraw.

The words were as contemptuous as though he had been flicked with fingers. Long-legs drew himself up in swelled-headed pride.

"Cock of the hectors am I," he cried, and struck his right fist against his chest, "that can spit a running fowl through the neck; and am here," his lips writhed with the same sneer, "to do such for you, little man."

"Lug out!" snarled Sir Nick, "Lug out, cock of the hectors, and see!"

Both blades whipped from their scabbards at the same instant.

The thin shaft of sunlight flashed on each, a brief dazzle, before it faded into a grey sky. Long-legs gave a little hop to the left, a little hop to the right, as though to circle round his opponent and take him off side. But the quarters were too cramped; he dared not risk it.

Sir Nick had fallen on guard: body sideways to his adversary, right foot out with a knee a little bent, left foot back and at right angles. But again, though his blade slanted straight towards Long-legs, his guard seemed too close to his body.

"Nay!" muttered the apothecary. "Nay, now!"

83

Long-legs saw it too. He dropped to the same guard position. But the blades did not cross or touch. Sir Nick's remained motionless. Bully of Alsatia snaked out his long arm, feeling with the point, feeling again, drawing back, edging closer in . . .

Then Long-legs, with all his reach, shot forward in a full-length lunge in tierce, at his opponent's right chest. There was a *clack* as Sir Nick, hand moving horizontally, jerked the hand six inches to the right and parried. But even Long-legs's agility could not dart his own right foot back to guard position before Sir Nick flung back a half-lunge in quarte.

The point struck and drew blood, very near the region of the heart. But it was so shallow a wound that it only infuriated Long-legs the more.

"God rot ye!" shouted Long-legs, and lunged, also in quarte, for his opponent's left chest. Sir Nick's hand swept to the left across his own chest. *Clack!* and he knocked the thrust wide, yet so close to the body that the blades hissed together.

Twice more the blades darted and rattled, making Master Wynnel's scalp crawl. Then he saw a terrifying thing.

It was a "secret" *botte*, or sword trick, only because men were as yet too overwrought to study it. If you fight closed-up, and venture little more than a half-lunge, your antagonist comes far to underestimate your reach. But, if you draw your right-angled left foot up close to the right foot, as Sir Nick was doing now, you will have an incredibly long leg-lunge when you go forward. Your body, almost horizontal, will be longer. Your arm and sword, rigid as a rod together, will seem far longer. . . .

And Sir Nick Fenton, sword-point aimed dead for his opponent's belly, shot forward at full lunge like a striking snake.

"Tchaa!" cried the apothecary. And his head jerked and his spectacles fell off into the water of the horse trough.

Only Long-legs's acrobatics saved his life. He did not even try to parry. He gave an immense backwards leap, one leg in the air and then two, which carried him a full six or seven feet under the arch. Sir Nick, inexorable, moved slowly after him to kill or be killed.

Bully landed staggering, but still a-snarl for battle. He landed beside the double line of red fire buckets on his left, inside the tunnel. He moved still further back, but stopped when he saw the periwig and pin-skewered hat of Sir Nick—nostrils flared, lips back in a fixed

84

grin—shuffling towards him in silhouette against the grey light of the arch.

"Sta-a-nd!" murmured Sir Nick, drawing out the word. "Stand, cock of the hectors! Or are you?"

The breath whistled through Sir Nick's nostrils. He seemed to be having trouble with his periwig, which was slewed towards one eye, and he brushed at it.

Long-legs crouched at guard. But his small mind ran red with delight. Unobtrusively his left hand crept towards his left pocket, in which lay prepared a good handful of gravel mixed with dust and grit.

"Cock of the hectors?" roared Long-legs. "When there's a hole in your own guts . . . "

His left hand must sweep over, flinging the dust and gravel straight into Sir Nick's eyes, an instant before Long-legs launched his own thrust. Yet he must thrust low and not high, lest his own dust blow back in his eyes. It was, at the time, a quite fair trick.

"When there's a hole in your own guts," he screamed, "you'll know who's master, who's cock, who rules the roost!"

Dust and gravel spurted from his left hand. Sir Nick, whose left thumb was already well under the periwig while his fingers gripped it from above, yanked the periwig forward and over, his broad-brimmed hat ducking like a face shield. Instantly he flung both periwig and hat into the air—just as Long-legs drove a full-length lunge in seconde at the upper part of the right thigh.

Sir Nick's rapier whipped over, knuckles down, pointed vertically at the ground. The two blades whacked as he swept Long-legs's sword to the right in parry. Then, before the head-down Long-legs could quite jump back to guard, Sir Nick's point drove out and up at an oblique angle.

The point caught Long-legs, whose head was a little back, through the upper throat not far under the chin. It ripped up behind the teeth, crashed through the roof of the mouth, and lodged in the brain.

In the next instant Sir Nick was tugging at it, tugging back and forth with both hands, so that he might loosen and dislodge it. It came away in a gush of blood which spattered heavily on his hands and cuffs but at least it was out.

For a half-second Long-legs stood upright, hardly swaying. A thin film of blood crept over his eyes and blotted them out. Blood gushed from his nostrils, foamed over his mouth, and ran from the throat-wound. This gaunt corpse tried to take a step to the left, but he was already dead.

Long-legs fell at full length, face down, across the double line of red-leather fire buckets. Most of them held his weight, though slopping. Two fell over, one creaked and swayed, sending out a splashing of foul water mixed with blood to spread a pool across the dirt.

Sir Nick looked down at him, using velvet sleeve to mop the sweat from his face. Across the tunnel, somewhat dusty, lay his fallen periwig and hat. He moved towards it.

"A man is ill advised," he was thinking, "should he intrust but the hat against matter of the kind. Periwig must go too, after masking the face whilst you may count one. It sweepeth away other dust, which might blind him in . . . . "

Suddenly his head went up, alert for a noise. Then, head bare except for black stubble, his hands and sword and cuffs bloodied, he raced out of the tunnel and back down the lane. On the way he passed a gabbling apothecary, with water-dripping spectacles, who had cast aside caution and run out from behind the horse trough.

George was in trouble.

Anyone could hear George's panting breath gulp in and out his mouth. His back was towards the turning and the spiked iron gate. His opponent—the second Bully of Alsatia—had his back to Sir Nick, and pressed hard. A thin dust cloud hovered round their waists.

Sir Nick stopped, measuring the distance with his eye. Then he lunged. The point struck under the man's left shoulder blade for a distance of just one inch. The man's body jerked like a hooked fish; then steadied on guard against George.

"Drop your point!" said Sir Nick. "Drop it, else your heart will be burst before you can say 'Laard.' —George! Drop yours too, but not before he shall do it!"

Slowly Bully the Second's hand fell to his side, still gripping the sword. When Sir Nick saw that sword, his friendship and admiration for George grew along with his black vindictiveness against Bully.

It was a very old-fashioned blade, longer and a good deal heavier than George's, with sharpened double edges as well as a point. To deal with it was child's play if you had knowledge. But George, who knew only modern swordplay, had fought like an overdressed, high-heeled, stout-bodied fiend and held him off for the enormous long time of three minutes.

Across Bully's shoulder he could see George's white face, a mask of sweat bubbles inside the periwig. George panted too much to speak.

"I am Nick Fenton," said Sir Nick, and twisted the sword point in Bully's back so that the man's flesh writhed. "Ye know me, I think?"

The faint nasal twang in Bully's voice betrayed him, as did other things.

"I know thee," he spat out, "for whoremaster and dog and swine, keeper of a Papist doxy . . . "

"All these I am, with much more that would shock and affright you. But doth repute say I ever broke my word?"

A hesitation. "Nay, I do not—"

"I will go back five long paces, rogue. Then do you turn and fight!"

"And the Laard grant me victory over the Philistine!"

Sir Nick's heels stamped hard in the dust so that all might hear the five paces. To break his word (save to women, in the way of lechery) he thought the only sin. For fair play he cared nothing, only wanting the fight for himself.

Round whirled the second Alsatian, a thickset man of about Sir Nick's height. His lank greasy hair, shot with grey, was cut halfway down his ears. A very old backsword cut seamed up the flesh over one eye, holding it slanted up. He had a very ill-fitting set of upper teeth, like bad gravestones.

"Art a Conventicle man, Scar-face?" Sir Nick asked politely. "Like to all rogues and knaves of Alsatia?"

Both used the familiar (or in this case contemptuous) "thee" and "thou" form, which is like the French *tu*.

"When thou wert yet unbreeched, a score and five years ago, I was of the mighty New Model army. If the Laard hath seen fit to visit me with misfortune, under an ill-got king . . . "

"Now who hath heard," said Sir Nick, and laughed, "of *any* Round-head could ever use a sword?"

And Scar-face, huffed to rage, charged in.

It was not a fight at all. Sir Nick merely played with him and laughed at him. Scar-face tried to fight in the new style, body sideways, remembering the warning against the overarm cut which his first opponent had found so hard to parry. He forgot that his heavier blade was no tougher of fiber than the new ones.

When he lunged heavily at Sir Nick's chest, he found his blade contemptuously slapped aside or feathered away with a slither that maddened him. Again and again he struck at nothing. "Lightly, lightly," thought Sir Nick, who then darted in and stung his nose so that a single drop of blood oozed from it. It acted on Scar-face exactly as Sir Nick hoped it would.

Scar-face's arm whipped back and up for an old-fashioned cut—leaving wide open the whole right side of his body. Out went Sir Nick at full-length lunge. The blade skewered the armpit, driving a little to the left, and struck on some part of the backbone.

Rocked back on his heels and all but overset, Scar-face struggled up just as the rapier was tugged out. For half a second Scar-face stood motionless. It may be doubted whether he could lift his right arm, yet his fingers clutched the blade.

"'Ware the dog behind ye!" he shouted, in the oldest trick known to duellists, and pointed with his left hand. As he shouted, his false teeth flew out of his mouth and landed unbroken amid swirling dust.

Sir Nick, for once off guard, glanced over his right shoulder. Instantly Scar-face, doubtless protected by his Laard, ran hard past Sir Nick's left, and sped like a winged deity towards the mouth of the lane. Blood drops spattered after him on the ground.

Instantly Sir Nick gave chase, running mightily and stabbing at his back. But Scar-face, who seemed to pray, went at inhuman speed. He dashed through the arch into the tunnel past his dead companion, not even slipping in water because it had dried into the ground. He attained the crowded Strand; and once more saw a miracle of luck.

To cross that street, in the ordinary way, would have been difficult to the edge of impossible. But a brewer's wagon, loaded with heavy casks and drawn by two Flanders mares towards the west, had locked wheels with a vegetable cart going in the same direction, while the drivers cursed and belaboured each other with their whips. Approaching westwards, two sedan chairs and a long cart heavy with sacks of barley (the chairmen hugely amused) stopped briefly to watch the belabouring.

Into that narrow space dashed Scar-face, still holding his sword, and disappeared across the road just as wheels unlocked with a bumping crash. Vehicles flowed together again as Sir Nick leaped to follow, and could not manage it.

Meanwhile George, who had returned sword to scabbard, sat against the brick wall and panted until his breathing returned. Though sweat-rumpled and grimy, he had forgotten this. When the other two raced up the lane, he bounced to his feet as though made of rubber. Picking up Scar-face's false teeth, apparently as a memento, George dropped them into his pocket and tore after the others with (also) unexpected agility.

Dashing through the arch, he paused only to pluck the hat with the green-ribbon rosette from the head of the dead man and crumple it into the same large pocket. He picked up Sir Nick's dusty hat-cum-periwig and was brushing it as he reached the outer arch.

There he found his friend, sword in hand, stamping and raving before a solid wall of vehicles.

"This dog, this—" Sir Nick swallowed hard. "He made 'scape through there. How do I seek him now?"

"You can't, Nick! Gently, now; be persuaded!"

Fitting the periwig in some tolerable fashion over his companion's head, which seemed only to confuse Nick, George attempted to soothe him.

"Nick," he said, nodding in the direction of Temple Bar and beyond, "there are above a score and three score of twisty alleys or lanes (d'ye follow, Nick?) which will take him back to Alsatia. Once there, the rogue is safe."

"Because 'tis a sanctuary?"

"More, Nick. Scratch me, a whole trainband—nay, a company of soldiery with flintlocks—durst not venture in there!"

"Then here's one who will!"

"No, Nick," George said quietly. "I'll not let you."

"Not let me? As how?"

"As—thus!" said George, and suddenly, behind him, locked his arms round Sir Nick in a powerful wrestling grip.

"Let be, curse ye! Let . . . "

Sir Nick tried to open his shoulders and break the grip, but he could not do it. As they reeled and thudded back against the wall, there was not one yell or howl of interest.

At least one Abram-cove saw the bulge of the heavy money purse in Sir Nick's pocket; of ordinary, he could have slit down the middle of the pocket with a knife so swans-down light that the bag would fall out unnoticed into his hand. But even the frantic held back; even the urchin did not cry out.

When you see a court gentleman, with mad eyes above bloodied sword and hands bloodied well above the cuffs, a-struggle with another of his breed in silent ferocity, this is too serious. The hand of Jack Ketch squirms through all. One constable (such were the breed) saw it and immediately disappeared. Only a magistrate—magistrates for the most part were stern inflexible men—would have dared to interfere.

"No!" panted George. "'Fore God, Nick, I'll hold you till your brain cools and the vapours are gone!"

"Will you?" panted Sir Nick, wrenching one arm free.

George instantly locked it again. They reeled out towards the kennel and the crashing wheels, they staggered back, turning again—and Sir Nick's left leg struck something or somebody.

The only one who had dared approach (since most sidled past with heads down and gaze on the cobbles) was a very young shoeblack, carrying his many rags together with his shallow tin vessel of soot mixed with rancid oil. Sir Nick's knee sent him sprawling; the soot-and-oil mixture splashed out and ran along the street into the kennel.

"Nay, now!" said Sir Nick gently. His arms went limp. George, swinging him round, saw that his eyes were conscience-stricken. "I meant no harm. Truly I meant no harm."

George let him go altogether. Sir Nick knelt down, to help up a frightened and black-faced urchin. "This sword; you are afeared; nay, back into the scabbard." Back it went into the scabbard. "Here . . . here's money; a gold angel; stay, take a handful; they are yours."

He closed the boy's hand on the coins.

"But be advised," he added. "That is all I would tell you. When you are grown up, and are become a man, this you must do: towards the weak and helpless, you shall shew humility, which is of the angels. But if they be proud and insolent,"—his fingers began to tighten on the boy's arm, but unloosed before they hurt—"then smite them across their sneering faces, and have no mercy!" His tone changed. "Stay, I would not harm you! I . . ."

Slowly Sir Nick straightened up. His knees tottered. With George making room for him, he stumbled and set his back against the wall. One arm went up and covered his face, elbow across the eyes. He remained there for a little time, and then dropped his arm.

"Er—George," he said.

Lord George Harwell gave a start which was almost a jump, and a shiver of superstitious dread went through him.

It was a different voice, an utterly different voice from old Nick's!

Stay! It was the same grave, courteous, kindly voice, pitched in Nick's tone but like that of an older philosopher, which had perplexed George all day until it altered in the apothecary's shop.

"How came we back here?" asked the voice. "I remember, in the apothecary's shop, I began to grow a trifle vexed with you—but over some absurd matter, a mere trifle—and I can remember nothing more."

Thus Professor Fenton opened his eyes, and looked round him. He felt shaken, as though he had been through a bad experience. That was all.

George desperately wished to pray, which he would have died rather than have admitted. But he could remember only a prayer for the dying, which did not seem applicable.

"Come, now!" he exclaimed, with false heartiness. " 'Twas a matter of less than ten minutes in all."

"Ten minutes!" repeated Fenton.

His wandering gaze travelled across the hanging gables across the street. As he had seen before, both lattices of one window were open. The pretty, tousle-headed slattern of sixteen, who wore no attire to speak of, was now lazily leaning both elbows on the window ledge and had not yet even finished her beer in the tankard.

"Why," George told him soothingly, "you did but kill one man and wound another. —Come, don't look at me so! Or down at your hands! You'll not be taken up: whosoever finds Long-legs's body, they'll shake his hand because someone hath saved the expense of a hanging. He's an Alsatian; his life was already forfeit."

"But . . ."

"Your great need, Nick, is for food," George said heartily. "Scratch me, my own guts growl for my dinner! Come, there's a cookshop, the Fat Capon—not ten yards from here—will do us well for such. Take my arm; man, you're weak; and I'll tell you the story as we go."

"Yes, by all means! But . . . "

George, glancing to his right, stopped abruptly. Slowly his large face grew crimson.

"Nick!" he said in a low voice. "Look there! Here's your own coach approaching, and Meg York inside it, a-tapping on the glass and smiling. Nick, Nick,"—there was a tremble in the voice—"durst I meet her, d'ye think?"

91

CHAPTER VIII

THE LORD OF

THE GREEN RIBBON

THE premises at the sign of the Fat Capon, though fairly wide and deep, were smokily dark except for the bed of red-glowing coals in the vast iron-and-brick chimney at the rear. Its heat flowed out heavily, past perspiring walls, and through the open lattice at the rear.

" 'Hell is murky,' " Fenton quoted to himself, as George drew out a chair at one of the black, long tables. It would be, he decided, an admirable smoky red-glowing place to met the devil. But would he meet the devil again?

"Sit you merry, gentlemen!" said the landlord, a very fat man with up-rolled sleeves and a broad belt with a brass buckle round his middle. "And how may I tempt your appetite?"

"For me," answered George, "a good capon and (say) four good pigeons." He gave the other a sinister look. "They are fat pigeons, ripe, and melting to the teeth?"

"Sir," the landlord retorted haughtily, "they are so, else you would not find them here."

"And for this gentleman," said George, who saw that Nick's periwig was lowered and that he stared in deep thought at the table, "hah! I have it! A meat pie, large with rich gravy and a fine beef or the like. For each of us, a pot of your best canary."

Fenton was only just beginning to enjoy himself again since they had seen Meg's coach lumber to a stop.

92

That conversation with Meg, a few minutes ago, had thrown the dice at a new and more dangerous fall. Was he never, Fenton wondered, to be at ease, without fangs all about him? His mind went back to the Strand, when he and George had climbed into the coach at Meg's bidding.

"To go on foot is so horrid!" Meg had said. "You go but a few yards? Nay then! you must sit here for a merry discourse with me."

The coach, a monstrous great box with wheels higher than a man, was curved underneath and slung on heavy leather straps. It had a periwigged coachman and was drawn by two heavy bay horses. It was painted bright gilt to its pinnacled roof, save for mudstains and Sir Nick's arms, four quarterings, under the glass windows.

"S—sweetest madam," bumbled George, his face fiery in the presence of one he adored, "I have no desire to—to intrude . . ."

Whereupon he fell all over his own feet on the step up to the coach, and dropped (to his further embarrassment) on the soft wine-coloured upholstery just opposite Meg, who took fiendish delight in teasing him.

"George!" her voice caressed softly. "Could you ever intrude?"

Fenton swung lightly into the coach and dropped into the farthest corner opposite Meg.

As for Meg, she gave the impression of a fine lady after an exhausting forenoon without buying anything. Her fur cloak, muff, even hat were cast aside on the seat. The scarlet skirt with golden arabesques was spread out round her; the upper part of her gown, of vertical red-and-black with a very low corsage trimmed in black ruffles, had the same effect of weariness.

Yet there was a smouldering quality about her, too. Fenton knew what it was; and, despite himself, it disturbed him. Her grey eyes, masked under long lashes, slid sideways towards him, and then away as though uninterested.

"This New Exchange," she said wearily, "is in higher repute than the goods it sells. I had desired to buy some simple gown, like this old thing, which some say none the less does become me."

And in weariness she lifted both arms above her head, all but emerging from her corsage when she lowered them, and apparently unaware of it. Fenton had tried to hide his bloodstained hands by putting them into his pockets. But Meg had seen them, as she saw all things concerning him. Suddenly she bent forward.

93

"Foh, you have been a-duelling again!" she said, shrinking back with a look of disgust and fright. Though the fright (for him) was real enough, anyone except George could have seen the fierce pride and pleasure underneath. "But lackaday! You won, which was most uncivil. One day you will be killed, and I shall be—oh, so horrid merry!"

"Nay, now, scratch me!" protested George, who was scarlet in the face.

"Sweetest George, would you know the difference 'twixt death and life?"

Fenton sat up.

"George," he said, "she but feebly tries to mock at you. Should she try it again, set a barb in it and fire it back as you would fire a petronel. 'Twill do the doxy good."

Meg leaned swiftly towards Fenton.

"Ay, and your own waspish tongue—!"

"Would you dance at my funeral, Meg?"

"Indeed I would. And sing too. Just as once . . . " Meg paused. She sank back into the corner, and her eyes wandered away. "Nick," she said presently, "have you no remembrance at all?"

"Of—of what?"

"Of the time, not two years gone, when we had a house at Epsom? Your friends would be there: George (I am sorry for what I said, George!), and my Lord Rochester, and Sir Carr Scrope, and the old stout man who bade us call him 'Mr. Reeve.' And all of you fierce Royalists, sons and grandsons of those who were there since the royal standard was raised at Oxford."

Real tears shone on Meg's eyelashes now.

"Nick, Nick, I say no word against Lydia. But my sire and grandsire were no canting Puritans like hers. My father, the brother of Lydia's father, was Captain Charles York. Even when they were beaten, and long afterwards, there were many who would neither flee to exile nor own Oliver as Lord Protector. They had no hope; but they would not yield. Whenever they saw an Ironside, they flew at him, backsword against backsword, until one or t'other was slain. Presently all were gone. Captain York among them."

Meg had sat up straight, shoulders quivering, eyes lost in a dream.

Fenton began to speak, but checked himself.

"And don't you remember, as a boy, how the Sour-faces stood straight at every lane, with pike or sword? And Royalists, under their eyes, drank

94

the toast? *Crummle* they lengthened to Crum-well. And they threw a crumb of bread into a pot of wine before they drank it. 'God send this Crum-well down!'"

"I—I well remember the custom."

"But not Epsom, Nick? You do, fie on you! The little dining room, with your friends there?" Meg had kept back her tears; she was proud. "I stood on a chair, with my other foot on the table; ay, and my petticoats thrown above my knee, and a cittern in my hands, thus. But I did not sing bawdry, Nick. I sang the old Cavalier songs, that set all your faces a-glow like a fire. I did it thus!"

Meg sat bolt upright. She herself was all a-glow, from her own heart or spirit. Carelessly she threw back her head, its lustrous black hair dressed down the sides to little curls that almost touched the shoulders, and in a fringe across the forehead. True colour flamed in her cheeks. Her mouth and eyes, through the run of the verse, threw out every emotion from bitter contempt to triumph. Her right hand swept across imaginary strings.

> "Come, fawn on disaster! Call Oliver master,
> And lick-spittle, shiver, and crawl!
> The breast-plate, the back-plate, the gorget and tassets,
> The sword that did smite them, now hid in a wall?
> The lobster-tail helmet, the wine of the well-met,
> The red and the gold of the Crown?
> 'Tis a dead comrade's ghost that shall give ye the toast—
> God send this Crum-well down!"

There were other verses, but Meg could not finish them. Half the fever went out of her. She sank back, her hands over her eyes.

George regarded her with hypnotized admiration and awe.

"What a woman you are, sweetest madam! And what an actress you would have made!"

"You forget," Fenton said politely, "she is one already."

George turned a face whose redness was now wrath.

"If any man but you had said that—!"

"Oh, her Royalist feelings are true enough. Charles York was a good and valiant man; may the grass be green on his grave!" Coldly Fenton's mind weighed the matter. "And do you think *I* don't feel the allure of her? Don't you think, even with the crowd round us now and eyeing us, I don't burn to take her in my arms?" Here Meg's fingers trembled a little. "But don't you observe, George, how she watches through her fingers the effect she has made?"

Meg dashed her hands away from her eyes and looked at him, through tears, with hatred.

"I go," she declared, keeping her lips straight, "to Mr. Plover's great shop, The Jillflirt in Cheapside. Will you favour me by leaving this coach?"

Fenton ignored the speech.

"If you be only jillflirt—" he hesitated. "Well! You do but inflame and baffle men's minds. George, for example, has a question he would put to you . . ."

"Nick!" whispered George, in an agony of fear when he approached the brink. "Nay, ss-s-t! Not now!"

"Question?" asked Meg in genuine surprise.

"Nay, ss-s-t! Nick!"

"Well, let be. It is a matter for consideration." Fenton paused. "Meg, did you dispatch Kitty to the Blue Mortar, in Dead Man's Lane, to buy arsenic?"

Meg's amazement was so great that Fenton could have sworn it was real.

"Arsenic? Poison?" Meg said. "And that, one presumes, to kill you? Think all else of me. But not that. And this—this 'Kitty'!" Her cheeks flamed again. "Must I be jealous of another too? What is her name? Kitty who?"

"Kitty Softcover. She is the cook in our own house."

Meg's shoulders lifted and writhed in disgust.

"*I?* To make confidante of a cook-maid? I have never even seen the wench. And besides!" Across Meg's lips curled that closed-mouthed smile he knew so well. "You think us conspirators?"

"What else?"

"I have many vices, as happily you know. But my interest lieth only in men."

"Now that," he told her dryly, with mock admiration, "I confess I had not thought of. But pardon me for reminding you that you have many jewels. This girl . . ."

"You are fond of her, I suppose?"

"No. She shocks me,"—he used the term in its old sense of *disgusts*— "as much as she would seem to disgust you. Yet she is thievish, and

96

fond of bright stones. Should you have given her a bright ring or bracelet . . ."

"And put my neck in danger? Faugh!"

"Yet the wench, unquestionably Kitty, gave to the apothecary a description of the lady who had sent her. 'Twas the true image of you."

Meg looked at him curiously.

"Nay, how much a dunce is the cunningest of men!" she said, shrinking into her most delicate manner. "Would any woman, sent to buy poison, give a *true* picture of the person who sent her, save that she wished to make suspect an innocent one? I hope this wench . . . nay, I will not speak her name! . . . is well and heavy flogged."

There was a pause.

"George," said Fenton, "Madam York is in the right of it. She makes zanies of us both. We had best go."

George opened the door of the coach, carried himself clumsily to the step, and jumped down. He was astonished to find this side surrounded by a silent group. Even the gaudiest coach was never stopped, nor had its windows broken by stones, if a pretty lady sat inside. The mob merely stood with lewd eyes and lewd expressions, seldom displeasing to the pretty lady herself.

Again real tears touched Meg's eyelashes.

"This is a true leave-taking, Nick," she told him. "You noted, questionless, I lied when I said 'twould take another night to gather my stuffs. You will find me gone from your house by early evening."

"And I will never cease to think," said Fenton, "that you are Mary Grenville."

He bent forward to kiss her hand, and found (unexpectedly) that he was kissing her lips instead. His knee slipped on the velvet-covered upholstery, and he fell against her. Before he could slip loose from her arms and get to his feet, his brain had become somewhat addled.

But he slid down and out to the coach step, and thence to the ground.

"Should you need me, as you will," whispered Meg, leaning out, "you shall hear how to find me. For we are bound together, you and I!"

Fenton gave a signal to the coachman, while George roared back loungers, who now seemed delighted. The coachman's whip cracked, and cracked again; the huge vehicle quivered, but could not move. Fenton and George, both now wary of slapping sword scabbards, moved away into the crowd.

"Nick," growled George, with his gaze on the cobbles, "she loves you."

"No! Attend to me. First, I care for none but Lydia. Second, you do not know Meg. 'Ware her temper; give her money; load her with jewels and gowns and baubles; and she will love you too."

George turned a face in which hope struggled above incredulity.

"Truly, d'ye think so?"

"I . . . am sure. Besides, I mislike the sound of this Captain Duroc: who, as I now recall, is named as of 'the French King's personal attendance.'"

Here George's left hand, as once before, dropped softly to his sword hilt.

"With you," said Fenton, "she will be in good hands. But you must make haste, George! She goes from my house earlier than I had thought; she goes this evening. You must be there; you must huff up your courage; you must speak bold and not stammer, or you'll lose her. Can you do it, man? Will you try?"

George hesitated. Then, through set teeth, he swore he would.

"Good! Now pray tell me what happened in Dead Man's Lane, when I . . . lost my memory?"

George told him, briefly but clearly.

All this, more swiftly than it takes to relate, Fenton analyzed and put each circumstance in its proper place. He saw that his worst danger was upon him.

They had been in the apothecary's shop: very well. The apothecary tells them Kitty's description of Meg. George raves and threatens the apothecary wildly. Whereat he, Fenton—who an hour or so before has been coolheaded under greater difficulty with the servants—then flies out against poor George. Sir Nick grips him then, and has complete control by the time he looks out of the window and sees the green ribbon of my Lord Shaftesbury's Country party.

But the real explanation, he knew, lay deeper. He did not really fly out against George. Wrath gripped him, and Sir Nick slipped in, because of the accusation against Meg. Both of them must be more fond of Meg, even if you called it lust, than either realized.

And there was worse, which made Fenton shiver. Each time Sir Nick was a-prowl, Fenton had heretofore sensed it; he had braced himself for that wrestling with the coffin lid and the remnants of the dead man inside.

Yet this time he had not even been aware of it. At the apothecary's he had felt only a mild surge of temper, a mere brush of it, not even as much as he had felt against Judith Pamphlin or Kitty Softcover. He could well remember looking out of the window and seeing the green ribbon . . . then nothing. He had never before lost his memory.

True, it was not completely a loss. As a very drunken man will next day recall only one or two hazy memories, he vaguely recalled swords clashing, and somebody very thin, and someone else shouting, "'Ware the dog behind ye!" At the same time . . .

What he had feared must be true. Sir Nick was growing more powerful.

"No!" his brain cried out. To have that dead lunatic creep into his bones, perhaps for longer periods than the stated ten minutes, would make the devil laugh and perhaps had been the devil's intent from the first. "*Within full of dead men's bones, and of all uncleanness.*" No!

Weighing it coolly, he knew he could defeat Sir Nick if he remained always, always and forever, on his guard. This he determined to do. And he was almost cheerful again when he followed George into the smoky Fat Capon, where George ordered a chicken and four pigeons for himself, a meat pie for Fenton, and pots of canary for both.

It was long past the hour for midday dinner. Very few patrons sat at the long tables, silhouetted like ghosts against the fiery red bed of coals. In the dimness Fenton's hands went unnoticed despite their bloodstains.

"George," he said, when the meal had been ordered and both of them sat pondering for a time, "I had forgot to thank you for. . ."

"Pah!" George said gruffly.

"Not to know that in these days one does not trouble to parry a cut, but thrusts home with the point as he lifts his arm," Fenton argued; "yet for three minutes to hold off a bully-Alsatia—!"

"Faugh!" growled George. "They cared not for me. You were their quarry."

"So I think. Yet let's discourse upon it. These bullyrocks creep from sanctuary to kill for pay. One flaunts his green rosette. Who set them on me?"

George looked at him in surprise.

"Why, are you in any doubt? My Lord Shaftesbury himself."

Now there flowed back to Fenton all of Giles Collins's forebodings and headshakings of this morning. "You would not take a cup of wine

99

at the Devil, so hard by the King's Head?" The latter tavern, of course, was the meeting place of the Green Ribbon Club. Most of all, Giles's dark words: "There is like to be bloody work this day."

Giles, in fact, had all but dressed him for a duel: without any lace encumbrances, without even a ring on his sword hand. Yet Fenton gnawed at his lip, here in the cookshop, and would not be satisfied.

"Granted," he admitted, scowling, "I hate my Lord Shaftesbury and all his works. But here's a man of high and mighty repute, a Lord Chancellor before he turned his coat against a King for the fourth time. Who am I to be his victim? Why?"

The colour drained from George's face. Slowly he turned towards his companion.

"Now God help us!" George prayed; and then whacked his fist on the table. "I had thought your humours gone. Nick, Nick! A good doctor of physick, now ..."

"I need none, George. Why should this little old man bear me grudge?"

George steadied himself, as though to speak to a child.

"You have no remembrance, Nick?"

"None."

"Parliament," said George, "was prorogued ..."

"In November of last year," agreed Fenton. "And hath not been convoked together even yet."

"Good! Good!" nodded George, eyes gleaming. "I'll have thee cured yet, good friend. Now to prorogue Parliament," he explained slowly, as to a child, "means but to terminate its session for a time, not dissolve it. Lords and Commons, in November, were at such a high pitch of quarrel that both Houses sat together in the Painted Chamber, which is common ground for both..."

"Devil take you, I know that! I desire to learn why my Lord Shaftesbury—"

George, a little shaken and awed, stared at the past.

"That night," he said, "I was in the public gallery of the Painted Chamber, which contains five great tapestries representing the siege of Troy. I cannot tell why I was there, having no head for such stuff. Stop; I recall; I went because I heard there would be troublesome affairs, and hence merry sport."

"Yes?"

"Jack Ravenscroft and I were a-laying wagers," George said defensively, "whether the candles would go out before the speeches ended. Indeed, the candles burned blue and dim, on high pointed windows and November fog over the river; but both fires were very bright. My Lord Shaftesbury was accommodated with a chair by the nearer fire. His Majesty was there too."

"King Charles? Why?"

"I can't tell. But he lounged by the other fire. This day, Nick, when we saw the face of the red Indian on the tobacco sign—curse me, seeing the face all long and brown, I had all but said 'Sire!' Save that he showed no teeth like the brown long face, and the curls of his black periwig hung a little forward, and his eyes moved everywhere. Ye do remember?"

"I—I—no."

"How you rose up from your seat," cried George, "pointing your finger at my Lord Shaftesbury? How you made against him the most ingenious speech that ever flayed the hide from a man's body?"

This time a cold shudder went from Fenton's head to his feet.

At the back of the sooty cookshop the fire bed glowed; they had long put George's capon and pigeons on the turnspit. A boy, himself called turnspit, basted the meat out of a ladle, hiding his face behind a damp cloth. Joints of meat, on iron arms and chains, were swung aside from the fire.

"No!" said Fenton. "No! My Lord Halifax will do this, in years to come. But not I! Not I!"

George had caught only the last words.

"Not you? Scratch me, but I was there! I heard you. Faces were all turned towards you, their mouths split; and all dark but for yellow firelight. Your temper was corked down like a miser woman's bottle. 'There he sits, my lords and gentlemen. "My Lord Shiftesbury," some call him . . .' "

"And—and what else did I say?"

"Nay; don't perplex me!" fussed George, with a heavy frown. "The beginning I recall, and the very end. Yet. . ." Suddenly his eyes narrowed with a look of deep cunning. "Was it truth, Nick, when you spoke of my Lord Shaftesbury's past life?"

"His past life? How?"

Since Nick was bemused, it appeared, George sought to trap and test his madness.

"That my Lord Shaftesbury, in youth and at the beginning of the

101

Great Rebellion, was a most zealous Royalist, and fought well in the army of Charles the First, until. . ."

Fenton sat up straight.

"Until," he retorted, "the man smelt in the air, smelt like a dog, that the King's fortunes were changing and the King's star would fall. Just before Naseby fight he deserted to the Roundheads. He became the most fervid, the most pious, the most zealous at psalms . . ."

"And at Abbotsbury?" prompted a hoarse-voiced George.

"At Abbotsbury," said Fenton, "he was so zealous a Roundhead that he desired to burn alive a captured garrison in a Royalist house."

As the turnspit basted the fowl, drops of grease dropped into a coal bed now flaring. There was a vicious hiss and sputter, and low red light shot through the cookshop.

"But his nose was ever a-sniff," Fenton continued coldly and quietly. "At the Restoration there he was, in some fashion turned Royalist again, bowing and smiling (for he is sometimes a merry man) among the Commissioners who welcomed King Charles the Second."

Again the grease drops sizzled in the fire.

"And do I need tell you," inquired Fenton, "how his fortunes grew high? Until then he was but Anthony Ashley Cooper, 'the little man with three names.' How his zeal for the new King pushed him up in titles and favours to being Earl of Shaftesbury? But he scented the wind again. This rising clamour of 'No Popery,' this determination to be rid of the Duke of York because the duke is a Catholic—or so my lord thought—would loose a tempest to blow away the King. He deserted again."

Hitherto Fenton had been quoting facts, coldly and without emotion. For the first time, now, he copied what he had seen that day. Turning his head aside, he spat on the floor.

But George was bouncing with excitement.

"You remember!" he kept repeating, and plucked at Fenton's sleeve. "Nick, this is no madness. You'll put no bubble on me! You were but drunk—faith, as I have seen ye guzzle for five weeks on end, with no memory left—when you spoke thus before Lords and Commons! And, now I think of it, you were drunk today; yet denied it."

Again it was the simplest way out. Fenton's wry smile implied assent.

"And 'gainst my lord and his Country party," said George, shaking his head dubiously, "you made six points. Here was the matter of the body politic, and beyond my wits. But sure there were needles in the bundle, for some did yelp and cry out; and you silenced them with a great voice, or some cunning retort that made them appear foolish. But the very end of what you said! Nay, that I can recall to the word!"

George rose to his feet. His hand, outstretched in red-shot gloom, might have been pointed at a ghostly Shaftesbury.

" '*Four times turncoat, four times traitor. Three times husband, thrice advancement. Twice ennobled, twice ignobled. Once dead, soon damned. And here's the sword would speed it on!*' "

George sat down, and stared with large eyes at the past.

"Ecod, Nick! The shout that went up, from both sides, was like to crack the gilt off the roof. In all this my Lord Shaftesbury sat still in his chair by the fire, making play with a lace handkerchief. He is little, but wears an extravagant huge flaxen periwig greater than mine. Only once he turned his face to ye, as calm as a god's. Only once he spoke (but this I heard later by report) to my Lord Essex. 'I mislike this fellow,' says my lord, as languid as a well-bounced wench: 'let him have a lesson.' "

"A lesson," Fenton repeated slowly.

Automatically Fenton's hand brushed up to go over the back of his head, as always when in reflection. Again he found the periwig and the hat. As he was about to remove the hat, he remembered that it must always be worn in public places, and stayed his hand.

"A lesson," agreed George, half-smiling. "It occurred but three nights later, you'll recall. Here was you, riding home alone through the loneliest part of the fields, with only a paring of a moon to guide you, after a carouse at the White Horse by Chalk Farm. Out of ambush, three brisk rogues flew at you and pulled you from your saddle."

Fenton made no remark, but his fist slowly clenched on the table.

"Come!" said George, half-apologetically. "Unless I much misread it, they had no intent to kill you. They did intend but to slit your nose and give you a heavy beating with cudgels, as a great lord customarily orders."

"Now how I admire my Lord Shaftesbury's moderation!"

George glanced at him, as though scenting some sarcasm here. But he forgot it in a chuckle.

"Admire your own," he advised dryly. "One rogue was found next morning in the ditch, half dead of a skull blow with his own cudgel. The second contrived to crawl back to the White Horse, with a sword-thrust through his middle. The third made escape."

"So I recall," lied Fenton.

"Now come, good hornet!" urged George, moving closer. "You can intrust me; I'll not betray it. Many wondered why you took no vengeance for that. For months you have done little but brood and drink at home, going abroad only to ride in the Mall or . . . or pay respect to Meg York at her house in King Street, before you moved her to your own. Some said 'twas Meg ensnared you. Some might have thought you afeared—"

"Did they so?" inquired Fenton, in a curious voice.

Again George looked at him quickly, and with apprehension. But Fenton turned on him a smile of such politeness, white teeth showing under the narrow black line of moustache, that he was reassured. Fenton himself knew his mind to be quite clear, with no trace of Sir Nick.

"Ah," breathed George, and gave a belch of relief. "Here's our dinner come!"

Up marched the landlord, a fat outline against a heavier gush of heat, with a smaller man following him. They carried the smoking meat on big trenchers. Holding open the left side of his coat, George disclosed a single-edged dagger, for eating purposes, slung in a sheath under his left arm.

"Nay, I'll pay our shot!" he said firmly, as Fenton's hand went to his pocket. "You sling away too much gold, hornet. Bear up, and here's to you!"

When you ordered a "pot" of wine, Fenton discovered, you received a good quart measure. If you had forgotten your own knife, the cook-shop could supply you with a knife in addition to a pronglike fork.

Lifting the quart of canary, Fenton took a deep pull and all but gagged. The brownish-white wine was heavy, potent, and so oversweet that his nose and palate only just received it. But what fascinated him was George's lightning-swift disposal of a capon, using only the dagger and dropping bones into a box on the floor. His manner of eating pigeons also interested Fenton, who had read of the practice.

Skewering a fat pigeon to the trencher, George cut it into four quarters and devoured each quarter by itself, bones and all. "Why, then," Fenton triumphantly cried in his mind, "here you are; here's your century; dig in!" And his knife drove deep into a meat pie which, as he had anticipated, was almost as big round as the mouth of a salad bowl. His new, dog-strong teeth ripped away at pieces of meat which were lean but very tough.

104

It was only the rich, soupy gravy, containing heaven knows what, which told him he would vomit if he did not leave off. He put down knife and fork, considering the plan in his mind.

"Er—George!"

"Wh'?" or some such noise emerged from crunching sounds inside puffed cheeks. George's face had grown red and shiny. His eyes beamed appreciation of the food.

"I believe," Fenton remarked carelessly, "my Lord Shaftesbury dwells at Thanet House in Aldersgate Street. Is ever a time appointed when he is always to be found at the King's Head tavern?"

Swallowing the last quarter of the last pigeon, George washed it down with a pint of canary.

"Why, as to that," he said, and reached up under the back of his coat to wipe greasy hands on his satin waistcoat, so as to have the stains out of sight, "my lord is there on most afternoons. Save when the Lords sit, or His Majesty's council. Come, I had forgot! My lord is always at the King's Head on Tuesdays," added George, forgetting this was a Tuesday, "from one of the clock until midnight. He. . ."

Fenton rose to his feet.

George's eyes, unexpectedly realizing, showed a look very like horror.

"I have a mind," said Fenton, "to visit the King's Head now."

CHAPTER IX

"HERE'S A HEALTH

UNTO HIS MAJESTY!"

THE dead men's heads, stuck on poles above Temple Bar, were not those of traitors. They were merely heads of unknown men whose bodies had been fished out of the river or found dead in field and lane. If none knew who they were, their heads were cut off, pickled in a mixture of vinegar and cumminseed, and thrust high so that somebody might identify them.

But, as the heads wagged in the wind, or looked down over stout grey-black-stone Temple Bar, their eyes and mouths were no warming welcome to the City.

Temple Bar, with its great arched opening through which wheeled vehicles crashed with even greater din, had on each side of it a stone wall containing an opening for those who went on foot through to Fleet Street.

Just beyond, at the corner of Fleet Street and the off-turning of Chancery Lane, stood the King's Head, with its black timbers and its balustraded balcony on the floor well above the street.

"Well, I'll adventure it," Lord George Harwell said stoutly. "But, Nick! As touches my Lord Shaftesbury. . ."

Just inside the entrance in the wall to Fleet Street, Fenton paused and looked round to view the sights. But George's insistence would not be denied.

"No, now, curse it! What's in your mind to do against him?"

"Much!"

"But in what fashion?"

"My Lord Shaftesbury," said Fenton, "has been good enough to say of me, 'Let him have a lesson.' Good! Let us see how my lord himself enjoys a lesson."

"Nick, you durst not challenge him! He is a noble lord—"

"So is your own father."

"True, true; but the old hunks cometh seldom to London. He is nobody. Here's another matter completely! My Lord Shaftesbury, apart from his vigour and extraordinary fire. . ."

"Hath he vigour? Hath he fire?"

"When he desires to show them: ay, for certain! Be warned, Nick! Apart from this (I say) he is elderly and full of poison from the hole in his side. He would laugh at a challenge. Now hear the best of the reasons why you cannot attack him now!"

George stabbed his finger at the upper floor of the King's Head.

"There will be fifty swords about him, where he sits among his friends in the upstairs room. The house, I think, is already alive with daggers. They'll not even suffer you to go near him."

"We shall go near him. Be sure of that!"

The sun had come out in brilliance, and the wind was dead. Street signs rattled only to the shaking of Fleet Street itself. Chimneys against sloping roofs, so many chimneys that they were lost in haze, foamed black smoke straight upwards, letting fall a heavy rain of soot.

"Over there on the south side," thought Fenton, "is the entrance to the Temple, with the Rainbow coffeehouse hard by. On our side, beyond the King's Head, there's the Devil and also the Good King Wenceslas. With so many hospitable red lattices of taverns, it's no wonder the crowd is thinned."

Past him, walking east, rolled a stocky youth whom Fenton identified as a seafaring man by his red breeches, broad belt, and tucked-up periwig. There was even a gunpowder spot on his hand. At the edge of Chancery Lane stretching up left at right angles to Fleet Street, the stocky young man hesitated.

Just across the lane, as though shrinking from crossing the kennel, stood a demure young woman in a shabby gown, but with a broad flopping straw hat, the very lowest of low-cut corsages, and bright artificial colour in her face. She allowed one eyelid to droop, and the half-curl of a smile. The noble seafarer, galvanized, leaped across the lane—kennel and all—at one bound. Linking arms with each other, as in some rehearsed dance measure, they both swung to the right and strolled casually up Chancery Lane.

"Now that was handsomely done!" cried George, in high approval, and craned to look after them. "Faith, that's a credit to Mr. Pepys and the Navy!"

Fenton also glanced after them. Chancery Lane contained many fine houses, mostly those of high-placed lawyers, with porter holding a tipstaff at the door. There were mean houses too. He wondered in which house Meg, under the protection of Captain Duroc . . .

"Over the lane," he said to George, "while 'tis still open. 'Ware the scissors-grinder's wheel. Across it . . . so!"

They were now beside the lattice and a few paces from the door of the King's Head.

"For the last time," George bawled, "you can't come at him with a sword . . ."

"Sword?" said Fenton, and swung round. "Who spoke of a sword? I mean to use none."

"Yet you said a . . . a 'lesson'!"

"True. Until he chokes on it! Stay; I had forgot the trophies!"

"What trophies?"

"The hat with the green rosette, and the set of ill-fitted false teeth. You told me you took them, and I see the hat in your pocket. Pray give them to me."

George handed them over, and his companion thrust both into his left-hand coat pocket. George asked no question, since again he was staggered. This man was not Nick in a temper, nor was he yet—quite— the grave, courteous scholar, though he might have been the latter.

Though Fenton's face was a trifle pale under its swarthiness, his eyes remained as passionless as those of a hanging judge.

"Being myself a lecher and swaggerer," he said, "can I judge my Lord Shaftesbury? Yes, I believe so. For I can pardon all things in all men, save one: an act of treachery. And this puffed-up fellow, as I remarked, has four times turned his coat."

"Nick, Nick, 'tis but the custom!"

"Not mine, I thank you!"

"Nick, for God's sake!"

Fenton threw open the door.

George, following him with head down as though to butt a wall, closed the door after them. At first it was certain that nobody, in the babble which burst out at them, recognized the outward seeming of Sir Nick Fenton.

It was a large room, with smoke-blackened plaster walls and, about

108

the middle of the right-hand wall as you faced inwards, a balustraded staircase ascending the wall. Though these were only small fry among Green Ribboners, they made enough clatter and brawl to account for the rest. There were long black benches, long black tables, small tables, short benches, chairs, and joint stools, all a-scatter. The reek of ale and wine and strong waters seemed almost visible.

Hats and periwigs wagged over leather drinking jacks, pewter pots and tankards, bottles, even cups. Some played at cards, half-rising and slapping down the card as though dagger-ready to fly at another's throat. A dicebox rattled under the stairs. Many smoked long curved pipes made of clay, with coarse tobacco whose smoke layers prevented Fenton from seeing much more than halfway down the room. Through this maze bustled the tapsters, or drawers of ale and wine.

"Anon, sir!" would cry the tapsters, or, "By and by, sir," while they seemed to scurry past, heads down; whereas, in fact, they did as little work as possible. Somebody was banging a tankard on a table, and shouting for a tapster who slid round an upright beam.

Though Fenton both smoked and drank, this overpowering gush into his mouth and nostrils stifled him.

"There's nothing here," he said. "Make straight for the stairs."

But George plucked at his sleeve.

"Look!" George muttered, eyes wide in surprise. "There! Just to the left of the door!"

At the left of the front door, behind a small table facing them sideways, sat an old and very fat man, with a stomach like Bacchus and gout-swollen legs ending in broad-buckled shoes. He was bald except for white hair, well kept and combed, which began about the crown of the head and fell down over his shoulders in the old Cavalier way.

He might have been Falstaffian, a gusty tun of laughter, except that his rheumy eyes seemed too old and weary. His clothes, once of fine quality, were ancient and rusty though carefully mended. From his left hip, on three straps blackened by years—Fenton's heart rose up for joy—hung the old cup-hilt rapier of the Cavalier.

And in front of him on the table . . .

"That's a cittern," George bent over to whisper in Fenton's ear. " 'Tis but a flattish box, much polished, and sharp cut on one side for longer or shorter lengths of string. Scratch me, Meg spoke of it today! The old gentleman is . . . "

"Why," Fenton was thinking, "that cittern is only an old-fashioned

109

simple zither, and I remember it when I was a boy. I could play a tune on it now."

"Venerable sir," he began aloud.

The old gentleman quivered and shifted his bulk. All of a sudden his broad face, somewhat drink-mottled, seemed to come alive. The film lifted from his eyes. Across his face went a smile which (perhaps) might have warmed the heart of my Lord Shaftesbury himself.

And his puffy fingers moved on the strings of the cittern, plucking out a tune which in that babble could be heard not four feet away.

> *"Here's a health unto His Majesty*
> *With a tow-row-row, and a tow-row!*
> *Confusion to his en-e-mies,*
> *With a tow-row-row, and a tow-w-w-row! . . . "*

These words were heard only in Fenton's mind. But again his heart rose for joy, of things never seen yet long held sacred. It was the song of the Restoration.

"You'll recall 'Mr. Reeve,'" George said jovially to Fenton. "And how oft he came to your House at Epsom, when Meg was there? Mr. Reeve is another," George added bitterly, "who melted his plate and sold his gold for the late King. Under Oliver his estate was sold, even his title filched away . . . "

> *"And he that will not drink his health*
> *I wish him neither life nor wealth,*
> *Nor yet a rope to—"*

As George spoke, the tinkling music stopped. Mr. Reeve's face grew expressionless. He spoke in a voice cracked and gruff, but still strong.

"Nay, now!" he protested gently, as one who finds a matter long gone and distasteful.

Fenton hesitated to put a question, because he knew and dreaded the answer. Yet he could not help himself.

"Your estate and title, sir: were they not given back at the Restoration? Or some payment made to you?"

"Boy, boy, that was fifteen years ago!"

"But, sir: did you not speak to the new King, and present your petition as others did?"

"We-ell!" said Mr. Reeve, moving one hand with a gesture of defensive apology. "I went to Whitehall, 'tis true. But so many flocked about him, so very many! And, no doubt, with better claim than

110

mine. And there were all of those we then called the 'confident young men,' so gay of plumage that they made me ashamed."

Mr. Reeve shook his head, so that from his bald crown the white hair trembled on the shoulders of his unpardonable coat. Though Mr. Reeve was now clean-shaven, Fenton could imagine his former tuft of chin whisker, and the two tufts of moustache under each side of his nose.

"To be open with you," Mr. Reeve confessed, "I wore the same clothes as I wear at this moment. I have now eighty years upon me. Even then I was a rusty old Cavalier, in want of coin and cuffs. Had I approached His Majesty, they would have laughed at me and mocked me. And so I slunk away, as I have never done (I hope) from field of battle, with my petition still in my pocket."

"And have never again been to court?"

The shrewd, penetrating look again appeared in Mr. Reeve's eyes, with a faint chuckle added.

"Come, I'll pay you out!" he said. "You are, I hear, among the hottest of the Court party. Are you acquainted with His Majesty?"

Two lines in Giles's manuscript came to Fenton's rescue.

"I . . . I have passed by him in the Park, and bowed to him. He hath returned the greeting most civilly."

"But not spoken to him?"

"I . . . think not."

"Only a few months gone, I hear, ye set all in amaze by a speech in Parliament that did much harm to my Lord Shaftesbury. Well! Did ye not go to Whitehall, next day (as would be but natural), to hear a word of commendation from His Majesty, or a friendly clap on the shoulder?"

"No!" Fenton spoke instinctively. He did not know whether this was true. But he felt that Sir Nick would not have done this, and he was certain he would not himself have done it.

"And wherefore not?"

"Damn me, but I'd have done it!" blurted George.

Mr. Reeve's bloated face turned without expression to George, and back to Fenton.

"Wherefore not?" he insisted.

"I can't tell," Fenton answered honestly.

"Why, then," said Mr. Reeve, "I'll tell! It was the black pride

111

in your heart. Lest you suffer the King perhaps to think you had done this for favours, for preferments, for a rung up the greasy ladder all climb, you would turn your back on His Majesty's own self! Do I say true?"

Fenton, who had drawn up a short bench and sat sideways to the old Cavalier, shook his head.

"I know not; I can't tell."

"Well!" Mr. Reeve said grimly. "There are things a man can't do, even if he should know himself in the right. Are you and I not much alike, then?"

Fenton's hand, surreptitiously creeping towards his money pocket, stopped.

"Nay, but stay a moment!" interposed George, who was rather red of face. "I am desirous to be civil, too. Yet why are you here? Sure you're not a sp—" George swallowed and stopped.

"Fie, now!" chuckled Mr. Reeve. "Where's the wrong in an honest word like spy? I am so, in my modest way. (Have no fear; they can't hear me.) I pick up a crumb or two here and there, for Mr. Chiffinch or even Sir Robert Southwell. For I loathe your Green Ribbon scum, even though they cry up the blessed Church Established like honest men. Eh, lad?"

All this time, strangely or not, Fenton had been thinking of Lydia. Against the smoke reek he saw Lydia, the Puritan by training but not by instinct. He saw her face: the wide-spaced blue eyes, the short nose, the soft light-brown hair tumbled about her head. For nine years he had cherished a pictured engraving, and here was living reality. He thought how much Lydia loved the man she believed he was; and he was not that man at all. He remembered what he had been thinking this morning, a sincere prayer, when first he left Lydia.

"O Thou," he had prayed, "if only a dry old stick in a boy's carcase could somehow be worthy of that, or live up to it!"

Well, he would live up to it now.

"I fear our talk must cease," he said quietly. "But will you render me a service, Mr. Reeve? Lend me your cittern for a quarter-hour or so."

"The cittern? Right willingly!" grunted the other, and pushed it across the table. It was about three feet long, with gleaming strings. "But to what purpose?"

"I go upstairs, to the council of the Green Ribbon."

112

The old gentleman showed no surprise as Fenton stood up, the cittern under his left arm.

"Oh, you'll do it," he grunted, after one look into Fenton's eyes and another at the dried, caked blood on Fenton's hands. "And I think, for the good kidney of it, I'll go with you."

"Nay, be still!" cried George. "To lose your place as . . . as . . ."

"Faugh!" sneered the wheezy voice.

With an intense effort Mr. Reeve hoisted himself up on swollen legs, tottered very slightly, and stood firm. His vast frame and belly made him seem round. His bloated face was a tippler's, his white hair that of an archbishop, and lovingly he patted the cup-hilt rapier.

"I am something weak in the legs for swordplay," he chuckled. "Yet there's a *botte* or two awaits the first lace-pantaloon who lets go,"—again he patted the cup-hilt—"against Dirty Bess. Where's to, lad?"

"Follow me, if you must," said Fenton. "But don't lug out, and don't speak unless you see a sign from me."

They moved towards the stairs in single file: Fenton leading, then George, then Mr. Reeve. At the foot of the stairs a tapster, with black plant-growing hair like a wild man's, skipped out to bar the way.

"Regret, sir. Can't go up."

Fenton looked at him in a mood more dangerous than any of Sir Nick's.

"I am Sir Nicholas Fenton," he said, and saw the name jump up with fear in the tapster's eyes. "Your health will remain good if you stand aside."

The tapster shrank back, but lifted his head as though to call upstairs. Fenton's right hand, concealed by the cittern, flashed to his sword grip; the blade leaped partway out; and the tapster saw he meant murder.

"I'll-be-quiet-sir," he muttered under his breath.

Back slipped the blade. A gold coin flicked over and landed at the tapster's feet. It was the first gold of his own he had seen for eighteen months. Scooping it up, he decided that silence was the better part of discretion.

Up the three went carelessly, save for Mr. Reeve's wheezing and the drag of his swollen legs. The wall was on their right hand. Fenton, keeping his head partly turned away, displayed the cittern very conspicuously.

The downstairs crowd, now roaring, wavered between intoxication

113

partial and intoxication complete. More than eighty pairs of eyes rose up enviously towards the stairs. But they saw only a musical instrument to entertain the Great Ones, and they turned back to pipe or tankard or card without further interest.

"Now I remember it," said Mr. Reeve, absent-mindedly aloud, "'twas Dirty Bess (my sword, gentlemen) we used to call Monk's wife: General Monk, if you please, before they made the big-behind Duke of Albemarle."

"Ss-s-t!"

Ordinarily, upstairs in a tavern, you found only private rooms. But the King's Head, as Fenton saw when his eyes lifted above the line of the floor, had only one long room like the taproom downstairs, save for a few private rooms at the back.

Its roof was supported by upright black beams, with gallows arms. Sunlight struggled in by latticed windows of sooty glass. Amid the same sort of furniture as could be found downstairs, about thirty gentlemen and a few noble lords—George had underestimated their number—sat and conferred gravely.

There was no heavy reek, except for the smoke which coiled up the stair well. There were no cards or dice, and only one or two pipes. The rich-gleaming finery of coats, waistcoats, and gold knee bands, as well as the glossier and bigger and more ridged periwigs under broad hats, told that here were men of dignity; or at least wealth. Most of them, crimson-faced, were pretty fresh in liquor.

There was dead silence. Though they could not have helped hearing footsteps on the stairs they made high-affected pretence of noticing nothing except their whispers to each other.

Only their anger could be felt, in a kind of concentrated breathing. Most were thoroughly honest men, believing in my Lord Shaftesbury's principles and dreading Popery.

The stair rail here, protecting the stairs below, also ran parallel with the far or narrower side of the room. There, so that its occupants faced outwards towards the stair rail, ran a long table like a high table for council. Only two men sat behind it.

"I know you," thought Fenton. "Only too well I know you from your portraits. Let us see if you respond to prod or sting, as they say."

On the left, behind the high table, sat my Lord Shaftesbury. His immense flaxen periwig was lowered; you could not see his face, as he contemplated a very small glass of white wine. Some of the severed heads on poles above Temple Bar were turned towards Fleet Street, and one of them gaped sideways at the window beyond my lord's left shoulder.

On the right sat the large, stout, florid-faced George Villiers, second Duke of Buckingham, growing towards his late forties and no longer so much fond of brawls or swordplay. He played with politics as he played with any other toy. He wore claret-coloured silk, with many waves and curls to his brown periwig, and a quart pot stood in front of him.

Fenton moved a little way along the stair rail, leaning his back against it carelessly and swinging the cittern up to his chest. George and Mr. Reeve ranged themselves on his right.

Still none moved, or looked up.

Fenton's fingers swept across the strings with a twang. He attempted to pluck out a tune, with each note loud and clear, a-jar against eardrums.

> "Here's a health unto His Majesty,
>   With a tow-row-row, and a tow-row!
>   Confusion to his enemies,
>   With a tow-row-row, and a tow-row! . . ."

So clumsily did he play, and so long ill-practised, that it was a matter of many seconds before anyone realized what the tune was. The first to recognize it, suddenly, was my Lord Shaftesbury himself. In the act of raising the very small glass of wine, he paused, set down the glass delicately, and pushed it away from him.

Afterwards all seemed to realize at once. His Grace of Bucks lifted the quart pot slightly, bumped it down on the time-smoothed table, and put it aside. There was a long squeak and scrape as my Lord Marquess of Winchester, near the high table but not of it, pushed a green glass as far away as possible. Scra-a-pe went two more. One stately Green Ribboner attempted to bring down his tankard with a crash, but he was whistle-drunk: it struck the edge of the table, letting fly a pint of claret, and clattered to the floor.

His Grace of Bucks spoke first.

"Sir Nicholas," he began, in his rich and not unkindly voice, "if you are come here to join a company of good patriots—why, sit you merry, and be welcome! Yet . . . "

Periwigs wagged together. Bucks now spoke in a stern tone.

"My Lord Shaftesbury," he said, "desires to know why you are here."

Fenton replied in the great voice which Sir Nick had used in the Painted Chamber.

"Then let my lord put the question for himself."

Shaftesbury looked up. At first glance it seemed a merry face, despite its razorish kind of quality: of long nose, pointed chin, and great starved-looking eyes. Though old as men then reckoned time, he was only fifty-four. He had much charm. His fluent tongue and art had won him three wives: not for love, but for political advancement. Always he kept his face smoothed out, his thoughts concealed.

At the moment he held a lace handkerchief, throwing it up and catching it. He did this two or three times, as though searching his memory for some elusive name.

"Er—Sir Nicholas Fenton?"

"My Lord . . . Shaftesbury?"

Through the whole room went a sudden creak: as of chairs or benches pushed back the shaving of an inch, and a tensing of leg muscles. My lord had thrown the first dart, and had got it straight back in the face.

But he appeared to notice nothing, merely tossing up the handkerchief.

"Come, Sir Nicholas," he said with an indulgent look, "you are a seeming hopeful young gentleman and, for aught I can see, a very ingenious one. Now how may I serve you?"

"First, my lord, I would make report on your second lesson."

"I fail to understand."

"At your first lesson, when you had three rogues set on me in a lonely field, I fear two may be dead and the third escaped; also, I took no notes. But here . . . "

Fenton handed the cittern to George, who in turn passed it on to Mr. Reeve. From his left-hand pocket Fenton pulled out a crushed hat with a green-ribbon. He straightened out the hat, even to its broken brim.

"This—" he began again. With a jerk of his wrist he sent it skimming over other hats and periwigs, to land on the high table some distance from my Lord Shaftesbury. "—belonged to the first Alsatian bullyrock you set on me this morning. He now lies across some fire buckets, with a sword-thrust from throat to brain."

My lord merely tossed up his handkerchief and caught it.

116

"These false teeth, too," said Fenton. He drew the false teeth from his pocket, and they now had an even more repulsive look, reflected in the eyes that watched. Fenton threw them towards the high table, but they landed and smashed to pieces on the table in front of my Lord Wharton, who leaped to his feet.

"They were worn," said Fenton, "by the other bullyrock, who was dealt with by my friend here, Lord George Harwell. I but finished the bullyrock, with a thrust which I hope will prove mortal." Then his tone changed. "My lord, your attentions begin to bore me."

Up went Shaftesbury's eyebrows.

"My attentions?" he asked softly. "Now there, I fear, you too much flatter yourself. And even were it so! Do you, a humble baronet, study revenge against me?"

"No, my lord. I am here only to tell you something about the future."

A derisive stir ran round the tables; yet, strangely enough, it died away.

"Sink me, can you tell my future?" demanded His Grace of Bucks, bending forward in deep fascination. Though Bucks in one season might be "chymist, statesman, fiddler, and buffoon," as Mr. Dryden was afterwards to write, Fenton found it impossible to dislike the man because of his wit and talent.

But Shaftesbury, himself faintly interested, silenced Bucks with a short gesture.

"A soothsayer, then?" he mocked. "Pray speak!"

"His Majesty, my lord, is the father of his people. Or at least, as his grace hath said," Fenton nodded towards Bucks, "of a good many of them. His illegitimate children swarm. But he can have no legitimate children, because Queen Catherine can have none. Not a fiend's tortures will make him divorce or put by the queen. His heir must be his brother, the Duke of York.

"And the Duke of York, they say, is become a Catholic. Your first move will be to exclude His Grace of York from the throne, by bill of Parliament. Your second move will be to drive out King Charles himself, mainly by your cry of . . . "

"No Popery!" shouted my Lord Wharton, and banged his tankard on the table.

"No Popery!" screamed my Lord Marquess of Winchester.

Others took it up. It penetrated to the downstairs taproom, where a thunder of "No Popery, No Popery!" blatted against the walls

117

and all but burst them. Tapsters raced up and down stairs, with more drink for the Great Ones. Bucks swallowed well over a pint of claret at one try. My Lord Shaftesbury, complacent, waited until the noise had died away.

Meanwhile Fenton lounged easily, his back to the rather low stair rail and a smile of serene confidence on his face. The Green leader spoke dryly.

"You tell us, in effect, of Father Adam and Mother Eve."

"Stay; but there is more." Fenton straightened up. "In a few years, my lord, you will rise mightily to power in this land. History shall know you," here there was a pleased gleam under my lord's drooping eyelids, "as the first great party leader, as father of 'campaign' oratory and of the 'whispering campaign,' turning the mobile party into the dread word mob.

"Stay; there is still more! In three years will come a great and malodorous liar, with a false tale of a 'Popish plot'; and you will use it to drive the town mad with terror. Blood will flow, flames rise, and there will be many murders by the hangman. And in the end . . . "

It is a sober fact that my Lord Shaftesbury almost smirked. Gently he waved the lace handkerchief to and fro.

"In the end?" he said, as though giving a slight push.

Out went Fenton's voice, like Sir Nick's in the Painted Chamber.

"You will fail," he answered. "The King, having given you rope enough, will first outwit you and then crush you in his five fingers."

A raucous laugh, which went up from one table, was hushed by a slight gesture from my lord. He seemed—almost—unmoved.

"Now here's much cloudy stuff," he complained, "as I could prophesy myself, or Orange Moll, or another. 'A few years'! Why not fifty? Or an hundred? Can you foretell nothing of somewhat closer date?"

"Truly, my lord, I can. What say you to . . . nine days?"

"Come, that's better! Well?"

Again Fenton leaned his back to the stair rail.

"At the moment, my lord, you are a member of His Majesty's council, the highest and most secret in the land. You account yourself too powerful to be dismissed. But in exactly nine days—nine days, my lords and gentlemen!—you will be dismissed from the council as a dog is kicked from a chair, and ordered to depart from London!"

Uproar broke loose at this; and eyes, a whole thirty pairs of eyes, slowly grew more menacing. Old Mr. Reeve slipped his right hand across to his sword grip. Still my lord's slightest gesture kept them quiet.

"Now would you make a wager as to this, Sir Nicholas?"

"I will lay my life on it," said Fenton. "If you be not dismissed on the 19th May, I vow to go alone, unarmed, into any lonely field outside London you may be pleased to name. Mark it well, my lord: the 19th May."

"See that it be writ down for him, good Bucks."

"And afterwards," Fenton flung at him, "when the Exclusion Bill is defeated, when you have lost your battle against the King, you will in truth be old, and withered, and crazed in your wits. You will shake a skinny arm, crying, 'I have ten thousand brisk boys at my command.' There will be none. You will be alone, almost friendless, all power gone."

Dead silence. For they had glanced at my lord's face.

"All power gone." None in that room, save Fenton and my Lord Shaftesbury, could guess what those words meant.

My Lord Shaftesbury's principles, as Fenton himself would have acknowledged, were very high. His hatred of the Catholic Church was quite genuine, near a mania. He cared little or nothing for money. He never took a bottle too many, or lost his head over a woman. All he desired was power, limitless power; and to get this, strictly on virtuous principles, he would commit any act from a small lie to wholesale murder.

He stood up suddenly behind the table, dapping his lace handkerchief on the edge. Casually, as though to adjust the fit of his green coat, he turned his face away. And, beyond the window lattice, he saw the severed head staring at him on the pole over Temple Bar.

All this time, swaying a little, it had been surveying the room. My Lord Shaftesbury turned back rather quickly, and sat down.

"Why, Sir Nicholas," said he, with a merry laugh, "you are in fact bold of your powers at soothsaying . . . "

"Nay, my lord!" Fenton said quickly. "I am no soothsayer or fortuneteller. I but judge what will happen by natural means, in facts known to me."

"Now I should wish," said my lord, "to make you acquainted with all my good friends here. That's impossible, I fear. But there is surely one with whom I must acquaint you!"

Instantly Bucks's periwig moved towards Shaftesbury's, while Bucks seemed to whisper and shake his head in objection. Other periwigs crept up to the high table, a garden of whispers among varicoloured hats with their flat plumes. Once Fenton caught a whisper, "No brawling." Another voice (they could not identify it) hissed out its sibilants so loudly that the listeners caught what was said.

"*Pox on it, you play your ace of trumps too soon!*"

"Be wary," muttered George, digging his left elbow into Fenton's ribs.

"Ay," growled Mr. Reeve from beyond. "That old knave turned his face away but to hide a screaming-fit. There'll be bloody work here, else I'm a Dutchman!"

Fenton, who had administered the lesson he promised, waited quietly.

But my Lord Shaftesbury was deaf to protests. He whispered back something which appeared to satisfy them. Except for Buckingham, the coloured hats slid back to their tables with only a soft slither of shoes on a board floor.

"Come, now!" invited my lord. Stretching out his hand towards a round table, where a number of Green Ribboners sat well back and towards Fenton's left, my lord lifted his hand insistently for someone to rise.

And up from among them rose the strangest figure Fenton had ever seen.

The man was very tall and lean, more so than Long-legs in Dead Man's Lane. But here all resemblance ceased. This man wore an enormous brown periwig, bigger and longer than any in the room, and powdered all over with gold: after the fashion of King Louis the Fourteenth.

Framed in the periwig, the man's liquid dark eyes were either mischievous or very sorrowful; it was hard to tell which. His long face was either very pale or else powdered; he wore an obvious spot of rouge on each cheekbone. His coat was white, with gold fleur-de-lis on it, in contrast to a dark-blue waistcoat with gold buttons; the tight-fitting breeches were white, above red stockings, and white shoes with high red heels.

So the immense figure threaded its way among the tables, at a mincing walk with one shoulder slightly lifted and the rouge plain on its cheekbones.

120

"That man," Fenton reflected idly to himself, "came here either in a coach or a sedan chair, else he would have been hooted and pelted off the street."

Yet nobody in the room, including Fenton himself, was deceived.

Many of the gallants, desperately trying to be in fashion, aped the effeminate airs of a few rich lordlings or of the playhouse. But, in that masculine age, it was nearly all pretence. Behind it lurked a deadly sword arm, and as much a man as King Charles himself.

Tap-tap went the red heels, as the man in the gold-powdered peruke worked towards the stair rail at its far end, and then turned left to approach Fenton along the side of the rail.

"Another led captain," whispered George in disgust. "Another bully. But this time the best they can buy. Have a care, Nick!"

My Lord Shaftesbury's voice rose up pleasantly.

"May I make you acquainted," he said to Fenton, "with Captain Duroc, late of the French King's personal attendance?"

Behind him Fenton heard George draw a deep, whistling breath.

"Now by God's death and Christ's body!" whispered George. His right hand darted from his sword hilt and slid under the left side of his coat, where the sheathed dagger hung below his arm.

"Gently!" Fenton said over his shoulder.

Then Fenton turned left, at the side of the stair rail, to face the Captain Duroc of whom he had heard so much.

Duroc, in his white finery spotted with gold fleur-de-lis, approached slowly beside the stair rail. His hard, long-fingered left hand rested lightly on the gold pommel of a sword slung on a baldric, after the French fashion, under the coat from right shoulder to left hip.

Still there was dead silence, while the ring of spectators looked on with watchful, amused eyes. Some kept their seats, some stood up, some peered past shoulders. Fenton heard the gurgle as my Lord Wharton, dark-faced and with black periwig, tossed down a pint of malmsey.

Captain Duroc stopped about six feet from Fenton.

"Monsieur!" he said almost tenderly.

He smiled, showing bad teeth, in the same tender way; the smile lit up his dark, liquid, mournful eyes, which might be full of sorrow or mischief. He made a deep bow, arm across chest, so that a few motes of gold dust sifted from his peruke.

Fenton gravely returned the bow without speaking.

121

"Alas," said Captain Duroc, straightening up like an actor, his hand on his heart, "eet ees most regret*table* that you and I moost disagree, yes?"

("You're no Frenchman," thought Fenton. "Your accent is overdone. You're probably some hybrid mixture from middle Europe.")

"But there must be no braw-ling," said Captain Duroc, looking shocked. "No, no, no, no! There must be de small hinsult; de seconds chosen; de place chosen; de time . . . today, tomorrow? When you like! *Tout à fait comme il faut, n'est-ce-pas?*"

Captain Duroc moved a trifle closer.

"*Hélas!*" he breathed. "Now is de question of de quar-rel. But it must not be of the nature politic. No, no, no! *Tiens,* I have it!" Duroc's liquid eyes grew bright. "We shall be like the knights of old, yes? Now I ask you!"

Here he thrust his long face almost into Fenton's. The rouge spots glared.

"Who is de fairest lady in de land?" demanded Duroc. "Queek!" He gave no time to think. "Who ees she?"

"My wife!" Fenton retorted hotly, and round him rose such a gale of laughter as nearly swept him off his feet.

To the ears of this generation, he realized, he could have said no more foolish-sounding thing. The Green Ribboners whooped or doubled up with mirth. Clanking their pots on the tables, they cried, "Bravo!" or lifted a tankard in mock toast.

Captain Duroc, who would have made a master playhouse comedian, turned slowly to his audience, lifted his shoulders to the neck in a shrug, and spread out his hands with his eyes a sorrowful blank.

"*Tiens,*" he seemed to be saying, "what can I do with such a man?"

Fenton's cheeks burned. "Keep your head!" a voice said inside him. "Keep your head! Keep your head!" And he steadied himself.

He had been a fool, of course. The strange look in Captain Duroc's eyes had been only amusement mixed with contempt. This tall pseudo Frenchman, with his painted face and his mincing airs, believed he could dispose of an adversary with two or three passes. Coolly, with a tinge of the comic, he was arranging a duel which should not involve the precious Green Ribbon Club.

Again Captain Duroc swung round dramatically, his hand at his heart.

"Monsieur," he said sadly, "I regret that 'ere is the place we dis-

122

agree. For de fairest lady, *vous comprenez*, is the sweet Madam Meg York . . ."

"Let me pass!" came George's hoarse-panting voice. "One chance; enough!"

For George, seeing before him only a contemptible French thus-and-so, would not have troubled his head with niceties of sword-drawing. George would have leaped straight for his throat with a dagger.

Perhaps, in the long run, that might have been best. But Captain Duroc continued.

"And now," proclaimed the Captain, "I moost give you de insult. But I would not 'urt you; no, no, no!" Again he looked shocked, all his features moving. "Not such fine gentleman as yourself! I geeve you only de small insult . . . so!"

He arched his lean body, lifting on the toes of his red-heeled shoes. At the same time he arched his right arm up and over, hand dangling with thumb and forefinger pressed together. Stretching out his arm, thumb over forefinger, he lightly flickered the forefinger against the tip of Fenton's nose.

"*Voilà!*" he said.

The gesture was at once so grotesque, yet at the same time so ludicrous at Fenton's expense, that the whole room roared again. Tears ran down from Green Ribbon eyes across Green Ribbon cheeks. Captain Duroc, well pleased, leaned his body negligently against the stair rail, and did not smile too much.

"Then that is the insult?" Fenton asked loudly.

"*Mais naturellement, mon ami!*"

This time Fenton did not forget the power of his shoulder and arm. Already his weight was on his right foot. His body pivoted. His right hand, palm open, cracked against Duroc's left cheek with a noise like a musket ball fired at heavy leather.

It would be a mild understatement to say that Captain Duroc, after an openhanded blow like the flat of an axe, merely tumbled over the stair rail and fell downstairs. For half a second his gilt scabbard, his white breeches, his scarlet stockings, his white shoes and high red heels, seemed to stand in the air upside down.

But this must have been an optical illusion. He fell at full length on the stairs, with a heavy and bony crash which set flying his periwig. He screamed once before he rolled to the foot of the stairs—all a whirl of sword, legs, lace, and ruffles—where he lay still.

123

One member of the Green mutineers rushed to the stair rail, keeping wide of Fenton. Below, a tapster and several others were bending over Captain Duroc.

"Well?" came the call from above.

"Can't tell, sir," yelled back the tapster, audible to everyone upstairs. "Don't like ut, though. Left leg's a-broke, thinks I. There's a barber-chiurgien three doors away, at the Healed Man. Like us to. . . ?"

The Green Ribbon man glanced back at Shaftesbury, who nodded. Assent was shouted down. And Fenton turned round.

"I would not 'urt you; no, no, no!" he told them, with heavy mock accent. "Not such fine gentlemen as yourselves, ah *quelle dommage!*"

"Lug out, both of ye!" snapped the gruff old tones of Mr. Reeve, in a low tone. "Deploy to the stairhead. These water-guts won't stay you."

Both Fenton and George lugged out at the same time. Fenton almost missed it, since Sir Nick had failed to clean the blade after the fight in the lane, and drying blood all but fixed it to the thin wood; but out it came.

Sooty sunlight ran along the blades as three men moved the short distance to the stairhead. Mr. Reeve raised his voice for all.

"George, be you first down the stairs. Dagger in your left hand, man; and carve meat if any stand! I'll go betwixt ye, with a song for the traitors and ninnyhammers! Nick, do you hold the rearguard. The first to come at Nick Fenton is a dead man, and they know it!"

There was a thump of footsteps as George started down, sword in right hand and dagger in left. Mr Reeve's hand ripped across the strings, and his hoarse tones went into the song.

"Here's a health unto His Majesty . . ."

My Lord Wharton, he of the dark complexion and black periwig, whipped out his sword. Fenton, at the head of the stairs, jumped round to meet him.

A strange exultation ran hot in Fenton's veins, because he was on his own. He had no Sir Nick to prop him up. He could use only his knowledge of the fencing foil, but carry it at them to the last thrust.

"Co-o-n-fusion to his enemies . . ."

At the high table, motionless, my Lord Shaftesbury sipped delicately at white wine.

"Now can any man," he asked with dry sarcasm, "in truth foretell the future?"

"Nay; 'tis foolish," grunted Bucks, his eyes on the stairs. "But were I ten years younger—"

"At him, Wharton!" snarled a furious voice.

My Lord Wharton danced out sideways, arm and blade extended—and then stopped dead, fully twelve feet from Fenton's dark-stained sword. Slowly my lord lowered the point.

"*And he that will not drink his health . . .*"

"Such cloudly stuff, as I remarked," murmured Shaftesbury, "could be mouthed by anyone. But this matter touching my dismissal from the council! Come: this Fenton is deeper in the King's confidence than I had believed."

"*I wish him neither life nor wealth. . .*" By this time Fenton had backed downstairs, still at guard. They could hear the clump of his swift footsteps.

"Make way, there!" George was bellowing, at a distance. "Set open the door!"

"*Nor yet a rope to ha-a-ng him-self . . .*"

Bang! went the front door, both leaves flying wide.

"When I mislike a man," murmured my Lord Shaftesbury, "he lives seldom long. I shall not fail a third time."

"*With a tow-row-row, and a . . . tow-row!*"

And so, with heads and hearts high, three King's men left the King's Head tavern.

CHAPTER X

OF ARSENIC

IN A SACK-POSSET—

LOOKING back on it afterwards, Fenton thought that the next month —or nearly a month— was the happiest time of his life.

Above all was his love for Lydia, his near-worship of Lydia. In those few weeks he had seen her change from a semi-invalid into a happy, laughing, sturdy girl, more beautiful of face and more healthily beautiful of body; and for some mysterious reason she adored him.

He himself was contented as he had never been contented. Professor Fenton, of Paracelsus, grew as young in spirit as his present age. For he lacked nothing he wanted.

"Why," he would think, "all I need is a daily bath and a toothbrush: and these, in clumsy fashion, I now have. Otherwise, is my living much different from what I found in the bustling twentieth century, when I took a cottage in rural England, and much enjoyed it?"

Or again:

"How strange," he reflected, "have been the minds of authors I have read, setting a character back hundreds of years in time! I think their learning is not wide enough. For they never allow the poor devil to have a good time. He must fret and fume because progress—accursed progress, and thrice-damned machinery—have not come to wreck men's lives.

"He is infuriated by the lack of telephones and motorcars. I felt no need of them when I studied, in rural Somerset, for some dreary degree or other. Our author, through his hero, is appalled at the sanitation, the harsh laws, the power of King or Parliament. Yet, in my heart, I confess these matters trouble me not at all."

Nevertheless there was one black spot at the back of his mind. This was the dread date, June 10th, when they said . . . well, they said Lydia would die. Every time this remembrance wormed into his brain, he blotted it out, swore Lydia should not die because he would prevent it, and kept the question at bay.

Also, amid the pleasant times of which we shall hear, a few ugly incidents struck into his life like a dagger. The first of the incidents occurred on the very night after he and George and Mr. Reeve left the King's Head, following their meeting with the Green Ribbon Club.

Fenton had wanted to go home, since late afternoon was drawing in. But George insisted they must take a cup of wine in sign of triumph.

"What's more, you must sprucify yourself," he argued, not unreasonably. "What! Return with those hands and those sleeves? You'll find a bowl of water at the Devil, for a surety!"

"A cup of wine, judiciously swallowed," declared Mr. Reeve with dignity, "improveth the digestion at all times."

So they had one or two at the Devil, where Fenton sprucified himself as well as possible. Then they moved on to the already long-famous Swan at Charing Cross. There, inside settles with high backs, facing each other across a table, George and Mr. Reeve fell to business with a will amid the roar and foulness of the tavern.

Fenton, whose palate as yet could not put down the wine or even the ale, took a desperate try each time. Then, half-ill, he used a stratagem.

Sitting on the floor beside his settle, legs outsprawled, was a hairy and drunk fiddler, whose eyes remained open but who could not move. Each time the tapster would arrive with fresh pints, Fenton would surreptitiously turn and pour his own down the throat of the fiddler, whose mouth opened automatically to receive it. As a result he drank himself almost sober; and, lifting the battered fiddle and bow from his lap, sawed away with much energy.

Mr. Reeve, nearly as boozy but more dignified, accompanied him on the cittern. The whole company of the Swan joined in singing ballads remarkable for great bawdiness and minuteness of detail with regard to female anatomy.

George swore (and six times he swore) that he would accompany

127

Fenton to Pall Mall, and ask Meg to wed him, after but one more pint. You may guess the outcome. Both George and Mr. Reeve fell under the table, as was the convenient custom.

With the assistance of two tapsters, Fenton paid the score and got them both wedged into different sedan chairs. Having ascertained that Mr. Reeve was well in the care of the "mine hostess of the Rising Sun, Red Lion Fields, being a kind willing dame of scarce sixty," Fenton sent two heavily snoring chairs in different directions. Before each ran a linkboy, his torch flaming against powdery-blue dusk. Since it was not yet dark, there could be small danger of footpads.

Afterwards Fenton hurried the short distance to his own home. The stately periwigged porter, with his tipstaff, stood very straight at the door.

"There is one question . . . er . . ."

"Sir," replied the stately one, "I am called Sam." Then rapidly he gave forth news. "Madam York hath departed, in a coach not her own, but with heavy boxes, not an hour agone. And I rejoice to tell, sir, that her ladyship, your wife, is well and mends in her health. A dozen times in the hour she sends Mrs. Pamphlin to seek you."

"Thank God," Fenton said slowly, and felt his heart contract.

The stately one bowed.

"I—I desired," Fenton said at length, "to learn how many letters were dispatched from here this day. But that's a trifle, now I learn . . ."

"Sir, there were four letters," returned Sam, reckoning up how many times he must seek a street porter. "One from her ladyship, to Mrs. Wheebler the dressmaker's, at La Belle France in Covent Garden. One from Madam York, to a Captain Duroc in Chancery Lane. One from Mr. Giles, to his brother by Aldgate Pump. One—hem!—from the cook-maid Kitty . . ."

"Kitty! Can she read or write?"

"One would not have thought so," frowned the stately Sam. " 'Twas so ill writ I could not discover the address myself, and gave it to a porter with sixpence, desiring him to be off."

"But this could not have happened in the afternoon! The wench (or so I think) was under guard in my study. . ."

"Nay, sir, all letters were sent in early morning."

"Oh, no matter!" thought Fenton, and, as Sam gravely opened the door, he dashed through the malodorous lower hall, up the stairs, and along the passage to Lydia's room.

The wax lights fluttered as he flung open the door. Lydia's room, over the panelling, was hung with tapestries which all but covered every inch of the walls. The heavy, sedate bed yet had gilt Cupids at its corners. Lydia, fully dressed in a low-cut gown for evening, sat in an upright chair beyond a golden sconce of five candles, a book in her lap.

Though she had undergone a bad time in recovery, as was plain from her pallor and the shadows under her blue eyes, still she was Lydia. She stretched out her arms. Fenton held her as tightly, cheek to cheek, as though he feared she might vanish.

"Dear heart," he said, when Lydia moved back to run her gaze searchingly over his face, "I hope I—I made you not too ill, so as to make you well?"

"Fie!" Lydia told him, her pink lips trembling. One eyebrow lifted a little, as though she would smile. " 'Twas nothing! Though troublesome at times, I'll own, especially . . . " Here she paused, embarrassed; and also she saw the imperfect condition of his right sleeve. "Oh, Nick, you have . . ."

"If I have, Lydia, you see me returned without hurt."

"Oh, I should have known that. I am not displeased. I—I am even proud. But I had not thought . . ." Her voice trailed away, as though horrified.

Across the room, her lean stiff back uncompromisingly turned to them, stood Mrs. Judith Pamphlin, holding high a plate so as to polish it.

Lydia's shoulders trembled very slightly. After giving a covert glance towards Judith, she pressed her lips to Fenton's cheek, moving back the periwig, and whispered.

"I shall have your company this night, shall I not?"

"And all nights!" he said aloud, and kissed her so that her lips moved under his.

"Then," he thought, "she is still frightened by her Puritan nurse?" This must be stamped on like an insect. He straightened up.

"Woman Pamphlin," he said, lashing her with the cold, even voice he had used before, "turn and face me."

Mrs. Pamphlin, putting down plate and cloth on a mirror-table, turned slowly. Her lips were a locked line.

"I warned you," said Fenton, "of ill consequences if you spoke one word of your Puritan cant to my wife. Have you done so?"

"Nay, she hath not!" cried Lydia. "I much wondered at it. Underneath all, I think, she is kind."

"Then you have done well," said Fenton to the rigid Mrs. Pamphlin.

129

"Take care you say no word of it to her ever again. Now go!"

Mrs. Pamphlin marched out of the room, closing the door.

"My dear," Fenton said gently, "you must not let these people affright you with their poisonous folly! I—I have an affair of moment, now, with the servants . . ."

"Yes. I am sensible of it. Nick, dearest heart, I have wondered . . ."

"But I will come back as soon as possible, and be with you at all times!"

Nevertheless it was a minute or two before he left the room, with Lydia's warmth tingling through him. He raced downstairs, round towards the study at the rear of the ground floor.

If he had looked only at the three candles in their silver candelabrum, atop the dark carved cabinet of the satyrs' heads, the room would have appeared just the same. But Big Tom, the sculleryman, lay sprawled on his back before an empty fireplace, his snores rising violently. Nan Curtis, the stoutening kitchenmaid in the cap, dozed in a chair with her head on one side. But, towards the carved cabinet where Kitty Softcover stood at one side and Giles at the other, he felt an atmosphere of hatred near murder.

"I make you all apology," Fenton told them, "for being longer than I had thought. Giles, was there no difficulty?"

Giles, pale but with thin jaws hard-set, rattled the coils of the cat-of-nine-tails.

"Sir," he replied, "they did wish for food and drink, and I took it as my responsibility to command cold meat and ale."

"Good! Have you complaints?"

He looked at the others. Nan Curtis, roused to wakefulness by his first words, kicked Big Tom to life with her felt slipper, and both sprang up.

Kitty, her eyes narrowed, leaned against the black cabinet with her arms folded. Her breast slowly rose and fell, a core of spitefulness; the light burnished her red hair and threw shadows of eyelashes on her cheeks.

"I ha' complaint," she snapped.

Again Fenton looked her up and down, wondering why he felt such intense repulsion for her.

"This bowse," she jerked her head towards Giles, the Alsatian thieves' cant thickening her voice, "did 'proach me in the way of amorousness. Did take his hand, thus . . ." She reached down towards her skirt, but Giles cut her off sharply.

130

"What the girl says," he interrupted, "is true. However, sir, she made a remark touching yourself. This, under favour, I would repeat to you privily."

"Giles," said Fenton, "should this happen again, and 'tis entirely a matter for your own conscience, be sure I hear nothing of it. Else I might be compelled to punish you, which would be a pity."

Kitty, in as much incredulity as wrath, screamed out at him.

"Th'lt not punish him?"

And Fenton realized, now, what his ear had not been keen enough to catch through Kitty's pronunciation. Before all of them, she had been using the "thee" and "thou" of complete familiarity.

"The matter of punishment, slut, we'll discourse of." Fenton drew the money pouch from his pocket and threw it to Giles, who caught it expertly. Briefly he took the packet of arsenic from the same pocket. "It was you bought this poison, one hundred and thirty-four grains of it. Nay," he added wearily, "don't addle your head to deny it. I have been to the Blue Mortar. Now: who sent you to buy it?"

There was a long silence while Kitty, still with arms tightly folded, studied him from between narrowed eyes.

"Th' hastna discovered," she decided. Up went her shoulders. "Then who can tell?"

"*I* can tell," answered Fenton with devilish quietness. "Giles! We do as I have ordered. Shepherd these people down to the kitchen. Kitty shall prepare a bowl of sack posset. The poison (of this I am certain) is in some ingredient already. Then it shall be drunk."

This time Kitty did not refuse. Her very small mouth, with its horizontal lower lip and Cupid's bow upper lip, made some derisive movement.

But Fenton, this morning raging with fear for Lydia, knew in his heart he had been too severe with those he believed to be faithful servants.

"Be not afeared," he said, looking at each of them in turn. "You will suffer no harm."

Reaching up on tiptoe, Giles fetched down the silver-branched sconce of three lights. Nan Curtis went out first, drying her tears, then Big Tom with his hand at his forelock, then Kitty expressionless of face. Giles's light sent a golden shining before them.

The stairs down to the kitchen, Fenton remembered, were across the hall and faced south so that it might lie beneath the dining room and be at the back.

131

"Hold!" said Fenton, whom Giles was about to light downstairs.

A hurrying of footsteps on the upper staircase stopped him. There was Lydia, in her evening gown of claret-coloured velvet outlined in white and gold, under the golden candle gleams.

"Nick, I would go with you," she pleaded. "I have a reason for this, truly!"

Already Fenton's nostrils had caught the heat and reek from below; he wondered whether he himself could manage it.

"Lydia, you can't go down there! Besides, you are in need of rest. Permit Giles to light you to your room!"

Lydia's blue eyes opened in wonder.

"Down there? It is nothing!"

"Nothing?"

"My—my father, as you are aware," Lydia lowered her eyelashes, "had no lack of coin or worldly goods. Yet many times he commanded me to scrub a kitchen worse than ours: so to chasten my pride and teach me humility. —Dear heart! Is aught wrong?"

"I wish the old swine were still alive," Fenton was thinking. "For I swear I would kick his behind from here to Ludgate Hill!"

"Lydia," he smiled at her, "I never command. But it will much please me if you do as I ask."

"Why, then—!" said Lydia, and did not pursue the matter.

"Giles, take the light. Do you give me the whip. Escort my lady. When you return, bring with you a clock. Any nature of clock."

And then, as their heels rapped away, he picked his way down the stairs. Of the odour we need say nothing. Since wax candles were too costly for servants, he could see below a gleam of tallow lamps with floating wicks, and a low red light from a coal bed not yet gone out.

Dull red light, and heavy dull heat. How many scenes, as he remembered them, had been played against a background suitable for his casual acquaintance, the devil! But the devil must be far away, busy amongst so many million other souls. On Fenton's right hand was a brick wall, on his left a wall of very dirty plaster . . . .

Then he gave a gasp, with that sense of the heart choking in the throat.

Something lurking against the right-hand wall, something as yet invisible, moved out against his side. Arms went round his waist. Small, rather chilly lips were pressed to the side of his neck.

"I knew th' didst but pretend," whispered the voice of Kitty, very low, and in quiet glee.

132

Fenton threw her away from him, flung her towards the left-hand, plaster wall. But it was hardly a foot away; her back made no noise as she landed there, except for a slight crackle of old plaster.

"I likes to be struck; I likes to be flogged; eh," whispered Kitty, her very large dark-blue and innocent-seeming eyes a-glitter. She nodded towards the steel-tipped thongs of the whip in Fenton's hand. "But not with that!"

Fenton was about to roar out and order her downstairs, when her next whisper stopped him.

"A comical gullery, was't not, when th' didst put Fire-Meg in a chamber opposite th' wife? And each kepit strict watch on other one, and forgot us?"

(Then here was the explanation of Sir Nick's odd conduct! But, in the name of all sense or even lack of sense, what could Sir Nick find attractive in this . . . this . . . ?)

"See!" flashed Kitty's whisper.

Now Fenton dared not move, in case he heard more information. They were about halfway downstairs, with the faint yellow tallow lamps and red fiery coals showing at the foot. Again Kitty sidled towards him, but this time facing down.

"See," she went on, "how I keep close t' gift th' gav'st me?"

Bending forward, holding open the front of her coarse blouse, she pointed. Round her neck, and slung down between her breasts on a grubby length of ribbon, hung a ring set with a triple tier of very fine diamonds. It curled round into a tiny snake's head, stretching as far as any woman's knuckle. The coils glittered wickedly.

"Pretty!" cooed the red-headed girl.

"I gave you that?"

"Th' didst. Who else?"

Again she sidled round him like a cat, attempting to get in front. Fenton did not push her, though his arms had become tense to do so. Kitty's own felt slipper dislodged itself from the wooden stair tread. She screamed out, fell backwards, and rolled heavily and all ways to the foot of the stairs, where she crouched unhurt with eyes glaring up.

A shout of laughter went up from the kitchen, dominated by the bass of Big Tom. Falling downstairs was considered an excellent jest. Also, from somewhere in the kitchen, there was a noise like the whack of light iron on a stone floor.

The laughter stopped instantly as Fenton appeared. Kitty sprang up

133

and bounced lightly away, a strange but triumphant look about her. Steadying his head and nostrils, Fenton looked round. This was not an underground room, as he had expected. Two heavily barred and dust-furred windows looked out towards a back garden and the edge of the stables.

The immense fireplace was much the same as he had seen at the cookshop, though nothing was over or near the fire, and more pots and kettles hung close to it. There were rats, too; he heard them scuttle. A long table, its cover a frayed tapestry piece discarded from upstairs, showed where the domestic staff ate. There was a tall oak carry-all, later called a dresser, on whose shelf stood the dim tallow lamps. Its shelves held upright dishes and cups: mostly earthenware, but some glazed or even china.

Big Tom, a heavy poker in his hand, suddenly leaped at one corner of the carry-all. There was a sound not quite to be described. In triumph, touching his forelock with it, Big Tom held up a dead or dying rat.

"Well done!" Fenton gulped out the words gravely.

Pleased, Big Tom went over to a heavy waist-high shelf, under which was heaped a pile of refuse. But in the board above was a large funnel-shaped depression, with underneath it a baked-clay funnel-shaped top and drainpipe as big as a chimney pot. About to throw the dead rat on the refuse heap, Big Tom hesitated and more delicately dropped it down the drain, emptying after it a little water from a large bucket. Nan Curtis nodded approval.

"Now," said Fenton, "let Kitty prepare the posset exactly as 'twas always prepared. Nan!"

"Good s-sir?"

"You shall watch her, close to her shoulder, and see nothing but what is usual shall be done."

Kitty, carrying her magnificent hair high, behaved with a contemptuous carelessness. She went to the carry-all, taking down a bowl of eggs and putting them on the dining table. She also took down a smaller earthen bowl, and a knife and fork from the drawer.

While Nan Curtis watched with screwed-up eyes, Kitty broke four eggs on the edge of the bowl and flipped their contents into it. With crossed knife and fork in two hands, she began swiftly to whip the eggs.

Footsteps descended inside the plaster-enclosed stair wall. Giles

134

appeared at the foot, with new wrinkles of anxiety in his face, and hugging a large clock. Behind him was Lydia, who peered past his shoulder without fully descending.

"Sir, sir," groaned Giles, "I fear your lady wife hath too wheedling and coaxing a tongue. She did persuade me that, though you said not in the kitchen, this did not include the pair of stairs leading down."

Lydia, holding high the candelabrum of three branches, looked at Fenton in so ingenuous and wide-eyed a fashion that he relented.

"Let be, then," he said, though he hated having her there.

"Oh, yes!" cried Lydia.

Giles, while Lydia casually sat down on the next to the lowest step, went over and set down the clock on the shelf of the carry-all. Everybody could see it. It had a bold face and a slow-swinging pendulum, inside an elaborate wooden case carved by Grinling Gibbons.

"Mr. Giles?" muttered Kitty, who had now whipped the eggs to a yellowish liquid.

From a bunch of keys Giles unlocked a cabinet, where the china used upstairs was set in racks. Taking a china bowl holding a good deal more than a pint, he put it on the table. Then he hurried towards a door at the front, presumably leading somewhere towards a wine cellar.

Nan Curtis fluttered her hands.

"Milk!" she said.

And, with unsteady hands, she took down from the carry-all a flattish earthenware jug, with a dish inverted on top to keep off flies or insects.

" 'Twas fresh-fetched from the dairy this morning, as I said," Nan insisted. "Yet, if it be turned—" Before she realized what she was doing, she tipped up the jug and tasted the contents.

"Good; this is sweet," she quavered. On the flash realization came to her; she looked, horrified, at the jug; then at her hand as though, like George, she feared it would swell up and turn black before her eyes.

"It can do you no harm," Fenton assured her firmly. "You took but a small sip."

Yet a start went through the hot room. Though this kitchen might be heavy with malodour, it was heavier still with evil. And all the evil, Fenton sensed, was concentrated in the small body of Kitty Softcover.

Carelessly Kitty poured the liquid eggs into the bright-painted

135

china bowl with gilt legs. After this she poured the half-pint of milk, and stirred the mixture. Giles, having returned with a quart bottle of whitish-looking wine, opened it with a corkscrew—the corkscrew being far from a recent invention—and put the bottle on the table.

From a wrinkled but bulging twist of paper, Kitty took out four small lumps of loaf sugar and threw them into the bowl. Measuring with her eye by holding up the bottle, she poured in exactly half a pint of sack.

"The' be th' sake pusset," she snapped. "Now drink of it!"

And she backed away. The pendulum of the big clock ticked loudly, yet so slowly that time did not seem to move at all.

Fenton's next move was so unexpected that all shied back, and Lydia pressed her hands over her mouth. Fenton tossed the heavy cat-of-nine-tails to Giles, who caught it gingerly. Then with both hands Fenton picked up the bright-coloured china bowl, tilted it to his mouth, and took a good drink. Afterwards he set it back on the table.

Taking from his breeches pocket the bloodstained handkerchief with which he had sprucified himself at the Devil, Fenton wiped his mouth.

"I order no servant of mine," he said, "to do what I would not do myself."

They stared at each other. Such a master merely bewildered them. Again, curiously enough, it was Big Tom who first understood.

"Good!" he growled out. Hitching up his trousers, he reached for the bowl.

"No!" Fenton said sharply "Stand back!" Big Tom, hairy and puzzled, obeyed. "No other person shall drink of it, save one." He made so imperious a gesture that Kitty ran to the table.

"Now, slut!" Fenton added. "Drink as I did."

Kitty hesitated. Her eyes, wide open, searched his face. Suddenly she lifted the bowl, took a good drink of it too, and set it down. Then, arms folded, she backed towards what might (roughly) be called the kitchen sink.

"Then it's not poisoned," thought Fenton, "or is it?"

Tick went the slow heavy pendulum; an interminable time until again *tick*.

Fenton was across the table from Kitty, who had leaned her back against the sink. Giles, in his sober black, stood not far from her; the

136

complexion of his face, against the upstanding light-red hair, seemed almost green. Fenton dared not look at Lydia.

"I fear," he said, "we must wait some fifteen minutes or more, should the symptoms of pain come on." He laughed. "Come: have you all a palsy on your chops? It's none so bad as that! Sure someone can tell a merry tale, and divert us by its relation? If—"

Big Tom, his iron poker ever ready, made another whacking leap and killed a rat.

Everyone gave a start; and Big Tom seemed surprised and hurt when they glared at him. Only Lydia gave him a smile of approval. There was a long scuttle and scurry of rats. Big Tom dropped the rat into the drainpipe behind Kitty, who did not even look round.

Tick; a pause that stretched out like elastic; *tick*.

If nobody wished to speak of the matter, Fenton decided, they had best remain silent. Once more he examined the evidence.

In that bowl, he felt convinced, there was arsenic. Judith Pamphlin, whom he did not like but whom he trusted, had sworn she had overseen the preparation of that bowl each day; and each day had carried it to Lydia, without being stopped or distracted.

Very well. Then it must be in one of the ingredients, since nobody had tampered with them today. Unless, of course, the poisoner had given up for a few days, as had also happened . . . .

Fenton's gaze strayed round the room. He looked at the clock on the carry-all, slowly beating against eternity. He looked at the dishes, and at long wooden spoons. At the back of his mind there obtruded some bump of wrongness in this preparation of the sack posset; something left undone or unnoticed.

Tick; and now the elastic seemed to stretch out until . . .

Fourteen minutes. A dozen times purely imaginary pains racked up through him. But once more he glanced at the clock as well as the other implements. Then, like the tallow-soaked spindle of a tinderbox scratching across his mind, it flashed up in a blaze.

"That's it!" he cried out. "That's how!"

Hurrying to the carry-all, he picked up one of the long spoons. At the table again, he thrust the spoon into the whitish-yellow-brown mixture of the china bowl. Round and round he stirred it. Then he looked at Kitty.

"Come here!"

Kitty approached as though hypnotized.

"Now drink of it!" said Fenton.

"Nay, do thou go first!"

"Drink it, damn ye! To the very dregs!"

"I'll not!"

Fenton's right hand swept to his sword grip. For the first time Kitty's face was pale, a glaring pallor against mahogany-coloured hair which had begun to loosen round her head.

"I'll drink," she muttered.

Fenton stood away. Kitty, fastening her hands round the bowl, slowly raised it to her lips. Whereupon, with a lightning half-turn, she darted four steps and overturned the bowl's contents down the drain. The china bowl smashed. Kitty bent over still further, her back to them.

"Giles, give her the lash!"

The steel-tipped thongs hissed. Fenton felt no qualm as they struck Kitty's body, which was flung forwards still further. Small spots and lengths of blood became visible against the back of Kitty's blouse, until her heavy hair tumbled down her back and hid them.

Releasing her grip, she sank face downwards against the heap of refuse under the sink.

"No more!" Fenton said quietly. "Until we determine what must be done."

Going over to the cabinet near where Kitty had stood, he took out what had so suddenly appeared in her hand: a wrinkled and bulging twist of paper. Fenton pulled it open. Out on the table rolled about fifteen small pieces of loaf sugar.

"Herein lies the simple secret," he said. "I were dolt and Jack-fool not to have surprised it! I have told you, I think, that arsenic is a white powder. It is without taste or odour. D'ye take my meaning, Giles?"

"Truly, sir! But . . . "

"Prepare a very thick solution of arsenic in not too much water," Fenton continued with disgust. "Dip your sugar loaf into this, taking care it shall be there only shortly; then it shall not even lose its shape, much less dissolve. Your arsenic is absorbed into it. If a white coating remain, this is not to be distinguished from the colour of the sugar."

He could see the superstitious awe of poison in their eyes as they moved back.

"You have all seen the girl Kitty do what was done," he added.

138

"When she stirred the bowl with a knife (d'ye recall?), she stirred only milk and eggs. She had not yet thrown in the poisoned sugar lumps. At the end, she did not stir the sack posset. Thus . . . "

"Stay, I have it!" exclaimed Giles. "The sugar lumps sink to the bottom and do not discharge their poison at once. Now I remember, you and the wench did drink immediately 'twas prepared. You drank from the top, as she must have known; and had no scathe."

Fenton nodded.

"Giles," he added, wrapping the lumps in the paper again, "I put these in your care. Guard them well. A dozen, taken all together, might well cause death. Here."

"Sir, I . . ." began Giles, hesitantly taking the twist of paper.

Giles ran his tongue round dry lips. For all the suggestions and insinuations he had made that morning, it appeared he had not really believed them.

"Why, then," he blurted out, "this means matter for a magistrate. Sir, this means Tyburn Tree!"

Kitty, in pain but still undefeated, slowly struggled to her feet and turned round.

"Cuffin-quire, eh?" she screamed out, meaning a magistrate. "What I could tell to a cuffin-quire . . . !"

Giles made a movement of the lash, but Fenton's hand stopped him. Kitty was not looking at Fenton, or Giles, or any person except Lydia, but she looked undisguised hatred.

Lydia, a girl of her time and generation, had not been in the least disturbed by anything she saw or heard or even smelt. Lydia had been sitting on the stair, on the step second from the foot, her elbows on her knees and her rounded chin in her hands. The silver sconce of three candles threw clear light on her claret-coloured gown, with the white and gold.

Now Lydia raised her head, cheeks a little flushed and eyelids lowered. She was not in the least commanding or dominating; she could never be this, and never wished to be. She felt no particular dislike of Kitty for the attempted poisoning; such things happened; what would you have? What showed under her eyelids was a shrinking abhorrence of another woman.

"If you mean," said Lydia coldly, "the diamond ring you stole from me . . . "

"Stole?" cried Kitty. "Th' husband—"

"You lie, for I saw you steal it. And truly 'tis mine, since you will

139

find my name graved inside. But pray keep the ring. I would not wish to wear it again. Even a ring may become . . . soiled."

At this, to Fenton's astonishment, Lydia turned on him a look almost of adoration.

"Dear heart," she added, "I have spoken because I must. Now do with her what you will."

All the servants were looking at Kitty, not pleasantly. Giles's fingers tightened on the handle of the lash. Big Tom slowly tapped the heavy poker against his hand, considering it. Kitty's eyes flashed round to each of them.

"Give her . . . " Fenton began. He paused, half-sick. How could he tell what had been the doings of Sir Nick? "Give . . . no, curse it! I—I can't have a woman flogged. Let be!"

"Sir," said Giles, "not far from here, in Hartshorn Lane off the Strand, there is a stern and upright justice named—"

"No!" said Fenton, "I want no noise of scandal. Worse, I want none of your filthy hangings. Law or no, none is dead. Give her . . . give her a couple of guineas, and turn her into the street within the hour. She has a ring; she may keep it, as my wife desired. But she must not return. I apprehend we have dogs?"

"Four mastiffs, sir, trained for short tempers and sharp teeth. White-boy, the terrier, hath distemper and cannot chase rats this night."

"That will do. Should she attempt to return, set the dogs on her. That is all. I bid you good night."

Lifting the silver candelabrum, he lighted Lydia's way as she went before him up the steps. All four in the kitchen were struck dumb.

They went to the ground floor, then slowly up the other stairs. Fenton, the light in his right hand, his other round Lydia, was in torture of more than one kind.

"I would have given all I have," he said wretchedly, "if you had not seen what passed down there."

He felt against him, rather than saw, Lydia's astonishment.

"Nick! Why, there I," her voice sank, "most admired you. In two quarters of the clock, you found and tore out this poison-secret like a buried evil thing which none else could see. And—and no master in London would have been so gentle in punishment."

"Lydia, as concerns that ring. I . . . "

"Hush! I have forgot it."

"But I durst not explain myself. It was not I, not myself . . . "

140

"And am I insensible of that? I know you—" Lydia's soft voice trailed away, as they went up the rest of the stairs and down towards her room, and Lydia puzzled her head. "But I don't know. Strange! Yet the one I love to madness is one I met last night, and partly in morning, and all this night. You are . . . no, I can't tell!"

"There is no need to tell."

Lydia sent a covert glance up and down the passage, as though to seek a lurking Judith Pamphlin, as they stood at the door.

"Nick," she whispered, "sure I have no need of a maid, have I? This gown is most facile to unfix; and the rest—well!" Lydia's cheeks grew flushed, but her eyes were very bright and her speech more rapid. "Nick, Nick, need we trouble our heads with having supper, this night?"

"No! No! No!"

The door closed after them.

And, in that house, presently all the lights went out. Towards the east, the vast old smoky huddle of roofs along the river had long been dark; most of its inhabitants went to bed at dusk, so that they might be awake by sunrise.

But Lydia, and certainly Fenton, could no longer be restrained. They passed the night in a kind of fury and violence. Once it occurred to Fenton, in a vague kind of way, that the Puritan girl knew more than most; briefly he cursed his other soul, before it was swept away by different considerations. Near dawn, when both half-dozed towards an exhausted sleep, Lydia clasped him tightly and fell into a fit of sobbing. He was wise enough not to speak, and presently she slept.

In a few moments he was asleep too. Birds bickered in the vines outside. A grey sky mingled with ghostly white. And so, from that night, they passed into the days of happiness.

CHAPTER XI

—AND THE GREEN

HANDS BEGIN TO MOVE

IN THE first fortnight, while leaves deepened their green with the flush of May, Fenton learned many things.

He learned to eat the food, mainly meat with heavy rich sauces, which his young digestion enjoyed. Vegetables you could have in moderation, potatoes, eggs, fish, and good cheese. Nobody, he noted in high pleasure, ever pestered you to eat vegetables for your health. Except for potatoes, he discarded them.

He learned to drink, for a beginning, a quart of the heaviest wine without a fuddled head or a noticeable slur of speech. George Harwell marvelled at his sobriety, and swore he was a cursed reformed fellow. Their pronunciation, too, slid more easily to his tongue; he could (almost) speak without thinking.

Tobacco smoking was easier. Though no pipe bowl, save a china one, makes hotter smoking than a clay, the Virginia tobacco was far better than he had expected. It crept up the long stem, deeply soothing to the lungs, without scraping off the roof of his mouth.

Big Tom constructed a toothbrush for him, and another for Lydia, after a design which Fenton drew on paper and carefully explained six times. It was instantly understood by an alert stableboy named Dick, who tried to teach Big Tom. As the latter would sit pondering over the design, Dick would rush at him with bursting words, only to be sent flying head over heels into a bush with one sweep of Tom's hand, while Tom continued to ponder.

On occasion Tom would put the design on the ground and merely

142

walk round it and study it from above. Fenton wondered whether he would ever get that infernal toothbrush.

But this came later. It is regrettable to state that almost his first official order to the household caused tumult and near-riot.

The tumult occurred on May 13th, only one day after he had gone to see Sir John Gilead regarding a cellar half-full of sewage. George, who came to dinner on the previous night, explained the matter.

"Why," exclaimed George, "where in all this is the difficulty? A small thing of bribery; no more."

Fenton, more as a historian that a householder, tested certain matters he knew to be true.

"I must bribe everybody, then?"

"Not shops or tradespeople, scratch me! But if it becomes inside the matter of a favour, or a preferment, or some work in control of a Whitehall office, too low for higher name . . . why, then, plump your money on the table in a bag, and have done with it!"

"An honest practical matter, then?"

"To all but the most squeamish, ay." George shrugged his shoulders. "My father . . . hem! We'll speak no names. Yet a practice so long established, when we buy their parliament men or they buy ours even among nations, holds no deep taint. Have a tack at it, and I'll tell you how to speak to Sir John Gilead."

Sir John Gilead's place of business was in the Treasury Buildings, on the west side of King Street. In his little office at the back, Fenton could look out at the Cockpit, with its red brick and its flattened conical roof painted white, vivid against the greenery of St. James's Park. There lived my Lord Treasurer, the Earl of Danby. It appeared, as a surprise to Fenton, that both Sir Nick's father and Sir Nick himself had been close friends of my Lord Treasurer, a financial genius and himself a master of bribery at keeping Members of Parliament hot for the Court party.

This, no doubt, accounted for Sir John's great civility when he welcomed Fenton. Sir John was a bustling man with octagonal spectacles all but hidden in a great grey periwig.

"And that is the problem," concluded Fenton. From a big leather box on the floor he took a canvas bag full of gold pieces, tied lightly at the neck, and containing far more than enough for his project. He put down the bag carelessly on his companion's desk.

"Hum!" said Sir John, placing one finger solemnly on his lip. "A good plan does indeed occur to me."

He then outlined a scheme whereby a pipe should be run downwards under Fenton's back garden, under the deep garden wall, so that the sewage should "seep away" under the terraces down to the Mall.

"Now scratch me," cried Fenton, who had picked up the term from George, "but this lacks good sense. 'Twill also seep upwards, an offence to all nostrils, in His Majesty's own park! And what if it should reach the Mall?"

"Questionless, there are difficulties."

"Now my first plan, a pipe run but three hundred yards to a main sewer . . ."

"It would be costly, my dear sir. Very costly."

Reaching down to the box on the floor, Fenton picked up a second canvas bag, somewhat larger than the first, and set it on the desk.

"Hem!" said Sir John, without seeming to notice. "Why, sir, after giving this matter deep thought," he added after a time, "I am sure I can dispatch your business." He arose and beamed through his spectacles. "And for a friend of my Lord Danby, the King's chief minister, it shall be done speedily."

And it was, too, beginning next morning.

On that same next morning, rather early, Fenton returned from Lydia's room, wrapped in his brown bedgown with the scarlet-poppy design. His step was springy, his eyes were bright, his shoulders had the swing of confidence.

"Hark'ee, Insolence," he bellowed at Giles, though smiling, "from this day there is a new order in the house."

Giles had opened a door, almost invisible against the panelling, towards the right of the bedroom door as you faced it. This opened into a small room or dressing closet, where the suits were hung, the linen and decorations stored. Being unable to decide which clothes to choose, Giles was in an impudent mood.

"Would move the beds, sir? 'Twould be more convenient if . . . "

Fenton silenced him. Fenton explained that he must go out and find the best bathtub, even if it had to be constructed, which could be procured. It should be large, and if possible lined with porcelain. It should then be placed in any room on this floor, to be called in straightforward fashion the *bathroom*, and all furniture cleared away save for a chair or two.

Giles made certain comments, and Fenton fired a heavy riding boot at his head.

144

But this was not all. In some room off the kitchen, say, there should be installed a bath for the servants: only one bath a week being required. This caused a true revolt among the servants, including six whom he had never even seen.

Here, actually, he met a generation of truly free Englishmen. In any public place—street, tavern, playhouse, cockpit, or any place that did not awe them—they considered themselves as good as any nobleman, and said so. They had no vote, but they had much indulgence because of their power to set up or pull down. They were the "mobile party," whom my Lord Shaftesbury smilingly hoped to use against the King.

In this battle of the bath, Fenton, who had expected opposition but not near-revolt, floundered out of his depth because he could not understand why they made such objection. Twice he sent Giles to put the question.

"Sir, they say the practice is unclean."

"Unclean!"

"I can but report what is said, sir."

Fenton's countermove won them over. A good master allowed his lower servants one suit of clothes and cloak, or woman's dress and cloak, each year. Their Sunday or best suits they acquired by various means into which we need not pry. Fenton offered two suits a year, together with a Sunday suit provided by himself. The servants, who worshipped this new Sir Nick because he would not allow them to be kicked or abused, still sent back a compromise.

"Sir," reported Giles, "all agree with groans to one bath a month. But, since 'tis you, they will shift their undergarments each week to the clean linen you vouchsafe to provide."

"I'll accept it!" Fenton said instantly, and so, while workmen still dug up the road in front of the house, the matter was settled without report spreading even to another house. Sir Nick had few friends, since most considered him a surly and murderous dog.

The upstairs bath was installed. Since a pump could not be managed, each day Big Tom carried up bucket after bucket of hot water.

And as for Lydia . . .

Even Lydia, at first, was disquieted by the notion of a daily bath. Fenton knew that gently, very gently, he must take from her mind the nonsense of her upbringing. Employing his knowledge of Latin authors, as well as French authors of the seventeenth and eighteenth centuries, he pointed out its possibilities in ways other than washing, when two persons were present.

She had been brought up to believe that too much washing was bad for health, as noxious as night air, and a sin because it exposed the body. But, when Fenton explained certain matters, Lydia's feelings changed almost instantly.

He had grown fatuous about her, as well he might. Thinking back to the night he met her, with paint raddling her face and her eyes dull because of the poison, he considered it an age ago. Each day, each week, he watched her change. The eyes were now bright blue, with luminous whites; they sparkled with mirth, or their eyelids drooped in a way he well knew.

Her hair, with all arsenic gone from the roots, grew softer and richer, light-brown with a sheen on it. Even her moods were different, because she was happy. Her skin, instead of being white, ripened into the pink-white of flowing health.

"I think I grow fat," once exclaimed Lydia, who had a horror of this.

"Not in the least degree or kind," he assured her truthfully, "beyond what is exactly proper to you."

"And it's because all arsenic hath gone from me?"

"In part," Fenton said gravely. "In part."

Meanwhile, on a clear blue afternoon when the lime trees made rich lacework in Pall Mall, Lord George Harwell and old Mr. Reeve rode up to his door on good horses. Though Fenton was no very able judge of horseflesh, he considered those he had seen for the most part as coarse-blooded, lacking line: well enough for heavy cavalry, no doubt, but not for a horse match at Newmarket.

When the horses had been taken round to the stables, Fenton led his guests into the long dark dining room, where so many portraits of Sir Nick's forebears were painted on wood instead of canvas. The latest to be added was a portrait of Sir Nick's father, with his sword and half-armour slung below it according to his wish.

Fenton thought it would please the old Cavalier, and it did. Yet, even as he stood before the portrait, taking off a very broad-brimmed hat which restored the saint-like appearance of his long hair and bald crown, Mr. Reeve's wheezing from his great stomach seemed a trifle worried.

George, drawing out a chair from the long table and sitting down, went straight to business.

"Nick," he said, "d'ye know what day this is?"

Fenton very well knew. Each day he marked down and crossed off in a book he kept locked away in a drawer in the study. Though he prayed that all danger had been removed from Lydia by the removal of Kitty, he felt in his heart that this could not be so. It was too simple, too easy.

"The day," he replied, "is the 19th May."

"So 'tis!" said George, and slapped the edges of his fingers against the table. "This morning my Lord Shaftesbury was contemptuously dismissed His Majesty's council and ordered to depart from London. Exactly as you prophesied."

Fenton looked down at the polished table. "Well?" he said.

"Report of it," said George, "went like fire through every tavern and coffeehouse from the Greyhound to Garraway's." (One was at Charing Cross, the other off Cornhill.) "In one day, Nick! Don't ye hear nimble tongues a-clack, many of them, and all Green Ribboners?"

"I can conceive of it, truly. But what's your meaning?"

Today George was all in red: red-velvet coat and breeches, even red hat, except for yellow waistcoat with ruby buttons, and yellow hose above shoes with gold buckles. He also looked down at the table, the yellow plume astir on his red hat, while he hesitated too.

"Nick, ye go seldom into company. Who finds you at a court ball at Whitehall, or at one of the great houses? Who finds you but at a foul boozing-ken, or among books in your study? Yet here's your miraculous swordplay. Here are you, last November, on sudden an orator to inchant Parliament as Mr. Betterton inchants a playhouse. And here's your prophesying to a very day!"

"I repeat, George: well?"

George gulped, with perspiration running down under his periwig.

"Some, who are fools, call you a black-a-vised dog who hath made a compact with the devil . . ."

Fenton looked at him strangely.

"Why," he thought with surprise, "these so-called fools are quite right. So I have. Yet I possess only ordinary knowledge."

"Now let's be open!" appealed George. "Men of sense know—ay, despite Sir Matthew Hale's hanging of poor crazed wretches at Bury St. Edmunds, because the law still runs so—men of sense know that these ghosties and witches are but our ancestors' foolery."

"And if this be so?"

147

"Why, scratch me, the thing's plain! Nick, you are deep in the counsel of His Majesty; 'tis but natural you should learn beforehand."

"George, that is not true."

George gave him a brief glance. Then he brushed his leather riding glove slowly across the table, and back again. Presently he fetched up a deep sigh.

"Some there are," he muttered, "who say an underground tunnel runneth from your house to Whitehall Palace, and that is why no man ever sees you there. This—" George paused, and smote the table. "Nay, Nick; forgive me; I'll not pry."

"You cannot pry, old friend. By God's body I swear I have never exchanged one word with His Majesty, and I have no more power of soothsaying than yourself!"

"Why, then," replied George with relief, "you say it; and I consent thereunto. There's an end to it. Besides, with my Lord Shaftesbury away from London, there can as yet be no danger to you . . . "

"Danger? What danger?"

"Oh, scratch me! There's my clacking tongue again! —Let be: I'll say it! Do you recall what else you prophesied before the Green Ribbon Club?"

"Some nonsensical stuff or other! I forget."

"*They* don't, Nick. They say ye prophesied that soon there would be a great and bloody uprising of Papists, who would cut our throats and burn London."

Fenton rose slowly to his feet.

First he spat out oaths. Slightly, very slightly, the fastidious ex-don was coarsening to meet the mood of the time in which he now lived. Then he walked up and down the room, a dim cavern twinkling with silver, to quell any spring of Sir Nick.

"I spoke no such words," he finally said, in an even tone. "To be more exact: they quote the precise opposite of what I said. I said there would be a lie and plot *against* innocent Catholics, many of whom would die bloody deaths."

Old Mr. Reeve for the first time turned round from the portrait and the half-armour hung below it.

Gently he had touched the breastplate, and the tassets, or thigh guards, which hung below. His bloated tippler's face seemed grotesque against the long white hair.

"I can testify as much," he said. "And so can Lord George Harwell.

148

What other man will do so?"

Dragging a chair far from the table to accommodate his stomach, he turned his shrewd old eyes on Fenton. His long sword scabbard rattled on the floor.

"This knowledge," and he gestured towards George, "comes in most part from me. I am, as they call it, an ear; a hired spy, though now revealed to the Country party as such. But have you taken thought, lad, to the meaning of all this?"

"I . . . I have . . . Nay, I . . . "

The rheumy eyes were still fixed on Fenton; gently, but steadily.

"When you spoke plain against my Lord Shaftesbury in that upstairs room," Mr. Reeve continued, "all men were vexed to raving, and confused of mind. They recall well the '19th May,' since you so often hurled it at my lord. But what else can they recall? Even the most honest, with a bemused head, is uncertain. They heard, to be short, what my lord told them they heard.

"If you foretold a bloody Papist uprising—why, 'tis clear you must yourself be involved in it, perhaps a leader of cutthroats. Assuredly (thus spake and smiled my lord) the Duke of York must be privy to the design. Perhaps His Majesty as well? Lad, lad! If my Lord Shaftesbury were yet strong enough, which I am sure he is not, you'd ha' opened the bottle of civil war!"

Still Fenton paced up and down.

"With myself," he asked sardonically, "as the cork?"

A look of puzzled impatience crossed Mr. Reeve's Bacchus-like face.

"Sir Nicholas," he said formally, "d'ye find no import in this? D'ye not perceive the offence they say you've committed?" He struck his fist on the table. "Treason, no less! Would ye see the inside of the Tower?"

Fenton stopped pacing, and turned to him.

"I—I am not insensible of danger," he protested. "But your news comes so amiss, so sudden and troublesome, that . . . that . . ."

"Come, that's better! A man would have guessed you cared not a groat."

"But what am I to do?"

"Why, this!" said Mr. Reeve, smiling and softly tapping his finger on the table. "If you have told us truth this day, it becomes simple. Seek a private audience with His Majesty, which is most easily attained . . ."

Here he paused slightly, wincing a little because he had never done

149

this for himself or in his own interest. But Mr. Reeve blew it away with a puff of his lips.

"Tell the King, if he doth not know it already, that you used your judgment and had but a stab of luck with that date of May 19th. Explain how my Lord Shaftesbury did twice have you set on by bully-rocks, and that you (good!) became bored by his attentions. Tell His Majesty what in truth you did say, pouring out moonstruck prophecies to affright my lord as though with an enorm spectre. Above all . . . "

George, at the other end of the table, could fidget no longer.

"Above all," he burst out, "why you made the statement, as flat as a man can, that this 'Popish plot' would begin three years from now. The Green Ribboners would have it 'three months'! You must say 'twas all lies."

Mr. Reeve silenced him with a stately wave of the hand.

"There is all you have to do," smiled Mr. Reeve. "His Majesty must be well disposed towards you. He was in the Painted Chamber, I hear, when you spoke against Shaftesbury. Tell him, and he will laugh at them, as he . . . as he tries to laugh at all."

For a long time Fenton stood motionless, gripping the high back of a chair, his eyes tightly closed. So many thoughts jostled through his brain that he could not sort them out. Yet on one thing he was determined. He opened his eyes.

"Sir," he said to Mr. Reeve, "I cannot do this."

"Cannot? Wherefore not?"

"That is what I durst not explain."

"Again I must softly remind you: would you see the inside of the Tower?"

"Yes! Rather than see the inside of Bedlam amid howling madmen! That is where they would put me. Besides . . ."

"We listen, Sir Nick."

"My heart, my life, my—my whole being has gone into naught but the study of history! Strange it may seem to you, and in truth," said Fenton, "strange to me. But I'll not mock or make sport of it."

"Sir Nick, what kind of madness is this?"

"Every word I said to Shaftesbury was true. I don't prophesy it; I know it! Would you hear the exact date on which first intelligence of the mythical 'Popish plot' will be communicated to the King? Let me tell you: it will be on August 13th, 1678."

George leaped to his feet, with terror showing in his face. But old Mr. Reeve sat quietly wheezing, like a patient schoolmaster, and tugged

150

at his small white tuft of chin beard. Even his gruff cracked voice remained soft.

"Now I suppose," he said, "when you were good enough to show me that portrait a while ago, you never imagined I should recognize it? Save as another old Cavalier like myself?"

"Well!" said Fenton, his wits now attacked from another side. "I remembered, certes, Meg's house at—at Epsom," he lied, "and your visits there. Yet, when we met that night at the King's Head, you did not seem to know or even recognize me."

Mr. Reeve's eyelids drooped.

"Know you?" he said. "Not know you?" And his gaze wandered away. "Boy, I rode side by side with your father in Rupert's charge against Ireton at Naseby fight."

Again, for a moment, it seemed that his wits had gone away too.

"We charged uphill, ye'll recall. On our right flank there was a hedge, with Okey's Dragoons (poor devils) a-sputtering and spitting at us with muskets that dropped scarce a man from the saddle. When we struck Ireton's line," and now a kind of glory shone in his eyes, "we broke it like a china plate; like a thunderbolt on a rotted tree; like . . ."

His lifted hand dropped slowly to the table, and he awakened.

"But these are old things," he declared wryly; "and, when all's said, we lost the battle. Lad, in the dust fog I saw your father's sword—that one on the wall—cleave through a lobster-tail helmet with one overarm cut. That night, when all was over, we lurked together beyond the campfires; we saw the pious Roundheads slit the noses of our women camp followers . . ."

Again, with hard effort, he stopped.

"Come; enough of that! But have I no interest in my friend's son? What strange malady is on you I know not. But, if you'll not help yourself, I swear I'll help you notwithstanding!"

Then George completely lost his head.

"You?" he shouted contemptuously, and looked at the patched, ragged clothes. "Worn-out tosspot? Soldier, yet spy? Who are you to help anyone?"

And at last Mr. Reeve was stung from his silence.

Slowly he pushed back his chair. Slowly he rose to his feet, towering half a head over George.

"I am the Earl of Lowestoft," he said, with terrible clarity in that quiet room.

He groped down for his ancient hat, but straightened up again.

"I was born to that title, and twelve generations before me, as I was born to my name of Jonathan Reeve. Rascals may filch away title and estate; I use them not; but they are mine." The strong voice hesitated and faltered. "I much fear, young sir, that the remainder of what you say is true. But there are some few who still remember."

Again, in deathly silence, he groped for and found his hat. A man of great age sees clearly only the past; that is green, that is bright; and he sees, with helpless clarity, the man he might have been. Perhaps, if you add old thin blood, that is why his emotions are so close to the surface. A thing happened which horrified him: tears appeared in his eyes, threatening to trickle down old cheeks.

"Under favour," he said, hastily turning his head away. "I must take leave. I—I have work to do."

Fenton threw his arm round the old man's shoulders, slapping awkwardly at his far shoulder.

"My lord," he said, with so deep a courtesy that it almost stung tears again, "allow me to escort you. This matter of title and estate shall be set right, I promise you!—whether I use the law or the sword, it shall be set right!"

"Nay, don't trouble. Nay, I beg of you! Yet 'tis God's truth I can help you. I go never to the court. But there are friends, the sons and grandsons of friends. They well know I won't pocket their money, and they tell me every whisper that's bruited from the matted gallery to the council chamber. You shall hear all; and thereby be at guard."

George, who knew the old Bacchus had been a man of title and had merely blurted out any words that came to his mind, was in an agony of remorse.

"Stay!" cried George. "I am but slow of wit; I meant no hurt!"

"And d'ye think," said the eighty-year-old, who had secretly got rid of tears for chuckles, "I was not sensible of that? You are young, lad, you scorn weakness. Nay, I'll ride wi' ye. Give me leave to go a little first. My foot is grown unseemly to the stirrup, and my right leg something painful in the heaving over. I would have it seen only by a stable-boy."

Then he added the old form of the salutation.

"God b'ye," said Jonathan Reeve, Earl of Lowestoft, Viscount Stowe, lumbering from the room, with a sting still behind his eyes, but as proudly as though he went to meet Prince Rupert.

Fenton detained George with a fierce gesture. No man on earth could look quite as guilty as George.

152

"And who are you," asked Fenton, "to call any man tosspot, drunkard, or the like?"

"Nick, I spoke wildly . . . 'twas in you own interest, because you would not see danger, and spoke like a Bedlamite!"

"Well, well! Let be. But, when we returned from the King's Head for a carouse at the Swan, you swore you would seek Meg and with honeyed words carry her away."

"Nick, I did but endeavour to advance my courage, and took a step too far."

Fenton gnawed at his underlip.

"I . . . the matter is not of import; but have you communicated with her since?"

"Ay; the next day, as I forgot to tell you. You'll recall the man-lass, Captain Duroc, the be-painted giant, the led captain you struck so hard he flew over the balustrade and fell downstairs. Well, yon tapster was right. He did break his left leg; and hath been since retained at the chiurgien's, a-raving in boards and bandages, but not yet well."

"And Meg?"

"Meg is installed alone in his lodgings—fine lodgings, I hear, with a Madam Somebody to preside—and Meg is pleased. I sent her a note, pleading; ay, pleading! She replied that she was prepared to admit only . . ."

"Captain Duroc?"

"Nay; yourself," growled George, his face darkening. If he had not been Honest George, Fenton sensed, George might have hated him. "I'll dally no more with her: here's a thousand jillflirts to be had for the rent of a pretty house and a few gowns! But Nick, Nick! A word of advice!"

"I am desirous to hear it, George."

"You are besotted with Lydia! You are as overfond, as doting, as old Pinchwife in the play! You spend so much time a-pleasuring her that 'tis wonder you have strength left to hold a knife at table. I say no word against Lydia; but 'ware your enemies. My Lord Shaftesbury will depart from town; but he can't be kept away. You lose your wits, as I heard with my own two ears a moment gone. Take care you don't lose your eye for swordplay."

And George, in his heavy-lined red silk, with his sword scabbard tilting up the skirt of his coat, stamped away in a huff.

"Your eye for swordplay."

Though Fenton was far from unaware of the dangers about him, still one matter lurked in his mind and forever scratched there. It was simply this: that he had never handled a true sword. Sooner or later he must fight. In his heart he knew he feared no wound, not even a bad one, but he would *not* show himself a blunderer, fool, incompetent.

Well, how far would his long experience with a feather-light foil avail against a heavier weapon, hard driven in a skilled hand? He must test that.

Hence that same evening, as he stood at the wall of his back garden, looking out over the Park, he sent word to fetch Giles Collins. Westwards, after sunset, the sky was a clear bright yellow, stretching lower to the south amid long low clouds.

"If I don't know it," thought Fenton, "I must somehow learn it. Somehow!"

The garden was broad and very long, of close-cropped grass, and shut away from the stables by high yew hedges. Along each narrow side ran a line of beech trees in bloom. Fenton now understood how the back of Pall Mall, as he knew it in the twentieth century, could go down so easily to the Mall below. One drop of ground floor was added by the kitchen of a house. A very long garden added length; and its wall dropped down in a brick wall to a shady walk beneath.

From this, grassy terraces sloped down to the reddish-yellow stretch of the Mall, along which by day lumbered leather-slung coaches of gilt or lacquer, and horsemen showing off their prances to pretty ladies at coach windows.

"You desired my presence, sir?" inquired Giles behind him.

Fenton started slightly as he turned round. Giles, hands folded, with white turn-back sleeves and white collar spreading down over his coat, stood lean in the yellow evening light.

"From certain remarks you have passed, carrot-top," said Fenton, "I hazard a guess you are, or were, a good swordsman?"

"Sir," Giles asked slowly, with the beginning of an impudent smile fading to dead seriousnous, "did your father never tell you who truly I am?"

"No; never."

"Then keep the riddle; don't read it. As for the rest, I accounted myself—ay, and still do!—among the very masters of fence."

"That's well. For I have it in mind to try for a little practice . . ."

Fenton knew it could not be foils, since the buttoned foil would not be invented for more than a hundred years from now. A glitter of joy leaped into Giles's eyes; but it died dismally away

"Sir, that has been thought on before. If you put great corks on the swords, the corks fly wide in play or the point pierces through. If you would blunt the point with masses of soft stuff in a glued binding, then play becomes ill and cumbersome. A wooden sword . . ."

"What do you say to breastplates?" Fenton demanded.

"Breastplates?"

"Yes! Sure there are many old breastplates in the lumber-room. True, we may thrust only between shoulder and waist, yet—"

"Ecod, sir, have done!" said Giles, somewhat upset. "Aside from saying the point will be dulled or the sword broken against a steel breastplate . . ."

"Then we grind a new point or buy a new blade!"

"Sir, 'tis not that. The blade, striking, will fly wide. Even though there be a gorget," and Giles ran his finger round the upper part of his throat, "the point may fly upwards into the throat or face. Or into an arm. Or," here the corners of his mouth went down, "it may strike downwards, with most unhappy result of all."

"Giles, I command you! Fetch the breastplates! I have the Clemens Hornn here; choose what blade you like from among mine."

Giles hesitated, bowed, and hurried away.

Since Giles was only an inch or more shorter than Fenton's present height, they soon found that several tolerably clean and polished breastplates would fit them. But how to fasten them to the body was different. They were compelled to wear a useless backplate as well, since each was a part of the other and the plates buckled together. It would interfere somewhat with lunging, but . . .

Kicking aside useless armour and discarded swords, they stood up and faced each other.

Under the still-fading yellow sky, Giles stood with his back to the tall thick hedge which fenced off the stable yard. The gleam of the breastplate seemed grotesque against Giles's black clothes and long face. Giles had chosen a blade of just the same length and weight as Fenton's, but with round convex guard of steel wrought to lace pattern.

The cropped green turf was firm under their feet. On either side of them stretched a line of beech trees. There was not a sound, not even from the stable yard. Then up went Giles's voice, not loudly, but with a queer raspy sound Fenton had never heard there.

"Sir, I would warn you," Giles said. "The moment we fight, we are no longer master and servant. I will hit you, and hit you as many times as I can."

Fenton's throat felt dry to the lips. His heart beat far more heavily than it had done when he stood before my Lord Shaftesbury.

"Agreed!" he said.

There existed, as yet, no formal business of saluting and engaging. They moved towards each other, blades feeling out.

Instantly Giles, very quick on his feet, darted out to lunge in low tierce. Fenton, as he caught the blade close to his guard and swept his hand to the left, automatically and without thinking gave a slight turn of his wrist to send Giles's blade wider. Back went Fenton's return lunge in quarte, aimed at an imaginary spot on the breastplate to represent the heart.

The point struck steel with a slurred *thud*, dead on the mark he had chosen. At the same instant his blade bent, hissed sideways, and flew wide without touching Giles's arm. Fenton had barely time to parry the return thrust.

"Not bad," he was thinking. "Not bad. Steady!"

On Giles's breastplate he had put in imagination a number of points in a shape like an X. He was fighting in regulation style, not closed-up like Sir Nick. Drawing a deep breath, he drove in to attack.

Fifteen minutes later, when the light grew so dim that play was dangerous, both lowered points and sat down. The play had gone in short, sharp bursts, of course, with intervals for breathing between. But Giles was very pale; new lines seemed to be carved deeply in his face, and he was panting.

Fenton, though not much winded, was so dazed with amazement that the grass, the beech trees, the whole garden seemed slowly to revolve round him, as in a dance. He still could not understand. Giles Collins, a highly skilled and dangerous swordsman, had not once touched his breastplate. And yet, after he had set a series of points drawn in the form of an X, he had scored dead to the mark on more than half of them.

This was fantastic! In his brain he could still hear the thud-slither, or only the sharpened thud, as his point struck. But, in a swift bout, men's minds grow confused. . . .

"Giles, Giles!" he said in hurried contrition, really seeing Giles for the first time. "I had forgot you were not a young man! You must go and lie on your bed!"

"Faugh!" answered Giles, with something like a sneer. He held himself propped at seated position until his breathing slowed. "Look to yourself! You have done me no mischief."

Fenton's mind circled, as so often his blade had swiftly circled Giles's.

"Giles," he stammered, "I regret that my swordplay today was not . . . not . . . "

"Hark to me, Sir Nick Fenton," said Giles, pointing a finger. "I am no flatterer, as you can testify. Rather am I a wasp to sting you, as your father wished. But, sir! You were today as swift of foot as ever. Your eye, perhaps, was a thought less than its best. But I have in my whole life never seen swordplay so good or so deadly!"

"What?"

Again Giles pointed. Incredibly something like pride glittered in his eye.

"This also I tell you. I would lay a thousand guineas, if I had 'em, that not a man in London could stand against you for twenty seconds!—Now enough of praise, sot and sinner!"

"Giles, you must take rest. Pay no heed to these bits of armour or swords thrown aside. Go."

Giles rose up stiffly, and tottered away.

Fenton, his sword still in his hands, walked at a dull step towards the low brick wall at the back of the garden. A single yellow line lay low and murkily along the sky.

And suddenly he realized the great blunder he had made.

In this present year of 1675, the art of fence was still in its age of clumsy development. It would not attain near-perfection until the end of the eighteenth century, a hundred and twenty-odd years from now. Present-day parries were mere slaps, though Sir Nick must be more skilled at this. Thrusts were unsubtle; in many lines but easy to parry. Feints were childish to anticipate. These people had never heard of wrist-turn in parry, or many sword tricks except those of foul play. Their guards were almost wide open.

Against this he could set his thirty-odd years' experience of foil play (a very competent man in any *salle d'armes*), together with the knowledge of several hundred years, in the catfooted and vigorous body of a young man. Some authorities maintained the lightness of the foil as of no value. But others pointed out that long practice counted most; that any stroke learned deeply and done with agility, all the craft of fence, could beat the duelling sword.

And they were right. What Fenton had believed his greatest danger was, in fact, his greatest strength. He was a better swordsman than Sir Nick.

Drawing deeply into his lungs the sweet-scented air of grass and trees, Fenton stood back. His bewilderment fell away. For some time Sir Nick had been completely quiescent; there was not even the rattle of a coffin lid. And he rested now, in fleshless satisfaction.

But across Fenton's lips went a curious smile, which was not like—at least, only very faintly like—the murderous smile of Sir Nick. It vanished; Fenton forgot it. Nevertheless he held out the sword blade sideways, so that the dim yellow light gave it a last glitter.

"Who comes at me now," Fenton said aloud, "is delivered into my hands!"

CHAPTER XII

THE JILLFLIRTS

OF SPRING GARDENS

AGAIN, within ten days, the enemy struck twice. The first attack began so mildly, amid such melody and even frolic with Lydia, that he scarcely knew when it began.

Often, with something like a laugh, he would recall George's bitter words:

"You are besotted with Lydia. You are as overfond, as doting, as old Pinchwife in the play."

Well, and why not? He was always with her, save when Judith Pamphlin stood guard while he sat in the study or walked alone in the remoter stretches of the Park: southwards, for instance, near the slums of Westminster.

The study enchanted him. To your true booklover, even the scent of old books is as heady wine. Sometimes the day would be wet; and, with a small coal fire burning, Fenton would sit before it with his long pipe drawing and five branches of candles at his elbow.

Again, a true booklover requires only that the book be old and full of good-for-nothing lore. Fenton had ceased to trouble his head with more changes to the house, even in its sanitary arrangements.

Therefore it delighted him to find the folio volume written by Sir John Harrington in the reign of Queen Elizabeth, over a hundred years ago. The nimble-minded Sir John, with as much sauciness as description, had invented the first w.c., with full plans and diagrams so that it might easily be constructed. He had the volume printed, dedicated to Queen Elizabeth, and presented the first copy to Her Majesty.

Queen Elizabeth, nothing if not progressive, had ordered the new apparatus to be installed in a room at Windsor, with a copy of Sir John's book hung on a nail beside it. But the apparatus never attained favour, even among the ladies, who preferred the old-style indoor accommodation. Fenton, musing over this while relighting his pipe about every minute with a glowing coal held in a tongs, decided against it.

"I am not one of those idiots," he thought, "who delight in staggering people of another age with modern inventions. Especially since this modern apparatus is more than a century old now."

Also, he noted, the four mastiffs were forever in the house. For the first minute when the dogs saw him, they hesitated: suspicion lurks ever in the canine soul. But, when they heard his voice, and sniffed, and he held out his hand to be licked, all suspicion vanished. The mastiffs flew at him like runaway cannon; they leaped up on him to lick his face and all but upset him; they dashed round him to the peril of all furniture; crouched down and uttered bubbling noises of joy.

They were the old English mastiffs, the fighting watchdogs who protected the family. In contrast to their long, heavy, thick bodies they had a fine line of leg; their flopping earlaps quickened at the faintest sound, their eyes were alert over hanging dewlaps, which concealed murderous teeth.

The highest of them stood within six inches of Fenton's waist. In colour they ranged from fawn to brindle. Their names were Thunder, Lion, Greedy, and Bare-behind. This last-named, Bare-behind, is given here as less frankly named, in old English terms, than he really was. Sometimes it raised Fenton's hair to hear Lydia's sweet voice, clearly upraised, calling him from a distance by his real name.

But it was the brindled Thunder, biggest and most powerful of the dogs, who attached himself most worshipfully to Fenton. Thunder was good to have at your side, though the most ingenious devices had to be adopted when you wanted him out of the room.

"Dear heart," Lydia would say, "you'll not forget their training, now?"

"Er—as though I could!"

"When you but speak with someone, not even an enemy but a friend, never put right hand on sword grip or draw blade in the least. Else—" and she lifted her shoulders.

160

Lydia, like so many of her Roman namesakes, was now taking more baths than she needed. She was reaching her full bloom of health; and, in his heart, Fenton swore that not a woman at court (which he had not yet seen) could touch her. There was one occasion, while he stood by to watch, that Lydia caught him off balance and tipped him fully dressed into the bath. Three doors away, where Judith Pamphlin listened with lips in a livid line, she heard the mighty splash, and Lydia's gurgle of delight, and the string of oaths.

Fenton did not really mind being tipped into the bath. Slowly he had all but removed the Puritan upbringing from Lydia's mind. Though she much enjoyed undressing, she had at first a firm notion that this must be done in the dark.

Instead he demonstrated the greater virtue of effect in full candle-light at evening, though as a concession with drawn curtains. Lydia, at first timorous, grew soon delighted with pride and pleasure and the knowledge that it pleased him. Her pink-and-white flesh, the development of her body, had aesthetic quality as well as, to Fenton, far more important considerations.

"Stand thus!" he would say. "Your smock fallen to your hip, a trifle bent forward . . . "

"Like this?" And he could hear Lydia breathe.

"Now let the smock fall. Altogether. Move towards me."

"Like . . . this?"

"I love you."

Lydia could not reply, her lips being engaged with his own, but she nodded violently to show she returned the sentiment, and made other demonstrations as well.

He guarded over her, watched, always in attendance, especially when they took their meals at home in the long dining room which at evening became all a shining fretwork of silver. Though Lydia revelled in this, too, after the neglect or brutality of Sir Nick, she was once moved to mild protest. After every course was set before her, Fenton would eat the upper half of it. He would turn his mind on the effect of every poison then known.

"Dear heart," said Lydia, "I have read tales of kings in olden times who had tasters to their tables. 'Tis no wonder they are gone now. The king on his golden throne must near have died of hunger ere he tasted a mouthful, which was indeed already as cold as charity."

June 10th, June 10th, June 10th. Now the day was drawing ever closer, it hammered so much in his brain that his reply was slow.

161

"This must be done, my dear."

"But who would dare try? With you so . . . so . . . "

Lydia was about to say "much changed," but she checked herself. The mastiffs snuffled round the room, except for Thunder, who dozed at full length across Fenton's feet.

"Where is danger from outside?" Lydia asked. "At night the house is locked like a fortress. The dogs are outside. Nay. You've guessed it. It was that . . . that . . . "

About to say "Kitty," Lydia again checked herself and lowered her eyes. She could not bring herself even to utter that loathed name. Then she glanced up, with an expression which would have enchanted Sir Peter Lely. The light glimmered on her hair, cut in a fringe across the forehead, and flounced out thick and soft at the sides. Without even speech, her blue eyes would have expressed what she meant.

"Doth it indeed matter so much to you," she asked softly, "what should happen to me?"

"Much, Lydia. My God, too much!"

Often they rode into the country, Lydia in sidesaddle on an easy nag, Fenton on a good high-stepping mare he had bought from George. They rode into the fields, thence up the high hills to Hampstead or even Highgate. There, in a private room of a cozy inn with drums of cheese almost as big as the ale barrels, they could eat and drink without fear of poison.

Afterwards, lost in tenderness, they would ride back through the sweet-scented night, under a bright half-moon. Softly Lydia would hum or sing. Once, amazingly, she sang a snatch from part of a Cavalier ditty:

"Come, fawn on disaster! Call Oliver master . . . !"

But she looked sideways at Fenton, under drooping eyelids, to see whether this reminded him of Meg. If she could have got the most-loathed name of Meg from her mind, Lydia would have been utterly happy. Fenton had . . . had *almost* forgotten Meg. In any case, he was too watchful of every bush or hedgerow. Unknown to Lydia, under the right side of his blue-velvet coat there were two pistols thrust into his sword belt.

Lydia sighed with dreamy pleasure.

Or at evening, when everybody else had gone, they would stroll in the dimness of St. James's Park. They would stand by the artificial lake which the King had ordered to be created there, with its ducks,

162

its cranes, even one droopy-looking flamingo. Late one afternoon, of bad omen, he took Lydia into the City to see a playhouse.

It was the Duke's House, some time moved from Lincoln's Inn Fields to a fine new building (so they said) in Dorset Gardens, Whitefriars. Fenton had no need to take Lydia through the screaming soot-blindness of Strand or City. They would go by water, the most pleasant way of travel if you had time and even small money.

Lydia was so wildly delighted, cheeks flushed and eyes sparkling, that she must wear her very best gown of grey and blue and silver. She quivered before a mirror while Judith Pamphlin, white-faced and white-lipped with rage, assisted her.

For she knew her mistress had intent to visit a playhouse, which was sin.

Fenton, watching Lydia dress, leaned idly against the wall. Judith would cheerfully have murdered him without a stain on her conscience, save that she did not dare try. She and Fenton were the personification of Roundhead and Cavalier, without a single meeting place.

Long ago Fenton would have got rid of her, except for her deep devotion to Lydia. He did not hate her as much as she hated him; only her Puritanism. When he agreed with the servants' compromise for one bath a month, he had known Mrs. Pamphlin would not agree. She had not agreed. Carelessly he ordered Big Tom to assemble the servants as spectators, then to strip Judith and hold her under the pump until sluiced down. Judith had yielded.

But now, with the playhouse as well as other matters poisoning her mind, Judith could not control herself.

"The man of blood," she said, nodding towards Fenton but speaking harshly to Lydia, "leadeth you still further down into lewdness."

Fenton waited.

Three weeks ago Lydia would have murmured some soothing words. Now she whirled round.

"Lewdness," she retorted, proudly and sweetly, "is a most excellent good thing. Am I not his wife?"

Up went Judith's admonitory finger.

"Wife or no, carnality for pleasure's sake is in the eyes of the Laard . . ."

"Stop," said Fenton, not loudly, Putting his thumbs under his satin waistcoat, he hooked them in his sword-belt and strolled towards her.

"Woman," he continued, "some while ago I bad you use no Puritan

163

cant in the presence of my wife. You have done so. Now depart from this room. You will never attend upon my wife again."

Judith Pamphlin opened her mouth to speak.

"Go!" said Fenton.

In her eyes, as she went out, Fenton saw that all Judith's thoughts were whittled down to the one point of revenge against him. Not (as she would think) personal vengeance, but only the vengeance of the Lord, because only she and her Independent sect understood His will. Fenton must again look sharp for murder in any shape that crawled near.

" 'Tis strange," muttered Lydia after the door had closed. She spoke in an astonished voice, with half-laughter under it. "I feel no pain of conscience at all." Abruptly she swung round, radiant, and dropped Fenton a curtsey.

"Doth—doth this mode of gown displease you?" she added. Her eyes grew desperately serious. "If it be so, I swear I will cut it to ribbons!"

"All pleases me, Lydia." A passion of earnestness shook his voice. "What you say, what you do, what you think, what you are! I . . . Well! As touches this matter of gowns—"

"Oh?"

"I would have you bespeak so many as would fill the house. And jewels, trinkets, watches, all you can call to mind! When next you send to your Mrs. . . . " he snapped his fingers to recall the name, "Mrs. Wheebler's, at the sign of something in Covent Garden . . . "

Lydia turned her head away, and gave a little shiver before she turned back.

"I have not sent to Mrs. Wheebler's" she answered, with his own passionate earnestness, "for well above a fortnight. I have sent to the New Exchange, or to Madame Beautemps, at the sign of La Belle Poitrine, in Southampton Street. I—I feared she was too costly."

Round Lydia's neck Fenton fastened a silver-laced cape lined in blue. Over his own left shoulder he flung a cloak, buckling it close to the neck. It could be buckled over the right shoulder as well, in foul weather; but this position left free his sword arm.

"Take no heed to cost. And," smiled Fenton, "we must have a *belle poitrine.* May I remind you, sweetest, that the play is at afternoon, not evening; and we must make haste?"

Whitehall Stairs, descending to the riverside, were open to the public; just as were all the many water stairs, by which you could travel to so many points down the Thames. Escorting Lydia down a length of oak steps, near rotted at the end, he steadied her into a wherry where a fat, jovial waterman sat with long oars towards the stern.

Since it ws near the middle of low tide, no high splash and swirl of water drenched the occupants. Sometimes it did, but they paid scant attention. Lydia and Fenton, sitting backwards into the prow, faced the river eastwards and also faced the waterman.

" 'Tis not a bright day, nor yet a dull," proclaimed that dignitary, who was cheerful by tradition. "I'll bear ye well towards midstream, away from soots and smuts. I'll give ye fair journey to . . . ?"

"Whitefriars Stairs."

The dull-grey Thames, with its smoky sparkle, was full of small craft: some of them with little whitish sails. The light breeze blew cool and clean, scarcely disturbing Lydia's broad hat. On their left, past the heavy stone watergates of noblemen's town houses, the tide crept up the mudbanks behind the backs of the high, huddled old buildings along the Strand and into the City, half-wrapped in smoke.

When eventually they reached the Duke's House, in Dorset Gardens, Fenton found much that he expected to find. He obtained a side box, which was little more than a cubicle of four bare posts against a brick wall. But the stage was of good size; and, since the death of Sir William Davenant, of Opera fame, his son maintained a splendour of background together with Betterton's invention of movable scenery.

Like all ladies of quality or respectability, Lydia had slipped on her dark vizard mask as soon as they entered the playhouse. It was the only thing she knew of the matter, and the mask seemed to fascinate her.

"Shall we laugh?" she whispered eagerly, plucking at Fenton's arm as they sat down in the side box. "Shall we laugh very much?"

In the small, crowded, malodorous house, many dim candles touched to magnificence the gaudiness of the Oriental scenery.

"Nay, love," said Fenton. "This is Mr. John Dryden's rhymed tragedy, *Aurengzebe*. You'll have learned that Glorious John was but recently much stung and hurt in a witty comedy, writ by His Grace of Bucks,"—the whole Green Ribbon Club rose in his mind,—"to ridicule him."

"I am so ignorant!" murmured Lydia.

165

When she had sat down, she had unfastened and thrown back her cloak. The fops, seated in chairs on both sides of the stage, had been listlessly combing their periwigs or crying to each other (so-called) witty remarks to impress the pit. The orange-girls, making a din as they cried their wares, moved forwards and back in so narrow an aisle between side boxes and pit benches that they almost invited pinches and certainly received them.

But now the fops woke up. A dozen gold lorgnettes were lifted at Lydia. Men and women stood up in side boxes to peer, the women's masks eerie in that heavy gloom. Men rose up from the pit, and almost all in the gallery. One drunk but forthright man in the gallery shouted her praises in terms sincere if bordering on the obscene.

This pleased Lydia; who, though in confusion, openly smiled. A hum of approval went up for such condescension from an obvious lady of quality. Then all settled down, somewhat restless.

"Now observe," mocked Fenton, "how all share my opinion. I am most damnably jealous."

"Nay!" cried Lydia; then her expression changed. "Nay, you are jesting. Pray don't. I like it not. Dear heart, you spoke of this play?"

"Why, there's but little. This is Mr. Dryden's reply to His Grace of Bucks's ridicule in *The Rehearsal*. Not by retort or repartee, mark that; only to show he can give of his finest. Hark; here's the prologue!"

The leading parts were taken by Mr. Betterton and Mrs. Betterton. Thomas Betterton, not yet middle-aged, in full strength of voice and presence, played with his audience's emotions as a master-swordsman plays with a novice.

" 'Tis easy," he would often say afterwards, "to rouse a house by a wild voice and mighty gesture. But to subdue it, render it so rapt and hushed you may hear a fop comb at his wig or a woman sniff at a pomander ball: this, I hold, comes closer to art."

And that is what he did.

At the end of it, for several seconds the house sat silent. Most were openly weeping. Then the hum of applause grew mightily to a roar which all but split the walls of the Duke's House.

Fenton had already read the play. Though he was as unmoved by the tragedy as would have been you or I, he had been held by the power of words: words a-blaze like banners on the march, making Bucks's poor footling comedy no more than a dying taper. But the tears were running down Lydia's face; and it took long jostling out

166

of the house, and fresh air and many words, before she regained her good spirits.

What with the crowd outside, and the people waiting at the landing stage, darkness had fallen by the time they were being rowed back towards Whitehall Stairs. The half-moon had risen, silhouetting far ahead the half-mile straggle of tall roofs and peaked roofs, a-bristle with chimneys, which marked the line of Whitehall Palace.

A fresh breeze blew in Fenton's face, so that he drew Lydia's cloak more tightly round her. Lights glimmered from the right-hand bank. The tide, at its full and on the turn, ran out swiftly. Far behind them, the water crashed and foamed under the piles of London Bridge.

"Dear heart," said Lydia in a voice he knew. Long ago she had removed her mask, but she had been looking at it thoughtfully as she turned it in her fingers.

"Yes?" prompted Fenton.

"Would you escort me to another place, if I desired so? I have heard report of it, but I have not been there. 'Tis called Spring Gardens."

For a moment Fenton moved away and looked at her.

"You have heard report of it, you say?"

"Oh, yes!"

"Well! At Spring Gardens, which is a vast place surrounded by a tall thick hedge on the edge of the Park, you will find other hedges, and bowers, and winding walks amid trees, like a maze gone mad. It is most discreetly lighted; in some parts, not at all."

"Dear Nick, I—"

"You may take refreshment there, or hear a trio of music. But in the main, Lydia, 'tis for young satyrs to pursue masked nymphs who are fleet of foot and yet not unwilling to be captured, in some dim nook, and brought down."

"I shall wear a mask," Lydia said innocently, "and my very *oldest* gown."

Fenton regarded her with mock severity.

"Mort," he said. "Bawd! Dell!"

Lydia merely tossed her head and looked away.

"No; shall I tell you what you are?" smiled Fenton. "You are a girl of the highest respectability, who longs to play at being the worst of the none-respectable. Would any in Spring Gardens think your pursuer is your husband?"

"Oh!" cried Lydia, and her mouth fell open. "How did you know . . . ?"

"Why, merely because so many women are the same, but won't allow to it."

"Willst take me tomorrow's night," pleaded Lydia, "if the weather be fine? I shall wear my very oldest gown."

"Do you see that star?" he asked, pointing at random. "I would take you there, if you desired it and I could contrive it. This is easily managed. Spring Gardens let it be!"

And so, all unknowingly, Lydia touched off the spring of evil omen.

"I shall wear my very oldest gown," she stated rather primly.

It is hardly necessary to say that she did nothing of the kind, but went out next day to buy her newest one.

At ten o'clock that night, after being dressed by Giles, Fenton went out into the upstairs passage, now dimly lighted by a few wall sconces. He wore his usual loose, comfortable, sombre-hued velvet, and shoes now made to his liking. Giles was always in agony at his lack of jewelled rings, diamond waistcoat buttons, even lack of more than a plain laced neckband.

At the same time, Lydia ran out of her bedroom and hurried to the head of the stairs.

Lydia wore a mask, but no hat. Her gown vaguely suggested the simple countryside, perhaps because of very small pink roses against vertical stripes of silver set off by sky-blue. But it had no shoulder straps, and was cut in such fashion that Fenton wondered how it stayed up. Beside her was her new maid, Bet, carrying a scarlet cape lined with dark blue.

"Indeed," Lydia declared, "it is my oldest . . ." She paused, peering at him.

Though he was in a merry mood, having drunk above a quart of malmsey at their evening meal, doubt filled his mind. Also he felt jealousy (of what? Of anyone.) like a claw at his heart.

"In theory," he said, "this frolic gives no occasion of distrust. Yet in that roystering throng, if I set you loose to pursue you. . . "

Lydia ran to him, while Bet fastened round her neck the great scarlet cape.

"But you did permit me," she protested, "to go out alone this day in the coach."

"That's none of the same matter. Whip and Harry were with you."

168

Whip was the heavy-shouldered coachman, and Harry one of the downstairs porters who was a very tolerable swordsman and practised each day with Fenton.

"What if I should lose you in that throng?" demanded Fenton. "What if some brisk fellow should make at you and seize you?"

"Oh, that?" said Lydia without inflection or even much interest.

She drew back the left side of her cloak. In the padded lining was a small pocket for a light chamois-leather sheath. A thin, light dagger, hardly four inches long but with sides razor-sharp to its point, nestled there with a light gold haft.

"If any man but you were to touch me," said Lydia, stating a simple fact, "I would not try to kill him. I do not think I could. But for months, it might be years, he would regret the day he saw me." Beyond the mask her eyes opened in wonder. "Sweet heart, were you not sensible of this?"

Lydia could not understand why he kissed her so hard.

"I am a moody fool!" he laughed. "Why do we wait?"

As they hurried down the stairs, Fenton glanced over his shoulder. At the far end of the passage stood Judith Pamphlin, motionless, arms folded, watching.

It was only a short distance to the main entrance of Spring Gardens, which Fenton had noticed when he crossed the open space with George Harwell on his first day in Old London.

Not long after they had gone, a street porter loped along Pall Mall and asked of every tipstaffed porter if this would be the house of Sir Nicholas Fenton. When he reached Sam, still straight-backed with periwig and tipstaff, Sam snapped his fingers. The porter handed over a squeezed-up letter and received sixpence.

Sam summoned Giles, who took the letter under the wall candles of the ground-floor hall. Its superscription, in neat handwriting, was to "Sir Nick. Fenton, who resides in Pall Mall." It was sealed on the other side, with "Jonathan Reeve, Esq." underneath.

Giles, biting hard at his lower lip, weighed the letter in his hand. Deliberately he broke the seal and read. His features sharpened, though not with his customary satiric expression, and his face grew a trifle pale. For a time he stood motionless in thought. Then he hastened away.

Meanwhile, Lydia and Fenton discovered the high iron-railed gate almost hidden in the tall hedge at the main entrance of Spring Gardens. Dropping money into the hand of an attendant, clad all in green and with leaves and twigs fastened to her hat, Fenton found that the attendant had vanished as though by magic.

"Oh!" whispered Lydia.

The waxing moon rode high above Arcadian woodland. There was a little open space inside the gate. Then a second crooked line of hedge, not so high as the first but still higher than a man's head, showed several openings into the deeper woodland. The illumination here, as presumably to a small distance inside, was just enough so that you should not stumble. At long intervals were set in brackets torches chemically treated so as to burn faint yellow-blue, or dim coloured paper lanterns with a small candle inside.

But what caught both of them was the atmosphere of Spring Gardens on a summer night, as palpable as the scent of dew-wet grass or hedge. At first the gardens seemed very silent. There was no music of a string trio. Then little noises crept out at them. There were whispered voices, so faint or far away as to be nowhere. A very quick, soft patter of running feet, fading away. The crackle of a twig. A girl's low, trembling laugh.

Fenton's heart beat heavily. He kissed Lydia again, with intensity, before she gently moved back.

"See, I shall not stumble," Lydia whispered, displaying shoes which, though very small and silvered, were yet heavy and flat-heeled. "Now I shall run. Do you count slowly to five; then follow."

"Yet if I should . . ."

"I shall never be far from you, love, though you may see me not. Now!"

And Lydia went skimming away, her scarlet cloak flowing out, holding up the sides of a sky-blue gown with vertical stripes of silver a-twinkle. She did not dart into one of the open spaces before them, as he had expected. She ran for the farthest side of the inner hedge, rounding it between the inner and the outer hedge, and disappeared.

"One." Fenton had already been counting in his mind, with a double beat between each. "Two . . ."

It never occurred to him to wonder how grotesque this would have seemed to Professor Fenton, of Cambridge. He was a young man, and accustomed to being so. The old world seemed slowly to recede as his sense of values shifted and altered. . . .

His ear was alert for every noise. At the count of three he could still just hear Lydia running on grass. Gathering up the folds of the light cloak, he grasped the sword scabbard among them so as not to impede running.

"Five!" he said aloud, and raced off in pursuit.

As he whirled round the turn, some very remote flicker of yellow-blue showed him a narrow grassy path stretching straight ahead for what appeared to be some distance. As he ran along it, he kept an eye to the left for openings in the hedge. He almost passed one before he stopped and turned.

A low arch opened into what they called a "bower." It was so densely thick with leaves overhead that not a chink of moonlight entered. For a pace or two it was floored with gravel, then grass. From a far corner Fenton heard two voices faintly whispering together, but in such terms that he hastily backed out of the bower. Besides, he would have heard Lydia's footsteps on gravel.

On he plunged, finding another and higher opening in the hedge. This led him into a confused space where opened out three walks of real blossom, scenting and concealing rustic walls. He raced into the first, and was brought up against a dead end by a nailed rustic door. Sweeping into the second, he somehow got into the third: where he stopped, remembering something he should have remembered from the first.

Doubtless Lydia did not know it. But anything coloured red, in darkness or even semidarkness, is all but invisible. Doubtless she had passed him several times.

"Lydia!" he called.

"Won't I do?" softly inquired a feminine voice, almost at his elbow, and so unexpectedly that he jumped. A hand, not unwilling to be pursued, reached out and touched his sleeve. Softly shouting, "Lydia!" he plunged in another direction, followed by a giggle, and emerged again into the main alley.

This was hopeless. If this were some kind of maze, he could use his reason. But it was deliberately confused. Very soft, padded footsteps ran hard in his direction. He turned to see, in unsteady moonlight, a wench in a white vizard and a white short dress of sprigged muslin, hotly pursued by a fop in a periwig, who wore a cloth mask painted to represent a satyr.

171

They flashed past, as in a country of illusion, the satyr leering fellow-ship and encouragement.

"Never wear a sword, sink me!" whispered the satyr.

Then, not a minute later, Fenton caught sight of Lydia. He had turned into another side opening, resolved to explore each. Two paths divided. Instinct and experience told him that the path to the right would lead to a dead end or another bower. But at the end of the narrow, grassy walk towards the left he could see, against a faint yellow-blue spark, what seemed to be a high and thick circular hedge well above a man's head, and with a high arch cut in it toward this side.

Something darted round by the side of the hedge and inside it. Against light Fenton saw the flash of the scarlet cloak; he saw Lydia's gown, with silver stripes against pink rosettes, and her silver shoes. She peered right and left, poised for flight.

Fenton, after all but falling over a dwarf tree hung with artificial oranges, moved forward with swift, noiseless strides. He had been right about the hedge. It was large and thick and circular, having an arch on each side like the four points of a compass. Inside lay a slightly cup-shaped depression of smooth grass: the centre a flat circle, with sides gently sloping up to the hedge.

It swam in half-gloom from a torch placed outside one of the arches: to the left of the one by which Fenton approached, he thought. Lydia still hesitated, the hood of her cape drawn up, poised for every direction except the right one.

Fenton's blood had heated in more than one way. He thought of bringing down Lydia with a flying tackle. She would not have minded in the least; women were used to such treatment.

Instead he darted swiftly across the glade, picking her up in both arms. He swept her across the flat circle, fifteen feet across. He deposited her, face up, in the sloping grass of the other side. Pinning her there with his arm and shoulder, he threw back the hood and lifted the mask to her forehead.

"Did you think—" he asked, breathing heavily; and stopped dead.

He was looking down into the grey eyes and curling half-smile of Meg York.

CHAPTER XIII

FROM PLEASURE GROVE

TO DANGER SIGN

MEG, to be more comfortable, writhed out of the cape and lay against its dark-blue inner side. Her thick, sleek, black hair had been disordered by the removal of the hood. He noted—curse these disloyal thoughts!—that her shoulders and breast were more full than Lydia's, though her figure was more slender. Her hair lay dark against the whiteness of her skin.

Why, in sanity's name, was he struck with a kind of madness whenever he met Meg?

"Nay," she whispered, moving to draw farther under his arm and shoulder, "do you think my small gullery so very ingenious? For I tell you I was at a large shop, La Belle Poitrine, as was sweet Lydia this day. When I heard her cry in stage whisper, 'No made gown; this must be done today; 'tis for Spring Gardens tonight,' why, then, I had but to imitate gown and cloak. I had an even dice-throw to find you, if I covered my hair."

Fenton cast a quick look round. The grove hedge, pale green in its gloom, might have been "a wood near Athens" in the play. Never in his life had he been so tempted. And, since he received nothing but encouragement, he bade temptation to the devil and yielded to it.

" 'Damn her,' " he quoted in his mind, " 'I'll have her if she lie under a bed of thorns!' "

His lips pressed down on Meg's moist mouth, and his arms tightened round her. Suddenly she seemed to recall something; she held his

173

head back with both hands. Her long-fringed grey eyes looked straight into his.

"Nay," she said, though he could sense the warmth (or call it what you like) rising from her, "This glade is too open; I'll lead you to a bower I know. And first I have a question for you." Hatred rose now. "Art satisfied with my sweet cousin Lydia?"

The old problem jumped into his mind.

"And I have a question for you," he retorted. "Are you Mary Grenville?"

"Of course I am," she answered, in ordinary modern speech and accent.

Propped on one elbow, Fenton stared at her.

"But, oh, dear!" said Meg, still in modern speech, "you gave me some awfully bad moments, once or twice. And why were you so beastly and awful to me, when I planned it just the opposite? You even kicked me out of the house; and I couldn't do anything about it, except hint."

To Fenton, very briefly, it was as though all material things— hedges, grass, Meg's maddening, curving smile—all dissolved together. It was as though a vast eye had opened, in one comprehensive wink to show him a damp London street in 1925 and a grey-eyed quiet girl in a cloche hat.

"If I treated you badly," he answered, in the speech of 1925, "it was because most of the time Sir Nick was in charge. My—oh, call it other soul. Why didn't you speak out when I called you 'Mary' the first time we met?"

He heared her draw in her breath.

"I wish I had. Oh, God, I wish I had! But I was too unsure of myself. Don't you recall how I helped you with your *Dictionary of Seventeenth-Century Language*, and your records? But I was uncertain. I hesitated too long."

"I don't understand anything," cried the bewildered Fenton. "Look here: you didn't even have those engravings of people I had to help me, or any evidence. How could you be fitted into all this? How did you know?"

Meg pressed her cheek close to his.

"Listen," she whispered fiercely, "anything about *how did I know* is the one kind of question you mustn't ask me. Not yet! Later you'll learn and soon. You'll learn that my character, my soul if you like, are exactly the same now as they were before; but I kept silent, and nobody knew. Now we'd better return to a sweeter age."

174

The eyewink closed. The twentieth century vanished as it dwindled to remoteness. The only realities were soft-scented airs under the moon of Spring Gardens, and hedges or grass which could be touched as material things. Meg's expression subtly altered, no longer with an evasive smile, but tender.

"Nay," she said in those drawled tones, "we should do well to utter this speech, as fit as a pudding for a friar's mouth. I did put this trick upon you, Nick, in the main to give you this."

Partly raising herself, moving a little away from him, she threw her skirts above her right knee. Meg wore few if any petticoats. From the top of her garter, above the knee, she took out a small folded piece of paper.

Ever since their return to this age, Meg's movements had become more quick, her eyes more bright. It was the same with Fenton.

"Here," she said, "are my two houses, where you may find me."

"Two houses?"

"Faugh! You'll not find me often in the first. They are the lodgings of a French captain, named Duroc, who is horrid and shuddersome. Only this day they brought him home, on crutches, with his leg in boards and bandages. And (oh, fie) this monster would be at amorous tricks! To see how I did elude him would ha' made you burst a-laughing!"

"And the other?"

"That," whispered Meg, her tone changing to rapture, "is my own little house. Nobody knows I am there. None can find me, or trouble me. 'Tis in no fine neighbourhood; but what better? None will seek me, except . . . will you come and wait upon me soon? Soon?"

"I will! I swear it!"

"The house is kept, on my one floor since all else is empty, by an old woman called Calpurnia. But speak your name to her; she will admit you." Meg's tone changed. "You'll not be spiteful to me? Or harsh of word? Or use me ill?"

"The very reverse of all that, if you still desire!"

By this time Fenton would have said anything to any woman, yet even in his befuddlement he knew he spoke truth. Both voices spoke quickly.

"You spoke," said Fenton, "of a bower. . . ?"

"Yes, yes, yes!" Then Meg remembered. "Stay; you've not answered my question. Are you, completely and in all respects, satisfied by my cousin Lydia? One more kiss before you answer!"

175

She rolled towards him, and for the next few moments matters became somewhat chaotic. It was Fenton, periwig jostled to one side and part way near to calling the bower unnecessary, who glanced over his left shoulder. He saw the yellow-blue light blotted out by shadow, diagonally across in the arch to their left. He raised his head. Meg, also becoming sure it was too much trouble to go to the bower, raised her head too.

In the arch, so tall and gaunt that its top reached his flat hat and gold-dusted periwig, stood a corpse-faced man in white, with crutches under his arms and a swathed leg bent behind him. Just in front of him, still masked and cloaked but with lips deadly under the short nose, stood Lydia.

Meg sprang up, leaving behind her long-discarded cloak. Fenton, for certain self-conscious reasons, sat there but did not get to his feet— and later wished he had. Lydia moved with blinding swiftness in that blind, greenish light. Her hand slipped under the cloak, to the thin sheath with the double-edged gold dagger. She flew at Meg, holding the blade underhand, to rip up the middle.

"I can use a dagger," whispered Lydia, "as well as you."

At just this moment the orchestra, a trio composed of harpsichord, viol, and bass viola, arose in dreamy melody. The trio might not have been twenty-odd feet away, in a straight line; but where was a straight line here? Softly they played "I Pass All My Hours in a Shady Old Grove," for which King Charles the Second had written the words.

"Bitch!" screamed Lydia.

A dim spark struck on the dagger as it whipped up. If the light had been better, there would have been murder done. Silver stripes tore and pink roses flew wide. Meg screamed, backing away. Lydia, herself somewhat appalled, threw away the dagger and flew at Meg with a hand to slap and a claw to tear hair.

Though neither girl could in any sense be called tall, Lydia was the smaller. Meg, head down in butting style, ran at her with a violent shove of both hands. Lydia, staggering, caught her shoe in her own gown and fell. Meg instantly, and with sleek feline grace, ran out through the arch where Captain Duroc stood on one leg with his crutches.

Lydia, bouncing to her feet and not forgetting the gold dagger, dashed at the arch after her. Captain Duroc, a crutch planted on each side but none too well balanced, barred her way.

176

"Madame!" he pleaded with his liquid eyes wide, and all his comedian's courtesy, *"je vous implore!* Two ladies: no, no! This is not the *délicatesse!"*

Lydia looked him up and down.

"May I be a punk," she said almost sweetly, "if you are not the painted Nancy Ann with whom my husband dealt ere this?"

And Lydia, lifting the front of her skirts, kicked him so viciously below the belt that Duroc, with a half-scream of pain, doubled up backwards with his crutches slipping away, and fell into the outer hedge.

Fenton, still with nerves twitching badly from contact with Meg, had to find an outlet in some sort of action. He strode out of the glade through the same arch towards Captain Duroc.

"Sir," he began, voice still shaky, "though we be enemies, and must fight when your leg shall be healed, will you allow me the courtesy of lifting you up?"

Duroc spat at him. Duroc, famous for his manners, lay back into the thick hedge, all twisted, his face upturned to the yellow-blue torch. The lean face, framed in gold-dusted periwig, was chalk-white except for spots which seemed dark instead of red.

"Monsieur," he said airily, "I cannot see you. Of me, *me* you 'ave made a fool; and thees is not done with impunity. I don' know you. Go, fool, until I kill you."

"A word of advice, then," snapped Fenton, whose hands quivered to be at the other's throat. "I beg you won't dishonour a noble nation by posing as a Frenchman. Your accent, sir, is abominable."

Swiftly he turned back towards the glade, and entered the arch again.

"I believe," he said, "Madam York left her cape, scarlet lined with dark blue, on the bank where . . ."

Meg's cape was a little way down the short and shallow slope which led to the centre of the circle. Some distance away, the mellowness of strings mingled into "I Pass All My Hours in a Shady Old Grove."

Then Fenton paused. He was not alone in the glade.

There were four entrance arches, like the four points of a compass. He was near one. At the other three, straight ahead and at equal distance left and right, three men now stood motionless. All wore cloaks, but each had sword scabbard outside the cloak—blade about six inches drawn.

They stood just inside the arches, watching him. Their broad hats

177

concealed their faces, as the cloaks concealed what might have been good clothing. But in each hat was a large rosette of the Green Ribbon.

Fenton's joy, releasing all energy into this, sang through his veins in pure happiness.

"Well met, gentlemen!" he said, trying to keep his voice low in accordance with the whispering of Spring Gardens. Instantly he unbuckled his cloak from the left shoulder, and threw the cloak aside. "But sure this ever repeated move of my Lord Shaftesbury lacks something in subtility?"

The man opposite him never spoke. He gave only a high, giggling laugh, a very unpleasant kind of laugh, as though he were too cunning to speak.

"Sir," retorted the man on the left, who seemed (to Fenton) to have a very short beard and moustache, "my Lord Shaftesbury is from London. Of this he knows nothing."

"No no!" mocked Fenton. "Never!"

"Put by the notion," cried the third man on the right, "that we were hired or sent. Sir, we are honest patriots and gentlemen, who think you traitor and better dead!"

Each of them, at one time or the other, had flung the cloak back over his left shoulder. Each began to move forward out of his arch, slowly, down the slope towards a flat, good fighting circle fifteen feet across.

"Honest men?" Fenton called softly. "I rejoice to hear it. Then you'll come at me fairly, which is to say singly, and not three at once?"

The man on the right had a young, shaky, nervous voice.

"We would ensure the business, no more," he said. "Only a simpleton goes singly against the devil in velvet!"

"What?"

"Well, so they call ye. Have you ever donned attire save velvet?" huskily demanded the bearded man on the left. "But you are Papist and conspirator and spy! Can you deny it?"

"Yes!"

"Yet you will die. Even if you be devil . . ."

Fenton whipped out his sword. He jumped down to the flat surface of the fighting turf.

"Why, then," he said agreeably, "all three shall sup tonight in hell. Lug out!"

At that moment he or somebody was thinking:

178

"Come, here are easy odds. If I be quick enough, one bound—body turning left in the air—carries me off side of the right-hand man. Before he can bring round his guard, my point is through him. I use him, in left hand, to impede the second man's arm: striking swift at the second man's heart. 'Tis short; and the third man I dispatch at leisure."

Three opposing swords came out, all but colourless under moonlight and pale green. Fenton took a short leap to the right, nothing as yet to put them on guard. At the same time . . .

Three swords, as they were drawn, stopped motionless. Three broad hats, with the Green Ribbon rosette, turned as though each man looked behind Fenton's back.

The thing was too spontaneous, too quick, to be any kind of prepared trick. Under the fourth arch, as Fenton glanced behind him, stood Big Tom.

Big Tom's heels were dug in, his immense shoulders extended. On a double lead, with a pair of mastiffs to each lead, he held back Greedy and Bare-behind in his left hand, and Thunder and Lion in his right. Their powerful haunches seemed to coil; their heads were set between heavy shoulders; a low bubbling growl went up and down as their hides shivered.

The man opposite Fenton uttered his thin, giggling laugh. Slowly be began to move backwards, up the little slope for the arch. His unsteady fingers tried to put the blade back in its sheath. Fenton unobtrusively slid back the sword into his own scabbard. He did not like the Giggler.

"Tom!" he said.

"Aysir?"

"If I give the signal to loose Thunder and Lion, can you hold back the other two?"

"Aysir!"

Fenton pointed his finger straight at the Giggler. "There!" he indicated.

Then he brought his sword quickly up from the scabbard.

"*Thunder! Lion! Go!*"

Even though Big Tom had expected it, the lead ran harsh and blood-scraping through his hand. As the two mastiffs, haunches uncoiling, shot across the turf like brindled and tawny figures of nightmare, Thunder's snarl ripped out against the sweet, tireless strains of "I Pass All My Hours in a Shady Old Grove."

"Tom," said Fenton, quickly catching up his own cloak and Meg's

179

cape, "I think we'd best make haste from Spring Gardens, else there'll be public riot and ourselves haled before a justice. We—"

He stopped. The Giggler had turned round and bolted into darkness just as Fenton pointed at him. The other two men had prudently vanished too. All that saved the Giggler from annihilation was the darkness which baffled the mastiffs' sight, their sense of smell overcome by an overscent heavy with flowers, and trees.

One of them snarled and stumbled on stones. Amid furious patterings, an artificial tree went down. Then came the noises that indicated their quarry was in sight. They were on the view halloa, and their victim screamed.

"Tom," said Fenton, "I much fear they make towards the trio of music. This music . . ."

The music did not seem so much to stop as to explode. There was a crash as the harpsichord fell over backwards, all its strings leaping and jangling. The viol screamed like a pig, amid wild screams in the Italian language. The bass viola—much smaller than of later day, painted and with a scroll like a man's face—the bass viola shot straight up in the air for a distance of fifteen feet.

"Gotta heem!" a male voice cried ecstatically, as the viola descended and was caught.

"Thunder! Lion! Here!"

Three times Fenton bellowed at the top of his lungs. There was a pause, as of dying excitement. All through the woodland, as though Spring Gardens had become sentient, rose low laughter, which swept over the walks and died away.

The mastiffs padded slowly back to the glade. Though each had blood on his dewlaps, Fenton knew they had done no great damage. They were dispirited, almost slinking; Thunder raised one eye that looked almost as guilty as George Harwell's. Both Thunder and Lion felt they had done something wrong; they had not killed; or had they disobeyed? Fenton cheered them up.

"Quickly!" he said to Big Tom. "We must try, if it be in any way possible, to discover my wife!"

Big Tom, who had been given a bad time by the madness of Greedy and Bare-behind, found all four mastiffs tractable. He whisked them out of the glade, sending them trotting at random to the right.

Fenton, hurrying after them, came almost face to face with Captain Duroc. With the aid of the hedge and his one good foot, Duroc had

180

propped himself upright on the crutches, his weight upheld by the hedge. The torch in its bracket burned like a corpse candle beside him.

"I say a good night to you," remarked Duroc, lifting his upper lip. "We 'ave more to settle between us than a broken leg. There is also a lady, Madam York. She—"

"Prefers another?" Fenton asked softly. "How very foolish of her! A good night!"

He raced along after Big Tom and the mastiffs, seeing that last look in Duroc's eye and knowing it would be no easy fight when they met. Abruptly Fenton stopped and looked round, realizing where he was. The tall, thick hedge on his left was the outer hedge of the labyrinth.

"Tom," he said, "the mastiffs could rip us a hole in this. We should be out of it, though I can't tell where. If only my wife . . ."

That was the moment he saw Lydia, who also kept to the outer hedge, running towards them. She was flushed and breathing hard from running. As Fenton saw her, he suddenly felt far guiltier than any sentiments he had ever attributed to Thunder or George Harwell.

Yet she seemed unconcerned, almost smiling. He had completely forgotten Meg's cape, hanging over his left arm. If Lydia noted it, she gave no sign. At Fenton's signal, Thunder, Lion, Greedy, and Bare-behind ripped such an opening in the hedge that their masters could step out rather than crawl out.

"Why, curse it all," exclaimed Fenton, "I've come back on my tracks. Here's the begin step of Pall Mall. I had thought to emerge somewhere in the Park. Did not you think so, Lydia?"

"Oh, we're't home shortly," murmured Lydia.

Giles, pale and sharp-featured, opened the street door with all the wall candles burning behind him.

"I thank God to see you safe," said Giles. "Sir, there did come a note from Mr. Reeve, who said he would always warn you of danger. Humbly I cry pardon; but I opened it. You were to be set on in Spring Gardens, Mr. Reeve did not know where or when, by three gentlemen." Giles moistened dry lips. "I thought it well advised to send Big Tom with the mastiffs."

Lydia, without comment, had walked straight back and gone upstairs. Big Tom shepherded the dogs downstairs, preparatory to letting them out for the night.

"Did the letter," Fenton said harshly, "tell the names of these 'gentlemen'?"

"No, sir. Save it hinted . . ." Giles's mouth drew together. "Sir, I have not the letter by me. 'Twill keep till morning."

Fenton agreed. Nothing could have been of less importance to him, and he flung it from his mind. Startled, he discovered Meg's cloak over his arm. This was worse and worse.

"You have done well, carrot-pate," he said, and gave Giles a brief account of what happened. Afterwards he hurriedly told Giles to get rid of the cape; then, hesitantly, he went upstairs.

Though he tried to frame words of apology, he found none. Lydia's door was closed. He knocked on it, which he very seldom did, and was told to enter.

Lydia, her gown rearranged and her hair all but in order, stood before the looking glass in the far corner of the room. A single candle burned.

Again Fenton tried to gather words. Then, swallowing, he asked her whether she would like to have something to eat or drink.

"Indeed?" said Lydia in a cool little voice, turning round to face him. "But sure we must tarry long at table before our guest shall arrive?"

"What guest?"

"Why," said Lydia, lifting her eyebrows in surprise, "who but your sweet Meg? What! Not wait for Meg? How tenderly you did press her cape to your breast!" A wilder note crept into Lydia's voice. "How cunningly you put the trick upon me, luring me to your filthy Spring Gardens, when I had no wish to go! I may not believe my own eyes, I suppose. Yet of a surety she was on her back, and you about to—"

"Lydia! You behave like a child."

Lydia's face slowly grew white, so that her eyes seemed enormous. Then, as though at the loosing of every gun in a ship's broadside, she began to talk.

Up to this time, if Fenton had noticed any sign of her fierce possessiveness and jealousy, he had been apt to be amused or even flattered. He had behaved like a husband in the fourth week of a honeymoon; which, in a sense, he was. Afterwards men learn better, as he did now.

It was a bad business, and it lasted half an hour. Carefully Lydia dissected Meg's character, dissecting his own at the same time. Any fine lady had a long vocabulary of short words; and used them, even casually, in public. Her voice rose when she tore to pieces Kitty and

182

Fenton, describing their conduct as she imagined it. When he protested in disgust, she demanded shiveringly to know whether *he* was not aware he had stolen her diamond ring to give to the slut?

As her voice grew wilder and wilder, so did her accusations against him. There was no contemptible act, from miserliness to murder, which she did not pour out. Lydia herself was horrified. She did not mean all this. But she could not stop. Being herself badly hurt, some impulse drove her to hurt and hurt and hurt in return. Once she flew at him with the gold dagger, stabbing blindly; and he had almost to break her wrist before she let go.

As for Fenton . . .

He had a worse task. As he tried to keep silent, still his own temper flamed; and with it, since this was so close and personal, came Sir Nick. The fleshless hand gripped at his vitals; fleshless arm, shoulder, side were rattling from that rotting wood.

For the most part pressing his hands over his eyes, he mentally put forth every ounce of strength. If Sir Nick were to gain possession now, he might run amok. As Fenton felt the black hood vanish from his eyes, he knew he had won again. He must leave; he must go away.

Fenton stalked to the door, somewhat marring the effect by slamming it after him. Immediately he heard Lydia leap at the door, to shut the latch and fasten the bolt.

Outside, upstairs and downstairs were all dark.

Fenton, staggering, fell against the wall. He felt his way along it, attempting to cool his head. Presently he shouted for Giles.

Giles, white face below red hair, materialized out of darkness and carried a candle in each hand.

"What is't, sir? Some new—" Giles paused.

"Put a light in my study, old friend. Then fetch a decanter of our best canary. No, stay: of our best brandy."

"Sir! If I might . . ."

Fenton merely looked at him, and Giles dematerialized down the stairs.

After a time, while Fenton mopped sweat from his forehead, he felt more steady. He groped his way to the stairs, and went down by holding the baluster rail. The door of his study was open. On the great polished desk, amid the walls of books, a taper in a silver holder burned unsteadily. He sat down in the desk chair.

"I love her," Fenton said aloud to the candle flame. "The fault was mine. I own it. I must in some fashion mend her humour. Yet . . ."

Before him in imagination floated the face of Meg York. He could not resist Meg, and now he knew it. But why?

Her intense fleshly allure? Yes; but Lydia had that too. True, he had never known Meg in the sense he had known Lydia; but she must be maddening if she surpassed the Puritan girl. Or was it Meg's fire, her elusiveness, her utter disregard for what she did—that touch of devil's brush which many men have sought and some found?

But now there was a new quality straining them towards each other. Meg was Mary Grenville. He had seen her face, heard her voice, which had been so much disguised by the pronunciation of this age as her appearance had been disguised by hair style and costume. Fenton in his old life had never seen Ma—no, call her Meg!—with her hair round her face, or ever particularly observed her figure.

Besides, she was a fellow-wanderer in another century. For all her swashbuckling, she must feel frightened and lonely. She was the daughter of his old friend. . . .

Fenton brought his fist down on the table.

"I must not see her again!" he said aloud.

In his pocket he had the paper on which Meg had written her two addresses. Fenton stretched out his hand to burn the folded paper in the candle flame, and then stopped.

"How did Mary Grenville become Meg York?" he thought frantically. "Why is she here? All my dozens of questions she either evaded or said I should know the answer soon. And these answers I must have!"

For this reason (or so he told himself) he got up quickly. He went to a bookcase, took down a volume of Tillotson's sermons—what a windy hypocrite Tillotson was!—and put the paper between its leaves. Closing the book, he replaced it and had gone back to his chair when Giles entered.

On a tray Giles carried a candle, a flat clear-glass decanter of Nantes brandy on which the light struck with brown-amber iridescence, and a clouded glass. You drank brandy neat. Everyone, from the Royal Society to the meanest man, knew that all water was undrinkable save for animals.

Giles hovered for a moment, making ugly faces.

"Now, then," said Giles, "if you have a mind to—"

"Much thanks; but I need no advice. I shall not be drunk for a night, much less a week."

When Giles had gone, Fenton poured the glass nearly full. After a few deep swallows, slowly, Nantes brandy began to deaden the ache that concerned Lydia.

Tomorrow he would somehow reconcile matters with her. Never, by God, would he be unfaithful! And this nonsense of poisoning? This was what he feared, and feared horribly. But it could not happen. Round Lydia he had set too many guards.

In front of him, as though in clear handwriting, he could see the record of his life as Sir Nicholas Fenton: *Born 25th Dec'r, 1649; Dy'd 10th August, 1714.* He and Lydia would see unroll the pageant of those times, in the main of treachery and turbulence, yet once or twice with a flame of grandeur; and, at least, he could die happy just before the first damned Hanoverian came forever to disgrace the British throne.

Seeking such happy things, Fenton realized that the brandy had well fuddled his wits.

But they must not remain fuddled, or he could not protect Lydia. Rising unsteadily to his feet, gripping the edge of the desk, he put a firm hand on the candle holder. Gritting his teeth, he lighted his own way up to his bedroom; he staggered only when he closed the door.

Then, blowing out the candle, he fell into sleep across the bed.

Next morning, though he had a throbbing head and a stomach of nausea, the hot strong sunlight dissipated doubts and made the preceding night's quarrel seem foolish.

After a good bath, after being shaved by Giles and permitting Giles to dress him more elaborately than usual (to Giles's high approval), he felt in the best of spirits. His toothbrush, carefully whittled by Big Tom, set firm with such good bristles that Fenton dared not ask where they came from, lay on the dressing table with its handle painted bright red.

A second one, painted blue, was on Lydia's dressing table. Though he could get no toothpaste, a scented soap had to serve; and it at least made the mouth feel clean.

"B—bl—b!" Lydia would say, looking reproachfully at him with the brush in her mouth.

This morning, as usual, he hastened down to the kitchen and swallowed draughts of Lydia's morning chocolate before it was sent up to her. Since a new cook had not been found, Nan Curtis was elevated to that position; she, utterly trustworthy, was so closely watched by Big Tom that more than once she burst into tears.

Then Fenton accompanied Bet, the new maid, while she carried

185

the chocolate service upstairs. He made certain that no person came near it. Though still scraped raw by Lydia's outburst last night, he had prepared his apology when Bet knocked at the door.

"Yes?" Lydia's voice, rather eager. Then she stopped. There was a sort of hauteur in what she did not say.

"It's Bet, my lady. With the chocolate."

"Oh." There was a long pause. Then the voice shook a little. "Is my husband by you?"

"Yes, my lady."

"Then be good enough, sweet Bet, to tell him that his absence is more prized than his company."

Fenton closed his fists and drew the breath deep in his lungs.

"Do as the damned woman bids you," Fenton said loudly and clearly to Bet.

And he walked away down the passage, stepping loudly on the boards. Out of the corner of his eye, in a darkish corner, he noticed Judith Pamphlin, arms folded, still watching. Much as he disliked her, still she was an added guard.

Punctually at noon, as always, he took a key and opened the locked cabinet in an under part of one bookcase in the study. With another very small key he unlocked the book of days, which he had never shown to another person.

Dipping the pen carefully in the ink, he wrote the date *June 6th*, though he did not consider it was past until midnight.

Four more days. . . .

He could defeat it. He knew that. *June 10th* would finally be crossed off. Great as was his annoyance with Lydia, he loved her too much to neglect anything. In his mind he tested his safeguards, and decided to double them; but he could see no flaw.

Nothing happened that hot day, Lydia refusing food and Fenton austerely doing the same. There arrived a courteous, almost humble note from the proprietors of Spring Gardens, countersigned by Thomas Killigrew, Esq., Master of the Revels to His Majesty. The note mentioned some slight damage, and begged to present its account. Though the bill was far too large, Fenton paid it by return messenger to be rid of the matter.

By nightfall, when the candles were lighted, there was no change. Fenton sat in his study, first reading Montaigne, who is soothing, and then Ovid, who is not. Slapping shut the book, Fenton made his decision.

186

Quietly he went down into the kitchen, from which he fetched a small axe with a short handle. Quietly he went upstairs, holding the axe behind his back. A few wall candles burned, and he could clearly see Lydia's bedroom door.

With two blows of the axe, which crashed and reverberated through the house, he smashed the bolt inside the door. One blow exploded the latch. Calmly, as though with artistic neatness, he broke off the hinges so that the door toppled into the room.

"Now attend to me, woman—!" he began, and stopped as though a cavalry charge had met only cloud.

Sitting up in bed, on the far side of it, Lydia was stretching out her arms to him. Tears ran down her cheeks, and her mouth trembled. He raced round to the other side of the bed, and their embrace grew chaotic.

" 'Twas all my fault!" both cried at once. Whereupon a listener could have heard no distinguishable word in the babble, since both talked at once, each pouring recriminations on himself or herself. Fenton called himself, and Lydia called herself, what amounted to lepers, pariahs, creatures so vile as to be unspeakable even in decent human sight.

In the passage, Giles patiently and sardonically affixed a large piece of tapestry over the open doorway, tapping nails so lightly that even Judith Pamphlin did not hear him, and wondering how long it would take Big Tom to mend the door.

From furious reconciliation, in all its aspects, they passed on to the tenderness which is the crown of all reconciliation, speaking together in low voices long after the last taper had burnt down to a blue spark and puffed out.

They told themselves how foolish they had been, and Lydia sobbed. They swore eternal love so many times that it cannot be counted. They swore that never again, never under any circumstances, would they quarrel again; never, never. . . .

Well, we all know it. Forever it is whispered in the ear of time. Yet its sincerity, for the time being at least, is just as poignant in any age.

"With all your heart, Nick?"

"With all my heart, Lydia."

Then, on the following morning, they lounged abed until past noon. Fenton had to go into the City on business in the afternoon. What he noted in his diary was the 7th of June.

It was an oppressive day, overcast with grey cloud, too hot for the time of year. Several times he heard what sounded like a commotion in the stable yard, and he sent word to inquire about it. As a rule he kept away from the stables. Being in his old life only a tolerable horseman, he did not know horesflesh as Sir Nick would know it. He feared a bad blunder.

Dick, the stableboy, reported that one of the coach horses was a-ailing, but nothing horse doctor couldn't cure. Fenton ordered his black mare, Sweetquean, to be saddled and brought round to the front door.

Since by some (to him) miracle, Big Tom had repaired the shattered bedroom door before noon, he hastened up for last instructions.

"Fasten the bolt," he said, "and open this door to no one. Should one knock without replying, cry out of the window to Whip, the coachman, or Job, the groom, bidding them come in haste with cudgels and faggot bats. Your promise?"

"Oh, I will! I will!" said Lydia, in a passion of meekness. But she crept closer to him, head down. "Nick! As touches her." Still she would not say Meg's name, or raise her head. "Didst not truly desire to—"

"No!" he assured her. By this time he believed it himself.

There was a broad sweep of earth before the front door, and a wide gap in the lime trees for the convenience of coaches. Fenton, mounting Sweetquean and taking the reins from Dick, went off by devious directions to spare the mare's legs among Strand and City crushings.

He would not have gone at all, except that he wanted a real cook, preferably a Frenchwoman. Though Nan Curtis did her best, Fenton longed for one who could prepare a meal and not murder it. Well he foresaw another domestic riot, but he must meet it.

At Will's coffeehouse, where he had once glanced in briefly to see Glorious John, red-faced, smoking his long pipe in the chair of honour, he had met one who evidently had been a friend, a youngish man of science named Mr. Isaac Newton. Mr. Newton had told him of an elderly Frenchwoman, once in bygone days cook to the Comte de Grammont himself, who might be found at an address in Fleet Street.

So he galloped the long, semirural length of the Oxford Road, with Tyburn Gallows in the open field far behind. Sweetquean danced along Holborn, slowing now over a long run of vehicles, until Fenton's ears, and especially nose, told him they were nearing Snow Hill.

Then he turned right, southwards, down narrow little ways until he found Madam Taupin's lodgings in a tolerably clean brick house in Fleet Street. Outside, when they talked, they could hear the roaring of Fleet Ditch as the refuse of many kennels poured into it down Snow Hill.

It took Fenton a very long time to persuade Madam Taupin. She was a small woman, with so much air and grace of deportment that Fenton put forth his lordliest manners and won her heart. She shrank from the position, having been not very well treated (you understand, monsieur?).

When he eventually persuaded her to take the position on June 12th, and rode back homewards, it was growing dark. Not only actual darkness, but the strange sky like a curdled sea, and puffs of air like puffs out of an oven. A storm hovered, but would not break.

When he returned home, he found Lydia, still soft-eyed from a nap, dressing to sup. After dark, mysterious draughts and currents crept into the house.

Fenton, going down to the study to glance at some accounts Giles had prepared, found the light so unsteady that he kindled eight tapers; yet their flames sputtered or widened and would not burn clear. That sense of oppressiveness hung over him, as over so many.

Within ten minutes Giles came into the study. At the beginning Giles's face was expressionless. He walked slowly up to the desk and delivered his news.

"Sir," he said bluntly, "the dogs are poisoned."

CHAPTER XIV

THE BATTLE

OF PALL MALL

"DOGS?" Fenton repeated dully.

In the draught a paper fluttered out of his hand and went a-sail into a candle flame. Giles's bony fingers pinched it out amid sparks as it caught fire.

"Since I must be precise of speech with so learned a man," retorted Giles, always at his worst when he carried bad news, "I will be more plain. I had reference to the mastiffs."

Fenton started to his feet.

"When? How? Why?"

"Sir, 'twas done last night. —Nay, don't fall a-cursing that we durst not tell you. There is yet hope."

"Hope? How?"

"Job ran like mad to fetch Mr. Milligrew, best advised of all for knowledge of dogs and horses; ay, thrice better than your ignorant doctor of physick, who knoweth but how to kill. Well! Mr. Milligrew thinks, in eventual, he may save Thunder and Lion and perchance even Bare-behind, though all are in sore plight. Whiteboy, the terrier, is not permitted abroad at nightfall. But Greedy, as you may judge by his name, is dead."

Fenton sat down behind the desk, pressing his hands over forehead and periwig.

"How was't done?"

"Poisoned meat," replied Giles. "Thus!"

190

From where he had been concealing it, behind his back, Giles brought a greasy piece of paper. On it lay a piece of good butcher's meat, raw, bitten-off but untouched, and half-smothered in white powder.

"Arsenic once more," said Fenton, and stabbed at it with a quill pen. "Come: I could make you a crude test to prove it so. But observe! It is odourless and powdered. There are no (in chymist's term) crystals of other white poisons: as antimony or strychnine. No! Here's arsenic."

Giles folded his arms. "If that be so, what then?"

"Why, it means I have been a fool!"

"Oh, questionless," murmured Giles, folding his arms. "But—as how?"

"In this," replied Fenton. He rose from his chair and began to stride up and down, amid the blowing candle flames and the thick heat. "My concern, all of it, is to protect my lady wife from poison. I have searched, studied, made scrutiny of all inside this house. Would any do her harm?"

"Nay," said Giles, looking down at his shoes. "My lady is much beloved."

"And therefore am I a fool. Mark it: I have stood on my guard against those inside the house. Not once have I thought to seek outside. To seek a friend—"

"A friend?"

"A pretended friend. Let that friend call out, so that the mastiffs may hear his—or her—voice; let them lick his—or her—hand; thus there will be no noise."

Giles altered his position. His eyes narrowed, and he stroked his long chin as though he wore a beard.

" 'Tis common practice," he admitted, "among fuglemen or those now called burglars. Yet from this house no thing, nay, not as much as a spoon, hath been stolen away. Wherefore poison the dogs?"

"As thus. Tonight, the mastiffs; they must not be there tonight. Last night they were poisoned. Last night someone was here to do a work as old as Rome; older, for aught I know. In fine: to take a wax or soap mould to the lock of some door, perhaps the front door. A locksmith can grind you the key in one day . . . ."

"And this night?"

"Why, someone (it may be our good Kitty, who was cook and

fed all the dogs) will be here for quiet plunder in jewel boxes, as well as to conceal some heavy dose of poison for my wife. Have I read it aright?"

Giles, though for some reason he winced at the name of Kitty, looked back at Fenton and shook his head.

"Nay, sir," Giles answered quietly. "You are too much caught up with my Lady Fenton. You have not sounded the depth of this matter."

Fenton did not reply, but merely nodded with a gleam of anticipation in his eye. All the mysterious draughts, which blew the flames, had died away into heavy sluggish air. Fenton returned to his chair.

"Sir Nick, this runs deeper than a matter of poison. 'Tis a matter politic; it may involve the throne itself! Here's my Lord Shaftesbury, from what I hear, building up from small starts a vast Opposition or Country party, their mark a green ribbon, and in especial with an eye to rousing the mobile party . . ."

"Call it mob, Giles. Soon all will call it so."

"Well! And here you, you alone, who would shout 'God for King Charles!' amid a hundred of them! Each time they have struck at you, or you at them, you have held them up to mockery and ridicule. Such high-placed men of the Country party must not be so dealt with, lest their power diminish. They must make an end on't."

Giles, rather white, backed away from the desk. Fenton raised his head. Giles, startled, saw that his master wore a strange smile, and that there was an anticipatory glitter in his eyes.

"To deal plainly," said Fenton, picking up a quill pen, "they must attack in force and crush me. To deal even more plainly, they must attack my house and draw me out."

"Sir, I do not say this will happen. Only that it may. But if so: ay, tonight!"

"For my part," said Fenton leisurely, "I pray they will make a tack at it. For I have devoted some thought to this business . . ."

"What?"

"And I have devised a small plan. Come; look across my shoulder while I sketch."

Giles moved round. Drawing a sheet of parchment towards him, Fenton dipped pen in ink and sketched rapidly what looked like a minor military campaign. As he sketched, his quick, terse words stabbed at every point in explanation. At the end he wrote down five names, including his own. He paused there, hesitantly, as Giles whistled.

192

"And yet . . . " Fenton said in despondency.

"Come, sir! What is't?"

"These men," said Fenton, pointing towards the names, "are my servants. Can I, durst I, ask them to risk their lives?"

Giles nimbly ran round to the other side of the desk and faced him in amazement.

"Why, 'tis required by all masters," he said, rather puzzled. "And here! Sir, have you once considered what your servants, men or women, think of you? Or have thought of you since a certain date," and Giles's eyes slid round. "To be exact, the 10th of May last?"

Fenton's laced band seemed to grow tighter round his throat. He did not look up, but made aimless marks with the pen. May 10th had been the first day of his new life in old London. But Giles, in a new kind of passion, spoke quietly.

"Since then," he demanded, "has any heard the old, 'Curse thee, what good art thou?' or 'Rot th' soul, be off!'—with a bottle flung at the head to follow? Or floggings with the whip, even the cat-of-nine-tails, for the lightest offence? Or maniac ravings in the stables, and one near murder?

"Since then," pursued Giles, "have you brought the lowest of bawds from Whetstone Park to this house? And bidden them carouse, drunken and naked, singing songs in your own withdrawing room facing the street? Whilst you sat back, with a bottle in either hand, and sang with them?"

Fenton's hand went up in protest, though still he did not raise his eyes.

"No more!" he said, thinking what Sir Nick must have been like. "Forebear; I command it!"

"As pleaseth you, sir."

Giles lifted his shoulders. Both were silent for a moment.

"Yet still I ask," Giles burst out, "what of those same servants now? They have all they desire, and more. In this house flogging is abolished. The stablemen have but to request; you grant, at the small severity of a bath. Some saw you pluck the secret from poisoned sack posset as though you had eyes could look through brick walls; they saw the slut Kitty conveyed not to the gallows, but set free with a couple of guineas in her hand. Sir, they would die for you! And have I no gratitude?"

"For the last time, leave off!"

193

Still Fenton did not look. He was wondering, from that curious glance of Giles at mention of May 10th, how much Giles knew or guessed. And, above all, Lydia! No; Lydia could not have guessed.

"Why, then," said Giles, "I alter my discourse. But, sir, one thing must be altered!"

He stabbed a bony forefinger at the five names Fenton had written on the edge of the parchment.

"Sir Nick, you well know me for near a fine swordsman. My dagger play, in old time, hath been considered even better. Why is my name not there? Why is it not sixth among those to defend this house?"

"Giles, Giles, you are not . . . not youthful. I observed it when we were first at practice. This business may be long."

Giles drew himself up.

"Sir, you cannot prevent it," he said quietly. "This night, God willing, I stand at your side."

Something stung at the back of Fenton's eyes, and he put up a hand to shield them. Though nearly all of the old Professor Fenton had gone, enough remained to feel heavily embarrassed, to look in any direction save at Giles.

"Well, well!" he growled, and quickly wrote Giles's name at the end of the list. "There is little now to be done. Pray go belowstairs; acquaint Big Tom, Whip, Job, and Harry with our scheme. Let the weapons stand ready as I have chosen them."

All Giles's briskness had returned.

"Shall I order the shutters to be put up, sir?"

"No! Never! That will warn them we expect them, if indeed they come. Every man to his bed, until roused. Let Harry stand watch; all lights gone by ten of the clock. And—and no word of this to my lady."

"Sir, that is understood."

"As for the mastiffs . . . "

"Now, come sir! They are poisoned; of no use to us."

"Am I not sensible of that?" demanded Fenton, throwing down his pen and leaping up. "But have them brought up to the withdrawing room . . . ay, carrot-pate, I said withdrawing room . . . where they may be in comfort, and Mr. Milligrew as well!"

Always, when Lydia's image came before his mind, the old Sir Nick maddened him.

"Have not others, called human beings but far beneath our mastiffs for sense and decency, used that room to be 'comfortable'? A truce to your impertinence; I'll hear no more of it; go!"

And Giles ran.

Fenton fired the pen at the desk, and then went upstairs to wash for supper.

Without doubt, he decided, this notion of a night attack was madness: inspired only by thick heat, a storm that would not break, and a sense as of lice crawling along open nerves. But it was a possibility. As for Lydia . . .

When he ate with Lydia, in the shining cavern of silver with the portraits, he tried to be too merry and laugh too much. Lydia, though she dutifully laughed with him, kept her blue eyes fixed steadily on his face, searching for his mood.

"Nick," she said, "is it danger? Are those your thoughts?"

"In all honesty, no." He smiled at her, pressing her hand against the table. "At least, I swear there is no danger attending you."

"But I know that," protested Lydia, in genuine surprise. "Are you not here?"

Again Fenton lowered his head, his hands out to cut straight portions from a vile omelette prepared for her.

"Lydia, dear," he said, "this I beg: be not deceived by these fine names they give me. I am the poorest and merely most lucky man who ever tried to stand on his guard in three positions at once. Never hold me high! Think only . . . "

But Lydia did not hear him.

"You would ask me some question!" she said suddenly, and drew in her breath. "Dear heart, what is it?"

Her instinct was near the uncanny; again the arrow went dead to the target. He was wondering how much she knew, or how much she had been hurt, by the former Sir Nick. But he laughed, and swore, by any oath she liked, there was no question.

"Well, then!" said Lydia, relieved but still doubtful. She glanced over her shoulder, as though to make sure none could hear. "Promise you'll not jest or make sport of me?"

"Have I ever done so?"

"For days," said Lydia in a low voice, "I have had a fancy. I think that I am going to die, and soon."

Fenton's knife dropped clattering on the table.

"Lydia! Never say that!"

195

" 'Tis but a fancy," answered Lydia, her eyes seeming to grope their way. "I do not wish to die, now that you and I have found each other." She turned to him. "Tell me this is folly!"

He told her. He told her at length, as in different fashion he had told her before, and presently he saw reassurance, even laughter, return to her.

"Foh, I am a simpleton!" said Lydia, tossing her head. "'Tis gone; and I'll forget it."

But Fenton could not forget.

That night they went to bed before ten o'clock, in Lydia's room as always. Still the sky was a hollow of thick heat; outside the windows, each leaf stood as still as though limned there.

Before going to bed he made certain preparations with old clothes and weapons, setting them ready. Since neither he nor Lydia troubled their heads about night habit, he could be dressed in a few seconds. Lydia watched him, but did not speak.

Both were soon asleep, though he fretted and fumed. One thing he could never do, with cajoleries or mirth or plain cursing; and that was to persuade Lydia to open a window at night. She swore, sometimes on her knees, that it would kill them. The uneasiness pressed down. Once, as he felt himself falling into a doze, he thought he saw a distant flash of lightning. . . .

Then his blackened dreams grew distorted; not quite nightmares, yet menaces he could neither see nor touch, but always hear.

One scene, briefly, went blurred and twisted through his mind. He heard, amid much noise, the thudding chest notes of a railway engine. The guard's whistle blew. He was at a carriage door, leaning out, in some kind of soup-plate helmet. As he moved along, a solemn-faced, pretty girl about fifteen years old, with black hair and grey eyes, was handing him a bunch of flowers and a silver-wrapped ounce of tobacco.

Blurred, the face swept behind, as others milled about him. "Major Fenton?" "Yes?" "Telegram, sir." He could recall his fingers opening out the rough whitish paper of the telegram and the unsteady words, "Fear shall miss you in crowd at station had flowers tobacco but if miss you all good wishes your friend Mary Grenville."

And, inexplicably wound through all this, there was a great noise of voices singing to music. It was a cheerful song, roared out with

196

mighty cheerfulness; yet underneath every word ran a strain of heart-break. So faint, so far away, he could barely hear the words.

"Pack up your troubles in your old kit-bag,
And smile, smile, smile . . . !"

The train still rumbled on. Somehow the sky was pitch-black. His eyes strained close to the luminous hands and numbers of a wrist watch. His feet were near the top of a muddy stepladder, or some kind of ladder. In his right hand, held partly upwards, was a . . . no, not a revolver, but some pistol-like arrangement he must fire upwards. Some distance ahead, artillery opened with a bursting crash, and the sky went white. . . .

"Nick!" Lydia's voice clove through his dreams, shocking him awake.

Instantly he knew he was in the outward semblance of Sir Nick Fenton, and where he was. That noise had been a long peal of thunder. Since the bed curtains had not been drawn close, every window of Lydia's chamber had gone white with lightning.

He himself was half-sitting up, Lydia pressing his head to her breast, holding her arms tightly round him.

"Dear heart," she whispered, not quite steadily, "you did have such horrid dreams, and did speak in your sleep."

"Oh?" said Fenton, his breathing grown more quiet. "What did I say?"

"Nay, I am not sure." Lydia tried to laugh. " 'Twas English; yes, to be sure; but so quaint and strange there was but one part I could make out, where you seemed to speak to a parcel of men."

"What did I say?" he insisted.

Lydia's own quaint pronunciation stood out vividly against a background of what should have been ancient curtains and dead dust.

" 'We must pass the machine guns and the wire! But if you will look at this map . . . ' "

Fenton laughed inside himself. That was the time when lowly Major Fenton planned each move of the British and French break-through which nearly smashed Jerry in '16, and for which General Fathead-Fathead-What's-his-name got the credit. Fenton hated it. It was lost, gone, forgotten!

"Sweet heart," Lydia added quietly, "that was not the true reason I woke you."

"Well?"

"I think there are many men before this house, and they cry out."

197

Lydia's body was warm and damp. He kissed her once, and in the next second was on his feet on the floor, groping for clothes.

"Strike a light!" he said harshly.

He did not trouble with underlinen. He found old velvet breeches, and thrust his feet into them. *Scratch, scratch* went the point of the tinderbox; the grease-ignited flame went up, the taper kindled blue, then into a glow.

Fenton stamped into a pair of high, heavy riding boots. From them he had detached his usual light spurs; now he wore heavy spurs with large, sharpened rowels. He buckled on his sword belt, but he did not wear the customary belt or his beloved Clemens Hornn sword.

The two chains held a new scabbard with a blade somewhat longer and heavier, double-edged, with a ring-hilt. Ready to hand was a *main-gauche*, or left-hand dagger—from long ago, when his forebears had fought with sword and dagger—which tapered two feet to its point, with a fine, curved shell-steel guard over the hand.

This he thrust into his belt. Finally, in breeches pocket rested snugly a round, very heavy steel length of seven inches: the axle of a giant coach, for blows with the right hand.

"Why don't they call?" he demanded. "Where the devil is Giles?"

Before he could complete the sentence, there was a quick knock at the door. Lydia, drawing up the sheet, shrank back. Giles stood in the doorway, neat and prim, except with a bared sword in his right hand and another *main-gauche* dagger stuck into his belt.

But, more than this, Giles wore the old Cavalier helmet: not much changed, except for sharper line, in this present day of 1675. It was open-faced, with steel flaps over the ears; the flaps could be left undone or buckled under the chin.

"It is prepared," said Giles. "Sir, where is your helmet?"

And now the blood ran smoothly but hotly through Fenton's veins.

"D'ye think I'd wear a helmet to fight that scum?" he snarled. "Dignify the swine with military dress against them?"

"Sir, you have commanded the rest of us to wear helmets. In full melee, any stray cudgel may strike you down." From behind his back Giles took another helmet and held it out. "I feared this," he said.

"Giles," said Lydia, "give me the helmet."

Giles hurried forward and handed it to her. With one hand holding the sheet, Lydia stretched out her other arm and held the helmet towards Fenton.

198

"Wear it," she said. "For if you die, then must I die too. And not by hand of any rioter, but by my own."

There was a bursting crash of glass as a heavy stone struck the front window of the upstairs passage.

"*No Popery!*" bellowed a dozen voices, seeming far away. "*Death to Popery!*"

Without hesitation Fenton put on the helmet. The inside of its skull piece was heavily padded, with leather crossings to hold it firmly. To protect the back of the neck there were lines of linked steel tapering to a point: the lobster-tail. Fenton buckled the chin strap. Then, not troubling with shirt, he pulled on an old loose velvet coat.

"Now!" he said.

Hurrying out into the passage, he raced towards the front for a view of the attackers from the broken window.

"Sir, I count their numbers as—"

"A moment's peace, Giles!"

Fenton could see them fairly well. Towards the rear, they had for light a lanthorn stuck on a pole and a linkman's torch curling up yellow flame. They were spread out thickly and raggedly in front of the house in straight lines. On the other side of Pall Mall, which was tolerably wide for such a lane, there were houses or high-sloping banks.

In the front line, which had come no closer than within six feet of the lime trees with their broad opening, Fenton counted eight swords. Many swords were raised in the centre; but they were useless for close fighting. There were bristles of heavy cudgels, innumerable stones. But the weight of the cudgels, Fenton rejoiced to see, was not in the front line or on their right flank.

"No popery!"

"*Hang the warlock!*"

"*Let him stand out! Wizard, Papist for his mistress, son of a Papist whore!*"

As they saw two figures at that window, their shouts volleyed out again. Their hatred was a physical wave; it could almost be smelt. But, like most mobs, they hesitated and snarled. They would not yet come closer than six feet of the opening in the lime trees.

Fenton, his brain swiftly sorting out each detail, had put all into place.

"Downstairs!" he said. And, as they hurried down, "Where's the rain? I hear none."

199

"Sir, no drop is fallen! If we stay ten minutes more, we shall fight in a great store of rain on a road like hasty pudding!"

Beginning with what seemed like splintering echoes, a great crash of thunder exploded above the house; every window stood out ghostly white.

But downstairs there was no light, save for the glimmer of one taper in Fenton's study. As he opened the door, four helmets turned slowly round, with the eyes beneath them seeming changed and evil.

Every man carried the rounded, murderous coach axle in his pocket. Big Tom, whose helmet had an old-style nose guard, carried a length of wood not as long or heavy as a fire log, though it seemed so. His immense fingers went round it entirely, and a cudgel was stuck in his belt. He would swing the somewhat dwarfed log, parallel to the ground, like a bat.

Whip, the heavy-shouldered coachman, carried a log much like it; there was an anticipatory grin on his blue-chinned face. Job, the groom, had once been a juggler at a travelling fair; he carried two very heavy cudgels, being able to hit with lightning speed from either hand, crosshand, or both together.

The third swordsman, including Fenton and Giles, was young Harry. All four helmets had an ugly shine, despite dark spots or rust stains, as Fenton came in to give them last orders.

"I will be short," he said. "But hear this! *They* attack us. We are protected. D'ye know what'll happen to them? They'll hang, every man jack of them! Fear not to kill them!

"There's but one way to deal with what I call *mob*. They hang back at first, if they have no leader; you hear them out there? When I give the signal, do you instantly strike! You are not come to parley. You are not come for gentle pushes. You are come to crush and destroy and kill! Is that plain?"

A low growl went through the group, and the candle flame was reflected in their eyes.

"Good; enough!" said Fenton, and flung a pile of books off the desk, amid dust and thuds, so that he could speak to them more closely above the table. "We make sure our design is set. First! I go out alone, and spit in their faces."

Young Harry, with sword and dagger, cried out at this.

"Sir, for God's sake! We are six men; they are more than sixty! Can we fight six against sixty?"

"Ay, and two against two hundred!" snarled Fenton, and whirled on him. "If you have no stomach for it, then go back and sleep amid the women!"

And now, from under those old helmets about Fenton, rose an almost animal snarl. Giles, standing quietly with motionless sword, might well have thought the old Sir Nick returned.

But Giles would have been wrong. Fenton was whipping these men, according to his plan, into the savagery of fighting animals.

"Stay, where was I? Let the lily-livered bitch's son sleep where he please!"

"Sir, I will stand!"

"Then hark to me! Thus! I go out alone. The house is dark. I set open the front door. Now the three who carry log bats and cudgels . . . we'll call them woodmen; 'tis nothing accurate; no matter! Tom, Whip, Job! Move now to my left!"

They did so. Big Tom's eyes, out of matted hair and helmet, had acquired a reddish shine. Slowly Job moved the two large cudgels. Whip smiled.

"When I am halfway towards the opening between the lime trees, you three woodmen slip from the house; all quiet; no sound. None will see you if you crouch down; they have but a watchman's lanthorn and a linkboy's light. You will move on my left side; my *left*. When you have come to the first tree at the street, crouch down unseen and wait my sign. Understood?"

"Ay, sir!" three voices together snarled back the answer.

"Now. Giles and Harry! You, with myself, are our three swordsmen. The same applies to you two as to the other three, except that you will be on my right. My *right*. Understood?"

Two replies shot back at him. From upstairs there was a loud, long run of clatterings as a shower of stones struck front windows, accompanied by an overset of furniture and yells from outside.

"Be easy!" said Fenton, and every man stood motionless. "They've not yet the stomach for a dash at it, else they'd not throw stones. Here's our design near complete!

"Here am I, in the middle facing out. On my left," his arm moved, "three concealed woodmen. On my right," again his arm moved, "two concealed swordsmen. When you see me raise my sword high in the air—*thus!*—both groups, crouched down, will turn (woodmen left, swordsmen right) round the tree, and creep out between the mob and
201

the trees. Be sure there is room for you. If possible, you may even try to seem part of the mob.

"When you move out, not an eye will see you. I'll contrive it; I swear this! All eyes will be on my upraised sword. That is all, save I hope you have not forgot your final order? Woodmen?"

He swung round to Whip, Job, and Big Tom.

"Nay, sir," snapped Whip, smiling as he fingered his log bat. "When you cry, 'Let go!' then we three turn their right flank,"—out went his left hand, facing him—"and turn it back, so we force all round to meet us in the narrower width of the lane."

"Good! Swordsmen?"

"When you shall cry, 'Swords!' then all of us leap at the line together," said a now-tense Giles, "and God for King Charles!"

"Good. Now but a final word to the woodmen. Never do you strike, you logmen who will catch three, or four, or five person at once, never do you strike at their middles or their chests. They may seize the log and pull it down. Let fly always, with all strength, at their faces; split me their skulls and open their faces like a pulped orange. Cudgeller with two clubs, kill by head-smashing with every stroke. When you are drawn into the mob, as we may all be, let go your log; meet them with steel coach axles and extra cudgels. Have all here sharpened spur rowels, as I did order?"

There was a low, fierce hissing of assent.

"Should any catch at your feet, you'll know what to do by grinding the spur backwards. Swordsmen!"

"Ay, sir?"

"I do command you: fight as long as you may on the fringe of the mob. Else your swords will be useless. Give me no adroit play of the fencing school; give me but a dead man every time your sword or dagger plungeth out. If you be drawn inside, as you will be, let go your swords; use the iron bar for heads, but never let go the long dagger. Keep it below; never seen; always striking. Strike for the lower belly; strike everywhere and always! —Now I have done."

Fenton saw, in their eyes and mouths, that they were now wrought to the pitch. Already he had drawn his long, double-edged sword. He pulled the main-gauche dagger from his belt, settling his left hand round the grip and his thumb in its thumb groove.

"Now I go out; stand ready," he said.

At the doorway, as he opened the door, he swung round once more.

202

"Never falter. Never cease to strike. This mob is a tyrant, is he? God's body, let's adventure it! Three swordsmen and three woodmen shall bring the tyrant down!"

And he closed the door behind him, in a pitch-dark hall. As he strode towards the front door, he had little hatred for mob in the abstract. What he saw before him were the Country party: rich, fat, landed gentlemen, who would upset the throne to gain more power and money—just as Pym and Hampden and Cromwell had done, more than a generation before—and whom Whig historians with flat lying sometimes called "the people of England."

People of England!

Fenton threw open the front door. The blast of shouting, as lanthorn and link torch picked out his figure, rolled over him like a wind. Two heavy stones, to which he paid no attention, whizzed past shoulder and head.

As he strolled forward to meet them, he let out his voice at full power.

"A good damnation to ye, scum! What d'ye want?"

Again, as though rattling together like an avalanche, an enormous peal of thunder split above them. Down the lift of the lightning, far behind the backs of the mob, ran a white crooked bolt; all heard or saw the crack, sizzle, and white flare as it struck a tree.

Fenton stood motionless, halfway between road and house, swinging sword and dagger with true pleasure, until that was over. Then he walked straight to the open space between the limes, looking out over them contemptuously.

"Where's your leader?" he demanded. Then, bellowing it out: "Stand back!"

The impact of personality, the bolt drive of one who knows his mind, will send even an overwrought mob slightly backwards. The straggling line, still six feet from the lime trees, moved instinctively back two paces, while a woman's voice screamed at them not to move.

Fenton, who sensed that his three woodmen were now on his left, the two swordsmen on his right, rejoiced that there was more room for them.

"Where's your leader, I say?" he shouted. Then up went his sword, high up, glittering in the light of a bobbing lanthorn and an unsteady link light.

Every eye was fixed on it for a moment, as eyes had been fixed on

203

his bared teeth and his inflamed eyes below the line of the helmet. He could barely see the crouched line of shadows which ran out, left and right, in front of the trees.

"I am the leader, sir," snapped a harsh voice from the eight swordsmen huddled together too close on the right.

Out stepped a man who was fat-bodied but very lean and dignified of face, an ideal Country party member, with fine clothes and with a green ribbon in his hat. The crowd half-stilled as he spoke out.

"I am Samuel Warrender, Esquire," he announced. "Are you a Papist, or no?"

"No! But your behaviour tonight is like to make me one!"

"Have you knowledge to foretell the future?"

"Yes!" bellowed Fenton, at the top of his voice.

He felt, he knew himself, the chill of superstitious dread which made cold the hearts of them all. Now, now, was the time to strike.

"Then you'll have war?" shouted Fenton, lifting his sword again. "Let go!"

Almost unseen, appearing gigantic in those shifting dim lights, three figures well spaced apart arose in front of the mob's right flank— to be exact, the left side as you faced the line. Two log bats, six feet long, smashed round from the shoulder, as two cudgel clubs in the hands of one man began to dance like the legs of murder.

The first line hardly even saw what came at them. All were concentrated on Fenton. But, as the second line glimpsed their attackers, one inhuman screech of terror went up from them. Instantly the log bats swung again; the cudgel clubs never ceased as Job danced along the line.

"Back!" yelled one long-legged man in a fustian cap, who had tried and failed to climb a steep bank on the far side of the street.

"Move back! Move back!"

"Back towards Charing Cross!"

Now the dead or badly wounded, before the woodmen attackers, either sprawled backwards or fell face forwards through the broad spaces between the three woodmen, amid a rising cloud of reddish-brown dust. Though dust settled on the blood, it was well if an onlooker did not see their faces. One man, in periwig and gold buttons, dived forward, for some unknown reason clutching the gold chain to his gold watch. He ran a few low steps, watch and chain flying out, until he dropped head down, face snake-veined with blood in the dust cloud.

Meanwhile, those on the left wing—or right side as Fenton faced them—hardly knew what was happening until a series of shouts in the din told them.

Fenton, as cool and detached as he had ever been, stood as though he held a watch.

"Right!" he thought, as the second hand ticked into place.

And out he ran, past the front of the crooked line, with Giles following and then young Harry.

Bang went a heavy club, thudding harmlessly off a woodman's helmet. The mob's wing had now been turned back so that it stood facing them across the road; and, as they pivoted back, automatically the swordsmen's wing turned with them.

Now the position was altered. Now Fenton's men faced a much narrower line, cramped up together, in the width of a none-too-wide lane. In the mob's original position, their line had been too thick and stretched across the lane in front of the house. They could have surrounded and crushed any force which ventured out.

But now it was different. Now the mob line, though still too wide to be covered by six men unless they hammered death across it, was huddled and packed with their backs to the east. . . .

"*Swords!*" shouted Fenton.

And six helmeted attackers, as one man, struck the line at once.

So vicious was the spring, so damn-you determined were the attackers, that they sent the mob line reeling back twenty paces in half as many seconds. The lantern swung wildly on its pole, the yellow-blue link light streamed out. Though no thunder could be heard amid those cries, the lightning cut out harsh, hard lines of eyes and mouths.

Eight swordsmen leaped out at guard against three, and all eight were down, dead or writhing, in shortly over a minute. It is only fair to say that all were none too expert, save one who gave Fenton six passes and nearly thirty seconds—until Fenton broke his feint with a time thrust and ran him through the throat.

Unfortunately, the first dash at Fenton was made by Samuel Warrender, Esquire. Mr. Warrender went out at full lunge, not well, at the belly; Fenton heard the hiss as he parried; then he shortened his sword and stabbed the Green Ribboner through the heart. Mr. Warrender went forward on the ground, twisting like a trodden worm.

Now the swordsmen, leaping over the fallen and kicking back with spurs at hands which would upset them, struck at the mob itself, which either stepped back or ran out to fight murderously with heavy

205

cudgels. Giles, cool and methodical, never smote out with sword or dagger without finding a mark. Harry, pale but with tight-set teeth, plunged in a-slashing with his double-edged blade; they saw it glitter overhead, and glitter again.

But now the attack was almost halted; the mob began to turn.

Having lost their heads at the outset, they planned the counter-attack. Even their voices were stilled. Fenton, drawing back, saw that swords and daggers and cudgels were being passed hand over hand to the front.

They had discovered that the heaviest cudgel blow on a helmet will do little more than make its wearer's ears ring with dizziness. But, if you swung for the ear flap, it may break the jaw. Again, one or two might spurt through with daggers, to stab the woodmen from the back. . . .

He saw, with horror, that Big Tom was down. Far to his right there was a crack as Harry's sword snapped in two. He, Fenton, must guard the whole line.

Even as he thought that, a tatterdemalion with a shock of black hair wormed through the line with a dagger for Job. Job, white-faced and panting, did not see it. Fenton leaped sideways to the left. His short overarm cut nearly lopped the hand from Shock-hair's wrist; the latter stared at it unbelievingly. Another tatterdemalion, this one with a broad-leafed hat and spectacles, fought through with a sword.

Fenton's rapier went through him from side to side, so that the ring hilt thudded on his left ribs and the point jumped out on the other side. As Fenton yanked it out and back, the man raced forward, hat and spectacles flying off, and seemed to burrow his head into the ground.

Back Fenton raced through the dust fog. And he saw, now, that Harry was down too.

"You can't do it, sir!" Giles's voice said clearly from somewhere. "If we fight now, we must fight forward!"

Yes, Giles was right. Fenton, maddened, plunged straight at the mob.

For some moments, now, you might think he had been gripped by Sir Nick. His dagger with the curved hand guard, meant for straight left-hand thrusts, stabbed everywhere for the lower abdomen. Despite what he had told his own followers, the mob could not even bind his sword arm.

206

The razorish blade edge chopped, chopped, and chopped to the right; then out the point shot twice into faces, and back again to chop. They could not hold his arm; it was too elusive; and when many hands seized for the wrist, they found sharp steel which sent paralyzing pain in fire up their arms.

So vicious was his forward assault that the whole section of the line staggered back, driving their elbows into those behind to make room. A heavy cudgel, swung against his right ear flap, for some reason did not even stun him. A dagger, lunging at the left side, drew blood but only ripped through the loose velvet coat and tore part of it away.

Suddenly he found himself in an open half-circle, with not a soul at his back.

He could hardly draw breath; he could barely see them; but Fenton's brain was there.

All about them it was almost quiet, except for thuds and grunts and hisses. Pervading all in the dust was the harsh, raw stink of sweat which, more than any blood, thickens the nostrils in close fighting.

Distantly, from the Royal Mews, Fenton heard drums beating to arms. He did not want the aid of the military. Having outlined this battle plan, he *would not* let it fail.

"If I had a minute to think," he prayed in his mind. "Thirty seconds! Even fifteen...!"

To grasp an instant's thought, he tried what in his age of 1925 he would have called bluff. He raised his head, turning it partly over his right shoulder.

"Set loose the mastiffs!" he bellowed. "Thunder! Lion! Greedy! Bare-behind!"

The group in front of him quivered, but held their ground. He could pick out only a heavy man, in the stained blue smock of a butcher, who carried a club; and a little Alsatian, all dirt and hair, with the dagger that had missed.

"Kill the devil in velvet!" snarled the butcher. "Kill . . ."

Then he, like all others, stopped as if struck dumb.

All heard the din of barking down the road, and the smashing of glass. All saw the three great mastiffs, seeming even huger by that weird light, leap out from between the poplars. Greedy was dead, and could not hear. But Thunder, Lion, Bare-behind—poisoned, half-blind, and sick—the fighting watchdogs answered their call.

They smelt the spilled blood. They knew this was no half-playful

207

savaging in a garden. Brindled, tawny, and fawn-coloured, they leaped with bared teeth for their enemies between their friends, and they sprang high for the throat.

One last command Fenton gave.

"Forward!" And then: "God for King Charles!"

Up over the mob, like a man out of water, rose the helmet and whiskers and immense shoulders of Big Tom, lashing out like a Titan with cudgel and coach axle. Whip and Job, spent and tottering, felt the hot energy which is a man's second strength. Fenton plunged straight at the mob, sword and dagger a-glitter. Casting off all coolness or caution, Giles ran beside him.

And the mob broke.

For a few seconds Fenton did not notice it. One small figure detached itself at the back, and ran hard towards the thoroughfare of hay and grain, generally called Haymarket. One figure was followed by two or three, then half a dozen and a dozen.

The lanthorn toppled and fell. The torch sizzled out of sight. Men, seen as hardly larger than ants, were running hard towards Charing Cross or down King Street. When the second or third line melted behind them, the first line could only curse. With a last shower of clubs, cudgels, stones, daggers, and swords flung at the attackers, they turned and ran hardest of all.

"Hold!" cried Fenton, lifting his sword.

Just thirty seconds after they had struck the mob line with a second thunderbolt, not one enemy was left. The lane lay deserted, even eerie, save for the many dead and wounded behind them. Some of the wounded moaned, or tried to crawl. The torch, which would not burn out even under a light rain, sizzled yellow and blue on its side.

But what came to them, just as Fenton was giving instructions, was not a light rain. With a last explosive crack of thunder, the skies opened and the storm tore down.

CHAPTER XV

THEY SUP MERRY, WITH
RELATION OF A TEMPLE OF VENUS

ON the eve of the dreaded 10th of June, thought Fenton, it was ironic that they should have a gay little impromptu supper party.

At noon, when he wrote in the date of *June 9th* for today, he went to one of the open windows of the study, which faced out on green shrubbery, and smoked his long pipe until the bowl burnt his fingers. As he looked back on that fight on the night of the 7th, and what happened when the file of dragoons splashed up in the rain, he could smile again.

"Eh, well!" he could say, even though his body bruises made him stiff and ached when he moved, like an often-aching head. "A night, a night!"

It was now certain that Thunder, Lion, and Bare-behind would become well. Though Mr. Milligrew had cursed him in language unbecoming from him to a nobleman, still the vet admitted that the mastiffs' exercise might have helped to clear more poison from them.

Then Fenton had hurried to the kitchen, to see to the hurts of his small army.

He was greeted with plain, if very respectful, derision.

Big Tom had carried back, over his shoulder, the senseless figure of Harry. Harry's right arm and leg were broken, together with other injuries. Since Big Tom's speech was all but unintelligible except to Nan Curtis, he did not mention that he had gone down for a minute or two of the fight because of a cracked leg on one side and a sword-thrust through the other thigh.

Nevertheless, he carried Harry home just the same.

"Brisk lad," grunted Job, nodding towards Harry as the latter lay on the floor. "Only afeared o' seeming afeared; there's an end to't; three deaders on top of him when he went down."

Though all of them would admit to bruises, all denied broken bones: but Job had a broken collarbone and Whip several cracked ribs. Questioned closely by Fenton, they said they'd not have their bones plucked at by a double-damned chiurgien who knew nothing; best let be.

Whereupon Whip had an inspiration. If master had so much concern, let it be Mr. Milligrew. They'd trust *him*. Ecod, if the horse doctor knew so much about bonesetting with dogs and horses, wouldn't he know much more about men?

The florid-faced Mr. Milligrew, who wore a neat black coat, a waistcoat with pewter buttons, and partly polished riding boots, regarded a corner of the ceiling. But plainly he was in accord with the sentiment.

"Then look well to it, Mr. Milligrew!" said Fenton, being rewarded by a grave nod from the other. "Cure them, and I warrant you'll find me not ungenerous." Slowly, with a gratitude he could not express, he looked round. "Is there no small service I can render you? Come! Not in the least measure?"

"Ugh!" Big Tom, who had propped himself seated against the wall to ease his legs, now made a pleading speech.

All looked at Nan Curtis for translation.

"Sir . . ." Nan stammered, now tearful.

"Speak, woman!" insisted Fenton. "What did he say?"

"S-sir, he did say the leech would now put them all a-bed, as leeches do. He asketh whether they might not all, for this night, become as drunk as ever men were. He asketh that each may have beside his bed a quart pot of strong ale, wine, or whatever he may choose; and that I shall refill these as often as they cry out."

"By the body of Bacchus, yes!" returned Fenton. "Giles hath the key to the cellars; but tell him this is my command!"

From Big Tom, from Whip and Job rose such roars and howls of approval that they could be silenced only when Big Tom made another speech, now impassioned.

Again Fenton called for translation.

210

"Why, sir," said Nan, her cap all awry and her tears flowing, "'tis much the same thing over and over. 'Tis: God bless you. And: Such a fighting leader as yourself he never saw; and, if they but made you commander in chief, two or three British regiments would pursue King Looey out of France and the Netherlands too, and not stop till they'd stuck him upside down in the Emperor of Chaney's rice barrel."

And now the cheers and whoops and yells redoubled. Though Whip and Job were scarcely able to stand up, yet they stamped on the floor and beat with wooden spoons on everything available.

Fenton was taken aback. In this age, when laughter or tears or savagery bubbled all so close to the surface, he did not know what to say.

"Nay, I did but little. Yet I . . . I thank you. I . . . "

And he hastened up the stairs.

When he mounted the next flight, to the bedroom floor, Fenton found himself feeling very guilty, and tried to walk on tiptoe (in spurred boots) without sound. For a long time he had been conscious of blood dripping on his shoulder from a damaged ear where some cudgel had caught the ear flap of his helmet; his stiffening body bruises ached; but he had not a broken bone.

So he tiptoed, expecting that Lydia would raise a fuss. But Lydia, fully dressed, waited for him at the top of the stairs. She merely threw her arms round him, despite his warnings as to his condition, and said she knew it would happen thus.

"Nay, dear heart, I did watch from the window upstairs. And when I saw you destroy above an hundred of them—"

"Lydia, dear! The whole of them numbered only . . ."

But she would not have it. It was Lydia and Bet, skirts and sleeves tucked up, who raced up and down the stairs with buckets of hot or cold water for a bath. When he had taken advantage of that, and was propped in Lydia's bed with a silk bandage over his ear and a silk one across scratched ribs, he felt almost soothed except for an aching head.

He could hear the rain still driving on the roof, splashing against windows and hissing in chimneys. Lydia, curling up beside him, pursued her curiosity at last.

"—And when the great store of rain began to fall," she told him, "up rode a file of dragoons, with broad plumed hats instead of helmets. The leader held a light, and exchanged words with you."

"Why, as to that," Fenton laughed, "we must be respectful. They were the 'First the Royal Dragoons,' writ as I have spoken it, of the

King's new army. The leader of this group, an excellent fellow and by name Captain O'Callaghan, was as hot against the Green Ribbon as I could ever be. He told me: if I so desired, I could have every one of the wounded hung up in a halter. Yet he counselled caution."

"As why?" murmured Lydia.

"Well! His Majesty and the Duke of York mislike these public brawls . . ."

"H'm," said Lydia.

"In any event, my captain was persuasive. Let me not trouble my head in the matter. Let him have a word with the nearest justice. Meanwhile, he would cause to be brought two great wagons. Into one should be piled the dead, he telling his cornet the cornet 'must be sensible of some public place where they could be buried.' I knew not."

"He did mean the plague pits, sweet heart." And Lydia shivered.

"Is it so? Finally, into the second wagon should go the wounded who could move or speak or in injury not serious hurt, as also the badly wounded. The first parcel should be carried home, and warned that a rope awaited them for another show of riot. The second should be carried to Christ's Hospital, with the same warning into the ear of the chiurgien in chief. Then are all things smoothed, hushed, kept dark."

"What! And no credit or honour for you?"

"Lydia, what wish have I for these? And I would have no man hanged, could I prevent it." Fenton brooded. "Of dead and wounded together, according to Giles's accounting, there are thirty-one."

"Then there's the reason!" whispered Lydia, moving up beside him, and now with a shiver of different quality.

"Reason?"

"I saw it from the window. I saw Giles moving among the fallen, holding the officer's lanthorn in the rain. I saw him return, delivering the lanthorn to the cornet and a bit of paper to the officer. I saw the officer look at the paper, and his great black hat and periwig lift as he looked at you. Then . . .

"The officer turned, and gave some order. Every one of their great long swords lugged out, and flashed up at salute. You returned the salute: hand to chin, blade straight up, and for a moment all rested motionless in the rain. Another command from the officer; they did execute as fine and pretty a file turn as could have any Roundheads!"

"As . . . who?" demanded Fenton. Even in this state, wrath stabbed through him like the slight wound across his ribs.

"As—as Prince Rupert's Horse themselves," Lydia answered gently, and put her head on his chest as he sank back. "Sleep, dearest one. Sleep now. Sleep."

Thus on the following day, with black reaction on him and feeling pain, Fenton dozed all of the day and night under doses of laudanum. Nevertheless, on the day after that he awoke to briskness. Being one of those patients who will not stay in bed, he insisted on getting up and being dressed. Yet Giles, still white and shaken, he sent back to bed.

On that day, with Lydia beside him in the study while he marked his record in secret, he brooded. He felt that there was too little life, gaiety, music; that Lydia must be bored. So he wrote to my Lord Danby, the Lord Treasurer. He wrote to several friends in the country (at least, George had named them friends), asking them if they could appoint some future time to dine or sup with him.

Next day, as he scored down the 9th of June and felt its deadliness, he was well enough. Or, at least, he would have said so. His wounds of side and ear were trifling; besides, his periwig hid the latter. Only bruises made movement difficult.

After taking a long walk in the garden with Lydia, in weather again turned fine and sunny, he brooded again. Yet Lydia, as always, cheered him up. From below on the Mall, they could hear players at the game of *pêle-mêle*, and the *thock* of the big, heavy mallet as it swung hard against a heavy ball. The object of the game was to send the ball whizzing, "as though," Fenton quoted, "as though from smoking culverin 'twere shot," through a hoop at the other end.

Even the shouts and curses of the court gentlemen who played it, together with another wooden whack as of small ordnance fired at sea, in time became soothing to the ear.

Late in the afternoon, still brooding, he decided on a stroll outside the grounds. Skewering a hat to his periwig, he had some trouble with the big key of the front door. Impatiently he drew out the key. After one close look at it, he put his finger tips gently (but himself in a cold sweat) inside the edges of the big lock.

Soap. Dirty and now almost churned away, but traces of soap. Some person of the mob, unquestionably, had poisoned the dogs. But someone else, perhaps under cover of this, had got a soap impression of the lock so as to have a locksmith cut a key.

Fenton said nothing, except that he went round to the stables and gave instructions to Job, who was now cheerfully at his work. Fenton told Job that an inside bar must be affixed to the front door in the

213

shortest possible time. Then he resumed his stroll towards Charing Cross.

An outside poisoner? Very well; but what could the enemy do? Lydia's danger point began only with the stroke of midnight tonight, which would become the 10th. And he first ate half her food and drank of her wine. She refused to touch anything when he was from home.

Fenton's mood of cheerfulness, so odd yet natural of birth, had risen when he walked back from Charing Cross. Just before his own door stood a large, sombre coach painted dull brown with gilt trimmings. He hastened round to the other side, where Sam stood mute with respect, holding his tipstaff like a pike.

"Nick, my boy!" said a voice inside the coach.

As he hurried to the other side, Fenton found that the coach door was open. Seated inside, but framed in the opening, was a tall, very thin man whose portrait Fenton knew he had seen, but whom he could not identify.

Ordinarily, you might think, the newcomer's bearing would be stiff and austere. And, in the public eye, so it was. From under his hat and his immense brown periwig looked out the thin, sickly face of a man who was ill, whose nose seemed to droop like the tired lines across his forehead.

"I should hold it an ill thing, my boy," he continued, being now not in public, "if Tom Osborne could not reply in his own person to a letter from Nick Fenton's son." For an instant he pressed long, thin fingers over his face. "It is the work, the unending work at the Treasury!"

(Thomas Osborne, of course! Earl of Danby, Lord Treasurer, the King's minister in chief.)

"My lord," said Fenton, "will you not step down? Better still, will you not stay and sup with us?"

My Lord Danby smiled, easing some of the weariness from his face.

"That," he said wryly, "was the sorry intelligence I came to impart. I must speed home to more papers, as on any night you might name. Yet will it please you to sit for a moment in the coach?"

Fenton mounted the step, sat down opposite the minister in chief, and closed the door.

"I envy your youth," said Danby. At first glance his smile appeared ghastly, then, at close range, only a look of friendliness. "No; I envy you nothing. Your lady is well?"

214

"Very well, thank God!"

"Also, in this matter of coming to sup, a doctor of physick has strange notions of health . . . such nonsense . . . yet I take but little."

Fenton bent forward.

"My lord," he insisted quietly, "it will do you a world's good if you will remain and sup."

My Lord Danby, his long body hunched back in the coach, regarded him out of dim, shrewd eyes.

"In some strange fashion you have changed." He shook his head. "I cannot tell how. Yet—here's a miracle! You really wish that I may stay!"

"Why, what else?" asked the astonished Fenton.

"Because all men hate me," said Danby, looking at the floor. "The Opposition party, even my own party hate me. Why do they hate me?"

"I tell you, these are only hobgoblin fancies, begotten of too much work!"

Abruptly Danby leaned forward, fastening long thin fingers round Fenton's arm.

"This keep to yourself," he said in a low voice. "Near four years ago I entered upon a near-empty Treasury. Soon, in no great time, I will have put a million pounds sterling into that same Treasury. I will have added thirty new ships to the navy, mightier sail-of-the-line than any we now possess: holding, as I do, that we must remain masters of the sea and no Hollander or Frenchman dispute us. I will have paid the seamen, and the greatest part of the debt stopped in the Exchequer; to say nothing . . ."

His hand dropped, and he mopped his forehead with a lace handkerchief.

"I have served the Treasury faithfully, I think," he added. "I do not know what these gentlemen would have."

Golden light through the lime trees dappled one side of the dusty coach. Fenton, glancing out of the far window, saw a sight as heartening as the sound of an old song. Up towards his house rode George Harwell, a blaze of finery, and Mr. Reeve, in patched and mended black, on horses like their owners' costumes. They seemed to be looking for bloodstains in the road, but rain had washed away such stains.

As they rode in, the noise of the hoofbeats turning left towards the stable yard, some fragment of conversation floated back even to a closed coach.

"Then you are possessed of a new wench," came the wheezy tones of Mr. Reeve, with a grave, judicial air. "Good; that's established. Now . . ."

"I told Nick Fenton I would find one," George declared proudly, "and scratch me, if I haven't! Ah, what a woman! Her lips like two cherries, one above the other! Her . . ."

More intimate detail floated away.

"See, my Lord!" said Fenton, nodding towards the sun. He was really troubled about Danby's state of mind. " 'Tis not yet evening. We sup very early. Your need is for diverting discourse which shall not deal with the body politic. Could you take hurt from (say) a capon and a glass of wine?"

It was as though Danby, weighed down by many coats or capes, threw them back from his shoulders.

"We-ell!" he said. "I dare swear, my boy, they would do me no harm."

The impromptu supper, like most impromptu things, was first pleasant and then hilarious. Lydia, managing all behind the scenes, placed her reliance on capons, hot and cold, more of them than even George could eat; on baked potatoes, and a great drum of cheese.

All this Lydia contrived so rapidly that Fenton stood in amaze. He was even more amazed at the quickness with which she dressed and swept into the room: in blue silk, with orange colour about it, a-sparkle with diamonds. All set off her glowing colour, and her eyes and hair.

My Lord Danby gave her so courtly a bow that George was envious of it, and Danby kissed her hand with a compliment of such nimble wit that Fenton himself grew envious.

Fenton sat at the head of the table, with Danby at his left and Lydia at his right. Mr. Reeve, at the beginning as stately as a battered archbishop in the presence of the Lord Treasurer, sat at Lydia's right. George, facing Mr. Reeve beside Danby, was nervous and inclined to make gravy fly when he bolted his food. But the wine did its good work on all.

No hats, of course, were worn at a friend's table. The coils of the great periwigs glimmered behind many wax lights on the table. Nan Curtis had burned every potato save one, but all cooks did this and no one observed it. A porter stood behind every chair; and Giles, bolt upright at the back of Fenton, directed the porters with severe eye flicks.

Nevertheless, whenever George or Mr. Reeve gave a serious *hem* and tried to ask questions about recent events, Fenton deftly turned them away with a pungent anecdote translated back into their own terms. This set the table in a roar. All others joined in, including Lydia and Danby, with anecdotes—as a rule concerning the apprentice and his master's wife—as the wine ran faster at the end of the meal.

But everything in the talk centered round George's new love affair. Lydia finally triumphed.

"George!" she pleaded, allowing her silver wine goblet to be refilled for the sixth time, "tell us of her! Else I vow I will not sleep for curiousness, truly I won't."

George, now stuffed to repletion, gave a royal wave of his hand.

"Then, *imprimis*," said Mr. Reeve, who had again assumed his air of a judge on the bench, "let us hear her name. Let us hear her name."

"Her name," said George, with pride and pleasure, "is Fanny."

"Come now!" said the judge, tapping one finger craftily on the table. "Here's mere evasion! What's her full name? Or doth she refuse to give it?"

"Why a fiend's name should she? She is Mistress Fanny Brisket."

"And may I ask, Lord George," inquired Danby, very courteously, but with a somewhat owlish look of too much wine, "how you were made acquainted with the young lady?"

George's large face, already red and polished, could have grown no more red.

"Why, as to that," he answered, with a little cough. "To say true: 'twas in a bawdyhouse."

A great hum of applause went up, mingled with the banging of knife handles on the table. George, who at first thought himself jeered, was soothed by Lydia.

"Was it so?" she asked eagerly. Her elbows were on the table, her chin resting on clasped hands; and she tried to peer across at George through a maze of silver candelabra. "George! Dear George! Tell us of the house, and how 'twas furnished! Do, George!"

"Ah!" said George. "Here's a matter of true import. For you must not be surprised. This was none of your abodes in Whetstone Park."

Whetstone Park was not a park but a street. It was supposed to contain half the doxies in London.

"Nay," asserted George, and threw aside Whetstone Park in disgust. "This was, and is, a true Temple of Venus, for the convenience of a man of quality." Suddenly he stopped. "Why, scratch me, Nick, I recall I spoke of it to you, on that day!"

Fenton had been taking a sip from Lydia's wine goblet. Of late he

217

had grown accustomed to drinking a good deal of claret at supper, and even kept a decanter in his own room. But tonight, as host, he drank sparingly and had a cool head.

"What day?" he asked.

"Why, curse it, the famous day when you and I sought the apothecary's in Dead Man's Lane! And you skewered two bullyrocks at once? Nay; stop! I had but begun to tell you, when you were so preoccupied you all but fell into the kennel."

"Yes. I remember it."

"Come, come!" interposed Mr. Reeve at his stateliest. "As touches this bawdyhouse. . . ?"

"Well!" said George, turning a somewhat glazed eye round the table. "I chanced, one day, to dine at the Rainbow. After dinner I fell to musing, as men will, whether there might not somewhere exist some such temple as I conceived only in fancy. Thus idly I put the question to a friend who dined with me. I'll not give his name, for he is an impudent jackanapes.

" 'Why,' says he, 'are you dolt enough not to know of the veritable house itself, not two minutes from here?' I replied as you imagine. 'If you doubt me,' says he, 'I'll tell you the very house, and instruct you what to say.' Being pushed on by my desire for novelty, and other curiosity too: '*Laus Veneris!*' says I. 'A hit!'

"And yet, when I came to the street, and saw the house, I verily thought my confidence abused by this jackanapes. It was a fine high house of brick, and a porter with tipstaff at the door. 'However,' thinks I, 'I have a pocketful of guineas; a certain curiosity upon me; and well the jackanapes knows, if he should deceive me, I'll pull his neck from his shoulders like a cork from a bottle.'

"Wherefore I approached the porter with the tipstaff. 'Fellow,' says I, though with civility, 'are there any lodgings to be let here?' And I was not deceived. 'Yes, sir,' says the porter, 'which you may view if you will give yourself the trouble of walking in.' "

George paused.

Observing that he had caught his audience, George refreshed himself with a long draught of canary from his silver goblet, which was immediately replenished. He beamed round with an eye unsteady but full of good will.

"Hem!" George said suddenly, to conceal the fact that be belched.

218

"Now where was I? Ah! I had no sooner entered the door, but I was met by a grave matron. This grave matron conducted me into her parlour, which was gallantly furnished, there to take a stricter view of me: as, to judge how well lined my pockets were."

George held out a beringed hand, from which flashed the hues of orange and sapphire and diamond. George himself was modestly attired in orange and silver.

"The matron was well satisfied. And I have no doubt, my lord," said George, turning a grave red face towards Danby, "she would have been well satisfied with your lordship's self."

"I am much honoured, Lord George."

"Scratch me, my Lord, why don't you seek the house yourself? Scratch me, I'll take you there!"

"Again I am much honoured," replied the Lord Treasurer, who was almost as tipsy as George and took all this with deep seriousness. "But, if it be not too troublesome to you, another question. Was it upon this occasion that you met your divine Fanny?"

"No, no, no!" intoned George, shuddering. "I met Fanny, that celestial creature, scarce a week ago. And when I saw her ('tis truth, my lord!), I was so overcome by her beauty, her divinity—curse me, I swooned away at her feet!"

" 'Twould much grieve me," interposed Mr. Reeve, shaking his venerable head, "to mar this pure nosegay of poesy. But were ye sober?"

"Oh, in moderation sober," said George, huffed. "Can you name a time when but four pots of canary, even perhaps laced with brandy, have made me fall down in a swound?"

Mr. Reeve said nothing. He had brought his cittern, as he sometimes did. At a short gesture, the porter behind his chair gave it to him. But he did not play; on occasion he plucked at a string or two, lost in old years.

"Lord George," intoned Danby, "pray continue your first visit."

"Hum! Well," said George, "being satisfied, the grave matron shewed me the way up one pair of stairs into a very large and fair dining room. 'Twas hung with rich tapestry, and adorned round with excellent pictures, the effigies of divers ladies (as I took them to be) renowned in all ages for the fairest of that sex.

"A servant brought us up immediately a bottle of sack, without any order given. Whereat the old gentlewoman drank to me, expressing

219

her welcome. 'Come,' thinks I, 'here's civility itself; but whence do we proceed?'

"No sooner had I thought this, but the old gentlewoman spoke. 'Sir,' says she, 'as you are a gentleman, you may have some knowledge of that noble art of limning, or painting, for it is much studied by the gentry of this nation. Wherefore your judgment, sir: which in these pictures is the best drawn, or hath the best features?' "

Here George, nearing his oratorical mood, rose unsteadily to his feet and clutched the wine goblet.

" 'Madam,' says I, 'I will freely give you my judgment. Which, in my opinion (pointing to one, thus) is this. For she hath a full large front; her arched eyebrows are black, without any straggling hairs; her eyes are of the same colour, yet deeply tinged with grey . . .' "

"George," Lydia said softly, "is it not somewhat a likeness to Meg York?"

"Now the devil fly away with Meg York!" shouted George. "I have learned she left the French captain; but where she hath gone I know not nor care! Besides, this was no picture of Meg!"

"Nay, George, I but . . ."

"Having made this judgment about the picture," roared George, seizing the narrative and not letting go, "it seemed to me the grave matron but faded behind a curtained door. In her place, with a rustle of silks, out stepped the very likeness ('tis truth) of the picture, yet modest and a lady of quality.

"While we drank the sack together, the lady with the full large front (by name Eliza) did acquaint me with the custom of the house. If you remained *not* all night, you were entitled to wine not exceeding four bottles, a taste of food, and a mistress besides, for the sum of but forty shillings.

"But if you wished to remain all night," continued George triumphantly, "the custom was thus. Under your pillow you placed ten golden guineas. On each occasion you did deal well and manfully with your mistress, you should take back one guinea for yourself. Scratch me, but wasn't it a noble game?"

Danby hemmed. "And if the question be not too intimate, Lord George, how many of the ten guineas remained beneath the pillow at morning?"

"My lord!" protested George, shutting up one eye in rebuke and

220

swaying on his feet. "There's a question no man of quality durst ask another in this bawdyhouse. Yet I upheld my honour," proclaimed George, "and with Fanny—curse me, now!" His face became one vast beam, and he addressed Mr. Reeve across the table. "What say you, good friend?"

Mr. Reeve nodded thoughtfully. The strings of the cittern glistened against its polished wood.

"Ay, you are in the right of it," he muttered. "I am too old a rake-helly not to know my brethern. Yet 'twas not thus, I think, at the court of Charles the First." ·

"Come, ancient do-well! Come, Earl of Shadows and Mist!"

"We sought not women in houses," said Mr. Reeve. "We sought the women themselves."

His old yet very skilful fingers ran across the cittern strings. Softly, clearly, he began to play. Though he did not speak or sing, yet there was no person at the table who did not remember words older even than Charles the First.

> "*Drink to me only with thine eyes,*
> *And I will pledge with mine* . . . ."

Instinctively Lydia and Fenton, at the corner of the table, turned towards each other. She stretched out her hands across the table, and he gripped them. Her rounded chin was up, her face a little flushed, and in her eyes such love that it frightened him.

"Oh, God," he thought, "what if I should lose her?" And the hours, the minutes, ticked towards what had been called the appointed time. He had sworn it before, and believed what he swore, yet now it was complete: he had never loved Lydia so much as at that time.

Though the music had ceased, these two did not know it. They sat looking into each other's eyes, scarcely hearing a word about them.

"But, scratch me," protested a puzzled George, "that song's the very heart of poesy I've been endeavouring to tell you as concerns Fanny!"

"Under favour, sir!" observed Danby, fixing his eyes somewhat blearily on Mr. Reeve. "Putting aside the small question of (hem) bawdyhouses, these times we live in are harsh and hasty. Would you have us ape our forebears in all things, and sing pride of it?"

Mr. Reeve's rheumy eyes blazed.

Sweeping back his chair, which was carried away by the porter, Mr. Reeve arose on gouty legs. With his immense paunch, his hair and drunken face like a battered archbishop, he looked Danby straight in the eyes.

"No, my lord," he said in a rolling voice. "But I would tear to pieces the Green Ribbon ere it grew too strong. I would sing of a time but a few nights ago, June 7th, when above sixty rioters attacked this house. And six men—only six, my lord—routed them screaming amid thirty-one dead or wounded. And not one step hath been taken to punish the rioters."

Again Mr. Reeve's fingers swept over the strings. The whole cittern began to dance with a lively air, and Mr. Reeve's strong yet wheezy voice went out with them:

> "There's a tyrant known as MOB, sir, in this town of soot and
>   mud,
> Sitting green-faced by the hob, sir, with his hands imbrued
>   in blood;
> And he howls, 'Down with the Papists,' at Lord Shaftesbury's
>   smiling will
> And the most, who are but apists, will howl with him! And
>   yet still . . ."

Once more, as inside the Green Ribbon Club, Mr. Reeve's fingers ripped across the strings as the voice went out:

> "Here's a cry for all ye goodmen,
>   Shout it joyous through the town—
> Three swordsmen and three woodmen
>   Did bring the tyrant down!"

It could not be helped. Two porters, unable to restrain themselves, let out a yell of cheers. My Lord Danby, as though with cold shock, was stricken sober. George applauded wildly.

At the same moment, the door to the hall opened. Lydia and Fenton, absorbed with each other, would not have turned even yet except for one thing. The door to the hall, where burned many larger and stronger candles, opened and closed swiftly. For half a second Giles, who had been mysteriously missing for a time, was silhouetted there; and his long shadow fell between Fenton and Lydia.

Lydia, for some reason, shrank back as though in fear. Giles softly moved round the table, to whisper in Fenton's left ear. All caught the whispered words:

"Sir Robert Southwell, the clerk of the council, is come in a coach . . ."

222

This blurred away. Mr. Reeve, who had yet another verse to his song, sat down and began to make the cittern tinkle softly towards Lydia, whose face was turned and who tried hard to listen to what Giles was saying. My Lord Danby, now straight-backed and more weary than before, turned to George with some murmured commonplace which George was too drunk to understand. Then Giles melted back into shadow, and Fenton stood up.

"I think you are sensible," he said, groping out with his right hand and finding Lydia's, "that I would not leave this company for any reason save one. I have been promised that I may return in an hour; I have not even time to shift my clothes. Meanwhile, I beg of you, be merry!"

With his left hand he took from his waistcoat pocket one of the huge, thick watches, and opened its case. The hands stood at five minutes to seven. Outside the windows lay clear daylight.

"I am commanded to Whitehall Palace," he added, "for a private audience with the King."

CHAPTER XVI

AUDIENCE AT

WHITEHALL PALACE

"Phyllis, for shame, let us improve
A thousand several ways
These few short minutes stol'n by love
From many tedious days. . . ."

THE voice, clear and sexless, was that of a French boy: one of several imported at the pleadings of the French Duchess of Portsmouth. Louise, fat as a Turk, with a head like a golden-topped sofa cushion, had wept from night until dawn; the King finally cursed and consented.

And the voice, accompanied by a tenor viola, rose up from a platform banked with flowers on the west side of the great Banqueting House. This hall, its wall supports painted brown with indentations of gilt, rose up to an immense, lofty ceiling painted with goddesses and Cupids by Rubens.

You may see the Banqueting House today, since this alone escaped the fire which destroyed all of old Whitehall Palace in 1698. Yet, as you alone pace the stone floor on a gloomy afternoon, hearing your own footsteps ring and echo back, you will not see it as Fenton saw it on that lost enchanted night.

Fully a thousand wax lights, in chandeliers or iron-gilt holders up from the floor, kindled it to a blaze. Its great arched windows, west-wards, were curtained with heavy dark-red velvet, trimmed in gold, and slightly looped back by tasselled copes of gold. The brilliant light, in places soft and unsteady, mingled with the scent of banked red and white roses, carnations, the arum lilies, the heavy orange blossom, as though in a mist of heavy perfume.

"We await Mr. William Chiffinch," observed Sir Robert Southwell, a dark, bearded man. "Hold! I believe I see him."

Over all the light murmur of chatter, as he and Fenton watched from the great open doors, rose the pleading string notes of the viola, and the voice of the boy on the platform, as they begged Phyllis to consent.

"False friends I have, as well as you,
Who daily counsel me
Vain frivolous pleasures to pursue
And leave off loving thee. . . ."

The words were by Charles Sackville, Earl of Dorset, one of the early roysterers who yet remained at court when others had reformed, or, broken in health, faded into the country. Then Dorset displayed his dazzling wordplay for the final verse:

"When I the least belief bestow
On what such fools advise,
May I be dull enough to grow
Most miserably wise!"

"Sir Robert!" intruded a heavy, rather hoarse voice. "Sir Nicholas! Your servant, gentlemen!"

Mr. Chiffinch, unofficial Page of the Back Stairs, was a hook-nosed Hercules in a dark-brown periwig, plainly dressed except for lace, and with a plain sword. Having a head like a tun, he could outdrink any man he ever met, and so filch away secrets for the King. Many persons here would have been surprised to learn how much more was Will Chiffinch than a mere procurer, in the secret service of King Charles.

"If you will allow me . . ." murmured Sir Robert, and melted away.

"Sir Nicholas," said Mr. Chiffinch, as he bowed Fenton through the door, "having summoned you in such haste, it were uncivil to keep you waiting. Yet, God's body, I cannot find the King!"

His big hand indicated the throng among the flowers. There were many fireplaces in the room: and, since the June night had turned cold, they burned high with logs. This, in addition to candle heat and closed windows, made the Banqueting House uncomfortably hot.

" 'Tis no matter," Fenton heard himself say. "I . . . I can wait."

225

"But you must be amused," Chiffinch insisted. "Come!" he added, indicating the east wall of the hall. "A moment gone, there were several tables at cards by the fireplace. Do you wait there, and I vow to discover His Majesty in two minutes!"

"I thank you."

"And—hem—a word in your ear, Sir Nicholas. Be not amazed at what you may see. 'Tis only the part of gallantry that we should permit the ladies to cheat." Suddenly Mr. Chiffinch stood on his toes, looking down an aisle of chairs towards the eastern fireplace.

"Nay," he added, with a smile broadening his heavy face and the little blue veins round the root of his nose, "there's but one table and one pair* of cards. Madam Gwynn plays alone against Mr. Ralph Montagu in the common people's game of put. Two minutes, I vow!"

And he hastened away.

"I have stepped behind the mirror," thought Fenton. "I see what none but dead men's eyes have seen. I must look well!"

For an instant the dazzle, the greasy heat, the too-thick scent of flowers in the lungs, even a babble of talk overpowered by music from a string trio, made his head swim as though he were really in a dream.

But he straightened up, and slowly looked about for a face he might identify.

There was none, at present. Peruked servants carried trays of sweetmeats among gallants of bright-hued attire and ladies, with George's "double cherry" mouths and arched eyebrows, languishing behind landskip fans.

Fenton, lifting his shoulders, went down the aisle of chairs towards the card table in front of the eastern fireplace.

He had several times seen Madam Gwynn, since they both lived in the same street. Madam Gwynn bade everyone call her Nelly, since, she said, she was as common as anybody. Fenton had caught a glimpse of her pretty face at an ivy-hung window, and again entering a monstrously bedecked sedan chair. It is regrettable to state that Nelly was not always sweet-tempered and not always sober.

But tonight she was at her prettiest and most charming. Before a blazing fire stood a very large round table of polished oak, so that the two players were at some distance from each other. In that heat the candles drooped, sending a rippling glitter on the vast pile of gold coins at Nelly's elbow.

* Pack.

226

Nelly's golden hair was piled up on her head, with crownlike effect in front, and sewn with pearls. In her violet-coloured gown, with many necklaces and rings, she was as slim as a nymph. Her oval face glowed with excitement and her brown eyes danced.

"Nay, now," she cried, "who deals?"

"I believe, madam," lightly replied her opponent, "that the deal is mine."

"Sweet Mr. Montagu!"

Some half a dozen guests, gallants and their ladies, had lingered near the fire to watch. But Fenton, who had missed the name of Mr. Ralph Montagu when Chiffinch mentioned it, stood now sharply alert.

Mr. Montagu, full of those airs and graces which women loved and De Grammont had admired, was an ugly-faced, medium-complexioned man in a flaxen periwig framed against red roses, with another great pile of gold at his elbow. Mr. Montagu was artful, ingratiating, avaricious, as coldhearted and treacherous as a tiger.

Fenton, from old brown handwriting and old brown records, could see past that ingratiating look into the man's very skull. If he were not prevented, Mr. Montagu would in future perform an act of treachery towards the King which . . .

"But, Nelly," softly twittered one of the attendant ladies, "this game of put: I understood it not, even when you played. Ombre or piquet I know; but this?"

" 'Tis a common game, and becomes me," said Nelly, with a swift bright smile. "Ombre and piquet are but slow, slow, slow!" She flexed her white shoulders. "That fat fireship, the Duchess of Portsmouth, would shudder."

Delicately, Nelly spat over her shoulder.

"But that monster," she added, "is from London and indeed on the continent. The other mistress in chief, the Duchess of Cleveland, whom I mind not so much, hath long ago departed in a huff for the continent."

"And is there no other?" inquired Mr. Montagu, with his silkiest smile.

Nelly's beautiful voice, trained for the playhouse, could give her the most ladylike air when she chose.

"I am the King's whore," she answered sweetly. "I have not yet heard I was another's. Mr. Montagu, I would shew my friend the play of put. Pray deal to me."

227

The gaudily painted cards were already shuffled and cut. Montagu rose up gracefully and with just as much grace set three cards face down before Nelly, each with an audible flick.

"This is my hand, sweetest Araminta," explained Nelly, to the coy girl with the fan. "Mr. Montagu"—there were three more audible flicks across the table—"deals to himself, and sits down.

"Now before we wager," Nelly rattled on, "each may put by one card and take another. Then the winner is he (or, split me! she) who shall hold the lowest hand."

"The *lowest* hand?"

"True, sweet bawd. But always in this manner! The winner must have two cards of the same number: as, two fives or two sixes. The third card must be different: as, four or trey. Ace is always lowest. Thus a hand of deuce-deuce-ace (oh, Lord!) could not be beaten save by ace-ace-deuce. But that's a dream. Now stand back, my angel."

Both players picked up their hands. Nelly snatched up the cards eagerly, Montagu coolly, with a printed smile.

Fenton had not crossed over to the group by the fireplace. He stood at the beginning of the open space, left hand lightly resting on his sword.

"Your devoir, madam?" inquired Montagu, lifting his eyebrows.

Nelly, her cheeks even more flushed, leaned forward. Taking one card from her hand, she sent it spinning across the table towards him.

"Put!" she said.

Montagu caught the card, setting it to one side. From the top of the pack, or apparently so, he took another card. Without troubling to rise, he sent it spinning face down to Nelly.

Nelly, desperately attempting to look inscrutable, gave a deep sigh of excitement and dropped the cards into her lap.

"Your own devoir, Mr. Montagu?"

"Nay, madam," replied Montagu half-apologetically, and tapped his closed cards on the table. "I'll not put to myself. Yet I'll hold a thou— nay, two thousand guineas on the cards I have in my hand. Do you play, madam?"

"God's fish!" breathed Nelly, unconsciously using the favourite oath of the King, "but indeed I do play!"

Using both hands, she shoved across the table the immense heap of gold; but sideways, towards Fenton, so that it should not interfere with the open space. Montagu did the same.

228

It was observable, Fenton thought, that they did not trouble to count the money. They judged by size and weight and sheer glitter, as children will. As Nelly's violet-coloured gown rustled, she ran one white arm through the heap, loving the gleam and hard smoothness of gold far more than the gold itself.

"Your cards, Mr. Montagu?"

"It grieves me," said that gentleman, as though boyishly begging her forgiveness, "to triumph over a lady. Yet such are the gods of chance, being blind even to the most lovely face."

And he set out his hand. It was trey-trey-deuce.

There was a murmur from the spectators. One heavily wigged and jewelled gallant cast a sidelong glance at a lady with too-red cheeks; she tapped her fan against cherry mouth, lips pursed out.

"Stay but a moment," Nelly said sweetly. "And look at these."

Card by card, delicately, she put down trey-trey-ace.

Dead silence. Both hands were cheats, and such blatant cheats, that the spectators immediately began a rapid murmur of small talk. Yet Fenton could feel the wave of delight from them at the defeat of Montagu, who never played at cards unless he was sure to win. Montagu sprang to his feet.

"Madam, I—" he began in a strangled voice; but controlled himself. Turning to his left, he moved round the table towards the aisle.

And Fenton stepped directly in front of him.

"Mr. Montagu," he said, in so low a tone that no spectator could have heard it, "do you question the correctness of the play?"

Montagu's face showed a different look inside the flaxen periwig.

"And who the devil are you, sir?" he demanded loudly.

"My name is Fenton," retorted the other, just as loudly. "In full, Sir Nick Fenton. Do you question the correctness of the play?"

It was as though those spectators by the fire congealed into cake icing. Though they might be life-size, their heads and hearts were of cake with bright-coloured icing. But very much warm and alive was Nelly, who winked openly at Fenton. Alive was Montagu, from his ashy-coloured face to his brandy breath. He backed towards the edge of the table.

"I question it not, sir," he replied, in a light tone and with a smile.

But he backed against the edge of the table, his fingers under its ledge. In the hush a gold coin fell and rang on the stone floor.

"Sir Nicholas, for God's sake!" a voice hissed close to his periwig,

229

and a heavy hand was laid on his shoulder. And: "I cry your pardon," the somewhat brusque voice of Chiffinch was raised, "Madam Gwynn, ladies and gentlemen, at the short fashion of our leave-taking. Yet Sir Nicholas has business of import."

Whereupon the hook-nosed Hercules led him back down the aisle, and through a variety of paths through flowers. Though Chiffinch remained deferential, it was as though he controlled a slight roar.

"So-and-so!" he whispered. "May I not intrust you two minutes alone, without a near duel challenge in Whitehall itself? Your reputation, Sir Nicholas, is no whit underestimated."

"No!" protested Fenton. "These things," he groped in his mind, "are all accidents. I know what is to happen," here Chiffinch glanced sideways, "and I . . . I try to intervene. No more!"

"Well, do you attend here!"

At the southeastern corner of the hall, Chiffinch led him into a shut-off space with a fireplace built in the very angle of the wall. As many as four high folding screens, of heavy leather with brass nailheads, and thickened with three inches of padding, had been drawn round the alcove so that it became a very small room. The fire burned brightly. There were several chairs of the sort called Oriental, draped and padded for comfort, as well as two footstools. Since there was nobody in the little room, Fenton sat down.

He had almost lost his anxiety as to time, as a quick look at his watch told him it was only half-past seven. He felt eager and alert. He had forgotten the ache of his bruises, even when someone jostled him. There was so much, so much, of which he must warn the King!

Then he heard, outside the alcove, the "great voice," now tuned to an amiable bass growl, of which so many had written, and the familiar long stride of Charles Stuart.

"Not until I call you, Will!" said the voice.

And into the alcove, past the side of a screen, stepped the living presence of the man of whom he had read so much. There was a catch to Fenton's breath as he stood up.

Charles was six feet tall, seeming taller by height of periwig and medium shoe heel. He was lean, and on the muscular side, in an almost shabby black suit rather roomy for him but with a dull red waistcoat and much laced.

His very large black periwig, which was carefully parted in the middle and had many coils, stretched down on either side almost to his chest.

His complexion was almost as brown as that of a red Indian; his nose long and straight, and under it, like Fenton, he wore a narrow line of black moustache. He had the Stuart cheekbones, the long Stuart mouth and chin. But his best feature lay in his eyes, of a red-brown colour, under high black brows.

And he gave Fenton a warm, welcoming smile.

"I fear, Sir Nicholas," he said, holding out his hand, "that, since you will not come to me, I must needs send for you."

Fenton touched his forehead to the hand, which bore three rings, and made a leg. For a moment he was tongue-tied.

"Come, man, be easy!" urged Charles, dropping into a comfortable chair and setting up one knee to put his foot on a gaudily embroidered footstool. "Or at least be comfortable. Be seated—so! Now I am easy too."

Yes, he had all the Stuarts' charm. With word or look they could inspire blind loyalty and devotion. For that devotion, in past or future, how many swords would be drawn, how many toasts drunk, how many *vivat*'s heard even in the cries of the dying!

"I had intended," said Charles, trying to frown and not succeeding, "to be very severe with you. In my reign, Sir Nicholas, I have issued three royal edicts against duelling. At times you have been very troublesome to me. At other times—God's fish, how it hath warmed the heart!"

Charles leaned back. His face was often more sombre than it should have been, and with heavier lines than at first appeared.

"Was it true, as I hear, that when you did smite home the last charge on the rioters, you set up the old battle cry, 'God for King Charles'? Come! Was it for me, or for my father?"

"Sire, I do not know. I can't tell. 'Twas for both, I think."

"Either," muttered Charles, "were honour enough." His red-brown eyes lifted above the tops of the screens, and he toyed with a ring on his right hand. "I . . . you are aware, as I conceive, that from a far window of this room, then a door, my father stepped out on the scaffold to . . . to . . . "

"Yes, Sire."

"Well!" Charles's expression, which could change in a flash, now regarded him with an idle, indulgent smile. "This soothsaying of yours. I warn you I . . . "

" 'Have no truck with such kind of cattle,' " quoted Fenton, his

231

hands tightly clasped, his gaze on the floor, " 'for, if they could tell you anything, 'tis inconvenient to know.' "

Charles's face was completely impassive.

"And why do you use such words, Sir Nicholas?"

"They were writ by yourself, Sire. They were writ long ago, in a letter to your young sister Henrietta, called 'Minette,' and then married to the very vile Duc d'Orléans of France. She is dead these five years, and her good soul at peace."

Charles rose abruptly to his feet. He walked over to the little corner-angled fireplace, putting his hands on the shelf above and tapping with his shoe at the small burning logs.

Only two persons, Fenton knew, had ever deeply touched the heart of Charles Stuart. One was his fragile young sister, the other his father.

Now he turned back to Fenton, his chin sunk into his neck lace.

"I will not ask," he said, "how you could quote from a private letter, carried by private messenger. A man of cunning might have contrived it." Charles frowned. "Yet I confess you puzzle me, Sir Nicholas. I find in you a quiet-spoken gentleman of courtly bearing. I had thought to find a loud-voice braggart, such as your public appearances have shown me, even when you spoke in the Painted Chamber."

"Are we not both deceptive," asked Fenton, "in our public appearance?"

"How?"

"Under favour, Sire! Do you think all men give credence to your deliberate pose as 'unthinking Charles, ruled by unthinking thee'? Or, 'a merry monarch, scandalous and poor'?" At these last words Charles pulled a wry face. "This may have been true in your hot-humoured youth. But it hath not been true for many years."

"Why, as to that . . . " Charles began, but stopped.

With his most urbane air he moved back to the chair, sat down, cocked up his foot on the footstool. His restless, satiric brain must forever be a-probing.

"Poor I am," he conceded. "Parliament manage that." He flexed his muscles. "The flesh still stings . . . oh, damnably! Who can resist a pretty woman? Or who trust her? Yet I have settled to a kind of domesticity among my small seraglio. I frolic no more, and I drink only for my thirst. I am grown gaunt, and long in the tooth."

"Naught else?"

"God's fish, yes!" said Charles, with something like a snarl. "My enemies must learn, soon or late, that I will not yield and I will not

232

be bullied. The rightful succession shall go to my brother James, though they set up my bastard son Monmouth or another. And (you are in the right of it!) for years my hand hath guided this cockleshell boat; and I will bring her safe home ere I die."

"You will, Sire. And more. But the sea will rise high."

All Charles's seriousness dropped away, as did the gleam behind his red-brown eyes.

"Ah!" he murmured, with his usual careless, lazy air. "You refer, I take it, to your prophecy before the Green Ribbon Club?"

"If my words have been twisted to Your Majesty . . . !"

"Nay; have no fear for that. I pay more spies than my Lord Shaftesbury himself. But why must you carry the news to him? Why did you not come to me?"

"First, Sire, I had a small grudge to settle with my lord. Again, I knew you would give no credence to this 'plot,' from the time you shall hear of it from a Mr. Kirkby. When first you meet their master-liar, a bloody rogue named Titus Oates, at the council board on September 28th, 1678, you will say flatly: 'I call the fellow a lying knave.'

"Oh, Your Majesty will outwit and destroy them. But there will be three years of terror and bloodshed. Meantime, whilst innocent Catholics are persecuted as they have seldom been persecuted, you will not lift a hand to save them. Being Popishly affected, you will have sympathy; you will take hurt. But to pardon one Catholic will mean civil war; and as yet there can be no reckoning. You will even cry, as you sign death warrants: 'Let the blood lie upon them that condemn them, for God knows I sign with tears in my eyes!' So inflexible, Sire, you can be."

Fenton felt sweated, and knew he was trembling all over, from the force with which he tried to compel belief. Charles looked at him strangely.

"All this," Fenton added, "will come to pass. Unless, in some fashion, it might be prevented."

"How?"

The deep voice, not loud, seemed to fill the alcove with the volume of a monosyllable.

Fenton played his boldest stroke.

"Your Majesty will not convoke Parliament until the year 1677—"

"And wherefore not?"

"Because the subsidies paid to you from the French King will not

233

be exhausted until then. Shall I touch upon a matter of one hundred thousand pounds, as arranged in 1674?"

Charles's eyes shifted slightly. Since the now not-so-secret Treaty of Dover five years ago, he had at various times taken bribes from his cousin Louis, Charles being always cheerful to advance the interest of England against that of France. But mere rumour of it made the Commons howl.

"Now here, Sire," Fenton went on, "is the ironic jest. The present French Ambassador, M. Savarigny, will be replaced by another, M. Barrillon. I much fear that the French King mistrusts you almost as much as you mistrust him."

"Come, what a suspicious-minded fellow!"

"M. Savarigny does a certain thing now. M. Barrillon will do it to far greater extent in the future. It is this. He will bribe the holy, pious Country party, the high-minded Green Ribboners, to cry out even more zealously and bloodily against you!"

Charles pursed up his lips. "Now if I could but prove *that* . . . !"

"Sire, all the correspondence between Barrillon and King Louis— which will be preserved—shall contain a list of almost all the bribe-takers. In the Commons, for instance, you shall find Harbord, Titus, Sacheverell, Armstrong, Littleton, and Powle. As for the lords: but why carry it further? My Lord Shaftesbury's chief attendants will have their price at five hundred guineas a head; save for His Grace of Bucks, who receives a thousand. Could you but seize Barrillon's papers, or in some fashion contrive to copy them . . . "

"Stay, man, you go too fast!"

There was a silence. Hitherto unnoticed, a light chatter of talk, the sense of movement and music, floated over the screen, while Charles sat motionless. His elbow was on the chair arm, his forefinger up under the side of his periwig, while he bit at his narrow line of moustache. Slowly he turned his head.

"Sir Nicholas," he said, "you state, and state again, that these letters 'will' exist. I ask but one question, and a plain one. How do you know that they will exist?"

"Because I have read them!"

"Read them?"

"Yes! Such secret documents, questionless, could not be made open at the time. Not, indeed, until towards the end of the eighteenth century. You will find them printed fully in the second volume of

234

Sir John Dalrymple's *History of Great Britain and Ireland*, which, published in the year 1773, is—"

Fenton stopped dead.

Now, at long last, he had made the one irrevocable blunder.

Yet Charles's voice and expression remained unchanged.

"Is there aught else," he asked kindly, "of which you would warn me?"

"There is, Sire, though you send me to Bedlam for it! It concerns Mr. Ralph Montagu. You must not appoint him Ambassador to the French court . . ."

"Mr. Montagu is a very ingenious gentleman, so I hear. Yet I have no intent that he shall be appointed Ambassador to the French court."

"But you will, Sire! You will! Now who is Your Majesty's ablest and most faithful minister? I dare venture you would say my Lord Danby? Well! When Mr. Montagu is recalled from France in disgrace, his spite will bring with him a number of letters. One of these, read before the House of Commons in 1679, will call the fall of my Lord Danby and almost the fall of Your Majesty's self."

"Now let us reflect," mused Charles. "I believe you, and your father before you, have been near friends to my Lord Danby?"

"I believe so. Yet that doth not in any degree affect the fact!"

"You have no great liking for Mr. Montagu?"

"Upon my word, I never set eyes on the man until a while ago."

"Then tell me. When did you last see my Lord Danby?"

"He—he supped at my house this night."

"This night," Charles repeated thoughtfully.

And Fenton felt the strength ebbing from him. For the first and last time in his life, he went down on his knees.

"*For God's sake, Sire, credit what I say! Every word of it will come true!*"

Charles rose to his feet. Going to his companion, he lifted Fenton with a great heave, set him back in the chair, clapped him on the shoulder, and returned to his own chair.

"One last chance!" Fenton pleaded, with all remaining strength. "Do you put a question. Nay, two questions! On those I stake what little hope is left to me, else allow myself but a poor madman!"

"Sir Nicholas, you will make yourself ill," protested Charles. "Well, well, if it pleaseth you," he added hastily, "let it be so. Come, I have

235

it! For this Christmastide I have planned a small journey. Now at whose house shall I be, and with whom, on the 25th December of this year?"

Again December 25th, which was Sir Nick's birthday and also, grotesquely, Fenton's own. It seemed to haunt him. Suddenly he realized that his thoughts, concentrated on political events, must seek the trivial instead. They scattered into all corners.

Yes, there had been something of the sort. But mentioned by whom? Ailesbury? Reresby? Evelyn? Burnet? Charles's own collected letters? Desperately Fenton searched his mind, as a man might seek old papers amid trunks.

"Well, 'twas of no import," Charles assured him cheerfully. "Nor will be the other. I can't recollect the day; but this day is the second week of June. Now where shall I be on this same date, say, in the year 1685?"

Carefully keeping from looking at Fenton, examining the rings on his fingers, Charles did not see his companion's face turn as white as a candle. For there could be only one true reply.

"Sire," Fenton would have to say, "on this date in 1685 you will have been dead just over four months."

He opened a dry mouth, but he could not speak. Literally, physically, he could not deal this blow. True, Fenton knew the date of his own death; but this was so remote, in his present youth, that it held no terrors. True, the King would not believe him. Yet always would remain that fang of wonder and doubt. To watch the days pass, to hear the ticking of the clock, to fear the illness that might strike. . . ?

Too well, in his imagination, he saw that cold dawn in the great bedchamber, and heard a weak voice from the bed order the last clock wound up, with grey February light stealing through the window curtains. And Charles, who had lived through days of agony with a jest on his lips, died at last with the Catholic faith in his heart.

"Sire," Fenton answered clearly, "I can't tell."

"And there's an end on't," smiled Charles. His tone changed. "Nay, I call you no madman. This strain of prophecy, on occasion true but more often false, hath run in all old families. Minette had it. Perhaps that is why . . . "

Pausing abruptly, he held up his hand.

"Stay; that music; that song! I detest these boys' voices which have

236

neither the vigour of the man nor the allure of the woman. Yet here, though 'tis strange for so idle, sauntering a fellow as myself, is the song I most favour."

> "The glories of our blood and state
> Are shadows, not substantial things;
> There is no armour against fate
> Death sets his icy hand on kings. . . . "

On it went, with its queer sombre rhythm of "Sceptre and Crown, Must tumble down," in the lyric by John Shirley. Voice and viol throbbed. Charles sat listening, his head forward in the gleaming peruke, his long chin in his neck lace.

But, when it had finished, he sat up as grim-faced as any City man of business.

"Now, Sir Nicholas. You say you are here to warn me. But, God's fish! How I must warn you!"

"Warn me, Your Majesty?"

"I need not tell you that you walk forever in danger. But are you sensible you have a deadly enemy in your own household?"

Fenton's heart seemed to turn over.

"Inside? Outside?" he exclaimed. "I have tried to sound the truth. Would I could find it!"

"As, for instance!" said Charles, setting the tip of one forefinger against the tip of another. "On 10th May you were set about the ears by two bullies in a small street, of no conspicuousness, called Dead Man's Lane. 'Twas Green Ribbon work. Yet how could they know you would be there, and at that time in especial? Someone warned them. Had this occurred to you?"

"Sire, it was the first thing I did think of! When I returned home that night, I questioned my door porter as to what letters had passed in morning. All seemed harmless."

"Then you are not aware who betrayed you? And hath betrayed you time after time?"

"I fear not."

"Sir Nicholas, it was your own wife."

There was a short silence, while Fenton hated what he had to do. He stood up, looking straight down into the red-brown eyes, half-hooded.

"Sire," he said quietly, "you lie."

Again a silence, while all light noise seemed blotted out.

Charles's heavy hand came down on the chair arm, his powerful fingers gripping the outer end of it. There was a slight crack of wood as he twisted sideways. His foot, still with indolent leg cocked up on the footstool, shot out and sent the heavy footstool spinning across to thud against a heavily padded leathern screen, all but toppling it over.

Still Fenton's gaze did not waver a hairline from his own. Fenton could see the Stuart rage, always dangerous and seldom predictable. In the half-hooded eyes he saw it turn slowly to a kind of bewilderment, then a wonder and doubt. "This man," the eyes seemed to say in perplexity, "is honest." The doubt, groping, became conviction and then a kind of admiration.

Charles stood up, towering six inches above his companion.

"Man, I love you for that!" he said in a deep growl, and with as much sincerity as he was ever capable of feeling. "What crawler, what flatterer at this court durst have said it? My brother, ay; but James is too honest for safety. Bruce, Chiffinch, Berkeley; but Berkeley is dead."

Abruptly Charles held out his hand.

"Have done with this foolery of hand kissing," he said. "Grasp my hand in friendship, man, and know that a thoughtless fellow may be grateful!"

Fenton's head was bent, his fists clenched.

"Under humble favour, Sire. I would not touch the hand of the Creator Himself, unless He denied or else proved the words He had spoken."

Charles bowed very slightly.

"Yes, you are in the right of it," said the King of England, with far more dignity in accepting the rebuke than any man alive could have shown in resenting it. "You shall have your proof. Are you acquainted with your wife's handwriting?"

"I am well acquainted with it, Sire."

From an inside pocket Charles took out a thin grey letter sheet, folded in fours for a seal but now much frayed and lined.

"This," he said, "we intercepted after its intelligence had gone by mouth to the Green Ribbon. Pray read it, Sir Nicholas."

Fenton tried to unfold it with steady fingers. His eye instantly caught Lydia's handwriting, the date of 10th May, and then:

"*He hath but a minute gone from me (in hys owne Bedchamber),*

238

where he saith my Ilnesse may be cur'd by a Doctor of Physick. But he is gone below-stayres to give a Brisking to the Sarvants, poor Wretches, with a good Cat-of-Nine-Tayles. I fynde time to write these, at past Ten of the Clock. The Brisking, as I think, may be above an Houre. You will fynde him in Ded Man's Lane, as He so said in my Hearing, which I take to be Strand, sure between Noone and One of the Clock; it may be earlier or later. Yours in the Good Cause!

"Lydia F."

It was curious. Something appeared to be wrong with Fenton's eyesight, and his knees shook.

"I—I observe," he said clearly, "that 'tis addressed to a Mrs. Wheebler, dressmaker, at La Belle France in Covent Garden."

Charles made a gesture of impatience.

"Nay, they must have a clearinghouse for their spies' intelligence; and of a surety not at the King's Head. Here is a fine fantastical one; for who would suspect a dressmaker?"

"Were there," Fenton cleared his throat, "were there other letters?"

"I believe so. One we all but intercepted, save that . . . "

"Save that my wife had—had found another dressmaker, at La Belle Poitrine in Southampton Street?"

"Nay, for all this you must go to Sir Joseph Williamson and Mr. Henry Coventry, my Secretaries of State. But this letter of your wife I well recollect. Our fellow had a tack at copying it, but was compelled to leave off in haste and reseal it. One line he had, which was: '*If you kill him not the next time, I will abandon the Green Ribbon.*'"

Mechanically Fenton repeated the words.

Then he tried to go down on one knee, but was restrained by the unsteadiness of his legs.

"Your Majesty," he said, "I would—that is, I would try at some apology for the speaking of vain and foolish words."

The King gripped his hand, pulled him to his feet, and stepped back.

"Your apology is accepted, Sir Nicholas," Charles said gravely. "Let's say no more of it. But you observe . . . Hold up, man! What's amiss?"

"Nay, Sire, I did but stumble against a chair. Any man, you yourself, may stumble against a chair. In my own home I have put a few of these betrayals, that's to say, chairs, for comfort's sake. Yet 'tis easy to stumble against a chair."

Charles looked at him, pondering.

239

"Now what's the matter for this? Hum! All my informants tell me you and your wife are in bitter disagreement, raging and skreeking at each other."

"Your informants, Sire, are . . . mistaken."

"Well, well, even so! God's fish, what's one wench or another, save that all are alike in what concerns you?" He hesitated, and turned away. "Yet I confess I remember the old, long-gone days of Frances Stuart. —Keep your heart locked up, man!" he said in a fierce, muffled voice, and turned back again. "There's the first and last rule of life."

"I shall try to obey it, Sire. Have I now leave to go?"

"Of a surety, if you so desire. But you have been a loyal and faithful servant, sir. Is there no honour, no preferment, with which I can award you?"

"There is none, though I am much conscious of Your Majesty's graciousness. I . . . stay, though! There is one thing!"

"I would hear it."

"On the fringe of Whitehall is an old man who calls himself Jonathan Reeve. Though his title and estates were stolen under Oliver, he is in truth Earl of Lowestoft."

"Was he not," Charles interrupted suddenly, "one of the three at the King's Head? One of you," and the deep voice shook with pride, "who sang my health as you held the stairs against thirty swords?"

"That is the man, Sire. But he is old, and helpless, and broken. He will accept no farthing from anyone; I have tried. Yet if, in some fashion, the Treasury might restore his title and estates?"

"It shall be done. But for yourself?"

(*If you kill him not the next time, I will abandon . . .*)

"Nothing, Sire, except to—to serve you as well as I can."

"Nay, but I'll take one precaution!" Charles said grimly. The mocking, satiric lines were in his face again. "Being an idle fellow, as you may have heard, I am perhaps overfond of tales and legends. Now there is one tale, told of several kings and one queen, which facts prove ever false. But we'll do better; we'll make legend come true."

Slipping a cameo ring off his right hand, he pressed it down over one of Fenton's fingers.

"If they come at you with swords, Sir Nicholas, we need have no fear. But my Lord Shaftesbury, upon his return, may have subtler shifts against you. Should he try such (treason, it may be), send that

240

ring to me. It was given me by my father; our names are graved inside. It shall not go unheeded."

(*You will fynde him in Ded Man's Lane.* . . . Lydia, Lydia, Lydia!)

"I thank you, Sire."

"Now hold; bear up!—Mr. Chiffinch!" thundered Charles, in a voice which caused an instant dead silence through half the Banqueting House.

Chiffinch slipped in heavily past the edge of one screen.

"Look to it," said the King, "that Sir Nicholas shall go to his home in one of my coaches. After that, return here."

Fenton, as he backed away out past the screen, contrived a grave, courtly bow despite the shaking of his legs.

"Your servant, Sire," he said.

When both he and Chiffinch had gone, Charles remained for a time indecisive, stroking his cheek. Then he went to the little fireplace, again setting his hands wide on the mantelshelf and looking down at a grate of fiery ash where the centre log had almost burned in two.

He was still standing there when he heard Chiffinch return.

"And what did you make of him, Will?" he asked without turning round.

"Nay, I can't fathom the man," growled Chiffinch, a privileged character. "But he is honest."

For a moment Charles was silent.

"If I am a cynic, Will, I have reason to be. Poverty and exile ever sharpen the wits. If also I intrust few men and no women, I have reason for this too. Yet . . . "

He kicked at the centre log, which burst apart amid a shower of sparks.

"I tell you this, Will! There goes a man with a broken heart."

241

CHAPTER XVII

AUDIENCE IN LOVE LANE

AND YET Fenton himself would not have thought this, or said so, in the darkness of the huge, velvet-stuffy coach which jolted him to his home.

He merely felt numb. Ordinarily, the coach would badly have hurt his body bruises, but there was nothing. He felt no pain in his heart; no tendency to rage or revile; nothing. But it was extraordinarily difficult to make his arms and legs move as they should.

"I must think this out," he kept repeating to himself. "I must think this out from the very beginning."

He remembered how, as he went out from Whitehall Palace into Pebble Court, with torches shining about and the great coach in attendance, he had taken out his watch. He was astonished to find the hour was not quite eight-thirty. All his audience with the King, all that went into it, had taken less than an hour.

How strange is time! Fenton felt his hand begin to shake badly; he knew, in horror, he might drop the watch. Gently Chiffinch had taken it from his hand, under the torchlight, and replaced it in his pocket. In his other hand, unseen, Fenton clutched Lydia's crumpled letter. He managed to convey it to the pocket of his coat.

And now the great coach drew up before his door.

"I must think this out," he doggedly repeated in his mind.

Though he was glad to be assisted down the steps, yet he smilingly pretended he needed no help. Afterwards he rememberd preaching a mild, calm-voiced sermon to Sam, the door porter, that he need not remain there so late. It was deepening dusk, not yet dark. Sam bowed, opening the door for him, and then vanished.

242

But Giles, ever present, stood in the hall and held up a candle. When he saw Fenton's face, Giles's thin lips tightened.

"A good evening, sir."

"And to you, good Giles. Ever a good evening to you!"

"May I take the liberty of an old servant, sir, in the asking of whether all befell as you desired at Whitehall Palace?"

"It did so. And wherefore not?"

"His Majesty was not—angry? If you would take but one look at your own face in the mirror, you would understand."

"Angry, you say? God's fish!" Fenton began in a roar, but controlled his voice to quietness. "Learn, malapert, how angry was the King. He offered me any reward, any preferment, I should name. For honour's sake I could not take it, as you apprehend. Still!"

"Do you know what was offered, sir? Nay? Then I'll tell you. His Majesty offered you a peerage."

"Now, pox on't, what should I do with a peerage? —Giles. Is . . . my lady well?"

"Ay, truly," Giles answered in surprise. But there was a sour expression on his lips at his master's contemptuous dismissal of a peerage. "The supper was abandoned near as soon as you had gone. Lord George, stupefied, was carried home in my Lord Danby's coach. I confess, sir, I misliked the manner in which the elderly gentleman did sway in his saddle as he departed. Your lady, sir, hath gone to her room. She requested . . ."

Fenton seized the front of Giles's coat.

"I don't wish to speak to my—to her; that's to say, not now. Not until a few minutes before midnight. Am I clear, Giles?"

"Questionless, sir!"

"Fetch me lights," said Fenton. "I would go to my own bedchamber. I would sit there and reflect. Nor must I be disturbed for any cause. Is this clear too?"

Giles bowed. Quickly he kindled the tapers in a three-branched candelabrum.

"Nay, I'll light my own way up, Giles! Give it to me."

With a powerful effort Fenton kept his hand steady. His mind had always been clear, and he kept it clear. But, as the sense of shock slowly diminished, his bruises began to ache.

When he reached his own bedroom, he moved mechanically towards the two windows at the back, those windows looking out over his garden, the Mall below, and the Park. His long and heavy dressing table slanted out from the left-hand window, against the angle of the wall.

He set down the three-branched candelabrum on the dressing table near the mirror. Against ghostly darkness he caught a glimpse of his own reflection; it seemed (at least to his own eyes) a trifle pale, but not much.

"Why did Lydia do it?" he inaudibly asked the reflection, in his own mind. "Was this love of hers all a pretence?"

"You know it was."

"I can't face it."

"You must face it."

The soft candlelight bloomed on the glass, the dark-red of the claret decanter, which he had always kept in his room of late. Hastily he seized decanter and goblet, with a passionate wish to be dead drunk and away from all hurt. But he put them both down; now, if ever, he must be clear of head.

Unconsciously Fenton's hand, tightly clutching Lydia's crumpled letter, let it fall on the dressing table. Drawn up to the table was one of those padded Oriental chairs, much like those in the alcove at Whitehall, which were draped to the floor in crimson figured silk.

On a sudden impulse Fenton lifted the chair and set it down facing the darkness of the right-hand window.

But he made his preparations too. It was almost three hours and a half before midnight; Lydia's true danger began on the stroke of midnight, the tenth. Not once did he think of striding down to her bedroom, bursting in, and flinging that letter at her as accusation.

He could not do it. His mind shrank back, as from a fire. If she were guilty, he wished to keep knowledge from him as long as possible. It did not matter . . . well, it did not matter too much . . . what she had done. He loved her. He would protect her, whatever happened.

Carefully he set down his watch on the table, within reach of his hand.

Then he sat down in the padded chair, facing a window dark except for the reflection of candle flames and the leaves of a tall beech outside. Curious! When he had first waked up in this room, he had thought them trees of the Park, whereas, of course, they were in his own garden.

"I don't believe all this," he told himself, with a stab at his heart now the shock had worn off. "It's not Lydia! It's not her character!"

244

The other side of his own mind, cool and assessing, seemed to answer in terms of the twentieth century.

"Stop this emotionalism," it said. "You wished to think. Very well; think. What is Lydia's background?"

"Her parents were Presbyterians. Her grandfather was a regicide: which must mean either Independent or Fifth Monarchy man."

"And do you think nothing was stamped on her mind and heart before she married Sir Nick? Remember, she thinks herself married to Sir Nick. When I say 'you,' I refer to you in the semblance of Sir Nick. Did nothing hurt her, even when you cut her off from her old nurse, though she made a speech she knew would please you?"

"Be silent! What zeal would Lydia—of all persons— have for 'the cause'? The Green Ribbon?"

"Have you forgotten the elementary facts of history?"

"No."

"Then you remember that my Lord Shaftesbury, once himself a hot Presbyterian under Oliver, was the first forceful supporter at the Restoration that all Puritan sects might be permitted to take the Oath and Allegiance and Supremacy, so that they might not be out-laws? Don't you know he welcomes old Presbyterians, old Independents, to the Green Ribbon? And their helpers?"

"But Lydia! She has no head for politics, or interest. She has said so a dozen times."

"Rather too quickly, don't you think? Remember how each time she has turned you quickly away from the subject?"

"Be silent, I say! On the very first night I met her, in Meg's room,"— his mind paused a moment when he thought of Meg—"I tried to apologize for Sir Nick's conduct, and asked forgiveness. And Lydia answered, 'You ask my pardon? I ask yours, with all my heart.' "

"Well? And what else could she say?"

"I don't follow that."

"No one paints her character as cold and evilhearted. She was touched. Why do you suppose she defied her parents and married Sir Nick? It was a physical attraction; no more or less. When she found Sir Nick was a murderous and blackhearted dog, she hated him. Yet the ghost of attraction remained."

"Yes, you can bet it did! When next day she hurried into this bed-room, with the poison rash on her forehead and arm, she was all tenderness and . . . and . . ."

"Certainly she pretended it. But do you recall what you said?"

"I have forgotten."

"Only because you wish to forget. Sir Nick, half-mad, burst into a torrent of abuse; and called down God's curse on Puritans and all their race. Because she seemed a gentle girl, you forgot she might be at heart as savage a Roundhead as you are Royalist."

"Yet afterwards she was tender. Why, it was she who asked for—for me to seek her that night!"

"Mainly pretence. For the rest, you know her to be a fullblood girl of strong passions."

"There was no pretence. You lie."

"Ah, is your vanity scratched?"

"Do you tell me that, immediately after making that assignation, she wrote the letter telling my enemies where to find me?"

"Of course. She does not love you. You are dangerous; you must be destroyed."

"Stop this nonsense!"

"Yet you wished to think it out. How many times, when she wished to give you false praise, has her tongue slipped with that word, 'Roundhead'? Why, think! 'As gentle as a minister of God, yet as bold as a Roundhead soldier.' Those words so inspired you that you struck dumb the whole Green Ribbon Club, and not a man dared lay a hand on you!"

"I did not think of them at the time. Yet surely . . ."

"Who wheedled you into Spring Gardens that night? And, on the same day, slipped out secretly to send a note that brought down three swordsmen on you? To buy a new gown? Nonsense! Because the shop La Belle Poitrine is a new clearinghouse for letters."

"I tell you, stop this torture! If Lydia cared nothing at all, what do you make of her jealousy, and above all her jealousy towards Meg?"

"That is more foolishness. Lydia is a woman. You are her possession. Do you think she would let any draw you from her? Least of all Meg; or, rather, Mary Grenville? Lydia knows that secretly Meg turns your brain; she can't abide it; no woman's vanity would."

"I keep telling you, I have turned all Puritan nonsense out of her mind!"

"In a month? Come, now! When with six men against sixty, impossible odds, you went out to fight . . . well, did Lydia attempt to stop you, as most would? No; all she could think of was the dragoons; how they made a file turn as well as any Ironsides."

"She trusted me to win!"

"Remember," cruelly the other side of his mind pointed out, "you are fifty-eight years old. Not in body. But in mind. Could not a pretty face, and pretty airs, and designing flesh, easily fool you? Might you not even become besotted?"

"Yes; I must understand the possibility."

"Then take heed, when she warns you against the only woman who is really fond of you: Meg York. Lydia hates Sir Nick, and thinks you are Sir Nick; she is only using on another man the crafts of love she learned from Sir Nick."

Fenton sprang to his feet, his arm across his eyes.

Wrath flared through him, but he knew he must control this. Quietly setting back each whisper at his ear, or hoping to do so, he sat down again in front of the black window and readjusted his thoughts. For a little time he looked out on blackness, and then the loud ticking of his watch on the dressing table reminded him.

It was ten minutes to nine. Already he had come to one resolve. He sprang up again, putting his watch back into his pocket. At the same time there was a light knock on the door.

Giles, very hesitant, peered in.

"Sir," said Giles, clearing his throat, "I should not have troubled you. But the woman Pamphlin . . ."

Judith Pamphlin, as straight-backed and harsh-faced as ever, stood gripping her hands together.

"My lady," she said, "would ask why you have not come to see her since your return." Mrs. Pamphlin almost sneered. "She would also ask . . ."

Fenton's right hand moved lovingly towards his sword grip. It was a very ill-chosen moment, as anyone could have seen in Giles's face, for Judith to be here.

"You have disobeyed my order," Fenton told her, "as to going near my lady. Later we will have discourse on this. Yet your one virtue, as I can perceive it, is that you are devoted and loyal to my lady. Is this so?"

"It is so."

"Then keep good watch. Inform my lady that I must go from the

247

house, on a matter of import, but that I shall return before midnight."

Mrs. Pamphlin's mouth opened to speak, but instead a wicked look came into her eyes, and she grudgingly remained silent. Giles, hastily thrusting one of the two candles into her hand, pushed her outside and closed the door.

"Is this truth, sir?" Giles asked quietly. "Do you indeed go from the house?"

"And why not?"

"Because of your mood, sir. You are ill."

"Now what could you know of my mood?" Fenton asked dryly. His side smarted from a shallow sword-wound, and a feverishness came on him. "Giles! I would be habited with less of the showy or the conspicuous. Stay!" Vague memory stirred. "The black, Giles! The black velvet I first wore on that day, May 10th, you did so strangely mention to me . . ."

"Sir," Giles cried in agony, "I am a bad servant. I have not cleaned the black, or so much as touched it. There were—there are bloodstains on the cuffs."

Fenton was in too impatient a mood.

"No matter for that! These," and he looked down over his sober grey clothes, with only a silver stripe to the waistcoat, "will serve the occasion well enough. Now go down to the stables, and bid them saddle my horse."

After one look at him, Giles hurried from the room. From the dressing closet Fenton brought out a pair of light, soft riding boots which came well above his knees and had light spurs. He buckled on both sides of his neck a light cloak and crammed down hat on periwig.

Snatching up the three-branched candle holder, he attempted to creep softly downstairs. Even with the utmost caution, spurs would rattle on a board floor. What he feared was that Lydia might come hurrying out of her room.

Breathing more easily when he reached the ground floor, Fenton set down his lights on the desk. He opened the door of the bookcase and found the book of Tillotson's sermons in which he had left the slip of paper with Meg York's two addresses.

"One of them," he thought, as he found the slip, "will be useless now. George said she had gone from Captain Duroc's. But the other . . ."

He smoothed out the paper and read it.

> "At the Golden Woman,"
> Love Lane,
> Cheapside.

Despite his bitterness, Fenton could have laughed.

A minute later he found Sweetquean before the door, her bridle held by Dick with a lanthorn. An ache, he could not tell whether mental or physical, went over him as he set his foot into the deep stirrup.

"A fine night, sir," said Dick.

"Ay," he said. "A fine night."

Riding the mare on a slack rein, at most times letting Sweetquean have her head, Fenton rode for Charing Cross. Though chilly, the night showed a great throng of stars and a slender new moon.

Fenton passed Charing Cross, into the sweep of the Strand, under Temple Bar, and down the long slope of Fleet Street. All the world's affront of the nostrils assailed him as the mare's hoofs thundered on the heavy planks over Fleet Ditch, and Sweetquean went up Ludgate Hill at the gallop. There Fenton reined in to look round.

Except for stars and new moon, it was intensely dark. There were no street lamps. Behind him, sometimes in the distance ahead, would glow the warm red lattice of a tavern. But Bow bells, in Cheapside, must have struck nine some time ago.

That was the signal for the apprentices to unhitch their folded shutters and button up their shops for the night. In the street remained only a few revellers. Before Fenton lay a vast openness, cleared of burnt rubble, where once had stood Old St. Paul's before the Fire, and the first brick of New St. Paul's would be laid this very month.

"Old days," thought Fenton, as he sent the mare clattering round to the left of St. Paul's Churchyard and rode down Cheapside. But he was not thinking of London in this age.

He was remembering how he and Mary Grenville—or Meg York—had ridden in the Park together in their old life: not St. James's Park, but the now-woodland Hyde Park, where stood grisly Tyburn. He remembered how they had swum in the river at Richmond. Mary, at eighteen, was a famous swimmer. But he, removing his pince-nez at over fifty, had gone all out and beaten her by three lengths.

No. He must not think of her as Mary Grenville. He must think of her as Meg York, a grown woman and a tigerish one.

Clack went his mare's hoofs on the cobbles of curving deepest Cheapside, and he reined in to study where he was. Not far away a watchman's lanthorn bobbed in the air like a dull luminous face.

It might be a pity that Sir Christopher Wren's plan for a finer, greater London had never been used after the destruction of the Fire. But they built back the ancient streets, old since the Middle Ages, on exactly the same sites and with the same names.

Fenton's memory could pick up, on his right and sloping down towards the river, Broad Street and Milk Street and Wood Street. They had bought these commodities in the streets before them, as they had bought the other commodity in Love Lane.

There were still gaps and scars from the Fire nine years ago. But most of the new buildings, high or low-and-trim, had been built of brick, with the plague burnt out of every hole. Fenton, as he guided the mare carefully down slippery cobbles, noted that Love Lane had become a district of the respectable poor.

"Nobody," Meg had whispered, "knows I am there. None can find me, or trouble me. 'Tis in no fine neighbourhood; but what better?"

Above the steep street showed a narrow path of stars. It was a trifle too close to Billingsgate Fish Market, Fenton decided. Suddenly a great red glare, over the houses, sprang up some distance away down the Thames, faded to pink, and died away. It was the immense soap vats and boileries, which he had forgotten; and, fortunately, the wind blew the other way.

But the glare showed him the house he sought. It was small, new, built of brick; and, like most others, it had a long staircase built up to the ground floor. Not a light showed. Tethering Sweetquean to a hitching post, Fenton ran up the stairs and banged at the door knocker until the little street echoed. Presently the door was opened by an ancient woman named Calpurnia, with one eye still open after a life of thievery and viciousness.

"Ay," she wheezed out, narrowly inspecting him in the light of a floating wick in a grease lamp, "you're the man. One pair of stairs up, then find ye a chamber overlooking the street. On Calpy's oath, the lady's not strayed from this house one minute, for fear she should not find you. Some hath one taste," shrugged Calpy, "and some another."

Fenton flicked a coin at her, and it mysteriously vanished in mid-air. He did not even see her catch it.

"Now begod!" she cried, holding the grease lamp higher and rolling

250

her one eye. "Here's a different thing! Here's a gentleman; here's a nobleman! I'll stand and hold the lamp for ye, that I will and so help me!"

But the lamp was not necessary. Fenton hastened up the stairs, and back again along the upstairs passage towards the front. The front room had its door partly open, and faint candlelight shone out.

And then Fenton stopped abruptly.

Someone in the room, unquestionably Meg, was softly playing a tenor viol. Meg's fine contralto voice, though low-pitched, rang out with a triumph of joy and pride.

> "Here's a cry to all ye goodmen,
>> Shout it joyous through the town—
> Three swordsmen and three woodmen
>> Did bring the tyrant down!"

Fenton held hard to the stair rail, now half-sick at the stomach.

Of all the things he did not want to hear, these were the worst. Each tawdry word somehow concerned Lydia, and brought Lydia into his mind. He stumbled down the passage while Meg still proudly sang of that cheap brash affair . . . .

> "If all held firm and stood, men,
>> No Shaftesb'ry rules the Crown!
> Three swordsmen and three woodmen
>> Shall bring THIS tyrant down!"

Fenton, his spurs rattling, threw open the door. The bow of the tenor viol slipped away from the strings. He and Meg looked at each other.

"You have been a mighty long time," said Meg, tossing her head with a careless air, "in coming to wait upon me." Then her tone changed. "Nick! What's the matter?"

At the front of the room there were two windows, with a fireplace between them. At each window faced out into the room a huge carved chair, covered with coloured swan's-down pillows. A single candle burned in a golden holder in the middle of the mantelpiece, above a light log fire in the chimney. Meg, fully dressed in a purple velvet gown with a heavy fall of Venice point lace round the low corsage, sat in the big carven chair to the right of the fireplace.

The tenor viol had fallen from her hand. That dim light shone on her dark hair.

Since Fenton knew her tastes, he was not surprised to find the small

251

square room as richly furnished as any at Whitehall. There were padded chairs, and an ottoman. But most of all, because of the tapestries and the amorous pictures, it reminded him of George's description. . . .

Meg sprang to her feet, letting fall the viol bow.

"Wait!" he said.

His face was as white as tallow, his legs unsteady. His right arm so ached with bruises that he could not have made a quick sword-draw to save his life. But he groped up for his hat, and found it gone. It must have blown off somewhere.

"First of all," Fenton said hoarsely, in the speech of 1925, "let's get rid, as we did once, of all this nonsense of word and pronunciation out of our own century. Let's speak as we were taught to speak!"

The dim candlelight, the struggling fire, made a shadow-play across Meg's white shoulders. But her eyes, lids drooping, began to gleam with understanding.

"Very well, if you wish. —Professor Fenton, why are you really here?"

"Because I'm beaten," he answered flatly. "I can't see what to do. I came here for . . . for . . ."

"For sympathy?" asked Meg, with poisoned sweetness. She crept a little way out, her breast rising and falling. Jealousy, hatred leaped at him. "You've had a tiff, I suppose, with that . . . that . . . the Lydia woman?"

"In a sense, yes."

"And now you come crawling to me for sympathy? Well, you won't get it!" Meg straightened up. "And you!"

Fenton contemplated the bright carpet.

"Probably you're right," he admitted.

"You!" Meg said bitterly. "Oh, I know Mr. Reeve too! Who doesn't? And I have a copy of his verses! They call you the hero of the 'battle' of Pall Mall. I was proud of that. Yes! And, in our other lives, do you remember how you planned General, now Field Marshal, Fatwaller's campaign that nearly broke the whole German defences? Yes! And led the opening attack yourself, with the First Battalion of Westshires?"

"Strangely enough, I dreamed of that the other night."

"And now you come for sympathy to me. I can't endure a man who crawls. Get out of here! Go!" she screamed at him. "Take your silly troubles and get out!"

252

"Good night, then; and good-by."

He had not seen, even before he turned towards the door, how Meg's expression suddenly altered. It altered even as she screamed at him. There was a heavy rustling of silks as she raced past him towards the door, closed it, and set her back to it.

"Nick! No! Wait!"

"Get out of my way, please," he said dully. "What's the use?"

"Oh, why must I always do this?" cried Meg, her grey-black eyes roving round the room as though she might find some answer there. "Almost every time we meet, I turn spiteful; I grow vixenish; I say things I don't mean. And I didn't mean what I said just now; I didn't!"

To his dulled astonishment, real tears gleamed on her long black eyelashes as she looked at him. Meg clasped her hands together. More than her physical appeal, more than contrition, she seemed to exude a power of sympathy which almost burned.

"Don't go," she whispered. "Nick . . ."

Once more he kissed her, and once more he lost his head.

"Now tell me!" said Meg, looking at him with her head held back. "What hath this woman done to you? Hath she cuckolded you?"

"Damn it, Mary, have you forgotten the speech of your own century?"

"I'm sorry, I'm sorry! But did she—deceive you with another man?"

"No."

"Then wherefore did you quarrel?"

Fenton was silent. He could not speak.

"Well, it makes no matter," Meg said presently. "I do not care. Come here, Nick."

A little way out from the closed door was a large padded chair, which faced towards the fireplace with its window on either side. A red glare sprang up behind the right-hand window; but he remembered, as it dimmed to pink and died, it was only the soap boileries down the Thames.

"It makes no matter!" Meg repeated in a shaky voice, though both knew she lied. Again she indicated the padded chair facing the windows. "Sit down, my dear. And must you wear a clumsy sword, a buckled cape, even here with me?"

Fenton loosed the sword and the cape, and threw them over on the ottoman. Then he sat down.

"I should ask you to remove that periwig too," said Meg. "Yet (foh!)

253

all men have their hair cropped beneath, or near-cropped, so that there may be no lice."

Fenton did not know why he laughed.

"You need not fear the cropped skull or the lice either. I have let my hair grow," he said. Taking off the periwig, he flung it over to the ottoman with a single bruise-twinge in his right arm.

His heavy black hair, parted on one side, had been pressed down by the periwig. As he threw the wig away, it was as though he came step by step closer, through the mists of the past, towards the future. But Meg, who had sat down sideways on his lap so that she might look at him and bend over him, for a moment would not allow him to think of this.

"Nay," she whispered close to his cheek, "you must never think of me as Mary Grenville; only as Meg York. My true self is Meg York. This was so even when truly I was Mary Grenville, though I must needs conceal it because you all thought of me as a small girl."

She bent over him. His intense mingling of desire, comfort, and sympathy again kept him silent. Meg persistently used the old speech; he knew he must do so too.

"Much of your perplexity," Meg said, "I caused by things I should have told you long ago, but durst not. Will you hear me now?"

"I hear you."

"Do you recollect that night—in your withdrawing room, two hundred and fifty years from now—when you told me you had sold your soul to the devil?"

Fenton felt a small, inexplicable chill. But he nodded.

"I recollect it well," he replied.

"And you discovered me not . . . surprised?"

"True! I felt so. Yet I can't tell why."

"It was of the heart, dearest, not the mind. You sought and found it ere you knew."

"Yet . . ."

"Stay; hear me! I had heard no word of these people, or this matter of poisoning, though you had studied it for years. Still do you recollect?"

"Yes?"

"I was in a rage; I was sore jealous; I could have bit the blood from my arm." Now Meg's low voice hissed at him. "Yet I must not tarry. I

254

loved you. I must learn, in haste and from a certain source, who these people might be. 'Three beautiful women,' " Meg quoted, with hatred; "that was what you said. Well! As one of these women, I must travel into the past with you."

"Travel into the . . ." Fenton stopped.

"Playing Meg York, but with my own self in her place, could I not indeed demonstrate I was no little girl?" Round Meg's lips curled the elusive smile with which he was so familiar. "Faith, Nick, did you not mark it the first night you met me?"

The glow of the soap vats, rising up red behind the right-hand window and touching the left-hand window as well, showed Meg's wicked little smile more clearly.

"By God's body!" Fenton swore, and gripped her arms so that the smile became more provocative. "Did you, Mary Grenville, make any pact to sell your soul to . . . our friend?"

Meg's voice was enigmatic.

"Of that," she said, "we must discourse presently. In Spring Gardens, not long ago, you asked me why I did not tell you I was Mary Grenville when first we were met. I replied: that I was unsure of myself, unsure even of my speech."

Abruptly Meg, despite her body heat, shivered. He put his arms round her and gripped her hard, feeling the pressure of her arms in return and her cheek against his. Both of them stammered in their speech.

"Y-yet," said Meg, " 'twas not all the truth. I must make you sure I could not be Mary Grenville. I must put by and delay. I must cause you to love me, or at least desire me, as Meg York."

"Tell me! Have you made any pact with . . ."

"I'll not say yes or no. Yet I travelled back in time in my own semblance, though I chose to be Meg York. Your lady mistress."

"A pity," said Fenton, "I have never been in a position to exercise my rights!"

"Why, as to that! 'Tis easily remedied. —Stay; touch me no more for the moment! I would have time to . . ."

"Unnecessary! Pray why defer?"

After a certain struggle, Meg rose to her feet. She settled her purple velvet gown, with the heavy fall of lace at the corsage. Hurrying to the mantelpiece, she picked up the single taper holder to light her way into another room. As she turned from the mantelpiece and went back towards the door, she held up the taper flame when she passed Fenton, who was on his feet now.

"I shall return very quickly," she murmured. "Do you much wish for my return?"

"Much!"

She glided past his hand, looking at him over her shoulder with her eyelids lowered. The door opened, and closed after her.

Fenton, his nerves twitching, sat down again.

Now the only light in the little room, with its tapestries and pictures, came from a fire which would not burn properly. Its small logs were burnt fiery red underneath, but with only a flick of flame over them.

Once this whole area (so the thoughts mumbled in Fenton's head) had been swept by a Great Fire which began in a bakery in Pudding Lane. But surely there was something peculiar about the little log fire here in the grate now? Or else the direction of the wind had changed. This fire seemed to let smoke into the room, curling upwards in odd style. Then a deep glow from the soap boileries beyond the right-hand window, with its great chair facing outwards, rose up to show him the truth. There was no smoke from the chimney. There was no smoke at all. He had mistaken it for what seemed a vague, shifting outline of someone sitting in the great chair.

A suave, familiar voice spoke across at him.

"Good evening, my friend," said the devil.

CHAPTER XVIII

THE FATHER OF EVIL

THE red glare faded to pink dimness and died away. There remained only the unstable, varying outline in the chair by a dull fire. The devil, as usual, spoke modern English with a slightly archaic flavour.

Over Fenton's mind again stole the sense he had known on the first night he had met the devil: a dreamlike quality, wherein voices were soundless and emotions felt only as impalpable waves; yet, at the same time, all seemed as natural and commonplace as two men talking in the smoking room of a club.

But this was not all. The devil's appearance could not prevent Fenton from jumping to this feet, stifling back a fine old oath, before the dream world closed over him. He settled back again, with a suavity to match the devil's own.

"Good evening, my dear sir," Fenton answered coldly.

There was a pause. The devil seemed distressed.

"Professor Fenton," he said, "have I in any way offended you? Is my presence unwelcome?"

"You are always welcome," conceded Fenton, "if only for your verbal rapier play. Yet you choose a most da—a most unfortunately ill-timed moment for your visit."

"Ah!" said the devil, enlightened. "You refer to the—er—young lady?"

"Who will return very shortly."

The devil was deeply shocked.

"My dear fellow!" he protested. "Do you imagine for one moment that I, of all people, would interfere with this laudable little affair of

257

yours? No, no, no! You horrify me. Such affairs, in nine cases out of ten, are most useful to me. —Ah, I see! You consider my presence, at such a time, embarrassing and tactless?"

"I do not say tactless. I merely point out that you are here."

"Come now!" chuckled the devil. "I had not thought to find you so conventional. In that case, you can postpone your trifling for some other occasion."

"In all your own vast experience, sir, have you ever found that argument quite convincing at the time?"

The devil's tone altered slightly.

"Does it not occur to you, Professor Fenton, that you are treating rather lightly some matters which concern your own soul?"

And now Fenton heard or, to be exact, sensed in the wave of emotion which flowed from that great chair the first hint of malice, like that of the cruel small boy. Yet here was the Father of Evil, who could upset real mountains and crush armies as the small boy might upset a toy mountain or scatter lead soldiers.

Nor was this all. The devil, metaphorically, had waxed and grown huge. Despite his casual behaviour, like a man in a club, the glimmer of his power blazed through. To put the matter in ordinary terms, he was like a man who holds a handful of trumps, and begins to let it be seen. Of course he had known all the time that Meg was there.

For a moment, as at their one previous meeting, his presence turned Fenton's insides into a cold hollow of fear. Fenton walked amid tall dangers, and he knew it. But, crudely to turn back the metaphor, the devil did not hold the ace of trumps. Fenton's play against him must now never falter.

"You are right," Fenton admitted, with a shade of humility in his voice. "I have treated these matters—perhaps too lightly. I ask your pardon."

"Granted, granted!" said the devil suavely, as though he might have waved his hand. "I wished only to remind you of your position. After all, we did sign a certain . . . a certain agreement some time ago."

"We did."

"Ah! Have I fulfilled my conditions of the bargain?"

"In candour, sir, you have led me one devil of a dance."

"But you wished to be Sir Nick Fenton; behold, you are. Still! I must remind you that some of your 'conditions,'" said the devil, "were beyond even my power to grant. Being absent-minded, I failed to remind you at the time."

"Oh?" Again terror swept through Fenton. "You 'forgot' to remind me?"

"Alas, yes," sighed the devil. "Yet you should have seen it. When you said, 'You will make me do thus,' or 'You will not allow that,' you should have realized it was beyond my power *if* it contradicted history. But, my dear sir!" The devil sounded hurt. "I quite fairly warned you that no one can change history."

"No one?"

And now the devil was complacent.

"Not myself, or my . . . my Opponent." Briefly he seemed to glance upwards. "Long ago, at a time (forgive me) beyond your comprehension, my Opponent and I planned the history of this very small planet. We warred, of course. Here He gained a victory; there *I* won instead. But it cannot be altered. I have almost forgotten it. It is no more than a dusty plan, rolled up like an architect's, and put away in some obscure pigeonhole of time."

Soothing, drowsy, almost hypnotic was the voice. Abruptly the devil chuckled, altering his mood.

"Come now, Professor Fenton!" he said amiably. "If I have made you Sir Nick Fenton, what have you to fear? Nothing. Not even when I . . . call for you at the time of your death. Let us speak of more pleasant matters! For instance, this young lady—"

The door opened, and Meg stood on the threshold.

In her left hand she held up a lighted candle in a brass holder. Her dark-gleaming hair was loosed round her shoulders. With her right hand she held loosely about her body the yellow bedgown she had worn when Fenton first saw her as Meg York.

Even with the candlelight, she could not ordinarily have seen that immense, shifting vagueness against the window. And yet, Fenton realized as he turned round, Meg knew.

Immediately the taper flame, perhaps in a draught, dwindled to a blue spark and vanished. Just before it disappeared, there seemed to be strange lines and alterations in Meg's face; but they changed back into her normal beauty before the room went dark, except for the fire.

Meg stood terrified, as though her knees would not move.

"Ah, my dear," said the visitor. "You need not be formal. You may join us, if you like."

His tone was that of an elderly uncle speaking to a girl of eight or nine years old, whom he will presently reward with a shilling.

"No, no, my dear!" he added, still kindly but with a note of warning.

"You must not occupy the same chair as my good friend Professor Fenton. My broad-mindedness, I think, is well known. But this would (how shall I put it?) disturb the concentration of you both. —Go and sit on the ottoman, my dear."

Meg, turning her face away from Fenton, walked over unsteadily and sat down, huddling the yellow bedgown round her.

Fenton spoke, but the horrors were on him and he had first to clear his throat.

"One question!" he said to the devil. "May I ask one question?"

"My dear fellow! By all means."

"When I foolishly asked to be carried back into the seventeeth century, did Mary Grenville sell you her sou . . . that is, offer to join your household, if she could accompany me? For my idiot's sake?"

The visitor did not commit himself.

"And if she did?" he insinuated, like a shopman in Cheapside.

"Sir," replied Fenton, "my own soul is a poor and mean thing. But I offer it to you freely, if you will restore hers."

Daring everything, Meg sat up.

"No!" she cried to Fenton. "He hasn't the power to make such a bargain, even if he would! Don't listen to him!"

Meg stopped, her hands over her face, and rolled back on the couch as though she had been struck by some immense hand. Yet nothing had moved in the room; nothing at all.

The shape in the chair seemed to turn suavely towards Fenton.

"Why," it said, "the girl is quite right. She has been, as you so delicately put it, a member of my household since she was about eighteen. She was converted, I think, in 1918, because she found the world insufferably dull and she was overfond of men."

Fenton began to speak, but could not manage it.

"She passed her novitiate long ago," the devil assured him. "In general she is a tractable girl and an admirable servant." Now his tone grew kindly and soothing. "Yet for some reason (forgive me) obscure even to myself, her affections have always centred on you. When she begged in her prettiest way to travel back with you, could my kind heart refuse?"

"Then there is no way to restore. . . ?"

"None."

"Yet if—"

"Would you insult my household, sir? The girl is quite happy."

And then the devil's tone became one of sharp mockery.

"But your own offer, professor! It was very handsome of you. It was even quixotic, as often you so foolishly are. Offer your own soul? Now why should I bargain for what I already own?"

Inside Fenton's head his thoughts seemed to speak almost audibly.

"Now," they whispered. "Now's the time. *Hit him!*"

And so Fenton spoke out very clearly.

"Oh, no, you don't!" he said.

"I beg your pardon?"

"You don't own my soul. You never did. And now, by God's grace, you never shall."

The fire popped and crackled. Fenton braced himself for an outburst, one of those terrifying waves in which the cruel small boy predominated over the suave philosopher. But the heavy silence seemed even more menacing.

"Your—er—evidence for that statement, Professor Fenton?"

"It is in your own theology."

"You must be more particular, I think."

"With pleasure. Sir Nicholas Fenton was born on December 25th. In case it has escaped your notice, so was I. December 25th is widely known as Christmas Day."

Fenton leaned forward.

"In my reading," he continued, "I discover that a man or woman born on Christmas Day *cannot* sell his soul to the devil, save that he lose it by free gift or believe your hoaxing: which I do not. Any pact I may make with you is null and void before it is signed. Do you deny this?"

"You have accepted favours from me. You must pay for them."

"Granted. According to rule, on each December 25th I must give you a Christmas gift in token. When the proper time comes this year, I shall be happy to present you with a silver toasting fork or an illustrated Bible. Come, didn't you know all this?"

"Oh, I knew it. But I wondered whether you did."

"Wondered?" echoed Fenton. "Are you not, in the popular mind, supposed to know all things?"

"Yes, I know all things. As you shall presently discover in sorrow and pain. But sometimes, when I deal with a foolish quixotic soul like

261

yours," the visitor almost snarled, "a bandage is briefly set across even my eyes . . ."

"By One far greater than yourself?"

"Not greater," the other replied silkily. "Such speech is dangerous, Professor Fenton. I advise you against it."

"Do you admit defeat?"

"Oh, I cannot take your soul on my own behalf. You must be judged by my Opponent. And He, I hear, is not lenient in these matters. — But you tricked me, Professor Fenton. That is what sticks in my throat. I cannot abide trickery! Why did you trick me?"

Again Fenton leaned forward, clutching the arms of the chair.

"Because you yourself are history's greatest cheat," he said. "You would not give fair play to a sick dog. And I resolved to win over you." Fenton was now shouting. "And how did I win over you? Because, like all evil, you are stupid and a fool!"

Then the outburst came.

Meg screamed, writhing on the ottoman, though it scarcely touched her.

The waves of wrath, silent yet deadly, struck at Fenton like an army. Soundlessly he could hear the small boy kicking a tin drum, as well as the towering presence of Sathanas himself. Physically it exhausted him. Yet he muttered certain prayers, and looked straight ahead at what he imagined might be the eyes of the presence.

Also, he looked at Meg and was horrified. She was now sitting up, back partly turned, knees drawn up under the bedgown. The fire had burned up brightly. Her face (how he should have interpreted it then!) was the same he had seen on the first night of his new life: sly, mocking, withdrawn, essentially of evil. You must not call the devil stupid; this is the one thing he resents.

Yet the waves beat round him, and he came to no harm.

Presently they died away, though this was only the end of an outburst. Menace still hung in the room, like fire or edged steel, with Meg's vicious face behind it. The devil seemed to be musing. When at last he spoke, it was in a tone of unfeigned amusement and genuine interest.

"Professor Fenton," he said softly, "did you really think you could outwit me?"

"I can't tell—yet."

"Indeed? You can't tell? But I can. Once I had a liking for you. That is gone. I am tempted to tell you the mistakes you made, and the very

262

unpleasant surprises in store for you. But I refrain; you will know soon enough. Let us take only the lightest, smallest thistledown of the errors you made."

"Your own lack of intelligence, sir . . ."

The visitor ignored this.

"You," he said, drawing out the syllable into a long cavern of amusement, "would change history! Yes? And several times, I think, you have already tried to change it?"

"Yes."

"In fact, you spoke to the two most—most intelligent men in England, King Charles the Second and my Lord Shaftesbury, who are even of opposing views. Every word you said will come true. But would either of them believe you?"

"No."

"The King liked you, and was even desirous of believing you. He gave you that cameo ring on your finger now; this, he said, would shield you from all harm"—here the visitor chuckled malevolently—"if you were in danger and sent it to him. Can you be shielded? I think not.

"Stay!" he added. "A final word. Now why were you so astonished, Professor Fenton, when you saw me here tonight? Surely you must have expected me?"

"Expected you?"

"Come! The really important date in history, which you were determined to change, was June 10th. On June 10th (as I know, since I know all things) your wife Lydia is destined to die of poison . . ."

Fenton sat as though paralyzed, suddenly choked and frightened as the visitor had never been able to frighten him.

Lydia! Midnight! He had promised to return before then! With fingers all thumbs, he shakily drew his watch out of his pocket. His arm trembled, and the watch almost slipped from his fingers. His tired eyes, by firelight, could not read the numbers on the dial. But it could not possibly be very late.

"The hour!" he pleaded. "I entreat you, sir: tell me the hour!"

It was as though the visitor in some fashion raised puzzled eyebrows.

"The hour?" he inquired. "But doth it matter?"

Subtly, almost insensibly, the speech of them all crept back to the mode of the later seventeenth century.

"Yes, yes, yes!" cried Fenton. "Tomorrow, beginning with midnight, will be June 10th. Yet must I be there from the stroke of midnight, lest harm befall Lydia!"

"Now scratch me," observed the visitor, in horrible imitation of George Harwell, "but I think this man is struck from his senses!"

Fenton raced forward towards the dying fire, holding the open case and dial of the watch towards red lumps and red embers. The watch had stopped at nine-thirty, the very time he crossed Meg's threshold.

Slowly, badly shaken, Fenton replaced the watch. Then he flung himself at the shape in the chair, lunging with both hands for the throat. But there was nobody in the chair. Afterwards Fenton backed slowly away; and there appeared again the shifting, varying outline, once more clearly seen as the red glare of the soap vats rose up.

And still again, maddeningly, the visitor chuckled.

"Observe, my child," he said to Meg, "how your Hector shrivels up like a burnt worm when he thinks of danger to Lydia, and how he is mad for love of her! Can I never convince you?"

Meg was now kneeling on the ottoman, her teeth exposed in rage and her mouth pulled square like a Greek mask.

"Stay but a moment, Professor Fenton!" purred the devil. "I ask your pardon for believing you bereft of your senses. For, now I think on't, there's a simple way of explaining what perplexed me an instant ago."

"There's . . . you said what?"

"I think, good fellow, you have kept your own calendar for the past month? In a plain book?"

Fenton, impatient with this, hurried to the ottoman to gather up sword, periwig, and cloak. Meg struck at him like a cat, but he threw her aside. He was buckling on the sword belt when the visitor's next words, musing, made him stop abruptly.

"The calendar, or diary, whatever you would call it, was locked. The cabinet was locked. You shewed it to no person; you compared days with none! Yes? To no one did you speak of the day, June 10th, which you so dreaded. Yes?"

"I . . ."

"And yet," continued the shape in the chair, "this very evening, at your own supper table, Mr. Jonathan Reeve cried out truly that the 'battle' in Pall Mall occurred on the night of June 7th. Now bethink you! For two days after this 'battle' you rested. On the evening of the third day, this evening, you held a small supper. Yes?"

Automatically, so hard hit that his fingers were steady, Fenton buckled the cloak on his left shoulder. He picked up the periwig.

"It was somewhat stupid of you," murmured the devil, "yet perhaps excusable. You have forgotten that, on the day after the 'battle,' you

264

dozed all day and night under doses of laudanum and did not touch your diary. Next day, you wrote '8th' for '9th.' Your record is one day short."

Fenton jammed the periwig down on his head, gripping at the sides.

"What in hell's name d'ye tell me?" he shouted.

"*Today* was the 10th of June. —And your wife is dying."

The silence stretched out unendurably.

"Liar!"

"A pox, Professor Fenton! Now why should I give myself the trouble of telling a lie? You will discover it ere long."

"The hour! What's the hour?"

"Let me say once more that it cannot matter. If perhaps I stopped your watch, this was but a gentle scratch to remind you: a month ago, you jeered *me* for tampering with dates and clocks. Stay but another moment," he insinuated, as Fenton went towards the door, "and I will tell you why your wife has been poisoned, and is dying now, partly by your own neglect."

"My ne . . ."

"Assuredly. You returned from Whitehall Palace this night in (shall I say?) low spirit. Someone, completely unsuspected by you, gave my Lady Fenton a monstrous large portion of arsenic. When the pains racked her, my lady sent a message to you by a Mrs. Judith Pamphlin. You have always believed Mrs. Pamphlin to be . . . loyal?"

"Yes!"

"In a sense, no doubt. But did you never wonder? That Judith Pamphlin would rather see her beloved lady dead than in your hands?"

Fenton stood motionless.

"Thus Mrs. Pamphlin brought word only that your lady wished to speak with you. Not one word more could be pressed from her though you used weights at Newgate. You should have suspected some bubble, some trick, when you knew Mrs. Pamphlin had been in your wife's room. But no. You made haste from the house, seeking solace of another woman."

Meg, again kneeling on the ottoman, cried out to the visitor in a different voice.

"I am the humblest of your servants," she pleaded. "But torture him no more!"

There was a sound as of a large, scaly hand rubbed on the oak arm of the chair.

"My child," purred the visitor, "you have a certain attractiveness,

265

in particular when you are so careless with that bedgown. But *I?* Torture someone? You horrify me."

And the shape in the chair, with vast inner amusement, seemed to turn towards Fenton.

"Go now," it said; "go too late. Your wife, I think—indeed, I am sure—is in her death agony at this moment. If you rode with the wind, if you flew, you could not be with her before she dies."

The door banged as Fenton ran out. They heard a plunging clump of boots, a rattle of spurs, recede away down the stairs. When the outer door also banged, there was silence.

Again there was a noise as of a large, scaly hand on the chair arm. Meg shuddered with repulsion. The fire was of blackening embers.

"And now, my dear," cooed the devil . . .

Twenty-five minuters later, any person near dark Pall Mall would have heard the black mare approaching at a lathered gallop. Sweetquean swept in, rearing up and almost unseating her rider before he dismounted. Fenton, himself corpse-faced, his periwig awry and his spur rowels bloodied, ran towards a front door which opened before he touched it.

In the lower hall stood Sam, the door porter, his tipstaff leaning against the wall and a candle in his hand. Near him was Giles, also holding a light, and with a face of collapse. It was so quiet that they heard the leaves whisper outside.

"This thing cannot be so," said Fenton, urging on them the reasonableness of what he spoke. "I dreamed it. It is not true. My good and gracious wife, the sweetest that ever . . . " He paused.

Giles, who evidently could not face this, turned his back.

"Sir," said Giles, after conquering shaky lips. "She—she died near to half an hour ago. She is with God."

For a time Fenton contemplated the floor, along a zigzag scar on the wood. A shadow moved on the floor, and he looked up to see that Giles had turned round.

"Sir," asked Giles, "we sought you everywhere. None knew where to find you. Sir, who told you that your lady was . . . dying?"

"The devil," said Fenton.

Sam shied back. The candle fell from his hand and smashed on the floor. Quietly, curtly, Giles ordered him belowstairs. Picking up tipstaff and broken taper, Sam crept away.

"Sir," said Giles in a low voice, "your pleasantness is ill-timed."

"Look at me! Should *I* jest? Well?"

266

The light wavered back from him. "Nay, sir, I but—"

"You accuse me, Giles."

"Accuse you? Of what?"

"Of neglect. And you are in the right of it. But who did this thing, Giles? Who poisoned her? It was Judith Pamphlin, I'll adventure?" Fenton drew his sword slowly, with fine whetted expectation, from the scabbard. "Where's the woman now, Giles?"

"Nay, sir! Put by your sword; I beg it! Here's no need to soil your hands, if you but listen to me!"

"Where is she, Giles?"

Frantically Giles clutched at his arm as he moved forward.

"Master, the woman Pamphlin is belowstairs, guarded by the servants. If—if Pamphlin be guilty, which is likely, she will die very horribly at their hands, because they love you. They await you; you have but to speak a word. But heads are too hot to act now. So is your own. Master, for God's sake!" cried Giles, and then his pale eyes seemed to find inspiration. "Would your lady have liked the woman to die thus, by your own sword?"

Fenton, who had been shouldering Giles aside amid wild-flying light, took two steps more before he stood still. For a time he seemed to ponder. Then, with an effort at steadiness, he let the sword slip back into the scabbard.

Afterwards he and Giles looked everywhere but at each other. It was Giles who spoke first.

"Would it trouble your heart to see her?"

"See . . . ?"

"Your lady, sir. We have cleansed all death's foulness from the room; the windows are set open, and sweet herbs sprinkled. I think she would have liked . . . "

"Damn you, a truce to speaking of her as though she were dead! I'll not have it!"

"Your pardon, sir. May I walk before you up the stairs, and light the way?"

"I . . . yes; I thank you."

Up they went, softly and slowly; Fenton stumbled only once on the stairs and not at all down the passage to the bedroom.

Well, it was soon over.

They had left Lydia alone in the dark. Giles, standing discreetly back in the doorway with his taper, allowed the room to lie in shadow. Fenton took two or three steps forward. Tears stung and burned

267

into his eyes; he hastily wiped them away with his sleeve, but they filmed over his eyes and partly blinded him.

In the shadow of the great bed, its curtains looped back, Lydia lay with her fleecy hair spread out round her head, her eyes closed, her arms crossed on her breast, and with one hand holding something he could not identify. To him she seemed just as in life. She did not look like that, but he was partly blind and it was better so.

Haltingly he walked round to the other side of the bed, where sweet night air stirred at the open windows. He bent over and gently kissed her lips, which were still faintly warm. At last he saw what she held in her hand, pressed to her breast. Incongruously, it was the blue toothbrush he had caused to be made for her; a foolish thing, but the only memento she had of him.

That broke him in pieces. Completely blind now, he stumbled back from the bed, turning round, groping his way, seeing nothing and feeling nothing until in some fashion he lurched against an open window. Then a firm hand held his elbow.

"Enough, sir," whispered Giles, in a firm voice. "Suffer me to lead you."

Fenton obeyed. He felt himself walking somewhere, a long distance it seemed, on boards, until the firm hand under his elbow stopped him.

"She is not dead, Giles. Her lips were warm when I kissed her."

" 'Tis even so, sir," lied Giles gently. "You are spent and tired. You will be well in the morning."

Through blurred eyes Fenton discerned his own bedroom. Giles had already set lights on the dressing table, where he vaguely saw a crumpled grey letter, the claret decanter depleted by one glassful, his own red toothbru . . .

Then he was blind again. With a last effort, as though seeking sanctuary, he threw himself forward, trying hard to land on the bed with his head towards its foot. But he was not strong enough. His body struck the top of the hard wooden bedstead, and he rolled back senseless on the floor.

CHAPTER XIX

OF EMERGENCE FROM

DARK HOURS, YET—

IT WAS a valley of peace. When Fenton half-opened his eyes, he lay there wrapped in contentment, with a mind untroubled and a sense that he had passed through evil days or nights, but emerged at last with a healed mind and heart.

"Why, then," he thought, "it was a dream after all. I made no bargain with the devil; he is a myth. I fought no bloody battles for what seemed a month in one night."

The name *Lydia* came into his mind. Pain touched him, but very slightly.

"I loved a woman," he thought, "who must now be dead for more than two hundred years. That is as well. It was very vivid. Having been the husband of Lydia, I could never care for another woman. And now the dream is over. I am glad, because it became towards the end a nightmare.

"I took too much of that infernal chloral. It kept me asleep one night, and until dusk of the following day. I am back in the present again."

This occurred to him because he opened his eyes and found himself lying in the same big four-poster bed with the curtains looped back. The southern windows were darkening against a blue and white sky.

"Though I swore I would never think so," he told himself, "it will

269

be pleasant to hear taxicabs honking in Pall Mall, and see solid men in top hats going to their solid clubs. My error lay in believing that, by travelling back into the seventeenth century, I should become for the most part a detached observer, all but a ghost. But no one can escape his emotions, his loves and hates and fears, especially when he is in the shape of Sir Nick Fenton. He . . . "

Then came the shock.

Trying to sit up in bed, Fenton found himself as weak as though he had suffered a long illness, and had to fall back. Running his hand over his head, he found his head still covered with heavy, fine-spun hair which could only be black in colour. His night habit, too . . .

At the same moment, two lighted candles appeared at the left-hand side of the bed. One light was carried by Giles Collins, the other held high by Lord George Harwell.

George's large red face, framed in a gigantic periwig with a foretop, suddenly altered as he glanced inside the bed. His brown eyes bulged with astonishment, and the red face grew shiny with delight.

"Now scratch me!" he cried, "but Nick's awaked! Nick, good fellow, you have sore troubled us! Nick, give me your hand!"

Fenton still felt that strange near-contentment and peace.

" 'And gi'e us a hand o' thine!' " he said, recklessly quoting a great poet who would not be born for nearly a century. " 'Tis strangely weak, though."

"Well, curse ye, what else? Here's you, falling into a swound like a dead man, and lying thus for eight days . . . "

"Eight days!"

"Ay; ask of Giles! They could give you no food, save by holding you up and putting liquids down your throat with a large spoon, and that's no easy matter. But I'll have a tack at it now!" swore George, puffing out his chest behind a wasp-striped waistcoat with diamond buttons. "Scratch me, *I'll* look to your vittles! Hot smoking capons, stuffed with oysters! A steak-and-lark pudding, with fine gravy! What d'ye say to that?"

"Not now, I thank you. Yet you warm the heart, George."

"Nay, curse it," growled George, embarrassed and speaking from deep in his throat, "I am but a great lout." He hesitated. "Hark'e, Nick. They bade me speak you no word as touches Lydia; but I'll not be silent! When I heard of this, I was so cut down with grief that I . . . I . . . "

Giles's voice flowed so smoothly into the gap that George never noticed it.

"My lord," he said with deep deference, "may I beg leave to remind you, as I did before, that these eight days we have had a new cook, a French cook, a Madame Taupin?"

"Hey?"

"And, for your lordship's pleasure, I did venture to bid her prepare a shoulder of mutton. With hot mushrooms, my lord, and mushroom sauce. It awaits you in the dining room."

George drew himself up indignantly.

"Damme, man, am I come to this house for meat and drink?"

"Alas!" said Giles, smiting his fist against his breast. "And now it is you, my lord, who remind me. I hold the keys of a noble wine cellar; I suffer no wine or any spirituous drink to be set out in the house, else shall I find some porter fallen snoring-drunk on the floor with the empty bottle in his hand."

"Ah!" murmured George, deeply impressed by this good husbandry.

"Yet, my lord, I have forgot to set out for you our finest sack. If you will deign to go downstairs, and fall to, I will bring it you when I have had a word with my master. My lord: mutton and mushrooms!"

"We-ell," said George. He glanced at Fenton, evidently trying to display affection by looking sinister. "I don't take leave of you, Nick! I am but in another room."

"That's understood, George. Eat well!"

When the door had closed behind the visitor, Giles looked sourly at a bedpost.

"Lord George," he said to the post, "is a rare good fellow. Yet a quarter of an hour more and he would have had you on horseback a-roystering to some tavern."

"It may be so. Set me up against a pillow, Giles."

Putting down the light on the bedside table, Giles quickly obeyed. Then, fists on his hips, he surveyed Fenton. It was clear that he too must have some outlet for relief. The lines deepened in his face, and his old impertinence returned.

"Heyday!" he sighed, making a face. "Here are you again in your senses to harry us. But for days it seemed to me we might fillip up, cross or pile, whether you lived or died. The Lord He knoweth why I gave myself the trouble to watch over you."

Fenton spoke softly and steadily.

271

"Then my wife is in truth dead?"

"She was buried," said Giles, inclining his head, "four days gone, at St. Martin's; and Dr. Lloyd himself preached at her funeral."

"Ah, yes. I see."

Giles darted him a quick look out of eyes red-rimmed for lack of sleep.

"For your swound," he sneered, "we have had doctors of physick by the parcel. And but one with a rattle of sense in his head."

"Oh?"

" 'Why,' saith he, 'I have seen this before. It is of the brain, or so I think, and not of the body. As thus: we have seen a soldier in battle fight with lion's ferocity, it may be day upon day. And yet, when he thinks the battle done, without any bodily hurt he may fall into a swound; and lie there two, eight, ten days, and recover with brain cool and healed.' Thus said Dr. Sloane."

"He said true. —Stay!" said Fenton, frowning. "You refer to Sir Hans Sloane?"

Giles lifted his shoulders almost to his ears.

"Nay, I do recollect his Christian name was Hans. But he is not knighted."

"He will be. No matter. Now tell me what has happened in the eight days I have been here like a dead man."

"That I will do," retorted Giles promptly, "else I shall have no peace. You are enough well fed; this day, all but awake, you did swallow good thick soup. Well!"

Without asking leave, Giles went towards the windows and trundled back a padded chair. When he sat down, again without asking leave, only his red head and long face showed above the side of the bed. It was, Fenton thought, unpleasantly like the talking-head illusion of magic.

"Sir," said Giles, "do you well recollect the night of June 10th?"

"Which," Fenton said to himself, "I believed to be the 9th." He nodded.

"You returned from Whitehall Palace at about half-past eight of the clock, and thence to your chamber here. A few minutes before nine, I had occasion to come upstairs for an errand. At the stairhead, in the passage, I met the woman Pamphlin."

Giles illustrated each movement, like a goblin, with a stab of his finger.

272

" 'Tarry!' says I, seeing her hotfoot for the door of this room. 'Nay,' says she, 'I bear word of great import from my lady to Sir Nicholas.' Whereat I wondered, recalling your command that none should trouble you. Nevertheless, I suffered her to enter. Do you recall what she said then?"

"Much of it, yes."

Giles's red head moved forward, upper lip lifting like fish's mouth.

"In exactness, the woman Pamphlin said to you: 'My lady would ask why you have not come to see her since your return.' Thus far, the woman Pamphlin said true. For your lady, having heard your footstep on the stair, and being faithful in love of you even to the death . . . "

Fenton opened his mouth quietly to contradict him, but remained silent.

" . . . did in truth say this. But recollect, now, Pamphlin in this room. Her next words, regarding your lady, were: 'She would also ask—' Here Pamphlin stopped, for you did lay hand on sword. Curtly you berated Pamphlin, as was just, for entering into my lady's room, where you had forbidden her to go. Yet you intrusted Pamphlin."

Here Giles's face grew bitter.

"You bade her go back," he continued, "and keep good watch. For, you said, you must go from the house, but would return ere midnight. Now recollect, sir! Saw you ever so ugly, wicked a look on Pamphlin's face as then? Did remark it?"

Fenton nodded. "I remarked it," he said calmly.

"And so did I. You made haste from the house more quickly than I had thought. I believed you ill, and would have prevented you; but who could have stayed you? Whereat I called to mind the hag's stamp on Pamphlin's face, and wondered, and went to your lady's bedchamber.

"Well, your lady lay on the bed, still in the blue-silk gown, with orange about it, and diamonds. She was sorely ill and vomiting, with Pamphlin by her side. 'Twas arsenic again, as plain as your nose. Now hear what was the other part of her word to you, which Pamphlin did not tell you! It was: '*Ask him to come to me, for God's sake, because I have eaten or drunk of poison at supper, and only he can save me.*' "

Giles paused, with another quick look as though he wondered whether his story might not be too distressing.

But Fenton remained quiet. It was not that no pain or grief was

273

inside him. Yet they seemed concealed, hidden away, so that only the hardest of blows could break the secret armour.

"Poison at supper?" he muttered. "Yet," he went on, only half to himself, "it was a very early supper. For sure the symptoms must have come on much sooner than that, unless . . . unless Lydia hid herself away while I was at Whitehall, and would not speak."

"That was what she did, master."

"Yet stay again! At supper I ate of her food, and drank of her wine."

"You have forgot. I was there; I heard; I saw."

"Saw?"

"You ate of her food, true. But of your own wine you drank but sparingly, and her wine goblet you tasted but once. —Did you shiver, sir?"

"No. No. Go on with your story, from . . . from the words, 'Ask him to come to me, for God's sake, because I have eaten or drunk of poison at s-supper, and only he c-can save me.'"

"Seeing this," said Giles, "a certain madness came over me. Says I, to the woman Pamphlin: 'Why did you not carry this word, before my master departed?' Never before had I seen her smile. 'Because,' says she, 'I would rather see my lady dead than in his hands.' Nay, even then I held back! 'Once he gave you remedies for this poison,' says I; 'and what are those remedies?' And she replied: 'I cannot call them to mind.'"

At this point Giles changed colour.

"Sir, I struck her to the floor, kicking her savagely. I upraised her, beating her head against the door. The woman Pamphlin's face was as wood, like this bedpost; a fanatic's; nor would she again speak, until I turned away to your lady, and the woman Pamphlin ran to hide herself.

"Nor have I seen any lady so sweet, or so kindly, as your own lady, even in her pain. She would smile if she could. 'I am dying, Giles,' says she; 'and 'tis a judgment on me.' And other things she told me, though once (you recollect?) she mistrusted me. Stay! Long ere this I told her I would fetch a doctor of physick and also a Presbyterian minister, knowing," Giles glanced at Fenton, "knowing this to be her faith.

"Well! 'No doctor of physick can help me,' says your lady. 'But if you would bring a clergyman, let it be one of the Church Estab-

274

lished. For that is the faith of my husband, and now it is mine.'"

Giles paused. "Did you speak, sir?"

"No. I— No."

"The Lord He knoweth I will not harrow you with much more. Yet here's one circumstance," Giles said persuasively, "with which I must make you acquainted. When the woman Pamphlin could steal but an instant from her duties, she would keep watch on my lady's door."

"True. I have often remarked it."

"Good! The woman Pamphlin hath since deposed thus: that, as she watched the door on the night of June 10th, she heard your lady crying and moaning in pain. She did then hasten to your lady's door, which she discovered unbolted, and so found your lady to begin with. Could the tale be true?"

"Yes. Of late," said Fenton, "Lydia . . . my wife and I passed much in and out of the room. No longer did—did she lock the door when she was alone."

"And yet," said Giles, "the woman Pamphlin *could* have given poison to your lady? Being her old nurse, she could have persuaded your lady to drink of some poisoned draught?"

Fenton attempted to weigh the scales coolly.

"This is possible," he replied. "Yet arsenic is a slow poison. Even taken at supper, there must have been far an overlarge amount."

"Ay, 'twas at supper!" muttered Giles through his teeth. "Though the way of it I can't tell. Damn my eyes, I have been troubled as touches Pamphlin's guilt. I hate the woman; therefore I would be just. There's the reason for't: why I persuaded you, when you returned half-crazed eight nights gone, not to kill her with your own sword. Yet you must know this:

"The hag lies locked in a cupboard, with a chain round her wrist, belowstairs amid the servants. Mortal man, or I in least, cannot longer hold them back. They would have her dead, if only because she did not tell you your lady was dying, and let you go from the house without knowing it. And there's reason in it, mark you. There's reason!"

Here Giles gasped, like one who has tried to rule but cannot do so.

"Master," he added quietly, "what shall I do?"

"As to the woman Pamphlin," Fenton told him, "I care little. Nay; no writhings; I will make some guess at it, and myself inform the servants."

"Ah!" breathed Giles.

"But, Giles, you have told me no'thing!"

Giles was taken aback. "Nothing, sir?"

"Only of the night when my good and gracious lady . . . went to her rest. What occurred afterwards?"

"Why, I retort upon you your own word," said Giles, with his old pertness creeping back again in relief. "I say: nothing."

"But a doctor of physick here? A death from poison? Surely a magistrate . . . ?"

"I will end my small discourse," and Giles grew grim again, "with relation of that. Still, mark you, the night of June 10th. First arrived the clergyman, a quiet good man. Then arrived the only doctor we could discover at that hour: Noddle his name, noddle his head. In he comes huffing and puffing behind a long beard, pompous and empty-pated, with a great long cane in his hand. Your good lady screamed when he did touch her. 'Hem!' says he, and 'Haw!' says he, and, shaking his head, 'This is a mighty mysterious business!'

"At length (forgive me) I could endure this clack no longer. I drew him out into the passage; I asked of him, in the name of the Saviour, could he aid or cure her? 'Why,' says Dr. Noddle, tapping his nose, 'here's inflammation of the bowel, or it may be poison; I can't tell until the poor lady is dead. Meanwhile, fellow, I am mighty uneasy and I had best fetch a magistrate.' "

Here the bitterness in Giles's face would have surprised anyone who knew him. His red head darted across the side of the bed.

" 'Master of Physick,' says I, 'you must do as you please. Yet, before you trouble a magistrate, let me relate to you the names of those who were at my lady's supper party this night.' And I named them. 'My Lord Danby?' cries out old Noddle. 'Nay, I'll not meddle with this; 'tis inflammation of the bowel, no poison; I'll depose it; bury her when you like.'

"Then, sir, we were helpless but for this booby. Job, having ridden hard to Christ's Hospital for young Dr. Sloane, found him gone forth on another errand. Yet your lady bore all with patience. When she could talk, which was not often because I think she held the poison inside her of intent, she could speak only of you. We must fetch the foolish thing, for bruising the teeth or the like, and she pressed it to her breast like a cross. And so, loving you as few women have loved, she died."

276

Abruptly turning his head away, Giles rose to his feet.

He went over to the dressing table. Here he picked up a small glass, nearly full of a darkish-brown liquid like a prepared medicine. Holding this up against the dim light, Giles studied it before he returned and set it down on the bedside table beside the candle.

Fenton remained looking thoughtfully ahead at the coverlet.

"You have spoken well," he said, "and done well. I give you much thanks."

Giles bowed.

"In your relation," said Fenton, "there is but one mistake. I must tell you, as a secret, that my lady did not in truth love me. Would God she had!"

And now, from Giles's look, it was as though a noiseless clap of thunder exploded over the house.

"Ah!" he said in a different voice. Though this was no sibilant, it seemed to hiss at Fenton. "And here's more that I suspected!"

"Suspected?"

Giles, a-quiver, leaned part way towards him and over him.

"It concerns," Giles said, "a twisted grey letter, which I found there—on your dressing table—next morning, in your lady's hand-writing. It concerns your return from Whitehall palace the night before, you swearing to me that all went merry and hearty, yet I seeing with mine own eyes an ill and disheartened man."

Fenton turned his head away on the pillow.

"You have good intent, jackanapes. But what can you know of this?"

"Why, merely that I probed the matter. Ay, and found the truth of it."

"You?"

"Stick a sword through your impertinence!" retorted the servant. "Truly, who but I? Did I not hear what your lady told me on her deathbed? Did I not read the grey letter? Did I not have the ear of Mr. Jonathan Reeve, your friend, and hath not he the whole whispering gallery of Whitehall, exchanging news for news? If I had need of gold to filch out secrets, was there not your money box? Say to me now: did I do wrong?"

"No."

"Sir," returned Giles, humble again, "you still think your lady's love was all play acting, and that she desired your death. Well, perhaps you have reason to think so." Suddenly Giles's lean arm went up as

277

though taking an oath. "Yet I swear by my immortal soul that never in her senses did she betray you to the Green Ribbon, and that her love was even as I have said! And this I can prove."

Fenton was propped up almost to a sitting position against the pillow, his head turned away. Giles saw his shoulders quiver slightly. Fenton, nevertheless, turned back slowly.

"And yet," he inquired, "Lydia wrote that letter?"

"She did," Giles agreed calmly. "She wrote it when she was confused, half-crazed, not knowing what she should do. Here was no idle jillflirt, all fondlings and sugar cake. Here was a woman, all joys and hates and griefs! Can you recollect—weeks gone now—what occurred on the morning of May 10th?"

"I have forgot nothing."

"How you summoned your lady here, that you might seek the cause of her illness? Which, though we knew it not and only you made the discovery, was of poison by arsenic? How she did lie down where you are now?"

"I have forgot nothing!"

"Is it so? To her at first (and so she told you) you seemed all altered, as though a good soul had come into you and did fight away an evil one. Then you must turn and out-Nick Sir Nick himself, calling down a curse on Roundheads and all their race. Look you there at the bedpost, sir! There's the scar in the wood where you drove the dagger as you cursed them!"

Fenton, his face a blank, did not reply.

"Yet you did struggle back, as it might be to the good spirit. What could my lady think? What was here? And then, as thus she told me on her deathbed, when you two fell close-kissing and all but lying together here, where are you now, she knew you were not Sir Nick Fenton."

"What d'ye say, Giles?"

Giles gave a curl of the lip, and shook his head.

"Sir, sir! Did I not know, from the first hour on that morning, that you were not Sir Nick in the least? Many strange things, certes, Sir Nick might have done. But he would have been hanged at Tyburn ere he went from home in old flat-heeled house shoes, as you did."

Fenton looked back at him, impassive, from the pillow.

"It is somewhat late, Giles, to call me impostor and cheat."

"Impostor?" cried the other. "Who said it? Not I! Nay, I all but

278

told you, on the afternoon before the fight in the street, what was in my mind."

"As—what?"

"Knowing naught of good or evil spirits," said Giles, moistening his lips, "I'll not discourse of them. Yet in some fashion I think this good soul came within the body of Sir Nick, and did change it. Else what I have beheld is Tam o' Bedlam's work.

"Where got 'Sir Nick' the skill of physick and medicine, that he cured your lady from her first illness as though by magic? Sir Nick had the Latin and the French, though but stumblingly; yet I have seen you, in the study, read both as though they were English. How learned Sir Nick that wrist turn (thus!) of swordplay, and half a dozen bottes he never knew? Who gave you the tongue of true prophecy? What hand behind the stars taught you even the craft of war?"

His voice rose up and stopped. The long silence was broken only by the flutter of the taperflame outside the bed curtain.

"Giles."

"Master?"

"Speak not of me. Speak of my lady! You own, you acknowledge, the letter to the Green Ribbon and their bullyrocks was writ by her hand?"

"I do," said Giles. "She hated Sir Nick, as she had reason. She was fast in her religious faith. Having no head for the body politic, she believed in this 'good cause' because she thought (wrongly!) it would have been her father's. She was half-crazed; she wrote it. . . . Now mark, sir, what she wrote to the same Green Ribbon but a quarter of an hour later! Look upon it!"

With an unsteady hand he reached inside his sober black coat and drew out two crumpled letters on grey paper. The first Fenton knew too well, and Giles flung it on the bed. Taking the candle holder in one hand, Giles flattened out the second letter and held it before Fenton's eyes.

Brightly the light brought out what was written there. It was Lydia's handwriting, far more agitated than it had been in the first note. It scrawled upwards across the page; it was as though he could hear Lydia's voice, or see her there beside him.

"*A quarter of an Houre gone, I did write to tell where you might fynde my husband. I cannot say now 'twas a Lye, else I be not believed. But I say I was a poor Madwoman and a Fool. To your Countrey-Party*

279

I say, if you do him any Hurt (which I think you cannot, for you fear his swordeplay! !), I will denounce you to all Justices as Murtherers, and owne my part in't. I send these secretly, by Job the groom, in hope to overtake the First. But I will write you no more, ever. God for King Charles! as he saith.

"And I do disowne you in my title proper,

"Lady (Lydia) Fenton."

Giles held the candle close until he saw Fenton had read it several times. Letting the note fall on the coverlet, he put the light back on the bedside table.

"Was it not natural?" Giles asked softly.

"Giles, whence came this letter?"

" 'Tis ill advised to ask," returned Giles pertly. "You see it: enough! If it came from the strongbox of Sir Joseph Williamson or Mr. Henry Coventry, his Majesty's Secretaries of State . . . why, 'twas your own money filched it out. Faugh! Their parcel of spies grow so confused or knavish they can't separate innocence from guilt."

"Yet there were other letters, I think?"

"Sir, there were none."

Weakly Fenton raised himself from the pillow.

"Is it so?" he demanded. "Not one which began, 'If you kill him not the next time, I will abandon the Green Ribbon'?"

"Sir," retorted Giles, showing his teeth and looking Fenton straight in the eyes, "no such letter was ever writ. Mr. Reeve hath proved it so. A certain knave who hates you, and deceiving even the King's own self . . . "

"What knave?"

"I'll not clap a name on him until you shall be stronger. This rogue pretended he had read a letter (which none other hath seen) and did swear 'twas from your lady. His tale? Faugh! We shewed 'twas a nosegay of lies. I can fetch ten witnesses, and the damned rogue himself, as my evidence!"

Fenton sank back against the pillow, closing his eyes. For some time he remained motionless, while he could hear the creak of Giles's shoes as the latter paced about. Evidently Giles could endure it no longer.

"Eh, well?" he asked.

To Fenton it was as though the sealed wound, far inside and quiet, had now broken and begun to bleed.

"Your lady believed you to be some other soul in the very shape and flesh of her husband," said Giles in a repressed voice; "and thus loved you. When she lay dying, and you not there, she thought that first letter a 'judgment' on her, and wished to die. Sir, do you not find this at all pitiful? Have I cleared her poor character, now that she is gone?"

Fenton cried out in protest.

"Giles, I have been the world's fool. I have not considered; I did not dream . . . "

"Nay, now," said Giles, his voice softening. "I had expected too much from you. And I plagued you too hard. For this, sir, I beg forgiveness."

"Forgiveness? You, to whom I owe all deliverance?"

"Well, well," growled Giles, and stared at the floor. Suddenly he became all a-bustle. "And now," he added severely, "I must look to my duties. I must go down and seek the wine I promised Lord George Harwell some time gone. There's not even a whet of barley water since nine days; my lord will be raving."

"Stay, I would . . . !"

But, leaving the light behind, Giles bustled out and closed the door behind him.

Fenton half-smiled. He leaned back and, for a longer time than he knew, pondered the whole matter. In every corner of the dusky room he saw some image of Lydia.

He thought of what absurdities his own mind had made him believe about her. He remembered how often she had suggested, almost in tears, that she had done him some "harm." Yet most clearly he remembered that night, in her room, when he was roused from sleep to fight the mob. Would a descendant of Roundhead fighting men have held him back, if he wished to go? He remembered how Lydia had given him the padded war helmet.

"If you die," she had said, "then must I die too. And not . . ."

In a strange way Fenton was happy. He had lived in the wind between the worlds. He knew that the devil existed; and, Master of all, the devil's Opponent. Lydia was not dead. Fenton's head turned sideways, as though he would look across the room towards the dressing closet where hung his swords and daggers. His hand sought the region of his own heart. He could join Lydia when he liked. He could—

"Sir!"

281

And Fenton was startled, forgetting his long thoughts, to find Giles again beside his bed. Fenton scented trouble as the mastiffs scented it.

"Master," said Giles, "you are your own self again. Now I seek your commands, as to how I must deal with two visitors who are newly come downstairs. They are separate; not upon the same business. The first, perhaps negligible, is Madam York . . . "

"Meg York?"

"Ay; and with a monstrous haunted look to her. Madam York I led into the withdrawing room, and bade her attend. But the other, a man whom we have—"

"Yes?"

"He comes, or so he says, on 'a matter of state.' He huffs as high as a City alderman, crying down my excuses of your illness and bereavement. This fellow would see you. How shall I deal with him?"

"I will deal with him," replied Fenton, with a happy but wicked smile. "Aid me to dress."

"Sir," exclaimed Giles. "You'd not go downstairs? You lack the strength!"

But this did not seem to matter. Fenton, forcing strength into himself by sheer damn-you determination, threw back the bedclothes and swung cramped legs over the side of the bed.

"A matter of state, eh?" he said, breathing hard. "Call it a matter of the body politic, of the Green lords at their mischief. And . . . Giles! When I was put abed, did you mark the ring on my left hand? A cameo ring, the gift of His Majesty? I must wear that, as also my Clemens Hornn sword."

"You are yet in no way of health for swordplay! You need it not! Already I have given certain small commands . . ."

Giles's voice trailed away. His eyes narrowed in speculation.

"And yet peradventure you do well," he said. "For I think you now meet your greatest danger of all!"

CHAPTER XX

THE FIRST THE ROYAL DRAGOONS

THE Clemens Horrín sword swung at his hip. He wore a coat of blue velvet, a buff waistcoat with gold buttons, and buff-coloured stockings between the blue breeches and the medium-heeled shoes. Out of his periwig looked a face of sickbed pallor, yet freshly shaven as every day Giles had shaved him, and the face was smiling.

Thus Fenton, on unsteady legs, went down to meet his visitor. Giles, who carried a seven-branched candelabrum to light him, either could not or would not speak the name of the visitor.

And yet, to Fenton's sensitivity, it seemed that the whole house was alive with stealthy movement. As he went first out into the upstairs passage, he could have sworn he saw Harry—the porter-swordsman who had been badly hurt in the mob fight—go limping up another pair of stairs towards the lumber room.

Furthermore, no sooner had he stepped out of his room than there was a scurrying and padding and whining; and the three great mastiffs were about him, with brindled Thunder hurrying first. They sensed he had been ill. Not even Thunder reared up to put paws on his shoulders. But they crowded close, frantically licking his hand as he patted them; they whined, their puzzled eyes upraised.

"Gently!" said Fenton, steadying himself. "Gently, now!"

He walked down the stairs after Giles, the dogs slithering at his heels. While Giles set the candelabrum on the newel post, Fenton turned from the stairs, took a few steps towards the front of the large lower hall, and stopped in astonishment.

The floor was swept and shining. All the wall tapers were glowing in their sconces with very bright but soft light. The hall was empty except for a man standing in the open doorway, the front door being thrown wide.

This was a rather tall, heavy man, whose scarlet uniform coat (with black frogs) stretched well below his boot tops and was half undone. He wore a heavy backsword, and lace sprouted at his throat. On his black oiled periwig was jammed rakishly the broad-brimed black hat with the curled scarlet plume. At the moment his big nutmeg-grated face was red with wrath behind so large a curled black moustache that the moustache seemed to mingle with the sides of the periwig. In contrast, his blue eyes bulged under dark, tangled eyebrows.

Fenton looked at Giles, who had put aside the candelabrum and followed him.

"Giles," he said, "here is some other grievous mistake." He smiled at the newcomer. "Sir, are you not Captain O'Callaghan, of the First the Royal Dragoons?"

"I have that honour," said Captain O'Callaghan, drawing himself up stiffly.

"Giles, observe!" requested Fenton, and nodded towards the open.

Outside, where the air was sweet to Fenton's oppressed lungs, path and lime trees were illuminated by a brilliant half-moon. Beyond the trees, motionless on their horses, sat a file of dragoons, facing the house. They wore the long sword at the left side; over the left shoulder to the right hip, on a leather baldric, was slung the flintlock musketoon, or light musket.

"Have you forgot, Giles?" demanded Fenton. "Why, 'twas Captain O'Callaghan who bade his men salute us, that night we fought the Green Ribbon!"

And Fenton stepped forward, holding out his hand. Thunder, biggest of the mastiffs, padded at his side.

"Captain," Fenton went on with deep sincerity, "I give you all a hearty welcome, if a poor one. I have been, you apprehend, the merest trifle unwell. My household is in confusion, since my . . . my wife . . . my—"

His voice trailed off. There was more here than something wrong. O'Callaghan, fiery with embarrassment, still remained stiffly and did not extend his hand.

"What is the meaning of this?" Fenton asked in a low voice.

"Sir Nicholas," burst out the captain, "I hold ye high in esteem; strike me dumb if I don't! I have little stomach for my errand here; nay, I'll confess that too. But 'tis me juty, don't ye see?" His voice was almost pleading. "And a word to ye first!"

Captain O'Callaghan's hand, in its black leather gauntlet, shot out and pointed at Giles.

"Your fellow there," he said contemptuously. "Stop his mouth, Sir Nicholas. Stop his mouth, else begod I'll stop it with a sword down his gullet!"

"When you are in my house, sir," replied Fenton, with too-suave politeness, "you will permit me to command the servants. —Giles, have you given cause of offence to Captain O'Callaghan?"

Giles pursed up his lips.

"I fear so, sir. But you are here now, and may judge of his 'errand.' Be sure, be very sure, that he comes not from the Green Ribbon."

There was a pause.

"The . . . what?" roared Captain O'Callaghan, in blank amazement.

"I refer, Sir Captain, to my Lord Shaftesbury and his Country party."

O'Callaghan's amazement boiled again into rage. His hand made a short, instinctive movement towards his sword grip. From Thunder, quivering beside Fenton, ripped so vicious a snarl that the captain's head twitched round again.

"Hold!" said Fenton, in (almost) his usual voice.

Lacking strength to control the mastiff, he bent over Thunder and spoke soothingly. But his eyesight blurred and blackened as he stooped; he was compelled to stand up straight.

"Giles," he said, "we have both blundered, you and I."

"Blundered, sir?"

"Yes." Fenton nodded towards the dragoon captain. "You have, in effect, asked of an Irish Catholic whether he would serve a body of murderers from the Church Established or a Puritan Conventicle that would kill him."

"Ah!" grunted O'Callaghan.

"But that's the least of it, Giles," Fenton went on. "Our guest is of the army. By no wheedle could my Lord Shaftesbury or any of his lieutenants have brought him. The army are held fast in the grip of the King, and are at command of His Majesty alone."

Giles's face seemed to be greenish, like that of a shrewd, subtle man who for once has fallen into a trap. Fenton turned back to the visitor.

"But a word to you too, captain," he said in a different voice. "Be not so bold with your threats to send a sword down my friend's throat."

"No?"

"No! And, over all, set not a hand on your sword as though in menace. Thunder here," and Fenton patted the mastiff, "is much too close to you. He would tear forth your own throat before you could so much as lug out."

"And would he so?" inquired O'Callaghan softly, with all swagger returning. As though in challenge, he half-darted his hand again towards the sword.

Thunder's snarl was now echoed by Lion and Bare-behind. Thunder, sensing only danger to his master, gathered his hindquarters and poised for the leap.

Captain O'Callaghan's face had become much less ruddy of complexion. His hand slowly fell to the side of his scarlet coat. But he would not budge an inch. He lounged there with his customary swagger, eyelids drooping, and twisted the ends of his moustache.

"Come," said he, "this might be matter for a wager, now. Begod," he roared, "I'd lay six to one I could cleave the brute's head from his body 'fore he touched me!" The roar died away, and he almost pleaded. "But I've me juty to do, as I said, and I'll do it."

Again he drew himself up.

"Sir Nicholas Fenton, sir. Strike me dumb, but I must from this time take you into custody and escort you to the Tower, there to remain in durance until such time as . . . well, that's the manner of it!"

Fenton merely stared at him, while the captain shifted his boots uncomfortably.

"The Tower?" repeated Fenton. And then, stupidly: "The Tower of London?"

"Ah, now, what other tower would there be?"

Fenton looked at Giles, whose face was as blank as his own.

"On what charge?"

"Sir Nicholas, I'm not permitted to tell ye that; and well ye should know it!"

"And yet, or so I understand, men committed to the Tower are sent there but on one charge alone? Treason?"

286

"Well," grunted O'Callaghan, giving him a secret, affirmative wink, "if ye should fathom the charge for yourself . . ."

"Treason?"

". . . 'tis no business of mine to deny it. Come, this could be worse! I've no doubt you'll clear yourself in a week or two."

"Captain," said Fenton, with a fever in his mind, "I can't deny your own good faith either. But this, I swear, is in some fashion the most monstrous error that ever was!" He touched the cameo ring on his left hand. "Ere you do this, may I have speech with the King himself? Or, if that be too much, may I send him a certain token?"

"You'd appeal to the King?" demanded O'Callaghan, and ceased twisting his moustache.

"I would so."

"But, Sir Nicholas! Stab me, this order was signed by His Majesty's own hand!"

Fumbling inside his uniform coat, Captain O'Callaghan drew out a tightly rolled sheet of parchment. He unrolled it only far enough so that the ribbons of the seal slid down, and the signature was exposed.

"Would ye be acquainted with this?" wondered the captain, in vast perplexity. "Well, look upon it!"

Fenton looked. He could not mistake that *Charles R.* Too many times had he seen it, on letters grown yellow when all these people were dust.

"It is the King's hand," Fenton assented.

While Captain O'Callaghan carefully put the scroll inside his coat, Fenton backed slowly away. Thunder followed him, turning and padding. Giles also followed.

When he saw the King's signature on that scroll, Fenton had felt himself for one eyeflash between the present and the future. Then he knew that a great door had slammed, with all the clangour of its bolts, and shut him forever back into the past.

Lydia had gone from him. The King had deserted him. He was charged with treason; and few thus charged escaped the rope and the quartering axe and the disembowelling knife. The beloved past had turned into a monster, and apparently the devil would win hands down. Fenton was cold and lonely and disheartened, but . . .

"I am not yet beaten!" he said aloud.

"Eh?" exclaimed Captain O'Callaghan.

Carelessly Fenton pulled the ring off his middle finger, not wishing to explain what it meant. Again he felt that sense of stealthy movement through the house. But, without turning round, he threw the ring casually over his shoulder. He heard it roll and tinkle towards the back of the hall.

"Giles," he said, "let it be swept up with other trash. Like the honour of the man who gave it, it is not worth a Birmingham groat. —And now, Captain O'Callaghan," he snapped, "what if I were not minded to be taken?"

"Then, faith," retorted the captain, "ye'll be taken whether 'tis to your liking or no. You're a fine brisk swordsman, Sir Nicholas, when you've got good legs under ye. But now what," he mocked, "could ye do against my dragoons?"

A new voice struck across the hall, a voice loud and yet lazy.

"Why, scratch me," said the voice, "but there's some of us think we could do much."

And George Harwell, heavy-footed and wine-flushed under the flaxen periwig, strolled out of the dining room. His silver-hilted rapier hung in its scabbard. But in his right hand he carried a backsword like the captain's own.

"Here's no business of yours, sir, whoever you are," said O'Callaghan, looking hard at him. And then: "Ah, bejasus, you're as drunk as a new-paid seafarer!"

"A trifle refreshed," said George, "I well may be. This but loosens the tongue and lends cunning to the sword arm." The single-edged backsword whistled and hissed as George drew patterns in the air. "But do ye think ye can take Nick Fenton, my bold dragoon? Look you there, at the back of the hall; and decide!"

Fenton himself, in the act of turning round, saw Giles at his elbow. He also saw Harry, the porter, with an armful of glittering weapons. Into Giles's hands Harry thrust the ancient double-edged rapier with the ring hilt, and the shell-guard left-hand dagger. With the same weapons in his own hands, Harry moved back a pace or two.

Fenton swung round.

Up from belowstairs, against a hot red light, came Big Tom with a log bat on one shoulder and a heavy flintlock musket in his other hand. After him came Job, the groom, with a weighty musket slung by leather belt across his shoulder and a cudgel in each hand. Then fol-

288

lowed thick-shouldered Whip, the coachman. And Sam, the door porter. . . .

Since flintlocks were new, replacing the old matchlock and supplied only to crack regiments, this must be some premeditated bribery on Giles's part.

"Sir Nick," whispered Giles, "glance but at the stairs leading upwards."

Though neither of them could see the stairs, Fenton had already caught the soft, swift noise of footsteps. Round into the hall, almost silently, came every male servant in the house. They bore swords from the lumber room, and they had five heavy cavalry pistols. Even Dick, the stableboy, was there. Fenton turned round again.

Framed in the open front doorway, feet planted wide apart, Captain O'Callaghan surveyed them.

"Then you're all so fond o' treason?" he shouted. "You'd defy the King's writ?"

"Nay, now," said George easily. "We but defend Nick Fenton."

"I tell you, man, 'tis folly! Why d'ye do this?"

Then George's voice bellowed back.

"Too long," George said, "hath he carried the burden of the fight on his own back, upholding those who stumble or fall! Too long hath God or devil, I know not which, crept unawares and stabbed him in the back! Too long hath he laboured in every man's interest save his own! He shall not lose that labour now!"

From all the group behind Fenton rose up a murderous cry which was intended for a cheer.

And outside, beyond the elms and shadowy under a half-moon, the troopers of the dragoon file also stirred. A horse whinnied and reared up, showing the feelings of its rider. Somebody was swearing hard. There was a light patter of hoofs as the cornet rode past and cried an order.

"Unsling your carbines!"

It was answered, by Whip and Job and Old Tom and Sam and even Giles, with a roar that could not conceal delight. Behind him Fenton heard the thud, thud-thud as his own followers' heavy muskets were set on their upright supports to fire.

George Harwell roared out again.

"Captain," he said, "here are the men who fought the battle of Pall

Mall, with more men besides. Now what will befall your poor dozen of dragoons? We'll twist their necks like pigeons'; and cursed well you know it!" Here George controlled himself. "Go from the house unharmed, captain, to your men. And we'll come fairly at you."

"Ah, you can fight me!" said Captain O'Callaghan, not moving a step before the aimed muskets. "But can ye fight the whole military of the land? You'll hang, every Jack-fool of ye, for justice's sake!"

"Justice!" Fenton said aloud.

Many thoughts suddenly rearranged themselves as he had time to consider, and reflect that he had spoken and acted. He did not even note the open door of the withdrawing room. Just inside, where she had been waiting ever since Fenton came downstairs, stood Meg York. She was wrapped in a black hooded cloak; her face glimmered white, her lower lip was a blood smear where she had bitten, and the look in her eyes was hard to interpret.

"Stop!" Fenton cried out, and raised his hand. As he raised his hand every angry mutter, even the snarl of the mastiffs, trailed off into dead silence.

The man in the doorway was some fifteen feet away. Fenton, brushing aside Giles's protest, sending back George with a fierce wave of the hand, went out alone to meet Captain O'Callaghan. O'Callaghan, hand hovering above sword grip, watched him warily.

"Captain," said Fenton quietly, "I desire . . ."

Then it happened. Fenton's weakness caught him and shook him as though with hands. He felt his head spin, and his foot slipped on the polished boards. Whereupon, with a horror of humiliation which burnt him like bodily pain, he fell face forwards at full length.

The Irish captain looked down at the stricken face of the man who tried to struggle up. Captain O'Callaghan, after a brief struggle with himself, felt his wrath melt away.

"Ah, strike me dumb!" he muttered. And then, with gruff respect: "By your leave, Sir Nicholas," he said.

Bending forwards, so that the black periwig and the broad-brimmed hat with the scarlet plume dipped like ship's colours, he assisted Fenton to stand up straight.

"Prince Rupert's own self," said Captain O'Callaghan in a loud voice, "hath oft lost flesh from wounds or lack of food, and been far weaker than you. Take no shame for this. By God, sir! I honour you that you are here at all."

It was as though a strange healing, a soothing of ferocity as a dog is soothed, stole almost imperceptibly through the hall.

"I thank you for your civility," replied Fenton. "I desired but to say that my words, a while ago, were hasty and ill-considered. As thus: the murderer of my wife . . ."

Again bewilderment smote the captain.

". . . the murderer of my wife is not yet come to justice. I must study how to accomplish this, and be no brawler. Further, no more blood must be shed for me by my household. I thank you finally for your patience, sir, and yield myself up as your prisoner."

Captain O'Callaghan looked at the floor. He eyed a corner of the ceiling. He looked everywhere except at Fenton.

"Well!" he said from deep in his throat. "Well!"

"May I suppose, then, that in report you will say nothing as touches my servants? No matter of hanging, or the like?"

"Sir Nicholas, I've forgot it this minute!"

"Then I am ready. Er—am I permitted to carry with me a few books?"

"Books?" Captain O'Callaghan was taken aback. "Oh, ay. Books. Hem! Well, they may follow you tomorrow, together with more important things: clothes (stab me!) and more bedding should you wish it. Meanwhile . . ."

At the back of the hall there was a savage noise like a struggle. Up spoke the harsh voice of Whip, the coachman.

"Sir," he called fiercely, "what of the woman Pamphlin?"

Fenton, glancing over his shoulder, saw that they had brought her abovestairs. Judith Pamphlin's hands were bound behind her back to a length of chain held in the hard grasp of Whip, who had discarded weapons. He shoved her violently forward out of the first rank.

It was plain they had clapped a clean dress on her angular figure, to hide lash weals or bruises. But her muddied hair was round her shoulders, and out of it peered a long face, dirty and bruised. It might have inspired pity if her rheumy eyes had not been alive and steady with malice.

"Nick," said George Harwell, his mouth working and twisting, "they must have told you what Pamphlin's done. She let you go forth without a sign that Lydia lay in agony! She would not even tell the remedy that might have cured!"

Fenton looked briefly at her, and swallowed.

291

"She is but as fanatic a Roundhead as I am a Royalist," he said, and looked away. "Let her go free in peace."

"Sir?" blurted Whip.

"Such is my command."

No other protest was raised, not even a word. But from the back of the hall came a soft noise, like the hissing of many breaths indrawn; and it was very ugly to hear.

"Let us go," said Fenton hastily. "Unless there be aught else for me to do?"

"I must ask for your sword." Again Captain O'Callaghan grew fiery with embarrassment; no moustache-twisting could hide it. "That's to say," he added quickly, "only that it be left here, apart from you. Certes you've a cursed odd household; but 'tis none of my affair."

Giles Collins moved forward softly. He thrust the dagger into his belt, but the bright rapier he fingered lovingly as he looked under his eyelids at the dragoons outside. Slowly Fenton unbuckled his own sword belt over the under belt. With an effort he threw the sword towards Giles, who caught the scabbard flat against his palm.

"I shall not need it soon again," said Fenton.

"That may be so. And yet I have a presentiment," answered Giles, "that there will be one last great fight."

All those in the doorway started a little and shifted their eyes, even Captain O'Callaghan, at the hoarse cry of triumph from Judith Pamphlin.

"Now is the proud man taken as a traitor," she sneered; and she screamed and screamed so that weapons clashed in the hall. "Behold, he that corrupted my lady into the ways of flesh, and all manner of sinfulness, is smitten low by the power of the Laard! As 'tis writ in the Book of Revelations, he shall drink of the wine of the wrath of God!"

The woman was violently trembling in sheer ecstasy, so that even the chain rattled with her angular body.

" 'And the smoke of their torment,' " she cried, " 'ascendeth up for ever and ever: and they shall have no rest day nor night, who worship the beast and his image, and whosoever receiveth the mark of his name.' " Malice gleamed through holiness and piety in her Puritan triumph. "It was writ for you and yours, man of blood. Can you quote a better text?"

Fenton, about to hurry out past Captain O'Callaghan, stopped and looked at her.

" '*Come unto Me,*' " he said, " '*all ye that labour and are heavy laden, and I will give you rest.*' "

Fenton turned away. Vaguely he noted, as the front door creaked, that no bar had been put up.

"A better text, I think?" he muttered, half to himself. "I must remember it, in future, for Lydia's sake."

"There's a horse outside for ye," said Captain O'Callaghan, looking at the floor.

"Then I am at your service, captain," Fenton said.

Late that night, long after Fenton had ridden away with the dragoons, many persons gathered together belowstairs. They made a circle, in the reek and red fire heat of the kitchen, for the trial of Judith Pamphlin. Few words were spoken. No flogging was done. The verdict was only a nod. Big Tom, gripping her by the hair, held her head and shoulders over a wooden tub, and slowly cut her throat while rats scampered unheeded. They buried her in the back garden, with such craft at turfing that no man has ever found even bones or dust.

And elsewhere, at the Tower, the game of wits ran fast to its final, deadliest move.

CHAPTER XXI

OF LION ROAR

AT THE TOWER

THE roar of a lion, not far away as distance goes, was answered by an even throatier roar from another cage. The squall of a catamountain pierced through both.

The menagerie at the Tower of London, housed inside the Lion Gate but outside both the main gate under the Byward Tower and then the western moat, was open to the public on payment of a small fee. High rose the babble of Jack and Jill, with their friends, as they clamoured towards the long, low menagerie house under a sky darkened even here by chimney smoke and soot from the City

Colonel Howard heard the uproar as he strolled along the sentry walk of the battlements on the wall, southwards, beside the river. Colonel Howard, Deputy Governor of the Tower, should never have been of the military despite his good service. His face, delicate, with shiny cheekbones and a domed skull half-hidden by his grey periwig, was the face of a scholar or a dreamer. Colonel Howard was both.

Though the late afternoon had become hot, he wrapped closer round him the long cloak from collar to boot ankle. Long ago he had caught an ague in the Low Countries, and was often cold. Colonel Howard's short pointed beard and small moustaches, against the thin face, also suggested Spain and subtlety. After him tramped one of the warders, a fat fierce man as most tried to look, clad in the red doublet and hose, with the flat black-velvet cap, which had been the traditional dress of warders since the time of Henry the Eighth.

"Colonel Howard, sir!" hissed the warder, with all mystery in his voice. Greatly daring, he touched the Deputy Governor's arm and advanced a good carbuncle of a nose.

"What's amiss?" the warder whispered. "What cully's work's afoot for this night? Is it murder, or the like? Tip me the wink, sir!"

Colonel Howard regarded him with a mild frown.

"*Latine loqui elegantissime*," he said in his soft voice, and shook his head sadly. "Or your English speech, I should have said." The frown grew still more mild. "Have you heard report of murder, then? If so, you speak late."

The warder shrank back, protesting hastily. He lacked the words to explain that through this old fortress, among the warders and the redcoat military garrison as well, there ran a swift rumour, a word behind hand. It said that something of dire import, like the blazing star which heralded the plague, would strike here tonight.

"Come," invited Colonel Howard, patient but with narrowed eyes. "Speak your mind!"

The warder, wildly at guess, pointed ahead. Along the sentry walk they were approaching the round, rough-stone squatness of the Middle Tower, with a heavy barred door opening on the sentry walk.

"Sir Nick Fenton, the devil in velvet," he said hoarsely, "is shut up in there since a fortnight. Ecod, sir! When they fetched him here, I thought him an old man."

"And so did I," the other said thoughtfully.

"Ah! But a fortnight's good food and wine? Why, he's fleshed out again, fighting-muscled, all a-prowl like the leopard at the menagerie. And with a look . . . a look . . ."

Colonel Howard, who had almost forgotten his companion, nodded with the same thoughtfulness.

"As though he had passed through some horror?" murmured the Deputy Governor. "And walked amid flame and foulness, like the Italian of Florence, and was his own man again, yet kept the memory of horror behind his eyes?"

Again the warder was deeply perplexed, as were others, by this Englishman with the Spaniard's face. As a weapon the warder carried only a short partisan, which the public always miscalled a halberd; and he stamped its shaft on the old stones.

"Under favour, colonel, a black ugly look is a black ugly look; no more! But which of us ha' heard," and he pointed, "of a prisoner in the

Middle Tower? Why not the Beauchamp Tower, as is usual? There you hold him safe and fast. But here's the Middle Tower with a door opening straight to this sentry walk where we stand! And look you there, under favour!"

The fat red-clad warder leaned through an opening between two of the battlements on the riverside. Below there was a heavy wharf, stretching the entire southern side. It was mounted with a long line of heavy ordnance, great cannon of iron or brass, against attack from the river.

But, so that the river should serve as a natural moat, the wharf had been built out a little distance from the wall. Under its smoke pall the Thames ran dark and placid. Inside the piles of the wharf and this wall, the water yet boiled and hissed white.

"There's but one door," said the warder, "between the devil in velvet and a leap from here. We could cross him with musket fire; ay. But . . ."

Wheezing, he turned round the battlements, and stopped short.

Colonel Howard was not even listening. He was looking back, musingly, over the inside premises of the fortress; harsh, yet touched with greenery; the Bell Tower at the angle of the inner ballium wall; and all dominated by the huge square bulk, grey-white stone with a lookout pinnacle at each corner, which was then called Julius Caesar's Tower.

"These stones are too old, and full of bones," said Colonel Howard. "Too many men have died and then walked here. William Brown, are you never affrighted?"

The warder gaped at him. "Me, sir?"

"You are a fortunate man. I am oft affrighted."

More lions roared from the menagerie, their noise mingling with the laughter of children. Subtly the Deputy Governor's face altered; and Warder Brown, who knew this cloudy-cove's fame in battle, felt disquiet.

"As to your warnings," murmured Colonel Howard, "I fear you must address them to Sir Robert." He meant the Governor of the Tower, a stern martinet. "Now unlock and unbar me this door to the Middle Tower. Stand your guard outside, while I speak with the prisoner."

It was done. Inside, as the bars again clanged behind him, the Deputy Governor stood in a circular room of stone blocks, very hot and oppressive, yet spacious and with windows. Prisoners at the Tower seldom suffered as they suffered at Newgate.

"I am the bearer of news," Colonel Howard said to Fenton.

Fenton, his periwig discarded for his own black hair, stood in a cambric shirt, with old velvet breeches and gold buckles to his shoes, beside a table in the middle of the stone room.

"I have long guessed your news," he said without amusement. "On the night they took me, I was too shaken to think. But a friend—call him Mr. Reeve—had already warned me of exactly what might happen. Now I am charged with leading a Catholic conspiracy (God save such nonsense!) to rise against London with blood and fire. Mark how every stone falls into place, from a so-called Catholic mistress to a French Catholic cook named Madame Taupin. I was even advised to seek audience with the King. He sought audience with me. Well, I am here."

Colonel Howard, without replying, drew out a chair beside the table and sat down. His sword scabbard rattled against the floor, but he did not unfasten his cloak. On the table were several long clay pipes, an earthen bowl of tobacco, and piles of books.

"No," he replied, "that is not my news." As though irrelevantly he added: "I believe I have visited you upon every day since your imprisonment?"

"For which I am deeply grateful."

"We have discoursed of history, literature, architecture, astronomy . . . ." Colonel Howard all but sighed. A red-clad arm reached from inside his cloak and sought the books on the table. "Nay, the pleasure was mine! Yet we have never spoken of your—personal affairs?"

"No. Never."

"Yet I venture to think," said Colonel Howard, and lifted sharply penetrating eyes, "that you now mistrust all persons on this earth?"

Fenton merely lifted his shoulders again, but did not reply. He was as tense, as watchful, as a hunting leopard.

"Come, I would not pry!" protested Colonel Howard, and meant it. "But I dare suppose," he added casually, "you have at least once met with the devil?"

Fenton, staring back at him, felt the first qualm in many days. Involuntarily he put up his hand to his face, shading it. Though he was permitted no razor, not even a blunt knife to cut meat (which enraged him, because of his secret determination), each day he was shaved by the Governor's own barber.

"Never fear betrayal from me!" said Colonel Howard. His voice grew soft again. "Though, since with you all men's credit is stabbed, you'll not believe me." He mused. "Now I have never met with the devil. But

I am sensible he exists, and walks the earth, and might appear beside us at any moment."

Fenton merely smiled, as though at a modest pleasantry.

"You said," he answered politely, "that you brought news for me?"

"True, true." Colonel Howard glanced quickly round, and rose to his feet with an air of haste. "Let us go apart to the window."

The old arrow slits had been fashioned into windows in Tudor times. They were still small, and heavily barred. Colonel Howard beckoned Fenton towards a window facing west, above a moat stagnant and malodorous because it did not join the river. A causeway crossed the moat to the Byward Tower; and beyond rose the babble of the crowd round the menagerie house.

"Now do you forget the devil," said Colonel Howard in a very low tone. He snapped his fingers, as though flicking out the devil like a bird over the ill-smelling moat. "I bring you word, privately, from Sir Robert himself. Very late this night you will have a visitor."

"Indeed?" Fenton's heart quickened. "What visitor?"

"A lady. Or perhaps say only a woman. Her name or quality I know not."

"A woman?"

"S-ss-t! There is a window close to the door giving on the sentry walk, and, outside, a warder fire-consumed with curiosity."

"Nay, but this visitor! Inside the Tower? After the drums beat the tattoo?"

"I can but tell you what I was told," said Colonel Howard. A breeze stirred his grey periwig. Lightly he touched his moustaches and pointed beard, more brown than grey; a thin amusement gleamed in his eyes and died. "Sir Robert knows little more, or so I think. Yet this piece of gullery (you espy?) could have been managed only by someone in high place and command."

Beyond the moat, not far away, a mountebank was amusing the crowd by playing two flutes at once, with a flute stuck in each corner of his mouth. Many persons hurried to him, away from a parson who had been preaching a sermon beside the gallows on Tower Hill. The parson was waving his arms and seemed to be calling down wrath.

"But what is this woman's errand?" demanded Fenton. "I can't imagine," he added dryly, "that mine host of this good inn will even provide a wench for my comfort."

"No. That goes too far." Then Colonel Howard's tone changed. "I

298

am instructed to say only that she will bring you a message of great import. You will listen, and obey her. She is trustworthy—"

"Indeed."

"—and in your interest. That is all." Colonel Howard dropped his half-whisper and spoke in a normal tone. "Now would you hear news of a friend you but recently mentioned; and who, I hear, laboured mightily for you in a certain cause? Mr. Jonathan Reeve?"

"Mr. Reeve!" said Fenton, gripping the bars of the window. His warmth of eagerness was apparent. "What news have you of him?"

"He hath been rewarded, Sir Nicholas. Precisely as once you desired."

"Oh? And by whom?"

"By His Majesty the King."

"Your pardon, Colonel Howard. But I beg leave to doubt that."

"Have a care, Sir Nicholas," his companion said softly. "I can pardon much, conjecturing as I do that you have fought the devil and won your soul . . ."

On the iron bars Fenton's hands tightened and wrenched.

". . . yet still I hold the King's commission; and I am Deputy Governor of the Tower."

Fenton spun round from the window.

"Now how you terrify me!" he said pleasantly. "A fortnight gone, I was sick and much ashamed. In candour, I would now administer a dose of the same physick to someone else. Summon your guards, good sir. Let us see what a man may do against them with a table leg or a chair."

Colonel Howard was not even listening.

"'Hunc igitur terrorem animi, tenebrasque necessest—'" he muttered; then he paused suddenly and looked up. "Then you would not hear how your good and steadfast friend came at last to his reward?"

Fenton hesitated, looked at the floor, and nodded. Colonel Howard went back to the chair by the table, where he sat down and took up a copy of Juvenal's satires.

"I was myself a witness," he said, touching the book as though idly. "Though I go but seldom from the Tower, I was dispatched two days gone with a communication from Sir Robert to His Majesty's self. The King, with some others, did play at *pêle-mêle* in the Mall below the green terraces and in the Park. Mightily they smote the ball, shouting like schoolboys, amid the yellow dust."

Colonel Howard turned the book over in his hands.

"Presently," he went on, "the King made a sign, as one who cries

299

stop. The dust settled down. The mallets were put by. I saw this Jonathan Reeve approaching, on his swollen gouty legs, and on the arm of my Lord Danby.

"He did not know what was in store for him. But you conceive how he looked? All in patched black, with his great belly and his old sword, and his countenance like a soiled archbishop's in the long white hair? So he limped straight to the King, very proudly until he was there. Whereat, in a thing not seen in public these many years, he went down on one gouty knee, and bent his white head low.

"One or two there were who would have smiled; but that the King looked at them, and they ceased. His Majesty's self, with the dust on his coat and periwig, seemed embarrassed. Yet, when I did glance again, he seemed like unto his father.

" 'Nay, I am not knighting you,' said he. And then his great voice was like a drum. 'But rise up, Earl of Lowestoft, Viscount Stowe, and take your rightful place among men. The return of your title and estates is but a poor repayment to one among many.'

"And this Jonathan Reeve, Earl of Lowestoft, whispered but one word, which was, 'Sire!' All crowded about him, that they might set him upon his feet and speak civilly to him. And yet, scarce a quarter-hour after his great happiness, Jonathan Reeve was dead."

Colonel Howard paused. Juggling with the volume of Juvenal's satires, he threw it on the table with a slap which roused the half-hypnotized Fenton.

"Dead?" repeated Fenton, raising a hand to his eyes.

"Truly."

"But how?"

"Come, the man was eighty." Colonel Howard spoke carelessly. "Such honours, after decades of poverty and jeers, overcame him. In the King's own coach, on the way home to some blowsy tavern in Red Lion Fields, he seemed to drowse until the coachman heard a weak cry of, 'God for King Charles!' And so he died."

Fenton went slowly across to the improvised wooden bunk with the straw mattress. He sat down on the bed and put his head in his hands.

"It occurs to me too, though perhaps to no purpose," mused Colonel Howard, "that you have another good friend. You name him Giles Collins. Nay; don't start up! He is safe enough. But are you sensible of who he really is?"

"Why," said Fenton, pressing his hands to his temples, "I recollect Giles did once ask me the same question, when we were at swordplay practice. Did my father never tell me who he was? Or something of like meaning."

"Heard you ever," asked Colonel Howard, "of Woodstock Palace?"

Fenton sat up straight.

"In October of the year '49," his companion continued slowly, "some eight or nine months after the murder of King Charles the First, a group of Roundhead Commissioners went down to Woodstock Palace. Their work was to dilapidate or destroy. And yet, by November 2nd, they were driven forth in terror by what seemed (I say seemed) the antics of evil spirits."

Fenton uttered an exclamation. He remembered the incident now.

"Ah!" murmured Colonel Howard, giving him a sideways glance. "Then I need not recount the Roundhead Commissioners' unhappy experiences, which they drew up in a solemn statement as comical as any play by Mr. Shadwell. There were in truth no enorm spectres to drench them with foul water, kick over their candles, fly away with their breeches, fire cannon, set great logs a-rolling in locked-up bedchambers.

"The author of all the mischief was their pious scrivener-clerk, a concealed Royalist. With two confederates, a trap door, some chymical salts and gunpowder, he had made a blue flame rise even from the pot-de-chambre. He called himself Giles Sharp. His true name was Joseph Collins, sometimes called Funny Joe, and all the countryside round Oxford still honours him."

"He was also a gentleman," said Colonel Howard, "first swordsman of Sir Thomas Draycott's troop of horse at Worcester fight in '50! Yet, being poor, he took menial service with the valiant. Can you put me together that man's two names?"

"Oh, without doubt," answered Fenton, gripping the sides of the wooden bed. "Giles Collins, who in my hearing hath played both Puritan clerk and Funny Joe, can distinguish between good and evil spirits."

Again Colonel Howard gave him a swift glance. Fenton's eyes were shining, but not with enjoyment.

"Pray let me tell you," said Fenton, "what those Roundhead Commissioners had done. They would besmirch all that belonged to King Charles the First. His bedchamber they used for a kitchen, his dining

301

room for a woodyard. They smashed the stained-glass windows, mutilated the statues, knifed the great paintings." His voice deepened. "All that was of beauty, all that was of dignity and grace . . ."

Fenton stopped abruptly. Colonel Howard's long fingers tightened round the stem of a tobacco pipe and snapped the pipe in two pieces.

"Good!" cried Fenton.

"What! You call that sacrilege good?"

"Nay, you mistake me. In all our discourse together, for the first time you have shown some heart or human feelings."

"Heart? Human feelings?" Colonel Howard was perplexed. "Upon my word, what have these to do with me? Indeed I have felt none for many years, since my wife died shrieking in the Great Fire."

"Is it so?" demanded Fenton. "You had a wife?"

Rising up from the bed, he went to the table and clutched its edges on either side, looking down strangely on his companion.

"I also had a wife," he added. "She too is dead. She was poisoned."

"Poisoned?"

It was plain, by the startled look on Colonel Howard's face, that this secret had been well kept. None of authority knew it.

"In this cell of yours," said Fenton, breathing hard, "I have thought much and much. I can tell you who poisoned my wife. Nay, I can prove it! But I cannot do so unless I be permitted to write or communicate with my friends outside the Tower. I am allowed no visitors; not even pen and ink and paper. Why am I not allowed these?"

"I can't tell. It is not within my orders."

Fenton shook the table until books tumbled off and spattered face down on the floor.

"You have heard, sir, that I guess the charges brought against me. Let me add to this Tam o' Bedlam list. Come! Did I not speak, in Spring Gardens and to a false Frenchman called Duroc, with admiration of the French? Did I not cry out, before a clot of the mobile party who attacked my house, that I might well be a Catholic? 'Have you knowledge to foretell the future?' said their leader. And I must reply, 'Yes.' "

"Hum! Did you make mention," inquired Colonel Howard, "of any pact with the devil?"

"No. But I might have done so."

"That I can credit. But not to the least degree in anger."

"Colonel, put by this sorry stuff of treason! In our world I desire only justice for the person who poisoned my wife. May I not send a letter, even a spoken message, from here?"

"It is not in my orders."

"May I have speech with the Governor of the Tower?"

"Certes, Sir Nicholas, you may apply for it."

"Which must mean," said Fenton, bending over him, "that I'll not get it?"

"I have no orders."

Though not in the least afraid of the prisoner, Colonel Howard pushed back his chair, stood up, and moved behind the chair.

"I regret," he said, "my time here is spent." For the first time he raised his voice and called sharply. "Warder! Open me the door!"

Outside the door to the sentry walk there was a scurry and a rattle of keys.

"I have been much diverted," remarked Colonel Howard, with a kind of maddening wistfulness, "by our discourses on history and poetry. I bear you no ill will. Remember what I have said; a woman will visit you late. Do as she shall bid."

A heavy door lock snapped after the bars were rung back. In the quarter-opening of the door appeared the sharp, polished blade of the partisan, with the red chest of Warder Brown behind it.

"Remember!" Colonel Howard said for the second time. When he raised one finger, he was uncannily like Charles the First on the scaffold. *"You have less time than you think."*

The door closed, and was locked and barred once more, as the Deputy Governor left him. Fenton stood staring at the door, his hopes gone as though he had swallowed moat water. Throughout a fortnight, never speaking of himself, he had tried to gain the confidence of Colonel Howard.

He went back to the improvised bed and sat down.

His gaze travelled round the hot room, which was not overclean despite its size, past a pile of his clothes on the floor. In the wall opposite him there was a second door, also locked and heavily barred. Outside the door there was a winding stair in the wall; Fenton's fancy followed it down to the room below, always full of warders and on its walls the heavy muskets of the military.

As Fenton's consciousness opened again, the noises from outside rolled over him. He could even hear from below—on the path under the arch which led to the other side of the Middle Tower—the trampling and merriment of visitors, who might see the sights if they were escorted by a warder.

From the menagerie a hyena coughed and barked. The long after-noon light, smoke-darkened, drew towards evening amid grey stones. The crowds must go soon. Apparently the flute player had already gone. But three other mountebanks, with fiddles and fury, struck up a tune which made Fenton raise his head quickly.

"There's a tyrant known as MOB, sir, in this town of soot and mud, Sitting green-faced by the hob, sir, with his hands imbrued in blood . . ."

It was no great coincidence, since everywhere in the City they now sang it. But the old Earl of Lowestoft was dead.

Let him sleep well. For Lydia, who was always with Fenton in imagination, returned to soothe him now. As a rule he saw her as he had seen her on that last night at the dinner, amid silver and wax lights, while Mr. Reeve made the cittern tinkle softly to Ben Jonson's old love song.

He knew he saw Lydia only in fancy, else he would have come to madness. But Lydia sat in the chair lately occupied by Colonel Howard. Lydia's blue eyes were open and eager, but sorrowful. A light was about her brown hair. Her half-parted lips made attempt to smile. Her hands were clasped together, arms a little raised towards him.

And Fenton spoke to her aloud.

"Wait for me; you'll remember that?" he asked. "This day's work was bitter, when I would persuade the Deputy Governor, but failed. No matter! I am not yet defeated. Since I know the name of the poisoner . . . "

Fenton paused, regretting his words. Lydia, despite what seemed a frantic attempt to touch his hand, fled from him at that word "poisoner," as she would have fled in life. His mind would not allow him to see her when he thought of poison.

But the poisoner, of course, was Kitty Softcover, his former cook.

Kitty, the Alsatian bawd, must be very much alive. Nevertheless Fenton pictured her as standing near him: small, grubbily clad, with her fine red hair and her fine white skin, but with bad teeth and greedy eyes. Her eyes darted everywhere for diamonds, for emeralds.

"My good slut," said Fenton, "it was you I suspected from the first, and spoke my mind to Giles. I found in the lock of the front door the soap traces of the mould you took for a key. Immediately I ordered a bar to be put up inside that door. But someone forgot it. As I saw myself, when Captain O'Callaghan took me in arrest, there was no bar inside that door."

It was as though Kitty lifted her upper lip, hating and yet writhing to cozen him.

"But where, good slut, could you have found another great heap of arsenic to poison my lady? Only here in the Tower did I call to mind the shop of William Wynnel, the apothecary, in Dead Man's Lane. And the occasion upon which I went there with Lord George Harwell."

In fancy the figure of Kitty laughed at him.

"*I* gave you good character," said Fenton. "*I* said naught was amiss. Even when George must fall a-ranting with talk of murder, I bade him be silent and confirmed my words by guineas in the apothecary's hand. You sought him first (I vow?) since 'twas plain the old man doted on you? Had you returned, he would have given you as much more poison as you wished.

"Upon that I lay my wager, little claw-hand. You hated me; you hated my wife. Did you not poison a bowl of sack posset before my eyes, with arsenic in sugar? On the night of June 10th you crept into my house. Didst come to steal? You remained to kill. My friends have but to seize Master Wynnel, choking truth from him; and we hold you fast for the law."

But Kitty had vanished, because Fenton's thoughts faltered.

He passed a hand over his damp forehead. The fiddlers were silent, their tune ended. Fenton, drawing himself back on the side of the bed, rested his back against the wall.

The intense heat was fading, though there remained the ill odour of the western moat. Fenton let his head fall forwards, again attempting to think. . . .

Almost immediately, or so it seemed, a voice in his brain seemed to cry out. "Take care, take care, take care!" it noiselessly keened.

Fenton sat up straight, with a twist of pain in his cramped shoulders. Momentarily he thought he was in pitch-darkness. Then, as he blinked his eyes open, he saw that the stone room was deathly clear in all its outlines from the light of a full moon through barred windows.

Admittedly he had been asleep, as though storing up energies for some combat. In all the rabbit warren of the Tower there seemed no sound, not even a whisper, except the faint lapping of water below.

In that quiet there was the emptiness and even skin-crawl of a late

305

hour, perhaps even in the morning. He had not heard the steady tramp-tramp-tramp along the path below, and the ceremony of the keys as the portcullis was lowered at the Byward Tower. He had heard no roll of drums from the parade ground. Nothing.

With a quietness he could not explain even to himself, Fenton edged forward and stood up. He walked on tiptoe, moving round and round as though some enemy might lurk in a shadow.

("Take care! Take care! Take care!")

There were three windows: westwards, southwards over the river, and northeastwards near the sentry walk of the battlements. The air was chilly now. Moving soundlessly, Fenton stole over to the northeastwards window.

The sentry walk was just beyond his line of vision however he tried to look, as it was meant to be. He could see the path below, but no firefly lanthorn bobbed in a sentry's hand. He could see the Bell Tower at the angle of the inner ballium wall, then the inner battlements set in a line towards the Bloody Tower and the Wakefield Tower, where the Governor had his lodgings.

Unearthly moonlight darkened the old stones to blackness, but set among them glimmers of white. Even the ravens must be asleep in the trees on Tower Green. Rearing above all was the square shape of Julius Caesar's Tower, grey-white, dead, as though dead since a dust age when above its pinnacles flew the red-leopard banner of Normandy.

Fenton shivered. Softly, again without noise, he stole back to the southern window above the river. Even the Thames seemed empty, except for a few craft moored against the Surrey shore across the river, some three hundred yards away. One larger ship, a square-rigger in shadow, carried two green-glowing lanthorns from her mainmast yard. Now Fenton could hear the hiss of white water under the wharf and against the wall. But nothing else.

Stop! There was another sound.

Someone, very softly, was moving along the sentry walk towards the door.

CHAPTER XXII

THE WOMAN AT MIDNIGHT:

A NAME IS PUT TO THE POISONER

ON FENTON'S table there was a great trencher of food and a bottle of wine, evidently left for him while he slept; the food as cold as charity. He picked up the heavy chair, weighed it in his hands, and decided it would do as a weapon.

Tiptoeing across to half-shadow beyond the western window, he held the chair at his side, and waited.

Someone, with determination to make no noise, slowly eased back one bar with a grinding slur of iron. Then the second bar outside the door began to move.

"Gently!" thought Fenton, and quivered with eagerness as he gripped the chair.

His first notion had been secret assassination. And yet, though he had been shut irrevocably into the past, it was the reign of Charles the Second, not that of Richard the Third. No longer did the rack creak, with a snap of joints torn from their sockets, as some wretch screamed in the dungeons below Julius Caesar's Tower. No black-clad men, faces dark except for teeth, crawled up the death-narrow stairs of the Bloody Tower.

The bar on the door went back. A large key rattled in the lock; when it turned, even slowly, the lock snapped like the hammer of an empty musket.

Briefly he saw a vertical line of moonlight shine and vanish as the door opened and closed. He could hear his visitor breathe. And the visitor was a woman, in a long black cloak with a round hood edged in fine lace.

Fenton loosened his grip on the chair and set it down. He should have anticipated this, and guessed who she might have been.

It was Meg York, yet a Meg in some subtle way altered: perhaps by moonlight. Putting down the key on the table, she threw back the hood of the cloak. Her hair, dressed in a new style, fell in long black curls about her shoulders. And her face, with no touch of hardness or irony, was the face of Mary Grenville.

Fenton went cold, because this must be a mask. Meg kept one hand inside her cloak, as though holding a weapon. His hands moved again to the chair, watchfully. She at least was flesh and blood.

Without sound she swept towards Fenton, and stopped close to him. In horrible grotesque, to his eyes, as a mask of flesh, her face seemed warm with pity and sympathy. She spoke in a voice just above a whisper.

"You can have no fondness for me, I know," she said. "Yet you must do as I bid, for I am here to aid you."

Fenton merely looked at her.

"I tell you," cried Meg in a whispery voice, and stamped her foot audibly on the floor, "you must make haste! You have not a night, not an hour, to lose; else you will die. I swear this!"

"Come, I think not. They hold me on a charge of treason, I grant . . . "

"But—!"

"But, in consideration of Sir Nick's high name and place, and also as sitting in Parliament, they cannot fling me into Newgate as a felon. They must bring against me a Bill of Attainder in the House of Commons. Parliament will not be convoked, my sweet, until the year '77."

"If you make not your escape within this hour," said Meg, "all hope is gone." Meg yearned towards him. "Can you not intrust me?"

Though Fenton did not laugh, his jaws and lips went through the movement of it.

"Again?" he asked politely.

Meg closed her eyes, pressing one hand over her face, as though with fierce effort she would draw to herself some mighty power.

"Am I again fallen in love with my winding sheet," said Fenton, "that I should intrust your warmth and your desire? What are you but a succubus of the underworld, whose true touch is as cold as ice? And where is your master?"

"My . . . ?"

"I refer to the devil. Surely he must be near us. Stay, I have a new notion: summon him up, my pet! I would have audience with him for the third time, and defeat him as I did before!"

Meg, now shaken by deadly terror, glanced everywhere about her and all but fell on her knees.

"Stop!" she whispered. "You must not say those woids! I beg it!"

"Why, then," and Fenton smiled like a death's head, "is he so very near us?"

"He is far and far away. He hath forgotten you. He thinks no more on you than on thousands of life in a drop of water. He did promise . . . "

"Promise?"

"Promise *me*," said Meg, "that he would trouble you no more, since he knoweth history must run out its sands. But if you do call him, or say that you defeated him—"

"Let him catch a pox in his own domain," said Fenton, "for I did at least half-defeat him. True, his gibes and wrath drove me in fear from the house, while you sat half-naked on a couch and hated me that I did yield. But my fear was fear for Lydia. It was history won; not the devil. You heard your master own that I kept my soul, which so enraged him. That was the victory. '*For what shall it profit. . . ?*' "

"Stop! Stop! Stop!"

But it was Meg herself who stifled her own muttering tone.

"What was that noise?" she asked, turning her head from one side to the other.

Fenton had heard it too, though only the moonlight seemed real.

"I think," he said, "that the lions out there, or it may be other beasts, are restless. I have heard them before. Or perhaps they scent your presence, great and small cats alike."

"Call me what you please," said Meg. "Yet at heart I am Mary Grenville, as you are Nicholas Fenton of Cambridge. I, who followed you back into the past, cannot but love you. I'll not see you die." Again Meg pressed one hand to her face. "Nay, now are all my wits scattered! But, if I offer proof of good intent as well, will you hear me?"

She moved closer. Unnervingly, Meg raised clear grey eyes (or so it seemed), untouched by craft or elusiveness.

"I . . . I will hear you."

309

"Well! Is not the door of your prison cell unlocked?" Meg threw out her free left hand to point. "You are a far stronger swimmer than I, though I was accounted good when in dim days we swam together at Richmond. Jump from the battlements, swim beneath the wharf, and you are free!"

"Free? To go . . . where?"

"Have you glanced this night from the southern window of your cell?"

"I have."

"Then did you mark a great ship against the opposite bank? With two green lanthorns at the . . . at the . . . nay, I cannot remember men's names for these things!"

"No matter; I marked the ship. What do you say of it?"

"It is his Majesty's line-of-battle ship *Prince Rupert*," said Meg, "carrying forty, sixty: foh, I forget the number of guns. It was ordered there for your sake. You have but to swim three hundred yards and be safe. The ship will convey you to any port in France you shall choose."

Fenton stared at her. He began to speak, but Meg darted the palm of her hand across his mouth.

"More!" she told him, and her voice throbbed. "This night all warders and military in the Middle Tower, as also in St. Thomas's Tower at the end of the sentry walk, are summoned to a great drunken banquet at the Governor's lodgings in the Wakefield Tower. They are there now, behind muffled windows at a whim of the Governor. This secret is intrusted only to him, and in part to Colonel Howard. Unless some sentry should descry you, the way is cleared!"

"I am fascinated," declared Fenton, without expression. "Now who hath ordered here a line-of-battle ship, for my poor sake, and also made the Governor of the Tower corrupt his duty?"

"The King himself."

After speaking those three words, Meg shrank back before Fenton's cold, courteous smile.

"Why, then," and he laughed, "the King plays a most confounded game against himself. With one hand he claps me into the Tower; with the other he builds a perplexed structure to get me out. Would it not have been more simple merely to release me?"

"No! No! Oh, you would rather toy with words than deal in sense! You have had audience with the King, I think?"

"True."

310

"Then you are sensible he will not allow his hand to appear publicly in any measure? Any measure! And my Lord Shaftesbury is returned to town since more than a fortnight? Dear fool, the King did not put you into the Tower to harm you. He did this to save you!"

"Save . . ." Fenton paused. "Almost you persuadeth me," he said.

"Dear heart," said Meg, startling him, and with her eyes darkening in all her strength of appeal, "I had hoped you'd intrust me. I was stupid. Would you have proof now?"

"Yes!"

Meg's left hand darted inside her cloak, where it was plain she held some weapon. Instantly Fenton swung upwards the heavy chair, to crush her head if she struck with dagger or sword. Then the chair wavered and wobbled in his hands.

What Meg held out to him, though still keeping something back, was a folded sheet of heavy paper. Fenton, torn between half-belief and a cold disbelief, lowered the chair.

"Once before," whispered Meg, with a shaken smile, "you all but killed me with a chair in my bedchamber at your house. And I, for my jealousy, would have slain you with a dagger. No matter." She shook the paper. "There's light enough to read what is writ here."

He took the paper hastily to the white radiance through the western window. Though there was no signature, unmistakably it was the handwriting of the King.

" 'Sir N.F.,' " Fenton read aloud. " 'You might have intrusted me. In candour, you are too useful to me to fall into the hands of my Lord S. Also I owe you something for deceiving you, as I was deceived and much wroth when I learned it, as to the false charge (against) your wife. M.Y. will tell you of a great villain. Obey her. You may return soon. Destroy this letter.' "

Fenton lowered his head.

Slowly he tore the letter into very small pieces, letting them go through the bars and float out over the moat. He had several times to clear his throat before he spoke.

"Meg, I do not understand all this. In some fashion I am gathered into a dance of statecraft, like a small puppet in a raree show. But you are in the right of it. I must go."

Meg, with tears trickling down her cheeks, put her hand again inside the cloak. What she held out to him was his Clemens Hornn sword, in the old shagreen-covered scabbard, with the thin chains tinkling to the swordbelt.

"Meg!"

Fenton drew a deep breath. As he buckled the sword belt round him, he felt such exhilaration as he had never known. He took two long strides towards that unlocked door, bumping into the table amid shadow bars on the floor. But he hesitated, and returned to Meg.

"My dear, I must deal fairly with you," he said. "I will make escape, yes. But—but I have no intent to swim to the warship."

Meg's eyes widened. Her expression had become one of sheer horror.

"No!" she cried aloud, so that the sound rang and echoed in the stone drum. Fenton wondered whether some invisible sentry had heard it. Meg clasped her hands round his arms.

"You must not!" she whispered. "You cannot! Else you will undo all!"

"Meg, hear me. My first design, when they brought me here, was to dispatch letters to Giles or even George Harwell. I would have shewn the poisoner of Lydia: Meg, this poisoner was Kitty Softcover; no other! Having done that, I would find some weapon; fly at my guards; die in fair fight. Thus to . . . well, to be with Lydia. What else have I?"

Violently Meg shook at his arms in the cambric shirt, but she could not move them.

"No! No! No!"

"But now," whispered Fenton, "I have a sword. I can make escape, prove the guilt of the Alsatian bawd, and taunt a dozen Green Ribbon swordsmen into fight for my own end. 'Tis writ in Giles's manuscript that I shall not die until 1714. Out upon it! The document hath told me nothing, nothing. I think it is a forgery or else a hoax."

"It is," replied Meg, shocking him despite his own words.

But this was swept away. "Tell me," said Meg, in so strange and intense a tone that he faltered, "tell me, by any oath! Have I proved my good faith? Have I?"

"Why . . . who could deny it?"

Releasing his arms, Meg ran to the westwards window. Strangely, he heard no noise of silken or satin petticoats in that hush. Meg seemed to study the position of the moon, and wrung her hands. But she ran back to him.

"The hour is going, and your life with it. But there is still time

312

left. If I tell you all, you will seek the warship and not swim to land."
Meg's eyes, greyish-black now, held him motionless. "I loathe to
tell you all. But I must."

"All?"

"Listen well, and give fair answer. When did last you see me?"

"I have told you. I . . . well, you sat half-naked and hated me because
I fled from the devil."

"On that night," said Meg, "there was within me all spite and horrid-
ness. And this because I feared the closeness of . . . of . . . "

"Your master?"

Her whisper, though close to him, was so faint he scarcely heard it.

"I'll not call him master," she said, "when you are here. Have you
no notion why I am come to the Tower? I would renounce him. I
would renounce him, since—" Tears blurred her eyes as she looked
at him. "Nay, no matter."

"Can you renounce him?"

"I know not. I can but try." Meg's sharp fingernails wrenched at
her breast above the gown inside her cloak. "You forget what aforetime was my faith. If I be received back, whatever my penance, he
cannot touch that faith. For against it the gates of hell shall not
prevail."

Meg lowered her head, so that the glossy curls trembled against
her cheeks. But she looked up, quickly, urgently, and spoke again in
that ghost of a voice.

"And yet I am still his creature. If his great eye and ear should
not now be turned to other inchantments far away, as once he watched
you like a toy, his hand would stretch from the end of the earth to . . . "

"Let him try," said Fenton.

"No! Think not on't! Would you have me hurt and at torture?"

"Now God forbid!" snarled Fenton, and pressed his arm round her.

"Stay, my wits are all addled again. 'Tis you I must persuade. You
saw me last, then, on that loathesome night in Love Lane. But I saw
you . . . "

"When?"

"At your own house, on the night you were taken as prisoner by
the dragoon captain. I bit my lips in blood to observe how ill were
you. I saw you fling away, with contempt, the ring His Majesty had
given you."

313

"Meg, how were you acquainted with this knowledge? That I had received such a ring?" Fenton paused suddenly. "Was it knowledge from the dev . . . from *him?*"

Meg nodded.

"On that foul night in Love Lane, when you had gone, he told me all your thoughts; what was to happen to you, then and in future. Before the relation of all this, he . . . but that's of no account." Meg shuddered. "Dear heart, *I* can prophesy the future."

"You know what is destined to befall me?"

"Yes. It is not pleasant. At last do you glimpse my purpose? I would aid you to change history, for your sake, as you yourself made high attempt to do."

"And failed." Fenton merely pressed Meg more closely to him with his right arm. His voice was steady. "Continue your relation. You saw me fling away King Charles's ring . . . ?"

"True. The servants being much preoccupied with Mrs. Pamphlin, by roguery I stole the ring from the floor and went forth with it. Next morning I was at Whitehall, desiring audience with His Majesty."

Fenton, despite unimagined dangers closing round him like a ring of partisan blades, felt only a piercing of jealousy.

"I dare suppose," he said, "as in so many romances, the King immediately fell captive to your charms? And did your bidding?"

"Nay, 'twas no such thing," replied Meg, with a faint touch of injury or even anger. "For days I could gain no audience; and for shame's sake durst not pluck at his sleeve when he walked each morning in the Park to set his watch by the sundial. At length, becoming desperate, I did force and wheedle my way into his very council chamber."

"And then?"

"Why, there he sat, with only two or three gentlemen about him, at the end of the council table, signing a great store of papers. His eye did kindle when he saw me, to be sure; and he dismissed the others. Yet he said but: 'Madam, a looking glass will shew you how much I regret my lack of leisure. What is your errand?'

"Whereat I recounted as much as was necessary, indicating I was aware of as much as he knew himself. 'I am sensible,' said I, 'that you condemned Sir Nick Fenton to the Tower to safeguard his life; since,' said I, 'you know my Lord Shaftesbury is returned to town. And your spies tell you that my lord hath a great and evil design against Sir Nick.'"

Fenton spoke huskily.

"What design?" he demanded. "What design of my Lord Shaftesbury?"

"His Majesty," Meg rushed on, with her hair against Fenton's cheek, but without putting her arms around him, "His Majesty was amazed when I spoke thus. Yet he concealed it as well as might be. I can see him yet, with his black face and blacker periwig, knees crossed, eyes all a-studying you without seeming so, and the sun on painted windows . . ."

"Meg! Hold your clack! What is the design?"

He felt a shiver through Meg's whole body.

"But the King was in pliant mood, having discovered by questioning that the charges against Lydia were baseless." On ran Meg in frantic whisper. "You no longer believe, I hope, that Lydia 'lured' you into Spring Gardens?"

"Meg, for God's sake!"

"When I myself informed you that Lydia, at the dressmaker's, spoke of Spring Gardens in a loud aside for anyone to hear? More! There was a great villain, as the King said, who pretended to have seen a letter from Lydia; and there was none such letter. Have you heard his name?"

The quick question took Fenton off balance.

"I have heard of the man and the nonexisting letter," he said. "Giles spoke of it, but would not tell the man's name. Who was he?"

"A man who thought you had shamed him before the Green Ribbon lords. When he was free of his leg injury (which was soon, as he said in Spring Gardens), he did slink away and offer his service to Whitehall. Being discovered in this cheat of the letter, he is now returned to the Green . . ."

"Not Captain Duroc?"

"My—my aforetime protector. Captain Duroc."

Over Fenton went such a pressure of rage that it seemed to him he could hardly draw breath. His left hand dropped to the sword pommel at his side. In fancy he saw the very tall figure, all in white, mouthing at him with Duroc's suave sneer.

"Thus I persuaded His Majesty," Meg's voice was louder, if no less rapid, "that he must dispatch a ship, any ship, to bear you hence. This day I had but to walk into the Tower, ogled killingly by a warder at my side, and seek refuge with Colonel Howard until—"

Without warning Meg went limp, and would have fallen if he had not caught her.

315

"Nay," she whispered, gasping but steady again, "I can no longer prattle this idle talk! I must tell you of my Lord Shaftesbury's design. Well! he plans to use . . ."

Meg stopped short.

The roar of a lion, shaking silence like a physical force, burst up in rumbling tremors from the menagerie house. Another lion answered, then a third and a fourth. Squalls, snarls, ran snakily beneath.

Both Meg and Fenton stood motionless. An upriver breeze, freshing off the Thames, stirred through the cell and set rustling the trees on Tower Green. But across the upper part of the northeastern window flashed a faint line of yellow light.

Fenton ran to the window. From an upper window in Wakefield Tower, undoubtedly the room where the Governor held warders and Foot Guards at banquet, a heavy muffling curtain had been drawn back so that the light pierced out. Someone's shadow appeared there. Since it was not a hundred yards away, the voice carried clearly in breeze and night hush.

"Ecod!" roared the voice of a Foot Guards officer, shouting as men will when uplifted in strong waters. "King Charles hath a good voice this night!"

"King Charles?" blurted Meg, at Fenton's side.

"Gently! Have no fear!" said Fenton, though his flesh crawled hot and cold. "The largest lion in the menagerie is named always for the reigning monarch."

The lion roared again.

"Stab my belly," yelled another voice from the window of the Wakefield Tower, "but too long we've abused Sir Robert's hospitality. It must be the quarter-hour to midnight."

A bellowing chorus denied this, like the sounds from the menagerie.

"Bear up, friend, and here's a last bumper to a cursed good war!"

"Ah bah lays fransay!" thundered the Foot Guards officer, evidently thinking he spoke a foreign language. "Eh, though, where's our guest? Ecod, he's under the table; else ecod he's vanished like Lady Jane's ghost!"

Meg whispered frantically at Fenton's ear:

"Sir Robert, being a sober man, cannot hold them past midnight. Else he will be suspect when you are found escaped. You . . ."

The breeze had strengthened through the stone room. And the heavy door to the sentry walk, its latch imperfectly caught when Meg

316

closed it, blew open and crashed against the round wall with a noise like a culverin shot.

From the Wakefield Tower, now crowded with figures, there was sudden dead silence.

Fenton hurried to the cell door. Outside he could see part of the sentry walk, the breast-high battlements with their openings waist high. He could feel the free wind in his face and hear the seething of the water below. Two strides, a leap, and . . .

"God's beard! What's amiss at the Middle Tower?"

"Middle Tower? 'Tis the keepers a-clapping-to their doors at the beasts' den!"

And what, thought Fenton, would happen to Meg if he left her? Deliberately he shut the door and turned back to her.

High up on Tower Green moved the lanthorn of a sentry.

"Lord Shaftesbury's design?" asked Fenton, breathing hard. "Or be more short! What death hath history in store for me?"

Meg's knees shook like her lips. She must grasp the bars of the window.

"Either you will be cut down in making escape from here," she said, "or else . . . "

"Come, there can't be two deaths!"

"You—you are familiar with the devil's diverting humorousness," Meg faltered. "'Tis one or the other, and you must change history and turn away both! For the devil would not tell me which."

"What's the other death? Speak short!"

"Oh, God help me!" cried the penitent.

"Meg!"

"You will be pelted with stones and filth, half-dead as you sit on your coffin in the cart from Newgate to Tyburn; and at Tyburn, amid more showers of stones, you will strangle slowly from the high gallows! Now do you see why you must haste to the ship?"

"No!"

"Kitty Softcover, the cook-wench, was in your house on the night when Lydia died. True, true, even as you have thought! But this cook-wench did not poison Lydia!"

"Not . . . Then who did?"

"You poisoned her," gasped Meg. "It is Kitty Softcover who hath denounced you to the magistrate and to my Lord Shaftesbury."

317

CHAPTER XXIII

THE LAST DUEL: AN END

IS PUT TO THE STRUGGLE

"MUFFLE *the window, damn ye!*" bawled a voice from the Wake-field Tower. "*A last bumper; we take our leave!*"

In the cold, shadow-barred moonlight, Fenton looked at Meg.

"Here is no time for jest," he whispered.

"Dearest heart, would I jest now?"

"Liar!" said Fenton.

Yet a crack of horror, opening in his brain, showed him what might have lurked below.

"Yes, you apprehend it!" It was as though Meg read his thoughts even now. "It was not in truth you, your own self, your mind or heart; it was the soul of Sir Nick.

"Once before that, at the apothecary's in Dead Man's Lane," Meg rushed on, "you hideously feared for—for my sake, that I might be a poisoner. Dost recollect? You fell a-raging at this. For ten minutes of the clock you lost your memory. The soul of Sir Nick triumphed; you became Sir Nick, and ran in frenzy.

"My dear, my dear, it was in exactness what occurred when you returned from Whitehall Palace after your audience with the King. You did return home at the half-hour past eight by your own watch. You were in a daze, stricken for Lydia's sake, easy prey for Sir Nick should your anger rise high. Thus, arrived at your house, you did go straight to your bedchamber. There you sat in a chair facing the window. Do I say true?"

318

Fenton nodded. He could not speak, or so he thought. Nevertheless his lips moved.

"Yet Lydia," it was all hoarseness, "was being poisoned lightly, by slow poison, ere I came into the person of Sir Nick! I cured her! I was not there before! Who, then . . . ?"

"Oh, do you not guess?"

"Sir Nick?"

"Yes!" replied Meg. "Though he did send Kitty to buy the poison, and 'twas her hand put it into the sack posset—as you proved for yourself, when your wits were sharp—still was Sir Nick the guilty man. Are you convinced?"

"I . . . I . . ."

"Hear me! Sir Nick, the true Sir Nick, was become near crazed for Kitty and her most odd kind of love. Did she not press him to be rid of his wife, and also of the true Meg York? Did not rat-mouthed Kitty describe Meg York (not yet myself) to the apothecary, as the woman who sent Kitty to buy the poison?"

"But I . . . returning home from Whitehall that night . . . sitting at the window of my bedchamber . . . !"

"Now do you recollect it! You came to your bedchamber close after half-past eight of the clock. Or say by your watch, which you put down on the dressing table. Of late you had grown accustomed to take a good deal of claret at supper; and you kept a decanter of claret, with goblet, on your dressing table. Now speak! Was that decanter full to the stopper, or no?"

Fenton shied away from Meg's intent, tear-stained eyes and eyelashes. But he looked back.

"It was full to the stopper," he said. "I seized decanter and goblet to drink, but—but put down both unused." Horribly, in black and white and splashed colour, the scene unrolled in memory.

"I sat down," Fenton muttered, his voice growing louder. "For a brief time, if it were writ down, I thought on all suspicions against Lydia. Yet I could not, I could not, credit them. I leaped up from the chair, in a flare of rage . . . "

"Rage," whispered Meg.

"Yet I sat down again! I . . . "

"*Looked out on blackness,*" said Meg, and now she put her arms round him. "That was your own thought. But in your rage (did this not happen softly, too, in the apothecary's shop?) the soul of Sir Nick

319

again triumphed. In a black ten minutes, when you knew not what you did, the black poisoning was done and over."

"But where was the poison? There! Ace-ace-deuce: a winning trick!"

"Dear heart, no. Have you forgot the black-velvet suit, with dried blood on the sleeves, you wore on your first day in the past? It still hung in the dressing closet of your bedchamber. None had touched it, as Giles did say when afterwards you called for it. You yourself had forgot (though the soul of Sir Nick had not) that in the pocket of its coat was an apothecary's packet with one hundred and thirty grains of arsenic."

For the first time Fenton began to tremble badly. Meg, head down, forced and stammered out words which hurt her.

"Sir Nick, when your mind was gone from your body, poured forth a goblet of claret. In this he did pour also above ninety grains of tasteless arsenic from the packet. In your body Sir Nick crept down, wearing your smile with the evil turned inside, to Lydia's chamber. Who should look upon him, since the servants were at supper?

"Yet Kitty Softcover prowled close, at the door of the chamber opposite; once my room. Kitty herself had crept in after you, with a key to the front door, at this early hour because the servants were away. Even Sam, thus obeying a command you had just given, was not outside the front door. Kitty would have her claws into Lydia's jewel coffers. Who could tell Lydia would have gone abed so monstrous early? 'Twas so that Kitty, all a burning lump of thievery, durst not enter her chamber. Yet Kitty saw Sir Nick, since he set the door partway open.

"The time was short, so very brief! You were in Lydia's bedchamber but two minutes, entering shortly beyond twenty minutes towards the hour of nine. Now ask of yourself but what a cunning magistrate would ask!"

Fenton shivered as she pressed him more tightly.

"Nay," he said, "I begin to credit—"

"Your persuasion over Lydia was complete. She too . . . that's to say, she loved you. She was of gentle and good character. She was fast in obedience to the one firm command you had given. From whose hand but yours, in all the world, would she have accepted any morsel of food or drink?"

"Yes, it grows bitter clear!"

"What drink, other than claret from your bedchamber, could have

320

poisoned her? Every dram of wine, as said Giles, was locked in the wine cellar. There was not even, as also he said, a drop of barley water. And this is truth, though it come from the lips of the devil!"

As Meg spoke of Lydia, Fenton could at times feel the very emanation of her hot jealousy, which she tried with success to hold in check. Also, as his wits returned, he saw what in his blindness he had never before seen. He was not the only person who struggled against the coffin lid of another soul. Mary Grenville—though already succubus, witchwoman, call her what you like—also must have within her the handsome, vixenish soul of the true Meg York.

He and Meg were like unto each other, and had ever behaved as such.

"In those two minutes in Lydia's bedchamber," he said, "what speech passed between Lydia and mys . . . that is, Sir Nick?"

"I'll not tell you! Not ever or ever or ever!"

From the menagerie rose again the roar of the lion named King Charles. The lanthorns of keepers now moved inside the windows, as the keepers quietened the lesser beasts. But Meg was again in fear.

"That tower!" She meant the Wakefield Tower, and caught at memory. "There was a man did call that drink a last bumper. The warders on the soldiery will be here!"

"I'll not go," said Fenton, still tormented and crazed with wonder. "One more word. I know not why, but you are mine and I hold you. If I go to the ship, you go with me."

Meg threw back her head, regarding him with a wild look which again brought on her tears.

"Much of this," Fenton went on, speaking rapidly, "I now imagine for myself. Sir Nick (in my shape!) took the poisoned goblet from Lydia's bedchamber. In my . . . his room he cleansed it, using water from the pitcher in the bowl on the dressing table, and flinging the dregs from a window. Nod if I say true! Good!

"Wherefore," he continued, "the poison was not swallowed at supper. It was swallowed at a trifle beyond twenty minutes to nine. Stop! Could Lydia die so soon as midnight? Nay, this is beyond any possi . . .

"Come, I had forgot! Ninety-odd grains of arsenic? Any one of the stomach cramps, striking hard and sudden after a few hours' weakening of the victim, may kill with the shock of it. And so Giles described her death.

321

"More! With so monstrous great a quantity of arsenic, the pain would come well within eight minutes; on Lydia, it worked swifter than with most. All was squeezed and compressed into brief seconds. The murderer had returned to his bedchamber. Judith Pamphlin, upon her coming upstairs, did in truth hear Lydia moan even before my wits were unsealed, and I awoke. And this, I think, was at ten minutes to nine. True?"

"So says the devil." Meg added: "He hath seen so many deaths!"

"And Lydia . . ." Fenton hesitated. "Lydia must certes have been sensible who had given her the poison. Yet even to the woman Pamphlin she said only that she would speak with me, not uttering a word of the visit with the goblet. She made no ado, Meg. Not even when she died."

"I allow of it!" said Meg, lowering her head and sobbing. "In part 'twas because . . . nay, I'll speak no more of her love. I won't! And in part because she thought it a judgment on her, since in truth she did once dispatch a letter to betray you."

"I killed her, Meg."

"Nay, thou didst *not!*" gritted Meg, using the familiar with her intensity of feeling. "I prove it . . . I prove it by a secret, unknown thing. When Sir Nick had at length committed his final foul deed," her voice was hushed, "his soul was drawn and plucked from him ere you opened your eyes. His soul was taken away . . ."

"By the devil?"

"Nay, or you would be dead. By Someone," Meg's eyes wandered in affright, "of whom I dare not speak. But since then Sir Nick's soul is gone from you. Yours is that of Nicholas Fenton of Cambridge, set forever in the flesh you wear now. Ask me no more. You are yet hounded by humankind. Kitty, the cook-maid . . ."

Fenton, looking back with a glare of revelation on his different behaviour of late weeks, threw it from his mind as he grasped after Meg's words.

"Would Kitty, the Alsatian wench and I think known to many magistrates, durst have denounced me for murder? Or be believed if she did?"

"What! Under the protection of my Lord Shaftesbury and the Green Ribbon? She *is* believed; and walks bedecked with jewels amid stout swordsmen to protect her. The design is complete to wrest you from protection of the King . . ."

"The King?"

"Oh, the King will yield. As always he does, against too vast a public outcry. Did you not so tell him to his face, as concerned another matter?"

Now Meg lifted her arms, as though in passionate and low-voiced agony.

"Fraud and cheat!" she said. "All against you has been fraud, since that dim, lost first night when you made your false bargain with the devil. Most readily he could agree to all your 'conditions' in the strict letter of them. For he himself (the devil's logic) would not do what was to be done against you. It was decreed by history. His rages came not from your 'conditions,' but because you mocked at him. You misread the rages, and were in quagmire where you thought yourself most safe. And yet, for all, you did defeat him. —What's amiss?"

"Giles's manuscript," said Fenton. "Also a fraud. And not even yet writ!"

"And if not?"

"Well, why shall it be writ? So that posterity—once Giles by bribery hath destroyed all broadsheets or pamphlets, and even the Newgate record—posterity may not see a great name shamed. Posterity shall read of a murder, with pages omitted by deliberation; but of a good-souled Sir Nick who died many years later. Why, it would appear I am to be hanged after all."

"Not so!" said Meg. "This shall not be, if you have the boldness to go forth and change history as once you had. Have you that boldness?"

The breeze from outside, still rustling on Tower Green, blew at Fenton with fine and cold invigoration, like a plunge into cold water.

"I have!" he said, happily smiling, and tapped the sword scabbard. "Are you prepared?"

"Prepared?"

"To accompany me; what else? Curse it, I have not yet seen you all a-sobbing and shrinking. *I* say we now run the hazard too close!"

Meg whipped back and threw open her cloak.

"It was I," she blurted out, "who persuaded the King I must go with you. Round my waist, under gown and smock, there is a belt of pockets: all of precious stones for money, and, wrapped proof against water, a letter from His Majesty to King Louis of France. Yet, when I saw you, I was *resolved* to stay here unless you bade me to . . ."

"Then I bid you!"

"For love?"

323

"Yes! But speak of that when we are safe. D'ye hear? There's no more noise of a carouse from the Wakefield Tower. They make their way here!"

"I am still the devil's creature," said Meg, who could not stop tears; "whether I be Meg York or Mary Grenville, I am still the . . ."

Fenton, who had started for the door, turned round.

"Do you think I, who have myself dealt with the devil, care one lead hog whether you are his servant or no? Yet I think Someone hath altered you. No matter! You cannot swim in that cloak and gown; put them by!"

Now it was Fenton, not Meg, who heard the clock ticking and saw the sands running out.

If they found her here, he thought, she would slip like himself into the grasp of my Lord Shaftesbury, who always smiled but never let go.

Still Meg hesitated. Throwing back her curls, she cast a quick, terrified glance towards the door to the sentry walk. Fenton summoned up every fibre of will.

"D'ye fear the devil?" He did not speak loudly. "Well, this I warrant. We will together make escape from the Tower, though the devil himself stand outside that door. Come!"

Meg flung off her cloak. Her black-and-silver gown she twisted upwards: bending forward, tearing and rending the gown, she brought it up over her head and away from her arms. Standing in silk smock, stockings, and shoes, she kicked off the shoes and hurried after Fenton.

Though the upriver wind was dying, Fenton held the heavy door as he moved it open. Meg slipped out past him, into the angle of the battlements against the tower. Closing the door carefully, he followed her, pushing her forward.

Far below them the water slapped high and seethed against the wall. Fenton cast a quick look to his left. In the windows of the Wakefield Tower yellow lanthorns began to move down.

"One hand atop the battlement," he whispered, gripping Meg round the waist to push her; "up to the opening between; then jump! 'Ware the tide and the wharf piles as you swim under the wharf. Now!"

Meg, about to comply, turned her head to the left. Then she stood as though paralyzed. Fenton also looked to the left along the sentry walk between here and St. Thomas's Tower.

Facing him on the sentry walk, some twenty feet away, dressed in white and with sword drawn, stood Captain Duroc.

Captain Duroc.

324

The moon, almost overhead, was brilliant and with flat shadows. But it played tricks with eyesight. Duroc's gauntness and height made him appear a giant. Out of his big periwig was thrust the bony lower jaw, lower teeth glinting in a jeer. Up swept his right hand with the rapier: elbow crooked, hand at head height, sword point extended straight towards Fenton.

No longer was his periwig gold-dusted or his voice comical. He was tall death on the sentry walk.

"No, I am not de devil," Duroc's harsh voice whispered. "And I am not sent 'ere by milor' Shaftesbury. I was a guest at dees banquet, eh? You 'ave not heard dem shout from the window of their guest that disappear? Leetle nobleman! Sweet Meg which was my bedfel . . ."

Nobody saw the fire hiss along the fuse of hatred between Duroc and Fenton. But Fenton's hands were round Meg's waist, and she felt the hatred through his muscles.

"Up! I'll swing you!" Fenton muttered to Meg. "Jump!"

"Will you follow?"

"In a moment!"

"Then I'll stay," replied a hard-breathing Meg, "whilst you stay."

Captain Duroc's low-pitched cackle of a jeer floated towards them, above the hiss of the water below.

"You will not leap dere. No, no, no!" he said. "I stand so far away (eh) to teach you how I am upon you, *voilà*, if you t'ink to try!"

Fenton darted out from Meg's side—and almost toppled over the side of the sentry walk, which was hardly wider than six feet. But he swung round to face Duroc.

"The leetle nobleman," sighed Duroc, "weel not fight. No! He weel run. I am Duroc! I have a *botte* too many for him!"

Fenton lugged out.

"God damn ye," he said, not loudly, "now shew me a *botte* I don't know!"

"Take care!" cried Meg.

And even Meg, who was very far from being squeamish, had to clench teeth on a scream.

For they flew at each other along the sentry walk, like two men in a famous duel on Calais sands, as though each would drive sword through the other without a stop. But instinctively both recoiled, their shoes grinding on the stones, within lunging distance of each other.

Out shot Duroc's sword point, with a moon-flash on the blade, striking to pierce through Fenton's left eye. Fenton, parrying high

325

with a *clack* which resounded towards the Wakefield Tower, heard Duroc's shoe slip and stumble. Fenton went out at full lunge for Duroc's heart. And Duroc's laugh croaked as both men darted back to guard position.

The pseudo Frenchman had too immense a length of arm and leg. The point of Fenton's blade, out at full length, had fallen four inches short of his opponent's chest.

"You see, leetle nobleman?" panted his opponent. "You cannot touch me!"

"No?"

"No!"

The hand guard of Duroc's sword, like a small cup of lacework steel, had on each side a quillon projecting and then curving back like a narrow hook at the end. Fenton saw it by moon-flash, as Duroc elongated like a white snake for a thrust below the belly. Fenton, parrying blade-downwards, whacked the sword aside and cross-lunged for the calf of Duroc's extended right leg.

Point and blade ripped white stocking and flesh from the edge of the calf, with blood that swelled grey-black. "Captain Duroc," now shrieking out an imprecation in the language of Hungary, flew in to attack with his immense reach. Four times he lunged without riposte from Fenton, and Fenton laughed and Duroc became crazed, because he could not penetrate Fenton's guard.

"Guard yourself!" Fenton yelled, and steadied for the most dangerous trick in swordplay.

For the fifth time, on this occasion in quarte, Duroc's blade streaked out. Fenton's left arm, swordless, swept inside and knocked the blade wide to the right. Darting inside Duroc's guard, now at murderous infighting, he again drove for his opponent's heart.

The point pierced and sank deep—but not deep enough for the hard fibre that surrounds the heart. Fenton, leaping back, parried by shaved second the long thrust towards his forehead over the right eye.

Then both of them, panting, drew back and studied each other. The befooling tricks of moonlight did not aid their swordplay.

Duroc, bleeding heavily from two bad wounds, still towered over Fenton. He swayed once, but he did not fall. No longer, Fenton knew, would he thrust for what seemed to be the eye: it was, in fact, to gash the eyebrow with his point so as to blind his opponent and finish Fenton with leisurely taunting. Duroc employed only an old trick of swordsmen, considered fair.

326

But Duroc dared not do it now. His breath was going. He must thrust for the heart, as Fenton did. At the same time, Fenton remembered a trick which would not be invented until the eighteenth century. As a rule, it was impossible to disarm your man. Yet . . .

"*Now stab my belly,*" bellowed a voice not far away, "*but there's Nick Fenton in fight on the sentry walk!*"

"*Where?*"

"*Look you there!*"

"*Ecod, who's the woman? Scant-clad, and a beauty!*"

Fenton's insides seemed to contract. Musket fire at close range could . . .

The light of lanthorns flooded part way into the very broad path between the inner and the outer walls. There were heavy footfalls on stone stairs in the narrow arch between the Bloody Tower and the Wakefield Tower.

Fenton, his eyes on the quillons of Duroc's sword, suddenly gave a great leap backwards. Duroc, gasping in triumph, pounced after him. And Duroc flung forwards, the moon white on his back, in full-length lunge at his adversary's heart.

Meg cried out. For Fenton stood wide open, both arms stretched out from his sides; and then he leaped sideways to the right, his sword banging the battlements. Duroc's point and blade cleanly ripped open the left side of his shirt; Fenton felt against his side the fire-burn of what was only the cold flat of the blade.

Then the deadfall snapped.

Fenton's left arm swept down. As the cup hilt of Duroc's sword thudded between his left arm and side, Fenton held it clamped there for the instant's time needed to bring his own blade up and over. Projecting from the left side of Duroc's cup-hilt was one quillon with its steel curved backwards and close inwards like a narrow hook. Fenton's blade shot vertically downwards inside the hook, locking and wedging the other sword. Duroc could not jerk it back.

Too late the pseudo Frenchman saw it in horror. Suddenly whipping away his left hand, Fenton wrenched his right hand over and high to the right. No man's grip, holding a blade forward as Duroc's did, could stand against such sideways leverage. Duroc's sword, torn from his fingers, sailed up and over the battlements in moon-silvered flight, and dropped whirling into the river.

"*There's the devil in velvet, sir!*" bawled a voice almost unnaturally close from below. "*Ga! See what he's done!*"

327

"Prisoner, stand and give yourself up!" called the curt voice of the military.

Now the whole broad path hammered with running footsteps. Up sizzled and curled the bright, wicked light of torches.

Fenton, sword poised for the last thrust, looked up into the dazed, terrified eyes of Duroc, bully of all Europe. And Fenton could not do this; his sword arm trembled. Duroc, misreading his look, stumbled round and ran. Fenton, with unsteady fingers sheathing the stained blade, himself turned to run towards Meg. But he found Meg not four feet behind him, motionless, her hand atop one battlement.

"Up!" croaked Fenton, so winded he could hardly speak. "Jump!"

Without hesitation, without assistance, Meg swung herself waist high and jumped over. He heard the splash in the seething water.

There was a crash as the other door to Fenton's prison cell, the door from the winding stair in the Middle Tower, was unbarred and burst open. Torches flared in the opening. Fenton raced back and shot the bars of the sentry-walk door, locking it from outside.

But, as he turned back toward the path inside and below . . .

"Muskets, sir? They've a-fetched 'em from the Middle Tower!"

"Muskets! A file along the path. Here! Loose fire at will if he . . . Prisoner! Will you stand and yield!"

"Come and take me!" croaked Fenton.

The whole path seemed a maze of torches that dazzled his eyes. The light pinned him in view like an insect against a wall. Two Foot Guards officers, swords drawn and periwigs askew, were running up shallow steps to the battlements near St. Thomas's Tower.

Fenton turned his back to the path and swung up between two battlements. From below came what sounded less like a musket shot than a heavy explosion. Just as the heavy musket ball, erratic, smashed into the battlements a dozen feet away, he dived over.

Dived . . .

Too late he remembered that the wharf, with its battery of guns, was built too near the wall for any but a very close dive. It flashed through his brain as the gun wharf, the white-laced water, sprang up at him. He fell so close to the wharf that its edge tore off the back of one shoe, skinning the ankle. Then the shock of water, a cold hammer, drove him down into mud-swirling depths.

His upcurved hands carried him up through blackness; and, as he reached the surface, the white rushing water banged his shoulder against a wharf pillar. He swam forwards, dodging obstructions and foul rubbish. The tide was not yet at flood; the current looked worse than it was.

Writhing his ankles together and kicking off both shoes, Fenton emerged from under the wharf into moonlight. His crawl stroke clove water with the startling speed of his twenty-six years. Ahead of him he could catch a white flash of Meg swimming hard for the two green lanthorns of the dim ship; and how it stirred his heart again to exhilaration!

The cold wind seemed to have shifted. He put on more speed, his head burrowing into water and sideways for breath. Then a musket ball smacked water beside him and skipped ahead, just as one part of the Tower wall exploded to the din of massed musketry.

"Dive!" he shouted to Meg, or tried to shout. "Dive!"

Down he went, deep underwater. The current softly pushed him, smoothed at him, but he swam forward for what seemed minutes, and rasped lungs nearly burst. When he reared his head, twitching back to clear hair from his eyes, he risked a backwards glance.

The musket fire had stopped. But sputtering lighted matches, each a long cord wound several times round the bearer's arm, moved amid the gun battery on the wharf.

Then Fenton looked ahead.

Kindled to full great shape out of the night, the line-of-battle ship *Prince Rupert* loomed up only a short distance away. The glow of the battle lanthorns, swung low against the rigging, illuminated the line of cannon on her upper gun deck. Then the high-built sterncastle was illuminated too. From the mainmast head flew the royal standard.

A heavy-set man in a periwig, one hand on the balustrade of the sterncastle quarter-deck and the other holding a sea trumpet to his lips, shouted with a rolling voice across sound-carrying water.

"Fire on a King's ship, would ye?" rang the voice. "Master-gunner! If ye see match move to gun over yonder, lay me a twelve-pounder on that battery!"

The waist of the *Prince Rupert* was alive with the hard clack of bare feet running on boards and moving shadows against the battle lanthorns. A rope ladder with wooden treads clattered over the side and swung close to water.

Far behind, a glimmering gun match stopped in mid-air as though at some order from the top of the Tower wall. A little space more, and

Meg emerged from water. She climbed the rope ladder, swinging wildly with her drenched hair pressed close and also her drenched costume, until a staring tar nipped down to give her a hand.

Over Fenton, too, loomed the curved side of the ship, and the grey canvas above. He steadied the rope ladder; then himself climbed. He knew, as he swung there, that his mind and soul were at peace. Despite those doubts, in this age he had found what he sought. Lydia, though loved, had been a romantic ideal which would soon have palled. Meg, for all her tempers, had been his own from the first.

"We have beaten the devil," he said, "and we have changed history!"

And the Clemens Hornn sword still swung at his hip as he climbed the ladder to safety.

NOTES FOR THE CURIOUS

FOURTEEN years ago, when I wrote a factual study of political events between 1678 and 1681 to surround the murder of a London magistrate, and called it *The Murder of Sir Edmund Godfrey,* I did not think I should ever return to the bustling and brawling of the later Restoration. But, through all those years between, I had not ceased to read about it. The amount of factual material on which I have drawn for *The Devil in Velvet*—especially as regards the minutiae of speech, manners, customs, background, dress, eating, drinking, swordplay—has grown out of hand.

To add an extended bibliography to a novel intended only for entertainment would overweigh the story and sound like frantic pedantry. The first duty of any novelist, a duty so often forgotten nowadays, is to tell a story. Yet these details of the story, as well as the characters of the genuine historical personages, are all true. The foreshadowing of the "Popish plot" is true. In case some of the curious might be tempted to probe further into this matter, I am happy to add some notes on matters colourful or picturesque.

CHARACTER OF CHARLES THE SECOND

"The King of England," wrote the French Ambassador, Barrillon, to Louis the Fourteenth, "has a manner so well-concealed and so difficult to penetrate that the shrewdest are deceived by it." (Barrillon to Louis, Sept. 9/19th, 1680, Dalrymple, ii, 204.) "The King," privately declared that eminent jurist, Sir Franics North, "understands foreign affairs better than all his counsellors put together." (Roger North, *Life of Lord Guilford,* 1816 ed., ii, 181.) "He is so shrewd," commented Sir John Reresby in his *Memoirs,* "that you never know what he is about." So speak a few of his contemporaries who knew him.

The Letters, Speeches, and Declarations of Charles II (collected and edited by Mr. Arthur Bryant, 1935) show his wit as well as his common sense and his policy. To young Thomas Bruce, later Earl of Ailesbury, Charles really defined his aim: "God's fish, they have put a set of men about me; but they shall know nothing!" (Ailesbury, *Memoirs,* 1890 ed., 112.)

Charles's whole intention was to keep the stability of the kingdom, ensure the rightful succession, and never again to go "on his travels." After the work of such later historians as Sir John Pollock, Mr. Arthur Bryant, Mr. Cyril Hughes Hartmann, nobody takes seriously the grotesque parody of him which for long had comic place in the schoolbooks.

The reason for this schoolbook notion is easy to find. In Charles's own lifetime his Court party became known as Tories, and Shaftesbury's Country party as Whigs. Now history, throughout the Victorian age, was for the most part written by Whigs. And Whigs, notably Macaulay, had no liking for a King who upheld the monarchial principle with such skill as did Charles the Second.

Drawing on such sources as Anthony Hamilton's *Memoirs of Count Grammont,* the *Diary* of John Evelyn, the *Diary* of Samuel Pepys (all obtainable in many editions), the Whigs drew on anecdotes which honest Pepys received at third or fourth hand as gossip from his hairdresser, and tried to picture the King as little more than wencher and fool. Wencher he assuredly was. The populace loved him for it. "God," said Charles, "will not damn a man for taking a little irregular pleasure by the way"; and Dr. (later Bishop) Burnet noticed that few things touched him to the heart. (Gilbert Burnet, *History of My Own Time,* 1833 ed., i, 23.) But the Whig historians achieved something of a feat: for years they showed as Jack-fool a King who was the shrewdest man in Europe.

By the way, it is a joy and delight to read the *History of My Own Time* in its edition of 1833, which of course was from a text published originally in 1724. But this one is reproduced as it was once edited by Dean Swift, Burnet's bitter enemy. While the text moves ponderously on, gleaming-eyed Swift runs riot with such footnotes as "Liar!" or "Scotch dog!"

CHARACTER OF LORD SHAFTESBURY

The character and a great part of Shaftesbury's career have been sketched out in this novel. One date in his life has been altered by a year; otherwise all dates and historical events stand as they are stated. Aside from contemporary reports of him by Bishop Burnet, John Dryden, Roger North, and Sir Roger L'Estrange (especially in L'Estrange's *The Mystery of the Death of Sir E. B. Godfrey Unfolded,* 1688), he has had his official biography in W. D. Christie's *Life of Anthony Ashley Cooper, Earl of Shaftesbury* (2 vols., 1871). And there is a fine analysis in H. D. Traill's *Shaftesbury,* in the *English Worthies* series (1886).

Tory and Whig united to condemn him when the fever of the age had gone, though Christie (*Life,* ii, 287-293) attempts to slur over some of his violence. But we must see him as he was. He was not a villain, except insofar as he was a fanatic. He would not take a bribe. But he would cheerfully have a man hanged on false evidence or privately murdered. That razorish face can be deciphered only if, to his fierce ambition, we add Traill's suggestion of an honest blazing belief that Parliament must triumph over the King.

Hazlitt, writing lectures in 1818, praised Wycherley's comedy, *The Country Wife*. Long afterwards, the editor of a 'new edition' of these lectures in book form, *On the English Poets and Comic Writers* (Bell & Daldy, 1870), endorsed Hazlitt's praise. But he endorsed it because "the drama is said to be the best picture extant of the dissolute manners of the court of Charles II."

Let us omit the word "dissolute" and proceed. *The Country Wife* really did cause a sensation on the stage, but not because it was found dissolute. In this play Horner (the hero) seduces Mrs. Marjory Pinchwife (the heroine), luring her into his bedchamber with a promise to show her his fine set of china. Mrs. Marjory, enraptured, calls for so much more china that presently Horner must protest he has no china left. As a real-life result of the play, it was months before any respectable woman in London dared venture into a shop and say she wanted china.

Now this was the sort of joke which made playgoers truly whoop: just as, on the other hand, they loved firework displays of wit. It was a combination of the adolescent and the sophisticated, which to a great degree sums up the Restoration.

The best comic dramatists of the time, Wycherley and Etherege and Shadwell—together with Congreve and Vanbrugh, who appeared much later but demonstrated that the spirit of the Merry Monarch was still alive—gave playgoers their best crazy situations and their best wit. Congreve, especially in *Love for Love* and *The Way of the World,* is almost too witty. He flashes in your eyes like Tinker Bell; sometimes you wish he would stop coruscating and sit down.

What we must understand is that the fine ladies and "men of quality," in real life, were not really like these glittering stage figures. They wished to be. They tried hard to be. They had the same blunt speech, the same frank amorousness. But they were not one-tenth as clever, or one-half as coldhearted.

"In our sins, too," cries Brass to Dick Amlet, in Vanbrugh's *The Confederacy,* "I must own you still kept me under. You soared up to adultery with the mistress, while I was at humble fornication with the maid. Nay, in our punishments too: when I was sentenced but to be whipped, I cannot deny you were condemned to be hanged. In all things your inclinations have been greater and nobler than mine." This is a compressed but not expurgated version of the speech.

Even true-life wits at the beginning of the Restoration, Buckingham or Sedley or Rochester or the King himself, could not have fired off such a string of *bons mots* as does Manly in Wycherley's *The Plain Dealer,* or made love with such splendour as does Valentine in Congreve's *Love for Love.*

The Spring Gardens (or plain Spring Garden, if you prefer) were the old and original Spring Gardens. You may mark a part of the site to this day in Spring Garden Street, behind Cockspur Street as you go down to Trafalgar Square. The place must not be confused with what Evelyn calls "the *new* Spring Garden at Lambeth," (*Diary,* 2nd July, 1661). This refers to Vauxhall Gardens (Pepys's "Fox-Hall") on the other side of the river. Through the years Vauxhall gradually outshone and destroyed the old gardens, because of much greater space, more arbors, quaint illumination, and music. It had nearly two centuries of gay existence. See John Timbs, *The Romance of London* or *Walks and Talks about London,* both in many editions.

The Tower of London has a bibliography in itself. The Lion Gate has long been destroyed; and "Julius Caesar's Tower" is of course the White Tower. As for the Royal Menagerie, which is described in this story, it was removed in 1834. Yet you may still have a drink, not far from its site, at a pub called The Tiger. Nine years after the removal of the menagerie, the stagnant moats on the land side were drained. A map as early as Tudor times shows the gun wharf built out from the wall on the river side. Ned Ward, writing of a visit to the Tower in 1698, tells how they stuffed the fierce lion called King Charles the Second, and preserved him after death (*The London Spy,* 1929, Arthur L. Hayward, ed., 225-236).

The plan of London in 1678, published by the London and Middlesex Archaeological Society, consists of so many sheets that they fill the whole wall of a room when you fit them together. On this map, with its thick guide, you will find marked the position of every building, house, or place down to those of the very smallest importance: the home of a minor nobleman, a tolerable tavern. To the student of minutiae it is invaluable, as is the plan of Whitehall Palace in the Guildhall Library. In passing, it may be remarked that a plaque still marks the position of the "new" Duke's Theatre, and of the King's Head tavern.

As for the ordinary speech of these people, see their own letters and books. For example: compare the few authentic letters of Nell Gwynn published in Peter Cunningham's *The Story of Nell Gwyn and the Sayings of Charles II.* (H. B. Wheatley, ed., 1892) to the dazzling speech of Millament in the play. Nelly merely prattles, as rapidly as she is said to have spoken, in dictating the letters; and her name may be spelled in three different ways.

Or compare the formal speech of their books against one I prefer: four books, issued variously in 1665, 1668, 1674, 1680, under the general title of *The English Rogue.* This is a work of fiction. You need not believe one-tenth of the author's (or authors') adventures. But its breezy speech is authentic, like its background. And you may trust its thieves' cant, which scarcely varies a word from "A Dictionary of the Cant Language" in the famous *Life and Adventures of Bampsylde-Moore Carew* (printed for Thomas Martin, 1738).

OF SWORDPLAY

It has been indicated in the narrative that the swordplay of the time *circa* 1675 was unlike modern fencing. It was undeveloped; full of jumpings, circlings, foul thrusts and tricks considered quite fair; yet it was far more spectacular. No trick used in this story has been invented: all were really used. What may seem the curious guard adopted by Duroc in the fight on the sentry walk was the guard of many swordsmen, who tried to scare opponents with it.

For this subject the comprehensive and in fact the essential book is Egerton Castle's *Schools and Masters of Fence, Illustrated with Old Engravings* etc. (George Bell & Sons, 1893). Here the wealth of engravings shows the exact details, as in *The English Rogue* the engravings give a far better picture of costume than some modern plate.

The *botte* by which Fenton disarms Duroc may be found in another valuable work, Mr. J. D. Alyward's *The Small-Sword in England* (Hutchinson & Co., 1946), which deals with the transition of the rapier into the smallsword as well as the smallsword itself. Granting Duroc's sword in the story to have such quillons, and there were many such swords, Fenton could have disarmed him in that way—but in hardly any other way. When in book or film you see the hero disarming his adversary by some weird slap or other, it is pure nonsense.

Finally, for a general survey of swords or other weapons, see Hewitt or Laking, both very fine standard works in their field, as, for example, is Taylor on medical jurisprudence.